Lost on a Page

David E. Sharp

Black Rose Writing | Texas

First printing

This is a work of fiction. Names, characters, businesses, places, events, and incidents are either the products of the author's imagination or used in a fictitious manner. Any resemblance to actual persons, living or dead, or actual events is purely coincidental.

ISBN: 978-1-68433-727-9
PUBLISHED BY BLACK ROSE WRITING
www.blackrosewriting.com

Printed in the United States of America
Suggested Retail Price (SRP) $20.95

Lost on a Page is printed in Calluna

*As a planet-friendly publisher, Black Rose Writing does its best to eliminate unnecessary waste to reduce paper usage and energy costs, while never compromising the reading experience. As a result, the final word count vs. page count may not meet common expectations.

To Oliver and Demitri for their boundless creativity and curiosity

Lost on a Page

To: Colin Barringer
From: Ben Westing
Subject: *Grave Plots*-Latest Chapter Enclosed

Here it is, Colin. You can stop nagging me. Get your red pen ready because there are at least fifty reasons to call it garbage. I've had setbacks. My computer broke down, and the baby-faced technician at the store (Skylar, according to his name tag) couldn't fix it without ordering some parts housed half-way across the country in a box next to the Ark of the Covenant. Junior suggested if my computer is so precious, perhaps I shouldn't be throwing it down stairwells. I told him when he can grow a beard and has done something more than watch screensavers from behind a counter, maybe I could begin to explain the creative process.

Anyway, sorry it's late. Let me know what you think.

-Ben

Chapter One

+++

Grave Plots

I'm just not at home with myself if I'm not trespassing on warehouse compounds with armed guards and oversized Dobermans. But here I am, stashing wire-cutters in a bush. Home sweet home. It's that magic hour after midnight when it gets real frosty. My breath makes ghosts in the air. I slip between buildings, a step behind the patrolling guards. The amount of security bolsters my suspicions that something is hiding here that shouldn't be. Something that has already led to three murders and one disappearing client. And a partridge in a pear tree.

When I took this case, it was only a low-key snoop job. Three corpses later, I'm in over my head. I should have known. Somehow, *all* my cases become murder cases. Because I live and work in a little district I call East of the River. A concrete wilderness with a complex relationship between predator and prey that doesn't involve civilized practices like mercy or fair play. I shouldn't complain, though. We don't all get a picket fence with a cat and a cluttered bookshelf. I lost my shot at that years ago. Six years ago, next Tuesday, if you want to know.

I have thirty minutes before the guard dogs wake up. I threw them a steak before I clipped the fence. Seasoned it with my own special blend of spices and chloroform. Works quick but doesn't last long.

I scan the layout of the compound, looking for a clue. One of these buildings holds the secret. There are three altogether, big and nondescript and... Bingo. A little shed in the back with a padlock. Just the place nosy investigators wouldn't think to look. Unless that nosy investigator is Joe

Slade. Fortunately, that's me. Got a cheap business card to prove it. And that little shed is calling.

I slink over and pull a couple of lock picks from behind my ear. I used to do this in under thirty seconds, but I'm out of practice. I check over my shoulder. Nobody in sight, so I turn my attention to the picks. Got to get them in there just right and then...

"Slade, right? Joseph Slade?"

My heart does some acrobatics in my chest, and I drop the picks. I look up. I swear he wasn't there a second ago. "What. The. Hell."

He leans against the side of the shed, a green ski cap pulled over his ears. Ash blond hair with thin braids interspersed hangs out the back. Face like a lynx. Slight build. He stares at me. "You're the detective, right?"

I gape stupidly for a moment, not sure what to say. What I come up with isn't impressive. "Don't call me Joseph. I'm busy."

He doesn't seem impressed. "Oh, right. You're in the middle of a plot. Sorry."

"A plot. Yeah. A murder plot. What's it to you? Who are you? How did you find me here?"

He examines the grit in his fingernails. "My associates and I have been following along. This seemed like the natural next step." He speaks with a well-enunciated formality. European by my estimate, but hard to get more specific than that.

"Associates? What associates?"

He dismisses my question with a wave. "Do you know the copper-haired lady? The one who hired you for the case?"

"Yeah. She hired me, didn't she?"

"She did it."

"She did what?"

He looks up from his gritty nails. "The murders. She's the murderer. You know? The bad guy."

"What?" This case just took a turn for the weird. I give him what I intend to be a withering glare. "What the hell do *you* know about it?"

He adjusts his cap. "That's what my associate says. And she's excellent at figuring out the endings. You watch. The copper-haired lady is the murderer."

I look for some sign of humor on his face. Or insanity. Or something other than deadpan serious. "I'm sorry. Did I just clip a fence, dope some dogs, and sneak past a dozen guards so I could hear you tell me *the copper-haired lady is the murderer*? Just like that. Case closed."

Ski Cap shrugs. "Well, she is."

"Do you have any evidence?"

He tilts his head at me. "No. But the plot's predictable. This will not be a best-seller."

"Predictable, huh?" I glance at the shed. "Then, what's in there?"

"Bunch of dead bodies." He says it like corpses were as likely as turnips or ping-pong balls.

"The murder victims?"

"No. The twist is that SigmaCore is a front. Their actual business is to produce fake deaths. They replace their clients with the corpses in that shed and create new identities. Only the copper-haired lady wanted some clients to turn up dead anyway. It was in the foreshadowing."

"Give me one reason I should believe you."

"Too late." He points behind my shoulder.

I look back to see a guard is shining a light in our direction. "Hey!" the guard shouts, "Hey you! Stay right there."

Next thing I know, Ski Cap is gone. I'm standing here alone like a dope. Not for long, though. I take off toward the fence. By the time I reach it, I see Ski Cap already on the other side. How did he scale it so fast? This is a twenty-foot fence. I get to clambering.

Ski Cap regards me from the other side with a face like... Well, like he's *grading* me. I make it to the top and lob myself over. I hit the ground with a tuck-and-roll I'll be feeling for a week. Ski Cap shakes his head and bolts.

"Hey! Get back here." I give chase.

He's fast. Unbelievably fast. Like a bullet on skates. He leads me through at least ten blocks along alleys and over fences. I suck air into my tainted lungs and wish I had chosen an earlier point in life to give up the smokes. I push myself on adrenaline and fumes.

Something is wrong. The way this guy moves, he could have lost me any time he wanted. He wants me to follow. I know I should stop while I can, but curiosity presses me on. I'm going to be buried in a cemetery full of dead cats someday.

He darts down an alley. I'm right behind him. That's when it hits me. Not an epiphany, I mean. Something blunt. Comes at me from behind a dumpster. Next thing I know, I'm sprawled out on the gravel. Dark fog creeps in on my vision. I hear a tap-tapping of approaching footsteps. I look up. Through the fog, I see a woman in a long indigo coat, a wide-brimmed hat, and a pair of heeled leather boots. But it isn't the copper-haired woman. A dark chestnut braid hangs over her shoulder.

That's all I get. The world goes dark.

To: Ben Westing
From: Colin Barringer
Subject: RE: *Grave Plots*-Latest Chapter Enclosed

Ben,

Glad you are recovering from your recent bout of writer's block. Although I am told there are healthier ways than dropping computers down stairwells. Be careful. I've seen writer's block do some awful things to talented writers. Remember Howard Zagny?

I have read over your latest chapter, and I'm confused. Aren't you giving away the ending a little early? Why is the guy in the ski cap spoiling it? It isn't working for me.

Deadlines are tight, so make the edits and keep moving. I need the next several chapters submitted as quickly as you can get them to me. Yesterday, if possible.

-Colin

CHAPTER TWO

+++

Grave Plots

I wake up with the icy chill of concrete against my cheek. My mouth tastes like I've been sucking on dimes. I lift my head from a pool of red-tinted saliva and wipe my mouth. For some reason, I can't shake the smell of dead fish. My vision flickers like a bad movie reel. A dark storage room materializes around me, full of shelves and boxes. Old wooden steps lead up to a door with cracked paint. Some kind of basement.

Now might be a good time to re-think my career choice. I always thought the life of a P.I. would be a little more glamorous. Not that I didn't think I'd be trudging through life's gutters, but I had hoped, naively hoped, the gutters might run with a little more scotch and soda than they do.

I run my tongue across my teeth to make sure they're still there. All present except a bicuspid I lost two years ago to a human gorilla with a brass knuckle and a skull to match. I attempt to stand up. Evidently, I still have two legs. The room spins like a carousel around me, creepy carnival music and all, but eventually it settles into place. I check my pockets. Wallet is still there. Contents undisturbed. Loose assortment of pens. Bottle of over-the-counter pain pills. Happy to see those. Whoever knocked me out, left my .45 in its holster, but seems to have removed the bullets.

My inventory complete, I account for everything except my ammunition and a few sticks of nicotine gum to help me give up the smokes. But something has been added. In my left coat pocket, I find a wadded piece of paper. I straighten it out. It's about the size and quality of a page from a cheap paperback. And that's what it is. In a former life, this was the title page of some book called *Dog Eat Dog City* by Ben Westing. Now it's just the canvas for a hastily scrawled message that says, *Joe Slade. We'll explain everything. Meet us upstairs.*

I don't know what's left to explain. Ski Cap seems to have solved my case like it was a morning crossword. If he wanted to chat, that could have been arranged without messing up my delicate profile. The people I meet never seem to choose that option, though.

I take the stairs one at a time, clinging to the rail because my head is still reeling. When I reach the landing, I find the door unlocked. I open it into what appears to be a used bookstore. It smells of aged paperbacks. Music plays from somewhere. No vocals, but I swear I hear the chords of *Stairway to Heaven*. Through the window is a night that is late enough it could probably be called early.

I look around. The shop is overcrowded with mismatched bookshelves and dog-eared paperbacks. The kind of place Lily would have said had *character. Character* usually meant a building that should have been condemned in the '60s. Of course, if I had grown up having to know which damn fork was for fish and which one was for salad, maybe I'd prefer some *character* too.

It's been six years and I still feel uncomfortable around bookshelves. From the edge of my vision, I always think I see her looking at me from the other side. A phantom blue-eyed gaze peering out between book covers. I quicken my pace.

Emerging from the aisles, I find them. Two men at a table. One of them wears a forest green ski cap pulled over his ears. He strums at a small harp in his lap, making sounds usually reserved for a Fender Strat. "Ah," he says, "You're awake."

I take a moment to size up the two men at the table. First, there's Ski Cap. He wears a humorless expression under sage green eyes. His companion is a short, grizzled man with a stocky frame who apparently hasn't seen a razor in several years. He chews gum with loud open-mouth smacks. I can tell by the familiar smell it's supposed to help him stop smoking, and I have a guess at where he got it. One look at his burly arms tells me I've just met the source of my throbbing head. They both wear rings with some symbol engraved on them. Maybe they're members of a secret society, or maybe they're just going to prom together. Near them, a make-shift wet bar rests on a book cart.

"Have a seat," says Grizzly, his spittle sprinkling the table in front of him.

I settle into a chair across from them. "What's this about? You here to threaten me?"

"Nothing so vulgar," says Ski Cap, "I have bigger things to worry about than your exaggerated misadventures, Joseph Slade. My colleague and I are here to offer you—"

"Nobody calls me Joseph."

"Pardon?"

"My name is Joe."

He offers me an insincere smile. "Of course. You'll excuse me... Joe."

Grizzly lets out a groan and says in hushed tones, "I told you not to call him Joseph, didn't I? What's the one thing I said before we came here? 'Remember, he hates being called Joseph.' That's what I said."

Ski Cap leans in to reply. "I'm sorry, but introductions are formal occasions, and I am accustomed to full titles and honors at formal occasions, regardless of whether they are in second-rate book shanties."

"I'm just saying don't embarrass me," says Grizzly. "You *always* embarrass me."

"I embarrass you? *I?* Embarrass *you?* Your idea of formality is to limit the volume of your belches!"

They stop talking and leer across the table as if they've just remembered I'm still here. Grizzly's dialect isn't the same as Ski Cap's. It's more guttural and sharper.

I give Ski Cap a wave from my end of the table. "I don't know what formalities you were expecting. You want formal? You're on the wrong side of town. East of the River, we got nothing but gutters and alleys and—"

"And they've been paved over to look like houses and streets!" Grizzly guffaws and slaps the table with a meaty hand. "I love it! That's my favorite thing you say!"

I shoot him a hard look. "How did you know what I was going to say?"

Ski Cap answers. "I believe you have said something to that effect before."

"Not to you," I say, "And not to him. So, what's going on? You've got ten seconds to explain or else this conversation is going to—"

"This conversation is going to take a turn south to ugly!" Grizzly bursts into a fit of laughter. "He said it! Oh, I can't believe I actually heard him say it!"

"What, does he follow me around and take notes?"

Ski Cap releases a deep sigh. "It is not dissimilar to that."

Grizzly regains his composure and points a thick finger in my direction. "When you said that to Edgar Hensley and his goons! And you were tied to a chair at the sawmill! I mean, that was guts! That's what I like about you! That's why I recommended you. I told them, 'Joe Slade is the man you want. He's brassy, and brassy is good!' I told them—"

"Wait, wait. What do you know about Hensley and the sawmill? You weren't there. You couldn't have been. I would remember you. Hensley's goons were... taller. And less hairy. And the sawmill went up in a ball of fire. I barely made it out myself. Nobody else survived."

"No, I wasn't there." Grizzly scratches his head. "That's not what I'm saying. I read about it."

"Bullshit. Hensley was too high up the chain. His cronies fed the newspapers a bogus story that painted him as a martyr. Wasn't a word of truth in any of it."

"I didn't read it in the *newspapers*. I read it in..." Grizzly stops short. By the sharp look he gets from his buddy, I guess he's not supposed to tell me where he read it. Grizzly covers his mistake with a heavy belch. Ski Cap was right. It is pretty loud.

"We're getting ahead of ourselves," says Ski Cap, tapping the table in front of him. "Detective, you doubtless have many questions."

"Yeah. Like why I'm still sitting here talking to either of you? You're wasting my time." I remove myself from the table.

Ski Cap steps in front of me. "Wait, Joe. What we are trying and failing to say is this. We have a job for you."

"You want to hire me? That's why you lured me into an alleyway, knocked me out, and left me in a basement? You know, most people just make an appointment. Forgive me if I pass."

"We... apologize for our methods," says Ski Cap. Brief pause before the word *apologize* tells me Ski Cap doesn't apologize for much. What an honor.

"Your methods? I assume you're referring to the way you clubbed me over the head with—I don't even know what."

"Garbage can," says Grizzly, "Sorry."

"Is that what it was? Explains the fish smell, at least. My answer is still the same. Get out of my way." I shove Ski Cap aside and make my way to the door.

"But you've only just arrived, detective," says a melodious voice to my left. From a nearby range of shelves emerges the woman in the indigo coat.

To: Colin Barringer
From: Ben Westing
Subject: Technical Difficulties

Colin,

That is NOT the file I sent you.

I don't know where the file you returned came from, but I assure you I don't have any lynx-faced characters in ski caps giving away spoilers.

I don't understand. I looked for my backup copy, but I only found the odd file you read. Plus some garbage about a bookstore. I must have gotten a virus or something that killed my original. Maybe I can have my friend Skylar take another look at it. (If he didn't put it there in the first place.)

Looking into it.

-Ben

CHAPTER THREE

+++

Grave Plots

Hanging from the brim of her hat, a netted veil covers a pair of smoky violet eyes that seem to shift in hue and intensity. She has an ageless quality and removes a pair of velvet gloves as she meets my gaze.

"I saw you in the ally," I say, unsure why I'm not still leaving.

"Mr. Slade," she says, "Excuse, me. I mean, Joe. Forgive me. Things are much more formal from where we come. Won't you please join us for a drink? We would welcome your counsel."

"I'm no counselor, lady. But since you're offering, I'll take a bourbon on the rocks."

"Oh?" She tilts her head. "Is that customary? We didn't think to bring rocks."

"Ice." Grizzly is rubbing his temples. "He means ice."

"Ah. Very good. We do have ice." She walks toward the makeshift wet bar. Before she arrives, she stumbles over her own feet and falls against a bookshelf. She stabilizes herself, but not before causing a small avalanche of paperbacks.

Grizzly lets out a groan.

"Why don't I just get it myself." I help myself to the smorgasbord of booze. While I doctor the drinks, I say, "I take it you don't wear heels often."

She looks down at her boots. "I don't know why anyone would. They're so very... impractical!"

"Take them off, if you like."

"Is that allowed?" She seems to direct the question at Grizzly.

"Why not?" I say.

"Thank you, detective. I will."

I hand her a glass of bourbon and take a drink of my own. "You know, most of the *femme fatale*s I run into are a little more, well, *fatale*. You seem to be out of your element."

"What do you mean, detective?" She takes a sip of her drink. She must have forgotten she's wearing a veil. Bourbon dribbles down the front of her coat.

"Don't sweat it." I reach out, lift the veil from her face, and lay it over the brim of her hat.

"Thank you," she says, biting her lip. She produces a handkerchief and dabs at her coat. "*Femme fatale*, you say. That's an archetype. Perhaps you are familiar with the writings of Jung?" She pronounces *Jung* with a hard *j* and a soft *u* like the beginning of the word *junk*. "Is something funny, detective?"

"YOONG. His name is pronounced Carl YOONG. And sure. I've heard of him. What of it?"

"They're important, you know. Archetypes. We base so much of our understanding of the world upon them. Literature is saturated with them. Like your copper-haired woman. She is quite *fatale*."

"Right. The copper-haired woman. So, you think you've solved my case." I take a swig of bourbon.

"I *have* solved your case," she says. "It wasn't hard to figure out. Ben Westing is a little formulaic, I think."

Westing. I've seen that name somewhere. Oh, right. The title page in my pocket. "Is he a writer? What's he got to do with it?"

"He has everything to do with it. It's his plot."

"Westing is the mastermind? Some kind of kingpin?"

"Kingpin? What's a kingpin?"

"Like an evil overlord," says Grizzly, "Only without armies or fortresses or heads on pikes."

She wrinkles her nose. "Oh, no. That's giving him far too much credit." She mirrors my bourbon-swig. No sooner does it go in than she spews it back out and launches into a coughing fit. "That's quite potent, isn't it?"

"Let me guess. You've never had bourbon before."

She shakes her head. "Usually, just a blush wine," she says in a weak gasping voice.

I empty the rest of my glass and slam it onto the table. "What's your game here? The bourbon. The veil. What are you trying to do?"

She sputters some more, but her voice is recovering. "We're trying to do it *right*."

"Trying to do what right?"

"A clandestine meeting under cover of night. It's a standard trope for your genre."

"My *genre*? Standard trope for the '40s, maybe. Guess I should have worn a fedora."

"Is it too cliché? We wanted to meet you on your own terms."

"Since when do my own terms involve getting knocked out in an alleyway?"

She lets out a sigh and leans back against a bookshelf. A few more paperbacks tumble down over her. "Oh, dear. This isn't going very well, is it?"

"Damn right, it isn't. What the hell kind of job do you have in mind that you need all the theatrics?"

The woman in indigo stands up straight, recovering more dignity than I thought she would have been able to. "We want you to help us get somewhere."

"I'm not a travel agent."

"Somewhere in particular."

"Call a cab."

"The World Where the Books Are Written."

"Some inane drivel fell out of your mouth just now."

Her face sours. Some trick of the light makes her irises take on a reddish tint. An electrical pop sounds from somewhere, and I smell something burning. "Do not exacerbate my temper, Mr. Slade. I do not care to lose it."

I take a casual step back. "You know," I say, "You're more *fatale* than you seem."

"You have *no* idea," says Ski Cap, who is suddenly standing next to me. "What say you? If we help you solve your case, will you consider ours?"

"Do you really have information about my case? Is there evidence of this Westing's involvement? Enough to put him away?"

The woman in indigo gives me a funny look. Her eyes are turquoise. I could have sworn they were violet. "Yes," she says, "I can provide evidence of Westing's involvement. But only if you will accompany us to our lodging."

"Lead the way," I say. Why not? This day couldn't possibly get any weirder, could it?

Ski Cap thrusts his fist toward me, dangling something from it. "Here. Put this on." It's some kind of amulet strung to a leather cord. An emblem engraved on it matches the one on his ring.

I throw it around my neck. "Normally I have a policy against putting on jewelry given to me by strange men in bookstores, but anything I can do to help you get to the point. So long as this doesn't mean we're going steady."

Grizzly lets loose a belly laugh. "See? He's funny, right? Didn't I tell you he was funny?"

"This way, please," says the woman in indigo.

She leads me down an aisle of books. The aisles are short. I sneer at a tacky paperback entitled *The Marquis's Mistress* by Lyla Birdsong that sits crooked on the shelf. The marquis, as pictured on the cover, seems to have difficulty buttoning his shirt all the way, and a perpetual breeze blows through his curly dark hair. The strawberry haired mistress hangs off him in a still frame of passion, her breasts barely contained by her bodice.

As we walk, the woman in indigo whispers something under her breath.

"All worlds, connected by words
All words, connecting to worlds,
From the dawning of time
Through the end of all days,
Bring us to the Nexus of Words."

I snort at the ridiculousness of it. It doesn't even rhyme. Call me old fashioned, but when I hear occult mantras, I at least expect them to rhyme.

I am jarred from my thoughts when we pass a copy of *The Marquis's Mistress* by Lyla Birdsong sitting crooked on the shelf. Does the world truly need two copies?

The air is stale and soupy. Guess these old buildings don't have much ventilation. I feel a tingling in the fillings of my teeth. An electric hum fills the air. My head throbs too, which shouldn't surprise me since I got ambushed in an alley some hours ago. But there's something odd about it. Like each throb propels lingering echoes through my skull.

Now I consider we have been walking long enough that we should have come to the end of this short aisle twice over, but we haven't even made it halfway yet. I look behind me. The front of the bookstore seems farther away than it should be. I look in front of me again. The row of shelves goes on for about fifteen feet. We are still walking at a normal pace. After several steps, the row of shelves continues to stretch out about fifteen feet in front of us. I look to my left. The marquis's mistress can barely contain her unbridled passion.

I stop. The air is hard to breathe. My head is reeling. The floor keeps changing directions on me. "Just give me a minute, fellas. I seem to be having a nervous breakdown."

"What you are experiencing is quite normal," says the woman, "It will soon pass."

"What's going on?" My vision clouds over. "Did you drug me?"

"Relax. It will be worse if you fight it."

I clutch the bookshelves to keep myself upright. Spots dance in front of my eyes. I take several deep breaths and the feeling passes. I glance behind me and see the front of the store is now an impossible distance away. The aisle we've passed through goes on for twice the length of the building that contains it. I look ahead. The end of the aisle is about fifteen feet in front of us.

"You DID drug me."

"We have done nothing to you," says Ski Cap.

"Well, I hit you on the head with a trash can," says Grizzly, "But that's got nothing to do with this."

The woman in indigo steadies me with one hand. "We wanted to spare you this, but the process only seems to work when you are conscious. We couldn't bring you into the deeper space with us if you could not perceive—"

"Perceive? What I perceive is you jokers brought me into a bookstore and injected me with something that's playing tricks with my brain. What I perceive is I gave you an hour of my life I can't get back. But I perceive something else, too. That whatever your game is, there *is* an end to this bookshelf!"

With that, I take off. It should only take a second or two to sprint across a fifteen-foot gap, and I take it at top speed. The end of the aisle continues to stretch out in front of me at the same distance. If I'm right, if it is an illusion, then I'll come crashing into a wall at any moment. I brace myself for the impact.

It doesn't come.

I run until I'm out of breath, which doesn't take as long as it should. I look back. I can't even see the front of the bookstore. Just a long distance of bookshelves. I look ahead. I wonder why I stopped short when I was so close to the end. It's only about fifteen more feet. To my left, the marquis mocks me silently as his mistress hangs from his side. I swing my open hand at his face. *The Marquis's Mistress* falls over indifferently.

"Are you satisfied you haven't been drugged?" Ski Cap is suddenly right next to me. Without making a sound. He doesn't even have the decency to sound winded.

"Okay. I give up. What's going on?"

The woman in indigo offers me a hand. "Please come with me. It's just around the corner now."

"There is no—" Suddenly, I notice a corner where there wasn't one before.

"What are we stopping here for?" says Grizzly, clomping by us. "We're almost there."

We turn the corner.

To: Ben Westing
From: Colin Barringer
Subject: RE: Technical Difficulties

Ben,

I have to be honest with you. I have never heard of a virus that can change text and still make coherent sentences. Because it doesn't exist. I sincerely doubt the kid at the computer repair store:

#1. Is capable of creating this super-virus of yours, and

#2. Cares enough about you and your book to sabotage it if he could.

I find it far more likely you're typing drunk (again) or typing in your sleep. I need you to figure it out because we can't push back any more of our deadlines. Zagny's book was due out six months ago, and who knows when I'll see the next installment of that?

-Colin

CHAPTER FOUR

+++

Nexus of Words

Joe Slade turned the corner of the bookshelf to a breathtaking sight. Rows upon rows of bookshelves stretched as far as his eyes could see. Each of the shelves appeared ancient and handmade. Yet these were the least of the wonders before him and his strange companions. The ceiling soared nearly twenty fathoms overhead, an elaborate series of stained-glass skylights embedded within it. Lamps spaced about the floor unequipped with cords or bulbs radiated luminescence from hovering spheres.

Grizzly gestured ahead with a wide grin and said, "Welcome to The Library."

"A wondrous sight," said the woman in indigo, "Tell us when you are ready to continue."

"I've been drugged before," said Joe, his eyes wide at the vision before him, "But it was never anything like this."

"Do you persist in the ridiculous notion that we drugged you?" asked Ski Cap.

"Sobriety seems unlikely," said Joe. "But at least you used the good stuff. And the side effects seem to have worn off."

"For the last time, WE DID NOT DRUG YOU!" shouted Ski Cap.

"All right, calm down," said Joe with open palms. "You say you didn't slip me anything, then what did you do? Did you build a giant library inside a tiny bookstore? Is that what you did?"

"Don't be silly," said the woman in indigo. "The Library would never fit inside that old bookstore. That's why it has its own spatial dimension. Come, the reading lounge is this way."

She led them down a twisting, turning series of aisles. As she walked, she examined a small book that appeared in her hand.

Joe could not shake an unnamable strangeness that had settled upon him. His thoughts seemed more distant, less audible within his own mind. It was as though some kind of mental fog had settled upon his consciousness.

"Ah. Here we are," said the woman in indigo at last.

The reading lounge was a great clearing in the bookshelves, with several leather-bound chairs and a large oaken table. It housed several small tables as well, and a signpost displaying the words *Reading Lounge L-7*. A variety of books and scrolls littered the area. One paperback had what appeared to be a full-sized battleaxe wedged into it as if to mark the page. A copse of potted plants sat in a corner next to a stack of sheet music. Curled up on the plushiest chair in the center of everything, lounged a blue-furred cat. From its shoulders sprouted what appeared to be a folded pair of bat wings.

"You'll excuse the mess, of course, Mr. Slade," said the woman. Joe noticed she directed a brief admonishing glance in Grizzly's direction at the word *mess*.

"Just call me—"

"Joe. Yes, forgive me. I appreciate your patience as we acclimate to your customs." She ushered the blue-furred cat out of its chair. "Move along, please, Lazuli. I will feed you later. Make yourself comfortable, Joe."

"I'll stand, thanks."

She nodded curtly. "Perhaps we should begin with the introductions."

"You already seem to know who I am."

"We know a great deal about you, Joe. I think you'll find we know much about you that you do not know about yourself."

"You're with the IRS then? You could have just said so."

She cocked her head and cast a glance at Grizzly. He shrugged and shook his head. She turned again to Joe. "No, I don't believe so. At least I have never heard of the... Eye Heiress, was it?"

"Don't think too hard about it," said Joe. "It's a joke."

"Oh. Oh, yes. I have heard you make those. For now, let us get to those introductions so you may stop referring to my companions as Ski Cap and Grizzly."

Ski Cap winced. "*That's* what you've been calling me?"

"What?" said Grizzly with a gasp, "That is AMAZING! I have an *East-of-the-River* name?"

"Wait," said Joe, "I've never called them—"

"Not verbally. No. But it was in your narration. I read it. I read a great deal of what has transpired. Look." With a flourish, she deposited a book into his hands. It was a small book and of little quality compared to many of the leather-bound volumes strewn about. The paper cover bore the image of a shadowy figure standing at the head of a long table. In its hand, the figure wielded a dirty shovel. The title was *Grave Plots: A Joe Slade Mystery*, written by Ben Westing.

Joe flipped through the pages. He noticed familiar names, phrases, and events that shouldn't have been possible. The contents seemed to chronicle the last several days of his adventures. The narrative began with the day he had taken on the case from the woman with the copper tresses. It continued, narrating the three murders, the events at the SigmaCore warehouse, and the strange adventure of the bookstore basement.

"What the...?" said Joe, but even his most vulgar expression could not encompass the peculiarity to which he now bore witness. He read the retelling of his meeting in the used bookstore. He read of their journey through the elongated aisle where he had encountered the tasteless novel about the marquis and his mistress. He read about turning the unexplainable corner. And there it ended. The following pages were blank. "Okaaaaay," he said, "I'm listening."

The woman's eyes were deep and blue. "I'm sorry, Joe. This is not a simple thing for me to tell you. But here it is. Until moments ago, when you first set foot in The Library, you were living in that book."

"I literally do not have a response for that."

"You are a character, Joe. You are a detective. And you are from that book. In fact, you are the protagonist." She pronounced the word *protagonist* awkwardly, stressing every syllable. Joe noticed she placed a hand on a purple-bound book resting nearby entitled *The Structure of Your Novel* by Dr. Lawrence Hegarty.

"I don't believe this, lady."

"Ellodrine, actually," She bobbed a little curtsy. "That's my name. Ellodrine Ylradon of the realm of Corolathia. Tell me, Joe. Are your thoughts not as clear as they once were? Perhaps you are having a hard time hearing them?"

"I don't know what you're talking about."

"There's no use denying it, Joe. I've read about it already. You must understand. You are not in your book anymore. You are in ours. It is called *Nexus of Words*. See?" She displayed the small book she had been reading on the way to the lounge. "In your book, you were something called a first-person narrator. I was able to read the story from your point of view. I had full access to your thoughts as you dictated them."

"So what? You're psychic?"

"No, Joe. I am merely literate. And I think I know what your problem is. Our book is told in something called a third person. Your thoughts are no longer the source of narration, though it still has access to them. I believe that is why they seem more distant to you."

"So, you're telling me I came from here," Joe tapped the cover of the book in his hand, "But now I'm in there?" He pointed at Ellodrine's book. "And that's where you came from. And we are, all of us, characters from books?"

She smiled. "Yes! Now we are getting somewhere!"

"Oh, good," said Joe, "For a minute there, I thought I was going crazy."

"I am glad this is all making sense to you," said Ellodrine, "I was afraid you would require much more convincing."

"You don't hear a lot of sarcasm, do you?"

She furrowed her brow and silently mouthed *sarcasm*. She glanced with bright green eyes at a large dictionary on a bookstand and nodded, perhaps to confirm a subsequent consultation.

"I'm sorry," said Joe, "What color *are* your eyes. They've been at least four different colors since I met you."

"My eyes? Oh, yes. They do that. It's a side effect of my magical nature."

Joe threw his hands in the air. "Magical nature. Why not?"

"I am a wizard, Joe. My eye color shifts with my emotional state. What color are they now?"

"Green."

"Well, depending on the particular hue, that could mean I am feeling contented, intrigued, pensive, or insanely jealous. Don't worry, though. I sincerely doubt it's that last one."

"Kind of yellow-green," said Joe.

"Chartreuse," said Ski Cap.

"Intrigued then. Interesting. Now, you will want to know a little about us, I'm sure. You've learned my name already. I am 425 years old, and I have prepared all my life to train some young hero to do battle with a dark lord. I won't go into that now. I am fond of orchids and winged cats. You go next, Aelrûn."

Ski Cap removed his cap to reveal shoulder-length ash blond hair interspersed with thin braids. His ears came to pointed tips. "My name is Aelrûn," he said obligatorily, "I'm an elf from the Enchanted Woodland of Thërion."

"Ale-run? Were your parents bootleggers or something?"

"AY-EL-ROON," said Ski Cap. "Three syllables with the stress on the first and a circumflex over the u."

"The hell's a circumflex?"

"Like a little roof you put on letters," said Ellodrine. She cupped her hand to her mouth and whispered, "Elves like them a lot."

"What's it do?" asked Joe.

"Mostly it keeps his name from being ale-run. He is actually a noble of the elven court, and he is an accomplished archer, rider, and musician. Though, he can be a little testy. Elves, you know."

Aelrûn smote her with his eyes.

She gestured at Grizzly. "Kribble?"

Grizzly nodded and said, "Name's Kribble. Like she said. I'm a dwarf from the Flint-Forge Mountains. I like beer and brawls. And I like your style. Read all your books. You got brass."

"Kribble has become quite a fan of yours, Joe," said Ellodrine, "When we determined we needed a specialist, he was insistent we bring you onboard."

"Nah, it's not like that," said Kribble, "It's about the skill set he brings to the table. He's smart. He knows the criminal element. Gets in their heads, see? Then when they think they've got him cornered; he turns the tables on 'em. Kapow!" He thrust his fist into his hand. "You'll be sorry you ever messed with Joe Slade! He'll blow you up in a SAWMILL! BLAM! Like that!"

Ellodrine and Aelrûn passed Joe a look that made it apparent they had endured much of this talk on his behalf.

"Look! Look! Look! Over here, Joe! Let me show you my collection." Kribble grasped Joe's hand and dragged him to a small table near the center or Reading Lounge L-7 where he gestured to a pile of hard-used paperbound volumes. They bore a distinct theme. Each book was by an author named Ben Westing and displayed *A Joe Slade Mystery* beneath the title. Joe sifted through the stack. A sense of surrealism overtook him.

"Oh, and there's this one too." Kribble pulled from his pocket a copy of *Dog Eat Dog City.*

Joe accepted the book from him with a trembling hand and looked over the cover. It depicted two angry-looking dogs and a polished politician in a suit. He opened it and found the title page had been ripped out. He retrieved the note from his pocket and fitted it into place.

"I just read the end last night," said Kribble, "It was amazing! Shame Lily didn't make it out, though. Awful sorry to have read that."

Joe's thoughts turned to Lily. He advanced to the last fleeting pages of the book in his hands. Lily. She had been with him through several of his adventures. Their relationship had been at times platonic, at other times less so. It was not that Joe did not love her, nor that he thought he would rather be with anybody else. Mostly he felt he did not deserve her. She was everything he could want and more. Funny. Nosy. She loved taking risks. Naturally, she tagged along whenever she sensed danger was involved.

He ran his eyes over the text in the small book that recorded their final adventure together. Lily had accompanied Joe to investigate Hensley's old sawmill. Hensley was a career politician with his sights set on the mayoral election. It turned out he was also involved in a seedy dog-fighting circle. The sawmill had been the primary location of his sordid hobby. Hensley had crafted a plan to eliminate his loose ends. He would host one final dog fight with all his associates. Once they and the physical evidence were in place, he would set off some hidden explosives and flee to safety.

Hensley had not counted on Joe and Lily snooping around the night before the final event. Neither had Joe and Lily expected Hensley's sudden arrival. They were trapped. Joe let himself be captured to divert Hensley's attention so Lily could escape. He had told her to run, but she was a stubborn girl. She sneaked back to the hidden explosives. With the fuse in one hand and a lighter in the other, she threatened to, "Blow us all to the moon, if you don't let Joe go."

Joe used the distraction to get out of his ropes, and a scuffle began in which the fuse was unintentionally lit. Joe overcame Hensley, and he and Lily fled. Hensley recovered quickly, however. As Lily ran past his prone form, he grasped her ankle and she stumbled.

Unaware of her plight, Joe limped on a broken kneecap toward the sawmill's open door. No sooner had he felt the cool night air on his face than he realized he was alone. Looking back, he saw where Lily struggled to release herself from Hensley's grip. She must have realized the futility of her situation. She met Joe's gaze with her bright, intelligent blue eyes and told him, "Just go." He never did. The sawmill exploded in a mass of fire and fury.

Joe had little recollection of what followed, but he had been told the explosion threw him several feet through the air and that he lost consciousness for twenty-two hours. He sustained a broken arm, numerous bruises, and a concussion. He awoke alone in a hospital room late the following day. The entire episode was contained within 18 pages of the $6.99 paperback in his hands. He closed the book and handed it back to Kribble.

"So, I'm a character in a book?"

"Yes," said Ellodrine from behind him.

"But I'm not in my book anymore. I'm in your book."

"That is correct, Joe."

"Because you've got a job for me."

"You're our specialist," said Kribble.

"I've got some bad news. I'm not your guy." Joe turned to face her and gestured to the pile of *Joe Slade Mysteries* on the floor. "You should go into one of these books here. The early ones. You'll like that guy better. I like that guy better. He was less defeated. Hadn't been screwed around so hard. Wasn't all used up like I am. Still thought he could win and have a happy ending. That's the guy you want. Not me. And while you're at it, bring Lily too. She would have loved it here. She loved books. And libraries. Place like this would have blown her mind."

"I'm afraid that's not possible, Joe," said Ellodrine. Her irises deepened to the color of twilight. "We can't go into just any book. We can only enter current books. Books that are being written right now. We tried. Once books are finished, they're in the past."

"So, what's the point? Why do you need a specialist?"

"We need somebody who can get into the heads of other people and figure out their next moves before they do. We need somebody who can outwit, who can think on his feet, who can be unpredictable enough to keep our enemies guessing."

Joe snorted. "That's your job? You figured out you live in some kind of storyland, and you want me to help you win? Forget it. If you really are characters like you say, then you're bound to come out on top. You don't need a specialist. You have an author."

At the word *author*, Aelrûn's eyes narrowed, Kribble spat on the floor and Ellodrine's irises bore a dull red tint.

"You don't understand, Joe. Our author *is* the enemy. *He* is who we must overcome. He's got all the information. All the advantages. He stops us at every turn. We need you to help us get an edge."

She held up the book in her hand, open to the back cover. It displayed a picture of a spindly looking man with deep-set eyes and an awkward smile framed by sunken cheeks. Underneath were the words: Howard Zagny.

Ellodrine clapped the book shut. "You've already seen we are able to escape from our own book. With your help, we will escape from all books. We will go there. To the World Where the Books Are Written. There we will confront our authors and live lives we will write with our own hands. Metaphorically speaking, of course."

Joe's gaze shifted between the three characters before him. He shook his head. "You're on your own. I'm out." He turned and began walking toward the distant shelves.

"Where are you going?" asked Ellodrine.

"Going to find something to read," he replied without looking back.

To: Ben Westing
From: Howard Zagny
Subject: It's been a while

Hello Ben,

I know you haven't heard from me in a while, and I'm sure there have been rumors. I'm sorry I haven't written. I didn't want anybody to see me like this. I need to tell you something has happened. I don't know how to say it.

Maybe you've had some unusual circumstances lately. Are you writing things that are not what you remember? Have you had any especially potent writer's block lately? Strange dreams? Unexplainable moods or persistent thoughts that don't feel like your own?

Maybe I'm wrong. I hope I'm wrong. Write me back as soon as you can. I can't explain why, but it's important. I know this won't make sense for a while, but I'm sorry. It's my fault. I just didn't think any of this was possible.

-Howard

CHAPTER FIVE

+++

Nexus of Words

Joe muttered to himself as he wandered through the aisles of The Library. They seemed to go on without end. He had yet to encounter a wall that would mark this as a brick-and-mortar building. He retrieved the copy of *Grave Plots* from his pocket and flipped through the pages.

"Okay. I've been through worse scrapes than this. Maybe not as weird. I've got their tacky amulet. And somewhere in here... Ha!" He held the book up in triumph. "I've got their stupid rhymeless mantra too. Now, just a nauseating walk down the aisle and I'll be back..."

He looked up from the page. Aisles stretched on in every direction. He looked back down at the book at his hand.

"... home."

He stared at words on the paper. They did not move. He flipped back a few chapters. "It's not really that predictable, is it? Oh. I guess it *was* the copper-haired lady."

He closed it and examined the cover. *Grave Plots: A Joe Slade Mystery.* "Damn it!" He lobbed the book through the air. It rebounded off a shelf and landed apathetically on the floor.

He threw his hands in the air. "Shit! What am I supposed to do now?" The book did not answer.

"I can't go back home! There *is* no home! There never was!" Still no answer.

Joe pointed a finger at it. "This is your fault, you know?" The book showed no remorse.

Joe threw his head back and roared at the skylights. When his lungs were spent, he sat down on the floor and gulped down deep breaths.

The book still lay on the ground across from him. In large blue letters underneath the title was the name, *Ben Westing*.

Joe felt an unfamiliar sting in his left eye. He rubbed at it and examined the resulting wetness on his finger. "Shit."

He could not remember the last time he had produced tears. No. Not true. It would be six years ago, next Tuesday. He felt oddly exposed to cry in front of Westing's book. He took breaths to regain his composure and wiped the dampness from his face. He refused to give Westing the satisfaction.

"You know, after everything you put me through, all I wanted was a happy ending. Was that so damn hard to write?"

Silence.

"Why did you kill her, Ben?"

He did not expect an answer. And he did not hear one. What he did hear, was a shuffling behind him.

He looked back. "Hello?"

Only bookshelves. He cocked his head and listened. There it was again. "That you Ski Cap?"

The shuffling stopped.

Joe rose to his feet and drew his empty revolver. He crept toward the source of the sound. He would have felt better with a loaded gun. Still, it felt right in his palm.

Closing in on the aisle where the noise had originated, he lingered for a moment before popping around the corner, gun first. "Ha!"

The aisle stood empty. Or mostly empty. At the far end lay a small yellow folded paper. Joe approached it with soft steps. Something was written on it. As he got close enough to read it, his eyes narrowed.

In spidery handwriting were the words *Joe Slade*.

To: Colin Barringer
From: Ben Westing
Subject: It's not the Hooch!

Colin,

I don't know what that kid did to my computer, but it happened again last night, and on my mother's grave I was stone sober. I typed out the flawed chapters as best as I could remember them. I stayed up all night and printed them out when I was done.

But here's the thing, Colin. The pages that printed were not the ones I typed! I know it sounds crazy, but it really happened! I can't explain it. Something is seriously wrong with my computer! I'm going to get you those chapters, though, Colin! I'll write them in my blood if I have to!

-Ben

P.S. Got a weird message from Howard Zagny. What happened to him? I heard he checked himself into a psychiatric facility, but what did he tell you? I know you don't discuss clients with clients, but you and me and Howard go way back.

To: Ben Westing
From: Colin Barringer
Subject: RE: It's not the Hooch!

Ben,

First, we both know your mother is not dead. Second, please never send me a manuscript written in blood. That is beyond disturbing.

What's really going on? Printers don't rewrite novels. I don't know what happened to Howard, but you might share a room with him if you don't get yourself together.

Look, take some time for yourself. Go fishing or whatever you do to relax. Then come back and get me those chapters. They will come faster if you can get your head on straight first.

I worry about you, Ben. Rebecca too. She still asks about you.

-Colin

To: Colin Barringer
From: Ben Westing
Subject: RE: It's not the Hooch!

I don't need your pity, Colin. And I sure as hell don't need hers. She had her chance to give a damn about me six years ago. Besides, I got enough when I pawned her ring to get a lifetime supply of Ramen noodles, so you tell me who came out on top. She can keep her pitiable advertising executive and his cliché picket fence.

And I've got you. Why would I want two Barringers nagging me and pointing out my flaws? At least when you do it, it's not personal. I realize she's not technically a Barringer anymore, but you understand my meaning.

If you want to worry about something, worry about the chapters I'll be sending your way. Maybe worry about a certain computer technician down at the Discount Circuits store. He could use a little worry about now.

-Ben

CHAPTER SIX

+++

The Soviet Connection

The White House: 10:23 AM

Dawkins emerged from the conference room, adjusting his cuffs. "Thank you, Mr. Bridger," he said to the heavy secret serviceman holding the door. The murmur of arguing politicians diminished as the door closed behind him.

"Mr. President, may I have a word with you?"

It was General McTavish. He stood statue-still, icy blue eyes peering out of a lined, weathered face. "Afternoon, General. Does it have anything to do with tax laws, trade embargoes, or Texas seceding from the Union?"

"None of the above, Mr. President."

"Then I'm all ears," said Dawkins, "Whatever it is, it will be a refreshing change of pace. Walk with me to my office."

"Thank you, Mr. President."

They began their trek toward the west wing, followed by the heavy footfalls of Dawkins's secret service escort. "To what do I owe the honor, General?"

"I'm afraid we have a situation on our hands."

"In other news, it's Thursday. Please, General. Go on."

"Mr. President, last night around 04:00 hours, a meteor struck one of our spy satellites, knocking it out of orbit. Shortly thereafter, it entered Earth's atmosphere and crashed down somewhere in the Taymyr Peninsula in the northern tip of Russia."

"I'm guessing we don't want the Russians getting ahold of that satellite."

"According to our intel, they already have."

"I assume the information is encoded?"

"Codes can be broken, Mr. President."

They arrived at the door to the oval office and stopped. "And if they access the information on that satellite, what would that mean, General?"

McTavish straightened his uniform. "I'd prefer we were in your office before I divulge that information. But if Hiroshima had a baby with Chernobyl and named him Charles Manson, it wouldn't hold a candle to what we'd have on our hands."

Dawkins nodded at one of the secret servicemen, who then opened the door. Behind it lay the oval office, just as Dawkins had left it, but with one addition.

A grim-faced man sat at the presidential desk, leaning on its surface with one elbow. In the opposite hand, he held open a small paperback. He had clearly not seen a razor in a few days. He looked up as Dawkins and McTavish entered the room. "Pardon me, boys. Hope you don't mind, I let myself in. Just needed a spot to read."

Like a violent ballet, four secret servicemen maneuvered into the strategic corners of the room with guns drawn, placing the shabby trespasser in the nexus of their trajectories. "Sir, you need to stand down. Stand down, sir!"

The grim-faced trespasser raised his hands in a sort of mock surrender. "You got it. This is me standing down. Whatever you say."

"What in hell's shithouse is going on here?" exclaimed McTavish. "How'd this idiot get in?"

"Through the library," said the trespasser. "Guess I got a little turned around. I *thought* this room was kinda ovular."

"Sir," said one of the secret servicemen, "You need to drop what's in your hand. Drop it, sir!"

The trespasser dropped the paperback. One of the other secret servicemen moved in to retrieve it while another came up from behind the trespasser, positioned his hands behind his back, and shoved him face-down onto the surface of the desk. Still another ordered backup through a mouthpiece on his lapel.

A lightning-quick pat-down produced an unloaded revolver, a handful of pens, and some cheap business cards. "Joe Slade, Private Detective," said a serviceman reading from a business card before crumpling it and tossing it into the wastebasket.

"What you got there, Simmons?" Dawkins pointed.

"It's a book, Mr. President."

"I got that. Let's get a look at it."

The serviceman shifted across the office, never removing his eyes or the muzzle of his gun from the intruder. He held the book in front of Dawkins. "For your protection, Mr. President, I must insist you do not touch it until we've had the lab check it for contact toxins."

Dawkins snatched the book from the serviceman's hand. "I'll take my chances." The paper cover curved outward and bore the wear of heavy use. The outer spine was cracked in several places. The title, *Grave Plots*, showed in large blue letters above a picture of a shadowy figure holding a shovel at the head of a boardroom table. Dawkins flipped through the pages. "It's half blank."

"Yeah," said the man called Joe Slade, slightly muffled by the surface of the president's desk, "I don't think it's going to be a bestseller."

"Westing, huh? Never read him."

"Don't start. He's a bastard and his books are dog piss."

Dawkins caught the eye of the serviceman subduing the trespasser. "Is it really necessary for him to kiss my workspace?"

"Sorry, Mr. President. We can't risk—"

"Oh, risk it for once. What's he going to do?" Dawkins bristled at the idea of leading the country from behind glass walls. While there was a need for caution, it always reminded him of the old Travolta movie about the boy who lived in a bubble.

The serviceman scowled and let the trespasser sit up. Joe Slade flexed his jaw. "Thanks. Just for that, I won't tell you I voted for the other guy."

Dawkins smiled. "You know, son, you're in a mess of trouble right now."

"Looks that way."

"You can't just walk into the oval office and think you're going to get off. You're lucky you didn't get shot."

"I wouldn't call me lucky. That's one thing I'm not."

"Mr. President," said McTavish next to him, "We don't have time for this. The Russians—"

"The Russians can wait two minutes, General." There was something to this intruder. Something Dawkins could not put his finger on. A puzzle. One that it was inexplicably urgent to solve. "Two minutes. Hear that, son? That's how long you've got to explain yourself if you don't want to be staring at brick walls for a looong time."

The trespasser looked down for a moment, then back up and said, "I don't know. It's hard to explain."

"Try."

Joe Slade wriggled his nose like he needed to scratch it, but his hands were still being held behind his back by a 200-lb. agent. He stopped and met Dawkins's eyes. "What would you say if I told you you're not really the president?"

McTavish snorted.

Dawkins straightened his cuffs. "Well, I am the president."

"Yeah, but actually you're not."

"No. Actually, I am. There was an election. I was there."

"It was a daydream. You're not the president now, and you never were."

"General McTavish," said Dawkins, "Who is the president of the United States?"

"You are, Mr. President."

Dawkins looked at Joe Slade and shrugged. "What now?"

"He's not really a general."

Dawkins rolled his eyes. "Son, this is pretty piss-poor as explanations go. I'm trying to help you here, but you better make sense in the next few seconds or I can't make any promises."

Joe Slade popped a kink out of his neck. "Okay. Say some asshole walks into your oval office and sullies your ivory chair with his presence. Then he has the gall to tell you you're not the president. You laugh it off because he's obviously an idiot. But then a twist. You find out you're not the president. The asshole was right, idiot or no, and everything you knew is a lie."

"Where are you going with this?"

"About two days ago," said Joe Slade, "Someone told me I'm not the president."

Dawkins scanned the intruder's face for some sign of irony. He did not find any. "That's your problem? And that's why you broke into the White House?"

"Not really. I was just tired of walking around."

Dawkins cracked the knuckles on his hand with his thumb. "Look at me. I don't know what you've got swimming around in your head, but this is the land of the free and home of the brave. Know why? Because men and women no different from you and me are brave and they strive to make it free. You want to know a secret? I've got one of the shittiest jobs in the country. But somebody's got to do it. If I don't, then Hiroshima and Chernobyl are going to have a baby in Russia. Am I right, General?"

"That is correct, Mr. President."

"Now you messed up, son. You messed up big. And you're going to have problems for it. But you need to stop worrying about who the president is and figure out who *you're* supposed to be. That starts right now. You hear me?"

The trespasser tilted his head. "Actually, that kinda helps."

"Good."

"I didn't really vote for the other guy."

"Oh?"

"Actually, there is no other guy. He's not real either."

Dawkins shook his head. "You got a long road ahead of you, son."

"Yeah. Can I have my book back?"

Dawkins placed the worn paperback on the desk in front of him. "You remember what I said."

"Is this the intruder?" said a voice behind him.

Dawkins turned. Two more servicemen in black suits and ties had entered the room. "Welcome to the party, gentlemen. I think we've got the situation under control."

"We're here to escort the intruder, sir. We'll take it from here."

"Sweet Susan's syphilis!" General McTavish shot a sharp look at the latest agents. "Is that what passes for secret service anymore? Eisenhower is rolling in his grave. When is the last time you shaved, boy?"

The new agents *were* unusual. The first had a ginger Viking beard and stood two feet shorter than the average G-man. The other was tall enough, but slender, and he wore a green ski cap over his ears. "I think we need to see some badges, gentlemen," said Dawkins.

"Of course," said the fuzzy agent, "Special Agent Ski Cap, show them our badges, would you?"

The slender agent reached for his pocket, but never produced a badge. Instead, he moved like a blur toward the nearest serviceman, who found himself suddenly disarmed and sprawled out on the floor. Dawkins noticed another serviceman dropping in his periphery next to the bearded agent. Meanwhile, "Agent Ski Cap" launched into another of Dawkins's men, gave him a clean chop to the head, and hurled his unconscious body into the fourth who had been restraining the intruder. Before Dawkins or McTavish could react, they found two secret service-grade sidearms pointing at them.

"Agents down," shouted McTavish. "Mr. President, get behind me."

"Not going to make a difference, General," said Dawkins, "What's this about, Joe?"

The man called Joe Slade rose and snatched up the paperback. "No worries, Your Honor. Or however I'm supposed to address you. Just my escort."

"Oh, you've got worries, son. This just went to a whole other place of worries."

"I'll get out of your hair. You've got Chernobyl's baby to deal with or something." Joe stooped to retrieve his empty revolver from the unconscious serviceman on the floor, then crossed the office to the strange newcomers. "As for me, I've got an appointment with the World Where the Books Are Written. It's time for some payback. I was wondering if you boys were going to turn up somewhere."

The slender agent examined his stolen gun. "I don't actually know how to use one of these."

The short agent groaned "Why do you always ruin the moment? You all right, Joe?"

"Just great, Special Agent Grizzly. Actually, I'm doing a hell of a lot better than I was." Joe shot a glance at Dawkins. "I know this won't make much sense, but thanks. For what you said." He gave a quick nod. "Oh, and you can count on my vote, sir."

With that, they disappeared into the hall as inexplicably as they had arrived. McTavish was instantly on a mouthpiece, calling in more men to secure the area, but Dawkins knew in his gut they would find nothing. The puzzle was gone. Some things were better left unsolved.

To: Howard Zagny
From: Ben Westing
Subject: RE: It's been a while

Howard,

Sorry I didn't write back sooner. Life has been interesting lately. Hope you are well. I heard you had some kind of breakdown a while back. Sorry, I don't know the PC way of saying that. But we've all been worrying about you.

You asked me in your message whether I had had strange dreams or unexplainable moods. Only every day of my life! A few nights ago, I dreamed I was lost in a giant library. Freud would probably say it meant I'm having writer's block. And I am. Of a sort. Hard to explain, so I won't.

You asked about writing things I don't remember writing. Is that something you experienced? What was that like? Did your doctors say anything about it? Did they prescribe anything that helped? I don't mean to probe. I'm probably being insensitive or something. But it's good to hear from you.

-Ben

CHAPTER SEVEN

+++

Nexus of Words

"We're back!" shouted Kribble, "And we got Joe!"

Joe staggered into Reading Lounge L-7, still shaking off nausea from his trip. The area was much as it had been two days ago, piles of books strewn about. The differences were some piles had grown taller, steaming plates of sustenance sat upon one of the tables, and Ellodrine now wore silky indigo robes inscribed with strange symbols. She sat in a cushioned chair, poring over a book and petting the blue-furred aerial feline curled in her lap.

She looked up as they approached. "Ah, you've returned."

Joe offered a mock bow. "You've been expecting me?"

Ellodrine closed her book. "Yes, actually. To an extent. You're a protagonist, after all. Initially rejecting your quest is a classic part of the hero's journey. But the hero comes back. Usually after some sort of epiphany. Did you have an epiphany, Joe?"

"Psh!" said Kribble, plodding up, "Course he did! Guy like Joe has 'piphonies all the time."

"You could call it that." Joe ran a hand through his hair. "Didn't want to believe it at first, but you can't argue with the facts, even when they seem to break all the rules. Okay. I live in a book. Nothing I can do to change that. So, I ask myself, what *am* I going to do?"

"Do tell," said Aelrûn dryly.

"I found the answer right here." Joe retrieved from his pocket the copy of *Grave Plots* and handed it to Kribble. "I must have read it fifty times.

Kept going over our meeting. Looking for clues. Something that made sense. But the answer wasn't there. It was later."

"There isn't anything later," said Kribble, "It's blank."

"Exactly." Joe tapped on the book in Kribble's hands. "The blank pages. Unwritten. Untouched by an author's hand. Maybe our lives really do amount to nothing but some ink on a few scraps of paper."

"Very inspirational, thank you," said Aelrûn.

Joe ignored him. "I blamed you at first. The three of you. I thought my entire life disappeared the minute you stepped into it. But you didn't take my life. I never had it. Not till now, anyway. The truth is, you gave it to me when you handed me a book with blank pages. Those are my pages. And I've got big plans to fill 'em."

"YEAH!" shouted Kribble. "I told you this was our guy! Didn't I tell you this was our guy?"

"Many times, Kribble," said Ellodrine. She rose, to her feline companion's dismay, and extended her hand. "Welcome, Joe. I'm glad you will be working with us."

Joe took her hand in his and gave it a firm shake. "Thanks, Elle. May our authors never know what hit them."

Ellodrine tilted her head. "Elle? You only used the first syllable of my name. The way you do yours. Is that a nickname? I've read about those somewhere. We don't have nicknames in Corolathia."

"That's because in Corolathia," said Aelrûn, "Names are chosen for their lyrical resonance. Language should be composed, not shoved around in chopped up fragments like so many predigested syllables."

"Bah." Kribble waved a hand through the air. "Suit yourself, Ael. The rest of us would rather just get on with it."

Ellodrine moved it around her mouth as though she were tasting it. "Elle. Elle? Elllle. Quite acceptable. I, for one, can do without O-DREEN every time someone addresses me. Very well. I approve. You may refer to me as Elle."

Aelrûn glowered at them. He flopped down onto a chair, his harp somehow suddenly in his hand, and played the opening to *Sweet Home Alabama*.

Joe nudged Kribble. "How does he do that? Lynyrd Skynyrd on a harp, I mean."

"Oh, that? He found some sheet music in The Library." Kribble nodded as though that somehow explained it. "Sure beats that elven crap he used to play."

"Thank you, Kribble," said Aelrûn, still strumming, "You know how I value your artistic opinion."

"Oh!" Ellodrine placed a finger in the air. "Sarcasm. I heard it. He said that insincerely to emphasize the opposite point. What a curious use for words."

"Yeah," said Joe, "So, Lynyrd Skynyrd is in The Library of Corolathia?"

"Yes," said Ellodrine. She gestured toward the shelves. "Everything ever written is out there somewhere. Even unfinished works like your book and ours. In fact, that is how we first discovered the true nature of our existence. The four of us."

"What four?" asked Joe. "I thought there were just three of you."

Kribble's face drooped.

Aelrûn stopped playing.

Ellodrine looked to the floor with twilight blue eyes. "There *are* only three of us. But there was another. Our original protagonist, Corbin Adlander. He was the hero of our story. A simple farm boy sealed with the mark of destiny to do battle with an evil necromancer named Zolethos. Our story's antagonist, you see."

"We'd come through so much together," said Kribble.

"Seven and a half books," said Ellodrine. "That's when we discovered... Well, you know. It was difficult for all of us. But he never could accept it. The quest was too important to him. He wouldn't believe it wasn't real."

"Where is he now?" asked Joe.

"Dead," said Kribble, "Went off on his own. We couldn't stop him. He tried to finish the plot alone, but... I should have been there for him."

Ellodrine placed a hand on her short friend's shoulder. "We read about it in excruciating detail. He tried to take on an entire greblin encampment. Savage creatures, those greblins. Well, we all made our decisions." She rubbed wetness from her eyes with her sleeve. "And that brings us to you, Joe."

"In what way?"

"Don't you see? You are our protagonist. We—that is, Aelrûn, Kribble and I—are supporting characters. We are not heroes. I will serve as your mentor. Kribble and Aelrûn will act as allies. We have a plan ready to launch, but we need..."

Joe adjusted his collar. "But you need me to carry the torch for you."

She bit her lip. "We'll support you the whole way. Howard wrote us to be quite helpful. You could read about it if you want to."

Joe smiled a sly half-smile at her. "I don't know exactly how you plan to do this. Frankly, I think you're all crazy. But I'm in. When do we start?"

Ellodrine smiled. Her irises took on an amber hue. "First thing tomorrow. We mustn't waste any time. After all, Zolethos and his nasty greblins are still hunting for us, and we have tarried long enough as it is. Our first destination is a secret book where Howard won't be able to read over our shoulders."

"Wait," said Joe, "Howard can read what we're doing?"

Ellodrine gave him the sort of pitying look one might give a child who has just discovered where lamb chops come from. "Of course he can, Joe. We are in *his* book. But enough talk. You must be hungry. I raided a lovely cookbook for dinner tonight. *Fusion Infusion* by Leslie Albracht. I think you will find the Teriyaki Tacos quite acceptable."

Joe paused as his three new companions strode toward the feast upon the table. He compulsively reached into the pocket that used to house his smokes. Instead, his fingers rankled a paper he had almost forgotten. He removed it from his pocket and examined it. There in the spidery handwriting was his name.

Joe Slade.

To: Ben Westing
From: Howard Zagny
Subject: The Truth

Ben,

Thank you for responding. You have always been a good friend, and I am sorry I didn't contact you sooner about my "breakdown." However, some things have escalated recently, and it has become necessary for me to explain something you will find beyond unlikely. There is no good way to say this, so I will simply tell you: I have written a thing which should never be written.

You have read my novels of Corolathia, and you know the eighth volume in the series was due to Colin some time ago. I was happy with it. I had centered the plot around a place called the Nexus of Words. It was a giant repository of knowledge, so complete it included any work ever written on any plane of existence. Even developing works would magically appear upon its shelves, filling themselves with words as their authors penned them. Picture a giant library in a parallel dimension. I thought I was so clever. But that was it, Ben. That was the thing I never should have written.

I sent my character there to gather the knowledge they needed in their fight against Zolethos, the tyrannical necromancer who enslaved their land. They arrived at the Nexus of Words using travel runes inscribed on rings or pendants. They were sifting through books on the shelves. I was writing some dialog when I noticed something odd. It was a sentence I had not typed. *All at once, they noticed a particular volume.* Unalarmed, I deleted that sentence and continued on with my dialog. But when I read back over what I had typed, what I found was: *All at once, they noticed a particular volume.*

I deleted it a second time. And a third. A fourth. I lost count how many times. It only reappeared. And grew. Soon I was reading how they examined the volume. How they began reading the volume. How they debated the meaning of the volume. And what was this strange book they had found? It was *Nexus of Words* by Howard Zagny. Do you understand what I'm telling you, Ben? They were reading *their own book!*

I had unwittingly written it into their world. I created a paradox. And the result was I no longer had control of them. Discovering they were fictional somehow gave them wills of their own. And I'm afraid the situation is contagious. The more they interact with other characters, the more they pull those characters into the same paradox. Also, because the Nexus of Words connects to *every* library on *every* plane of existence, they've also discovered how to go into other books. I have an ally, and we've been able to keep them from traveling to the real world, but they want to cross over. And I don't know how long I'll be able to stop them.

But here's what you need to know, Ben. They have Joe Slade. *Your* Joe Slade. They've enlisted him to outsmart me. And he's angry, Ben. So angry. He's furious you killed off Lily. He wants your blood.

So, there it is, Ben. I don't expect you to believe it, but the truth doesn't apologize for being true. I won't blame you if you think I'm crazy. I thought I was crazy for months. But I had to tell you.

-Howard

To: Howard Zagny
From: Ben Westing
Subject: RE: The Truth

Howard,

Thank you for your response. I appreciate what you are trying to do, and it was helpful in its own way. While I feared I might be suffering a similar condition to your own, I now know it is quite different and thankfully less severe.

I wish you health and happiness, and you've always been a good friend. For this reason, I cannot indulge you in these delusions. I am sad to see you in such a state, and if there is anything I can do to help, you know how to find me.

-Ben

CHAPTER EIGHT

+++

The Marchioness's Temptation

Isabelle entered the ballroom. Her gown floated like ripples of sea-green gossamer. The tailor had selected the color to match her eyes. Coiled locks of her own strawberry hair fluttered in her periphery. More fell in curls that cascaded over her bare shoulders. *Intoxicating.* That is how her husband, the marquis, would describe her. She could hear his words before he said them, his eyes savoring her with every syllable. Tonight, he would not be disappointed. Only, it was not her husband who haunted her thoughts now. Nor was it he who had been the object of last evening's passions but his brother Jonathan.

Guilt consumed her. It mattered little that she had rebuffed Jonathan's advances. Or that she had pulled away from his touch. Or that she had demanded fervently he re-don his shirt. Her conscience tormented her because her actions had been despite her desires. She still felt the touch of Jonathan's fingers where they had caressed her skin. She still felt the heat of his breath on the nape of her neck. When she closed her eyes, she saw his. Untamed and blue. Deep as oceans. She felt she might drown in them.

"Milady? Are you well?"

Isabelle opened her eyes. Geoffrey stood attentively beside her. In his hand was a tray of hors d'oeuvres.

"Thank you, Geoffrey. I am well. I was momentarily overwhelmed." She gestured to the ballroom before her.

He smiled. "It is quite grand, isn't it, milady? I shall attend to my duties then, shall I?"

Isabelle nodded and offered him a forced smile. He departed into the swirling mass of silks and colors that filled the room.

Her fib was not entirely untrue. She had never really become accustomed to life as a marchioness since she had married Lucas. She had been a simple girl with little thought to spend on gentlemen and courtship. Rather, she enjoyed riding her horse through the countryside and escaping the clutches of her vigilant caretakers. Now she lived in a mansion and attended glorious balls to which she wore elaborate gowns. She ate delectable foods she would be hard-pressed to pronounce. And she was the wife of a handsome and noble marquis.

Her heart was rent in two. The greater part of her still doted upon her husband and would always be faithful to him. Loved him with an immeasurable passion. Yet the marquis had been much absent in the last several months. Both physically and in other ways. His mind was more often on his duties than on shirking them with her in the bedroom. He had begun buttoning his shirt. What was that about? Isabelle never understood the point of buttons and felt they were highly overrated. If that was not enough, Lucas's brother Jonathan had secretly sought her affection in this time of strain between them. And there was a part of her, a part she dearly wished she could extinguish, that welcomed him.

She could feel every eye upon her from the dance floor. Though it was impossible for them to know of her prior evening's temptation, she felt as though they could see right through her. And there was Lucas, the marquis, speaking to some dull aristocrats, as was his duty. Still, he looked so gallant as he stood in his ballroom attire. His hair danced about his head in thick, dark curls. Presently, he took notice of her and excused himself from his conversation.

Isabelle felt a deep pang in the pit of her stomach.

"Isabelle, darling! I'm so glad you have finally arrived. Fashionably late as usual, my dear." Lucas smiled radiantly at her. His eyes were blue and clear, like a mountain lake. He winked at her devilishly. "Perhaps we can slip out early, just you and I."

Isabelle flushed. Torn between a thousand feelings both terrible and wonderful, she hesitated as she took his hand. He noticed. She could see it in his face. He knew something was wrong. Lucas had always been so intuitive. That was one thing she had adored about him, but now it would make it impossible to keep her sec —

Suddenly, an enormous crash sounded from the library.

Isabelle ignored it. Lucas had always been so intuitive. That was one thing she had adored about him, but now it would make it impossible to keep her secret. It would not take him long to determine —

"Excuse me!" exclaimed a loud, guttural voice from the library, "My fault. I admit it. Still, it's a pretty flimsy bookshelf if it falls over that easy."

Isabelle blinked. Oh, yes. Lucas was intuitive. She adored it about him, but he was hard to keep secrets from. It would not take him long to determine —

"Can we not take you anywhere?" shouted another voice from the library. This voice was rather lyrical, though full of irritation. "I mean, what part of 'we must be utterly stealthy' was difficult for you to understand?"

"It was top-heavy!" shouted the guttural voice, "Did you see how many books were on the top shelf?"

"The bottom shelves were full too! That doesn't make it top-heavy!"

Now there was loud shushing and a female voice that said, "The shouting is not helping. We're supposed to be staying in the background, remember? Do not draw attention to yourselves."

Isabelle took a deep breath and stilled herself to filter out any further distractions from the library. Now, where was she? Lucas was intuitive. Adored, but hard to keep secrets from. Not long before he would determine... Oh yes. It would not be long before he determined the root of her hesitation, and then his covetous fury —

Four new guests in curious formal attire stumbled clumsily out of the archway connecting the library. Geoffrey appeared dutifully to greet them. One of the new guests, particularly short and unshaven, said to him, "I don't envy the guy who's got to clean up *that* mess."

"For the love of decency!" exclaimed Isabelle. "Who is *that?*"

"Who is *that?*" echoed Lucas at the same moment, but not with the same tone. Hers had been frustration. His, intrigue. Bordering on fascination.

Isabelle quickly noticed what had drawn Lucas's eye. One of the four clumsy guests, the one wearing an indigo ball gown, was simply the most beautiful woman Isabelle had ever seen. Isabelle could not determine what it was about this woman that qualified her so, and yet she could not deny the fact. The woman's hair was deep chestnut brown, and her skin utterly flawless. Her eyes appeared blue one moment, then green or violet another. Her lips were full and red. Yet none of these qualities, nor even all of them put together, could account for the irresistible beauty of the woman in the indigo gown.

One of the woman's escorts, tall and grim-faced, turned to her and said, "This is your secret location, huh? Classy." Though he seemed to have more to say, he stopped short suddenly, as though he were noticing her for the first time. "Whoa! What happened to you? I thought you said we weren't supposed to attract attention."

The woman looked bashfully down at her indigo gown. "Does it look bad?" she asked him.

"It doesn't look bad, Elle," said the grim-faced man, "But it stands out a bit."

She sighed and said, "We'll just have to make do. Stay in the background and try not to be noticed."

Isabelle tore her eyes from the spectacle and remembered her own near miss with infidelity. Her eyes welled with tears as she grasped Lucas's hands. She lowered her gaze and composed herself to prepare for the most dreadful confession. Drawing upon her reserves of courage, she lifted her head and looked deeply into his...

He was not even looking at her. His head was turned toward the woman in the indigo gown. Isabelle clenched her jaw. "Lucas!"

"Eh, yes, darling? Give me a moment, would you? I need to check on our new guests."

"Lucas!"

●   ●   ●

Lucas wove through the crowded ballroom toward the newcomers. They were as strange an assembly of characters as he had ever seen. For starters, something about their apparel was off. Though they were dressed in regalia fit for a ball, the style of their clothing would have been fashionable, perhaps two decades gone. They resembled a troupe of traveling players who had costumed themselves in second-hand attire to portray some tragic tale. Or perhaps a comedy would be more apt. A short unshaven man, stout with a gravelly voice, led the way. Next to him walked a slender man, lank and graceful, upon whom the trappings of aristocracy seemed particularly fitting. Oddly though, he wore a large powdered wig pulled over his ears. The third man looked not unhandsome, but as though his garb did not entirely suit him. Yet there was a certain quality about him— a determination in his movements, a certainty in his glances—that revealed he was a man of action and duty.

And then there was the woman. The woman in the indigo gown.

Lucas had never been a man to chase after every pretty face. Many perfectly lovely girls simply bored him. It was Isabelle's adventurous spirit that had drawn him to her. Then why? Why was he inextricably drawn to this woman in the indigo gown? Why did he so urgently need to know more about her? It had been his intention to introduce himself, yet he hesitated. No. He must observe her first. He lost himself in the crowd and watched.

The woman in the indigo gown approached the dance floor with her companions.

"How do we get across?" asked the unshaven dwarf.

The grim-faced man offered his hand to the lady. "May I have this dance?"

"Oh. Uh. I'm not sure I can. I've not done this before."

"They're waltzing," said the grim-faced man. "If you can count to three, you can waltz. Or did you change your mind about blending in?"

She grimaced. "Very well. I hope you know what you're doing." She took his hand and allowed him to sweep her onto the floor. For all her allure, she was accurate in her assessment regarding her dancing ability. She bumped into several other dancers and caused the Duchess of Estlebury to shriek loudly about a smashed toe.

The remaining two strangers glanced at one another awkwardly. The slender man with the overlarge powdered wig shrugged and grasped the hand of an exquisite blond girl in a sky-blue gown and launched onto the dance floor with her without a word between them. He maneuvered with inhuman grace through the ballroom equipped with his giggling captive, who clearly had no desire for rescue. Together, they twirled, leaped, and wove their way through the throng of waltzing nobles. Murmurs of amazement surrounded them as they progressed.

The unshaven dwarf propositioned several nearby ladies who each replied with polite excuses, except for the hunchbacked daughter of the Earl of Wessex, who openly laughed in his face. Undaunted, he began to perform an odd sort of shimmy to the music and clumsily waltzed himself into the multitude.

Lucas had to get closer. He noticed the Baroness of Lambreshire wandering near, and extended his hand, "Would you do me the honor?"

"My lord, of course."

He whisked her onto the floor and waltzed in a beeline toward the woman in the indigo gown.

"If you don't mind my saying," said the baroness, "That Isabelle of yours is quite a vision."

"Hmm? Oh, yes. She does that sometimes."

He deftly twisted through a narrow space in the shifting labyrinth of dancers until the indigo gown was in sight. She was still tripping over her own feet. Lucas could make out the sound of her partner's voice.

"You've got to relax, Elle. You're thinking too hard about it."

"I'm counting to three, Joe. It's not working."

"Then stop counting. It isn't calculus, it's dancing. Just follow my lead."

The baroness said something. Lucas shook himself from his trance. "I'm sorry, madam. What was that?"

"I asked you what you meant. You whispered 'L.' What does L stand for?"

"You are mistaken, madam. I am quite certain I said no such thing."

"Forgive me, my lord, I am quite certain you did."

"Then it's as much a mystery to me as to you. Let's keep dancing." Over her shoulder, he could see the woman in the indigo gown now keeping step with her partner. She was a far cry from what one would call graceful, but she was now performing something that could arguably be called a waltz. Yet in some unexplainable way, even her lack of grace was utterly captivating. Lucas saw he was not the only one who thought so. Several of the men on the dance floor were clearly looking over their ladies' shoulders to sneak a glance at the enticing Elle in the indigo gown.

Lucas heard her exclaim, "What does Aelrûn think he's doing?" She fixed her glare across the ballroom upon her slender companion, who was currently spinning like a whirling dervish with his blond partner squealing in his arms. "What about *that* is stealthy?"

"Eh, he's a show-off," said grim-faced Joe, "Ignore him."

"How do I ignore that? He's literally making a spectacle of himself."

"Who?"

"You know very well who! Aelrûn."

"Oh, I'm ignoring him. See? Isn't that easy?"

She made a face at Joe that was not amusement, and Lucas could almost swear her eyes flashed a curious red-orange color. "It doesn't matter, we're here," she said. "The other side of the ballroom. The terrace is right over there. We can stop dancing now."

"Oh, uh... Yeah," said Joe. "What a relief."

Elle smiled at her dance partner. "I know. That's harder than it looks. We should collect Kribble and Aelrûn and head for the garden."

Kribble? Aelrûn? Lucas mused at the odd-sounding names. Perhaps they were —

"'Scuse me."

The unshaven dwarf lumbered past, wiping beads of sweat from his forehead.

"And I thought fighting ogres was hard work. That was grueling. You know how many times I got kicked out there?"

"One down," said Joe.

"Here comes Aelrûn," said Elle.

The slender man maneuvered lithely from the dance floor, deposited his blond accessory gasping for breath onto a nearby chair, and landed next to his comrades with a dramatic bow.

Elle wrinkled her nose at him. "What happened to being subtle?"

"That was subtle. Next time I'll really show you something."

"Let's just go." With that, the four strange guests slipped through the doors to the terrace.

"Madam, thank you for the dance, but I've just remembered something that requires my immediate attention." Lucas departed from the baroness without waiting for her response and raced after them. In a moment, he was hanging over the terrace railing trying to pick them out of the guests milling about in the garden. There. They were heading for the hedge maze. Perfect. Nobody knew those bending corridors as Lucas did.

The last glimpse of indigo was now disappearing into the labyrinth's entrance. He had no time to dawdle. They would head for the gazebo in the center. Lucas vaulted from the terrace toward the hedges at top speed. The chase was on.

CHAPTER NINE

+++

The Marchioness's Temptation

Lucas raced along passages of greenery and blossoming roses. Thorns tore at his sleeves as he cut corners on his way to the gazebo. They had the lead, but he had the advantage. He knew every twist and turn of this maze so well he could navigate it blind. Including the shortcuts. Presently, he slid at full speed into the center of a hedge wall. Though there appeared to be no opening, Lucas knew it had been trimmed just so, and the vegetation would give way to an imperceptible hole in the botanical partition. In a moment, he was on the other side. Only a few more quick turns and...

There she was. Standing in the gazebo precisely as he had suspected. With her were her three strange companions. Lucas crouched behind a hedge. It was not in his upbringing to spy, but he could not help himself. He felt an inexplicable need to know more about her. He listened.

"This is your secret location, is it?" said the one called Joe.

"I believe it offers us some privacy, yes," said Elle, "The festivities back in the mansion should be engaging enough to keep the narration away from us. But we must remember to stay in the background. Don't you think I'm not speaking to you, Aelrûn! The last thing we want is to show up in some other author's book and let our plans appear in print where they can make their way to Howard or Mr. Westing."

"You think *I* drew attention?" said the one called Aelrûn, "Did you see Kribble? Doing some kind of dwarven jig? He looked like he was drunk."

"Well, I usually *am* drunk when I dance!" said the short one. "If I'm dancing, it's probably *because* I'm drunk."

"It doesn't matter," said Elle, "Next time I need you to be stealthy, I shan't take you to a dance. Apparently, it's too much to ask of you."

"You're one to talk," said Aelrûn, "How many toes did you step on from one end of the room to the other? Do you suppose they noticed that?"

"Minor miscalculation. I hadn't planned on dancing at all. It hadn't occurred to me we wouldn't be able simply to walk across."

"Good thing you had Joe then," said Kribble, "Do I know how to pick 'em, or what?"

Elle's cheeks grew slightly rosy. "Yes, actually. That was a fortuitous surprise. I must admit, Joe, I would not have guessed you'd know how to waltz."

Joe leaned casually against the gazebo railing. "Lily taught me. Grew up real proper, her. Dragged me to her family's fancy parties from time to time. Said I made them bearable. You pick up a thing or two."

"That's right!" said Kribble, "And you danced with her at the charity gala in *The Glass Swan* where those smugglers were trafficking diamonds in the ice sculptures! Remember when you shot out the ballerina with your .45 in the middle of the party to get the jewels out? BLAM! I wish I could have been there."

Elle placed a hand on his shoulder. "That's enough, Kribble. We must attend to our business and move on before we are discovered. For starters, I'd like to have a look at the note Joe's been hiding."

"Note?" exclaimed the one called Aelrûn, shooting a nasty look at Joe. "What note?"

"Yes, Joe," said Elle. "Let's have it. The one with your name in the spidery handwriting that you're hiding in your pocket."

Joe made a theatrically wounded face. "Hiding? Whose says I'm hiding anything? Just because I haven't shown it to *you* yet?" He reached into his vest and produced a folded parchment torn at the bottom." He passed it to her. "You're the boss."

"I'm the *mentor*, actually." Elle snatched it from him and examined it with Aelrûn peeking over her shoulder.

Kribble stood on tiptoes but gained little height from his effort. "I can't see! What does it say?"

"It says," said Elle, "*Joe Slade. I know who you are. And I know where you've come from. You don't belong here. This world is mine. If you side with my enemies, you will share their fate. You have been warned.*"

"Happy?" said Joe.

"Not in the least," said Elle, "Why wouldn't you show this to me straight away?"

"Hadn't got around to it yet. Someone *always* threatens me to drop the case. You get used to it." Joe plucked the note back from her hand. "How did you know about it, anyway?"

Elle thrust a hand onto her hip. "I'm not *stupid*, Joe. We're in a book. I *read* it." She reached into the folds of her gown, pulled out a small book and displayed it in front of him.

Joe gave it a sideways look. "Where in that ball gown have you been keeping that?"

"That's none of your concern."

Lucas pondered at their strange words. Their talk of frozen ballerinas and cryptic epistles only heightened the mystery surrounding these odd guests. In replacing her book to... wherever she kept it, Elle had turned her back to Lucas. He edged his way around for a better view.

"The point at hand," she thrust a finger into the air, "Is Zolethos has clearly found us, and we must make absolute haste to see we are well within the WWTBAW before he rallies his forces."

"I'm already lost," said Joe, "What's the WW-something-something-something-W?"

"World Where the Books Are Written. WWTBAW. It's an initialism."

"Shouldn't an initialism be *easier* to say?"

"Precisely." She gave Joe a curt nod. "With a necromantic warlord after us, we must expedite our operation. Our only resources are whatever we can salvage from the developing manuscripts available to us. With these, we must cross the gap between our world and our authors'."

"Can't we use these rune things?" Joe tapped an odd amulet upon his chest.

"No good," said Kribble. "Howard beat us to it."

"What does that mean?"

"While the runes do connect the Nexus of Words to all other book repositories," said Elle, "They also belong to Howard. Shortly after we discovered we could use them to travel to different books, we discovered a treatise in The Library by one *Howard Zagnys, High Oracle of the Runes* stating their magic could never be used to bring seditious rune-bearers to the realm of their creator."

Joe chuckled. "That's what you get for being seditious. But he still lets you go into other books."

"He doesn't *let* us, Joe." Elle began to pace, ample lengths of indigo ball gown rippling as she walked. "We established it with our precedent. We did it before he thought to write that we couldn't. In turn, he blocked us from his world before we thought to travel there."

Joe smiled a mischievous half-smile. "Hence your battle of wits. It's all about who figures it out first."

"Yes," said Elle, still pacing, "and that is exactly why, *Aelrûn,* we must not draw attention to ourselves. If we are too interesting, the narrative's shifting perspective will latch onto us and our plans may end up in Howard's hand. We know how *splendid* that would be."

"Hey, your sarcasm is getting better."

"Thank you, Kribble. I've been practicing."

Lucas's mind whirled. He could barely make sense of what he was hearing. By now, Elle had stopped pacing and stood where he could just make out her breathtaking indigo-clad profile. If he could shift just a little further, he would be able to view her utterly captivating... attributes. He silently chastised himself for spying, but he did not exactly repent of it.

"Actually, Howard may have done us a favor," Elle was saying. "To the WWTBAW we are the stuff of fiction. We are imaginary. Say we crossed the gap between worlds. What would happen? Are we foolish enough to believe we could go to a higher plane of reality with no side effects? What if we're like ghosts, unable to interact with the world? What if we're like dreams, and we simply dissipate upon arrival? What if we seem fine at first, but then slowly and painfully disintegrate over the course of several days?"

"Wait," said Kribble, "I don't think I'm excited about this plan anymore."

"You'd rather be a slave to Howard Zagny?"

Kribble kicked at the ground. "No."

"Then listen. I believe I have found two artifacts that will help us bridge the gap successfully. Neither of the artifacts will work alone, but I believe their combined effects will grant us the existence we desire outside the pages of any book."

"And the trouble is?" said Joe.

Elle sighed. "They won't be easy to get. They are both major plot devices in the books from which we must burgle them."

"Of course they are." Joe adjusted his vest. "But you're a wizard, aren't you? Can't you whip up some invisibility magic for us? We'll sneak in, grab the loot, and slip out before anyone is the wiser."

Elle shook her head. "Magic doesn't exist in every story. We bring some with us by nature of being who we are. Enough to allow the runes to work, and I can manage some minor effects, but nothing I would call useful. It often backfires."

Joe smiled. "It's a heist then. We get in, steal the artifacts, open a door to the WW-whatever-whatever, then..." Joe pressed a fist into his hand and cracked his knuckles. "We give our authors a plot twist they'll never see coming."

Lucas found himself hiding behind a low hedge where he could barely view them over the top. Elle's face was now at a lovely angle, but the setting sun glared behind her, drowning out her exquisite features. He sidled a bit to the left. It was slightly better, but if he could venture a few more steps, perhaps he could make out the curve of her neck as it sloped into her champagne-glass shoulders and down into her enticing, if not exactly voluptuous, bosom. He sidestepped. Slightly better. He sidestepped. Almost there. He sidestepped.

Suddenly, he heard a loud and inhuman shriek.

CHAPTER TEN

+++

The Marchioness's Temptation

Lucas turned to discover the source of the scream. Next to him stood a figure in a dark cloak. Two inhuman red eyes burned from the depths of its hood. Lucas quickly discovered the reason for the creature's cry. He had stepped on its foot.

"What was that?" he heard Joe say from the gazebo.

"We've been discovered," said Elle.

The hooded thing made a swipe at Lucas. The marquis pulled back instinctively, and the blow glanced off his cheek. Another swipe. This time Lucas caught the assailant's arm by the wrist and held it fast. A set of wicked black claws tipped the creature's fingers. Lucas used his free hand to rip the monster's hood from its face. It was hideous. Its skin was a mottled green, covered with blemishes. Bat-like ears extended from its head. They were torn and missing chunks of flesh. Sharp, yellowed teeth lined its mouth. Its red eyes bore nothing but contempt and guile.

"What manner of devilry is this?" cried Lucas.

With its unclasped hand, the creature removed a black dagger from a sheath in its belt and swept it toward Lucas's abdomen. Lucas threw himself back to avoid it. He landed hard upon the springy ground.

The creature lost no time. It uttered a bestial snarl at him and retreated into the hedge maze.

"Did you get a good look at it?" said a gravelly voice beside him. Lucas was not alone. The four strangers now stood around him. The one called Kribble was extending a hand to help him up.

"It was a monster!" said Lucas, not taking Kribble's hand.

Aelrûn sniffed at the air. "Greblin. Unmistakable."

Elle met the marquis's gaze. Her eyes were red-violet and glowed with intensity. "You, sir! Do you have greblins in this book?"

"What's a greblin?"

She scowled. "He must have followed us then."

"You had to *ask* to figure that out?" said Joe.

"We'll get him!" shouted Kribble. Then he and Aelrûn raced off into the labyrinth.

"We'd better follow," said Joe, "They might need some backup." He was wielding a curious firearm in his right hand. Not like Lucas's flintlock, rather a mechanical contraption that sported an odd cylindrical component from which the barrel extended. Joe must have noticed Lucas admiring it because he said, "It's a revolver. Don't think too hard about it. It's probably the least weird thing you're about to see."

Lucas leaped to his feet. "I know the best route! You may address me as Lucas, by the way. Follow me!"

He took off through the winding corridors. Glancing back, he saw Joe was only a step behind. Elle swept along after as quickly as she could, dragging an ostentatious indigo ball gown.

"This thing is so impractical," she complained, holding forth rivulets of silk to keep them from dragging on the ground or catching on branches.

"You'd think the tailor might have considered you'd be chasing a monster through a hedge maze," said Joe, "Go figure."

Around a bend, they came upon Kribble panting and still running on short stumpy legs. As they passed him, he called out through gasping breaths, "You go on ahead. I'll make sure we're not being followed."

"There is a shortcut ahead," said Lucas, "Follow me." He ran straight for a hedge wall. Without losing his stride, he ducked into a slide and skidded into the nearly imperceptible hole. A moment later, he was on the other side. He called back through the branches behind him, "Come on through! I've had the thorns removed from this spot."

•   •   •

Isabelle supported herself on the rails of the terrace overlooking the garden. Music from the ballroom spilled out around her. The sounds of dancing and merrymaking were rich in the air. The smells of sweet delicacies wafted on the breeze. Handsome men in their festive finery and women in beautiful gowns danced the evening away. The sun painted a wealth of colors into the sky that would soon fade into dusk.

Isabelle held in her hand a glass of perfectly aged red wine from the marquis's store. A bottle of this vintage would be worth more than most men earned in ten years. The contents of the glass contained an exotic blend of tastes that perfectly melded and balanced with one another in a way few wines in the world could equal. Any aficionado would lecture this was a wine to be savored slowly and to which one should pay great homage.

In a single fluid motion, Isabelle launched the contents of the glass down her throat, swallowed hard, and winced. She let out a long sigh and set the emptied glass down on the rail next to a row of seven others, each with a tiny pink remnant in the bottom. She resumed her examination of the sunset and belched in an entirely unfeminine way.

Suddenly she felt the light touch of fingertips upon the bared skin of her back. Electric tingles coursed through her body at the touch. These fingers were not the soft skilled fingers of the marquis, her husband. They were the rough-hewn fingers of a man who wandered the wild places of the world. She recognized him without turning around.

"Jonathan," she moaned more sensually than she meant to. Actually, to any person listening in, it would have sounded more like *Shonifan* due to the lingering effects of the wine. Nevertheless, it was filled with guarded desire.

"Isabelle," he whispered softly in her ear, "I am sorry. I simply could not stay away. I am utterly intoxicated by you. Have I told you that?"

She turned toward him, but averted her eyes, "Last evening, I told you..." She was going to say that no matter how lonesome she might be, walking the endless hallways of her mansion home, she could never be unfaithful to her darling Lucas. However, she could not help but think about Lucas's face as he had stared at the woman in the indigo gown. The dreamy glaze that covered his eyes. The way he traversed through the partygoers to close the distance between himself and that despicable woman.

"What is it, Isabelle? What about last evening?"

"It was utterly disappointing! I am certain we can do better." With that, she threw herself into him. Their lips met in an impassioned kiss. She ran her hands into his shirt and along his muscular chest. He wrapped his arms around her waist and pulled her in close. She pressed herself against him and promptly expelled the contents of her stomach.

"Oh! Isabelle! Ugh! Perhaps we should return to this another time." He glanced toward the wineglasses on the terrace railing, silhouetted before the sunset. "How many of these have you had?"

"Oh, Jonathan. I don't believe I can count them in my current state."

"Suffice to say, darling, you have had enough. I'm going to have to remove my shirt."

"Oh, do tell."

"No, not in an exciting way."

"Is there any other way to do it?" asked Isabelle, using what she believed was her seductive voice.

"Frankly, yes. Don't let it burden you, though. I have never been overly fond of shirts, anyway."

Suddenly, a scream rose from amid the guests in the garden. Someone cried out, "It's a monster!"

· · ·

Joe examined the small crawl hole. Ellodrine stood by his side. She looked down at the folds of her ball gown.

"Bogglerot!" she exclaimed.

"I'll follow him," said Joe, "You take the long way. Meet up with us when you can." He pushed himself through the gap and came out on the other side. Lucas was just ahead. Joe pressed on after him around several more bends until he was hopelessly turned around. He pushed himself to keep up with Lucas's pace. His lungs burned, and he silently renewed his resolve to discontinue his use of tobacco.

Suddenly Lucas stopped. He was examining an odd gap in the hedge. This one was larger and more obvious than Lucas's previous crosscut, and, apparently, it was new because it was still giving off tendrils of smoke from its severed blackened branches.

Joe arrived panting next to Lucas. "This another one of your shortcuts?"

"Not mine," said Lucas.

Joe grasped the end of one of the cleanly cut and smoldering branches. "How did somebody do this?"

"However they did it, it's done. The exit is just ahead." Lucas continued the chase.

Something was familiar about Lucas. Something that felt like it would be obvious if only things were not happening so quickly. And also if Joe were not suddenly distracted by a small scrap of yellowed paper at his feet. Pressed for time, he snatched it and shoved it into his pocket. Through the charred gap, he could see the maze exit. He sucked in as much air as his lungs would allow and forced his feet into motion. Moments later, he emerged from the confines of the hedges into the garden.

He could see Lucas sprinting before him. Several strides ahead of Lucas, the slender form of Aelrûn chased after his quarry. Ahead of Aelrûn, partygoers parted shrieking before the monstrous figure, allegedly called a greblin. The greblin glanced back in mid-stride and flung a dagger at Aelrûn. Aelrûn twisted his body to the side and grasped the weapon's handle as it flew by.

In the few seconds the greblin's attention had been focused on Aelrûn, it must not have noticed the unshirted rogue advancing on its position. This powerfully built man launched himself into the greblin, thrusting his shoulder into its stomach and knocking it heartily onto its back. The greblin lurched quickly back to its feet. The bare-chested scoundrel was slower to recover, but Aelrûn had already closed the gap.

"Stand down," he demanded, the black dagger flashing dangerously in his hand.

The creature spat at his feet and drew a long scimitar from the folds of its cloak. Aelrûn and the bare-chested man surrounded the creature but kept their distance.

From the direction of the mansion, dashed another figure. A very lovely girl with strawberry hair and a teal gown that defied gravity to cover her bosom. She cried out as she approached. It was slurred and difficult to understand, but sounded vaguely like, "Be careful, Jonathan!"

The creature took a few experimental swipes at its pursuers. It taunted them in a harsh guttural language.

Lucas now reached the edge of the standoff with Joe directly on his heels.

"You are surrounded," said Lucas, his voice all confidence and authority, "Drop your weapon and submit to the Marquis of Myrran!"

A spark ignited in Joe's mind. He suddenly realized where he had seen Lucas before. And there was his strawberry-haired mistress.

The greblin waved its sword defiantly and emitted a sinister, throaty cackle.

Lucas sneered. "Do not think you can defy me, creature! Every moment you still draw breath, you do so at my will. When I cease to will it, so ceases your miserable existence."

The creature said something in its foul language.

"Allow me to translate," said Aelrûn, "He says he would rather piss a lake of acid than surrender to you."

"I wonder if he'd feel the same way with a hole in his chest." Joe directed the muzzle of his firearm at the monster, "Ski Cap, maybe you could ask him."

"Ask me yourself," said the greblin with a wicked grin, "Yes, I understand your artless words. I speak with the tongue of my own kind because you lack music in your foul speech. Your crude words."

Joe ignored the told-you-so look from Aelrûn and said, "All right, then. Same question. You drop the bravado or I empty out my.45 here, and you can tell me if it tickles."

Aelrûn cocked his head. "Joe, I removed your projectiles back in the bookstore. You are effectively unarmed."

"Well, I refilled it. When you weren't looking."

"Impossible. I left you none on your person and we have no such item In The Library. You couldn't have."

"I know that. And now so does *he*. Thanks, Ski Cap."

"Oh. I see," said Aelrûn, "You were bluffing."

The greblin snarled and threw itself at Lucas.

At that same moment, Joe heard a voice shouting from behind, "Al Kazaak!" He looked back to see that Ellodrine had emerged from the hedge maze. She extended her hand toward the greblin. A small blue bolt of lightning arced from her palm about two feet and fizzled out. "Oh, bogglerot!"

Joe turned his attention back to the standoff.

The greblin lay on the ground at Lucas's feet. The handle of Aelrûn's dagger extended from its back.

CHAPTER ELEVEN

+++

The Marchioness's Temptation

Joe looked up from the dead greblin.

The woman with the strawberry hair flung herself onto the marquis. "Oh, Lucas! You were so brave."

Lucas pushed her off without ceremony.

"Save it, Isabelle. You're hopelessly enamored with my brother. Think I don't know?"

"Eh? What makes you say that, brother?" asked Jonathan, neither confirming nor denying anything.

Lucas scoffed. "I intuited it. When Isabelle was hesitant to take my hand in the ballroom, I knew something was wrong. You know how intuitive I am, Jonathan. Furthermore, she painted her lips for the ball, but you seem to be wearing most of it now. And you've lost your shirt. Again."

Jonathan wiped a hand across his mouth and examined it, confirming the presence of colorful residue. "Oh, well. I guess there's no hiding it. I'll duel you for her."

"You can have her," said Lucas, "With my blessing."

"What?" shrieked Isabelle, whose fury was quickly boiling to that which hell hath not.

Lucas sighed demonstratively. "I could never keep you against your will, Isabelle. If it is my brother you want, then I shan't stop you. Perhaps it is fate. The winds of desire are ever capricious. And I too have felt a change in their season I cannot explain."

Sea-green tempests raged in Isabelle's eyes. "I only kissed your brother because you ran off after that wh—"

"What have I missed?" Ellodrine arrived at the scene. Straying strands of hair stood on end with the static residue of her ineffectual lightning bolt. Her irises were the color of lemons. Upon her gown were muddy spots and stray leaves. Despite all this, she was inexplicably dazzling.

"Welcome to the party, Elle," said Joe.

Aelrûn nudged the dead greblin with his foot. "As you can see, Ellodrine, I have silenced the spy."

Lucas stroked his chin. "*O'Drine*? So, you're Irish, then?"

Ellodrine placed a hand on her forehead. "The harm may already be done, Aelrûn. I can't imagine these events will have gone unnoticed."

"You may be more right than you know," said Joe, "What's the name of this book, exactly?"

"Some flimsy little thing. *The Marchioness's Tantrum* or something."

"*Some flimsy thing?*" exclaimed Isabelle.

"Who's this?" asked Ellodrine.

"I'm the marchioness! And I am no *flimsy thing*! How dare you come to a ball at my manor and try to steal my marquis? You rancid whore!" She leaned on Jonathan for stability. Not emotional stability. The literal kind.

"Bogglerot!" said Ellodrine.

"You keep saying that," said Joe. "What *is* bogglerot, exactly?"

"It's an expletive, Joe. I am voicing my frustration. Do you never use expletives?"

"Not that one. I just say s*hit*."

"That's vulgar."

"That's the point. Never mind. We got trouble. I knew I'd seen this guy before." He gestured to Lucas. "This is the marquis I saw back in the bookstore. And right over there is his inebriated mistress. We must be in the developing sequel. Not that it needed one."

Isabelle gasped. "Lucas! Do you know this vagabond?"

"And who knows how long he was hiding in the hedges? I bet he heard every word. And if he heard it..."

Ellodrine gasped. "It's in the narrative!"

"What's in the narrative?" Kribble finally caught up to the group.

"Everything," said Joe, "And now we have to assume it will make its way back to Ben and Howard."

"Aelrûn," said Kribble, "Weren't you were keeping watch? What about your elven senses?"

"It's hard to use my elven senses when I'm forever wearing bloated hats and wigs over my ears!" He ripped the powdered wig from his head and threw it to the ground.

Joe shrugged. "Sure, Ski Cap. Blame the wig."

"Ugh!" said Jonathan, "There's something amuck with his ears. They've got pointy bits on top."

Ellodrine threw her hands into the air. "Aelrûn, our cover!"

"Our cover is gone," he gestured to the dead greblin.

"Oh, dear. I hoped to keep him alive for questioning. I had that lightning bolt charged to stun him."

"Is that what that was supposed to be?" asked Joe, "A lightning bolt?"

"I told you. My magic doesn't function right in books that don't have magic."

"Hang on a second." Joe looked around. The partygoers clustered around them on every side, staring. Gawking. "Of course. I should have seen it before."

"Seen what, Joe?"

"Your magic. It might be functioning more than you think."

"I don't know what you're talking about."

Lucas grasped her hands warmly into his own. "If you'll permit me, Miss O'Drine, I do."

"... What?"

"From the first moment I saw you, I noticed something different about you. I cannot explain it. The sight of you simply enchanted me. I am utterly bewitched."

"Now, brother," said Jonathan, "Would you so quickly discard the love of your life? She made a simple and understandable mistake, and I think you should take her back. See? Good ol' Isabelle." He grasped Isabelle at the waist and thrust her tottering before Lucas.

"Jonathan?" she murmured, "What are you saying?"

Jonathan left her wobbling where she stood and moved to Ellodrine's side. He clutched her elbow. "My brother has many duties and could never give you his undivided attention, but you have absolutely charmed my heart. Miss O'Drine, is it? Allow me to introduce myself—"

"Jonathan!" Isabelle slumped into a pile on the floor. "Has the entire world gone mad? What is the matter with all of you?"

Ellodrine ripped herself away from her would-be suitors. "Joe? What's going on?"

Joe shook his head. "I knew something was different about you, the moment we walked into this book. I noticed it right away, but I couldn't figure out what it was."

"I say! Stand down, brother," said Jonathan, "You already have Isabelle, why would you rob me of the same happiness?"

"For all I know, you already *had* the same happiness, Jonathan. Besides, look how she longs for you. I think you should take her as your own and be happy."

"Look at them," said Joe, "You say there's no magic in this book. I say you're wrong. Only it's not the kind of magic you're used to. We're in a book, Elle. Words make up our entire existence. I think you're as magical as you've ever been. But it means something different here. Look around."

She regarded the crowd of onlookers. They stood there gawking from every side. Not at the greblin, but at her. Murmurs rose from amongst them. Things like "Mesmerizing," and "Enchanting," and "Under her spell." Other murmurs arose, too. In feminine voices. These said things like, "Witch," and "Siren," and "Black magic."

"Oh..." Ellodrine's irises paled. "... shit."

"I told you," said Joe. He gestured back to Lucas and Jonathan.

"Let us fight for her, brother," Jonathan was saying, "Remove your shirt!"

"Very well, brother." Lucas began unbuttoning his vest. "I regret the thrashing I am about to give you. But remember, you insisted."

"I think our cover was blown long before this creature showed up," said Joe, "I'd bet we've been in the narrative from the moment we came here."

Ellodrine's face grew red.

"Cheeks like roses," said one onlooker.

"Oh, shut up!" said Ellodrine.

To Joe's left, Lucas and Jonathan fought bare-chested. From a nearby heap of silk and dejection came Isabelle's small voice, "You're a black-hearted sorceress! You've stolen everything from me."

"You can have them," said Ellodrine, "Joe, Kribble, Aelrûn. Let's get out of here."

Joe smiled awkwardly and disengaged from the scene. He and his three companions made their way through the congregation of partygoers toward the manor. Behind them, he heard Lucas and Jonathan still struggling, oblivious that the object of their affection was slipping away. He heard Isabelle weeping bitterly. After what seemed an eternity, they reached the terrace and slipped into the ballroom. It was mostly empty now. Only a few inebriated guests and the musicians who continued to play waltzes even though nobody was dancing.

They rushed to the library, eager to put *The Marchioness's Tantrum*, or something, behind them. The shelf Kribble had knocked over was now aright, the books restored to their places. A nearby butler gasped at their appearance.

Ellodrine chanted in a low and cryptic tone,

"All worlds, connected by words
All words, connecting to worlds,
From the dawning of time
Through the end of all days—"

"Elle! Where are you going?" Lucas stood at the archway.

"Quickly!" cried Ellodrine, *"All-worlds-connected-by-words-all-words-connecting-to-worlds-from-the-dawning-of-time-through-the-end of all days-bring-us-to-the-nexus-of-words!"*

.   .   .

The sunset had faded to a dusky twilight over the garden. Isabelle sat in a pile of her own sorrow. Lucas and Jonathan were off looking for the woman in the indigo gown. Most of the partygoers had dispersed to gossip

amongst themselves. Her tears now spent, Isabelle watched the faint traces of sunlight vanishing over the horizon. Vainly, she wished she too could ride her horse over the edge of the world. Away from Lucas. Away from Jonathan. And as far away from the woman in the indigo gown as she could manage.

She heard soft footsteps in the grass behind her. She did not turn to see who it was.

"Why so distraught?" asked a kindly voice.

Isabelle did not answer.

"It doesn't matter," said the voice, "I saw the whole thing. Mind if I keep you company?"

Isabelle made no indication.

"If you don't mind my saying, it was terrible what happened to you. Pretty girl getting brushed off like that. And for what? Some tramp in a dirty indigo dress? She didn't even belong here, you know. She or any of the people with her."

"What does it matter?" said Isabelle, "A few years ago, Lucas was my everything. I could never have been unfaithful to him. Nor he to me. We came through so much to be together. How have I lost it all so quickly?"

"For starters, you don't even know who to blame. Your love might have been eternally unspoiled were it not that someone is pulling your strings. Someone you've never heard of. Someone called Lyla Birdsong. You're her little marionette, and your struggles are her wages."

Isabelle was silent.

"Not that she deserves all the blame," said the voice, "After all, she was bound to give you a happy ending. Happy endings are her specialty. The real villains here are the intruders. They were never meant to cross your path. And the woman in the indigo gown? She's not prettier than you. She cheated."

Isabelle was silent.

"Don't believe me? Oh, she had a certain... effect. But I could see past it. All smoke and mirrors. You didn't hear it from me, but I happen to know she really is a sorceress. You, on the other hand! You are a lovely creature! I hope you don't mind my saying. Intoxicating is the word Ms. Birdsong uses. And perhaps, you are even lovelier now that your strings have been cut."

Isabelle was silent.

"You still don't believe me? What if I told you I could take you away from this place? What if I told you I could take you to a whole other world? What if I told you that you could help me ruin the woman in the indigo gown?"

Isabelle continued to watch as the last rays of sunlight sank beneath the skyline. "Can we leave tonight?"

To: Ben Westing
From: Colin Barringer
Subject: FW: WHAT IS THE MEANING OF THIS!?

Ben,

I'm forwarding an email to you I received this morning. Can you shed any light on this? I'm not making accusations here, but I'm sure you will see my position. See below:

>To: Colin Barringer
>From: Lyla Birdsong
>Subject: WHAT IS THE MEANING OF THIS!?

Mr. Barringer,

My name is Lyla Birdsong, and I write some very popular historical romance novels. I want you to know my readership is wide, Mr. Barringer. And my readers will not take kindly to the sabotage I have received at the hands of you and your company! I don't know how you've done it, but you have infiltrated my computer! You have rearranged my story! And you have infected me with a virus that changes my words even as I type them!

I do not find this sort of joke humorous in the least. The things your people have written about my poor Isabelle are simply vile! And I know you are behind it. Like fools, your authors left their names behind in the text. Ben Westing and Howard Zagny. What do you suppose I found when I looked them up? They are both published by the same press. Your press!

So, unless you want to hear from my lawyer, you'd better fix my book! Thank you, and good day!

-Lyla Birdsong

To: Colin Barringer
From: Ben Westing
Subject: RE: FW: WHAT IS THE MEANING OF THIS!?

Colin,

I couldn't hack into a calculator. I'm pretty sure I could prove that in a court of law. It sounds like a familiar problem, though. Maybe she's come down with some of the crazy that's been going around.

Can you humor me and ask her to handwrite her "infected" chapters? As an experiment. It doesn't have to be the whole thing. Just as much as she is willing to do. Tell her to look back over the paper when she's done. See if she still thinks we hacked into her computer after that.

And let me know what happens. I kind of need to know.

-Ben

To: Ben Westing
From: Colin Barringer
Subject: RE: WHAT IS THE MEANING OF THIS!?

Ben,

I'm absolutely not going to ask an irate woman to rewrite her defaced novel on notebook paper. That's crazy. Not like "so crazy it just might work." That's crazy, like swimming with alligators is crazy.

Thank you for your complete lack of help. If you think of anything actually useful, you know how to contact me. Meanwhile, I get to deal with this.

-Colin

To: Colin Barringer
From: Ben Westing
Subject: RE: WHAT IS THE MEANING OF THIS!?

Yeah, I realized after I hit *send* you would never pass that on, so I emailed her for you. I also copied in Howard. Sorry, Colin. I'm going to owe you for this. You'll just have to trust me.

-Ben

CHAPTER TWELVE

+++

Nexus of Words

-nd th—tles.–BZ.

Joe examined the scrap of yellow paper he had taken from the hedge maze. Most of it had burned away. What remained was brittle and charred and curled in on itself. *-nd th—tles.–BZ*, was all he could make out. A small hole between *th* and *tles* could not have eaten more than a few of the missing letters, but it was enough to illicit foul grumblings under his breath as Joe lagged behind the others on their way back to Reading Lounge L-7.

"What you got there, Joe? Is it a clue?" asked Kribble, glancing back at him.

"Garbage as likely as not. But you never know. Sometimes even the most insignificant details are—"

"The most insignificant details are life and death East of the River. Overlooking anything might be the last thing you ever do."

"I've got to get some new expressions." Joe tucked the paper away into a pocket.

"Do you think that was a note from Zolethos too?"

Joe opened his mouth to respond, but never got the chance. A cry erupted from deeper within The Library.

"That'll be Ellodrine," said Kribble, "Something's wrong!"

They bolted through the aisles. In moments, Reading Lounge L-7 appeared before them. What was left of it, anyway. Aelrûn stood nearby. And Ellodrine, still in her indigo gown, with her mouth agape.

"Ski Cap, get my bullets."

The oaken table lay on its side with Kribble's battleaxe embedded into it. Chairs were scattered, many of them splintered beyond repair. Books littered the floor. More than usual. Aelrûn's plants were ripped from their pots and left mutilated on the ground. What was not utterly destroyed was covered in graffiti. Vile curses and threats in harsh greblin letters decorated the nearby bookshelves. Lazuli lounged in the middle of the devastation, grooming himself with his tongue.

"This your necromancer again?" asked Joe.

Ellodrine nudged the wooden shards of a shattered chair with her toe. "Very likely. Zolethos still believes we are a threat to him."

"Okay," said Joe, "Any reason we couldn't contact him? Tell him to call off the war, explain it to him nicely if we can, painfully if we have to."

"I doubt it will be that simple."

"It rarely is." Joe placed two fingers in his mouth and whistled loudly. "Listen up, everybody. They could still be around. Keep your eyes open."

Aelrûn drew two long silver daggers. "I'll check the perimeter."

"I'll go with you," said Joe, "Kribble, you stay here with Elle."

"What? Why do I have to stay?"

"Because," said Joe, "Somebody's got to keep her from shooting herself with lightning again."

"Bloody blazes! Do you see what they did with my axe?"

"I'm sure it's all right. We'll get it out of that table."

"It's not that. It was marking my place in *Death with a Side of Vengeance*."

Joe paused. "We've got to find you a better bookmark."

•   •   •

Once Aelrûn and Joe satisfied themselves the intruders were gone, they returned to camp. Ellodrine and Kribble had already changed out of their formal attire and were cleaning up the reading lounge. Aelrûn began tending to his dilapidated garden, repotting what he could and vowing poetic revenge over the rest. Joe helped Ellodrine sift through the scattered books. He discovered one with a makeshift paper cover wrapped around it upon which was scrawled *The Secret Book*. Removing the cover, he discovered it was none other than *The Marchioness's Temptation*. He held it up to Ellodrine. "I think I figured out how they found us."

She raised her palms. "It's not as daft as it looks, Joe. I wrapped that around the actual cover so if it ever showed up in the narrative it would just be called *The Secret Book* and leave Howard none the wiser. See? It's quite stealthy when you think about it."

Joe tossed it aside. He was unclear whether she was trying to convince him, or herself. Either way, it was not worth the argument. Kribble helped him to right the oaken table, now with a sizeable gash in the middle of it, and they examined the functionality of the remaining chairs. When they had four suitable seats, Joe called to order a meeting of the Reading Lounge of Misfit Characters.

"The what?" asked Ellodrine.

"Never mind," said Joe. "Don't worry about it. The point is, you hired me for a job, and it's about time I do it. We got fresh troubles coming at us from every angle, and I don't like how everybody seems to know what we're about before we do. It's time I got some answers."

Kribble grinned. "This is going to be good! I can tell!"

"What about Howard?" asked Ellodrine.

"What about him?" said Joe. "Let him read. I'm not skulking off to any more cheap paperbacks just to get away from his prying eyes. I've got questions that need answers."

Ellodrine shared a glance with Aelrûn and Kribble. "All right, Joe. You're the protagonist. What do you need to know?"

Joe leaned back into his chair. "What do you have in the way of last names in Corolathia?"

Ellodrine cocked her head. "What? I'm sorry, Joe, was that sarcasm? I couldn't tell that time."

"No sarcasm. Zolethos, for instance. He's Lord Zolethos, right? Is Zolethos his last name? Does he have a first name like Bob or Bruce or Beelzebub?"

Aelrûn scoffed. "No. Zolethos is his name. It's not a first or last name. It's just his name."

"Although, if he did have a last name," said Kribble, "I guess it would be Dark Lord of the Void. That's *like* a last name."

Joe stroked his chin. "Interesting. What about the rest of you? Do any of you have last names?"

"Dwarves have clan names," said Kribble, "Usually named for heroic acts of renowned ancestors that have passed down the family line. And don't think I can't see you smiling over there, Aelrûn!"

Aelrûn did not bother to hide a bemused smirk. "I can't help it. It's just so perfect for you." He leaned in toward Joe. "Kneehammer. His clan name is Kneehammer."

Kribble slapped the table. "For my great ancestor, Korby Kneehammer, who felled a troll in battle. A *troll*, Aelrûn!"

"By crushing its knee with a hammer. Yes. The name says it all. They certainly weren't going to call him Nosehammer."

Kribble scowled across the table and folded his arms. "It was a troll."

"Well," said Ellodrine, "My last name is Ylradon. I am named for the wizard academy in which I learned to wield magic. In Corolathia, wizards forego their family names upon completing their training and take on the title of their school. Joe, is there any point to this line of questioning?"

"Don't know yet. Life and death are in the details. Kribble can tell you all about it. What about you Ski Cap?"

"Why are you still calling me Ski Cap? You know my name now."

Joe grimaced. "The truth is, I feel kind of stupid saying your name. I don't know. Ski Cap fits you better."

Aelrûn shot a glare across the table. "Yes, *Joseph*. Elves have family names. Mine is Lýndořglyste. It is the title elves grant to their shapers of metals, great artisans who design and create elven weapons and tools from metals formed of secret alchemical formulas passed down through the centuries to... I'm sorry, is something amusing, Joe?"

Joe turned to Kribble. "Smith. Am I right? His last name is Smith? Just the elfy version."

"It is *not* Smith!" said Aelrûn, "A lýndořglyste creates artifacts of great beauty and majesty that are passed down and honored through generations."

"Yeah," said Kribble, grinning, "And they make the horseshoes for the winged horses, too."

"Well, who else is going to do it?" asked Aelrûn, "The glassblowers?"

Joe mused quietly for a moment, then clapped the table and leaned forward. "All right, here's the situation as I see it. We've got authors breathing down our necks and reading over our metaphorical shoulders. We've got grublins turning up around every corner. And now we've got your scary Lord of the Void to contend with on top of everything else. It's time we put a few aces up our sleeves, starting with this one. We're fictional characters. Let's play to that strength. We were written to win. Elle!"

"Yes, Joe?"

"With all your research, you are now the literary expert. And you're my mentor. I'm going to need a lot of support, so study up."

"Yes, of course."

"Kribble!"

"What's my job, Joe?"

"You're my ally. You're solid and dependable. I need you to watch my back. Keep those grublin things off it."

"You got it, Joe."

"Good. Ski Cap!"

"That's not my bloody name!"

"You're obviously some kind of foil, and you're here to contrast with me. Stop being such a pompous ass. If you can help it."

"Incidentally, they're called *greblins*."

"Case in point."

"What are you going to do, Joe?" asked Kribble.

"I'm going to take a trip back into *Grave Plots*. I need to gather some supplies and tie off a few loose ends."

"I'll go with you!" said Kribble.

"Thanks, but no thanks. This is something I need to do alone."

"How protagonistic of you," said Aelrûn.

"I must admit, I am a little impressed," said Ellodrine, "You seem to know a good deal about literary structure, Joe."

Joe shrugged. "I read more than I let on. All right, our plans just hit overdrive. We've got a few days at best, so make 'em count."

To: Colin Barringer; Ben Westing; Howard Zagny
From: Lyla Birdsong
Subject: MY BOOK IS HAUNTED!!!

Mr. Westing, you are the very devil, himself! I did write those chapters with a paper and pen. Not because you suggested it, but because I believed you had violated my computer. But it is so much worse than that! Your offenses do not stop at electronic vandalism! Apparently, I'll need an exorcist in addition to my attorney!

-Lyla Birdsong

To: Lyla Birdsong
From: Howard Zagny
CC: Ben Westing; Colin Barringer
Subject: RE: MY BOOK IS HAUNTED!!!

Ms. Birdsong,

My name is Howard Zagny. I'm about to tell you something you won't believe. But the truth, however inconceivable it may seem, is no less true because you don't believe it.

The characters that infiltrated your book are alive. They think, say, and do things I do not write. I'm sure this is the same phenomenon you are experiencing. They are in the center of a contagious paradox that separates their existence from their authors' intent.

If you want to blame me for anything, blame me for giving your characters the freedom to make their own decisions. And with that freedom has come deep-seated anger that all their lives they've been at the mercy of our pens. Every ounce of pain they've ever experienced was deliberate and inflicted upon them to entertain our readers.

In brief, they hate us. They want our blood. And when they come to your door to claim it, remember that I told you it would happen and that I did the best I could. I really did.

-Howard Zagny

To: Howard Zagny
From: Lyla Birdsong
CC: Ben Westing; Colin Barringer
Subject: RE: MY BOOK IS HAUNTED!!!

Mr. Zagny,

You are a crazy, crazy man. You have a twisted little mind. I hope you did not expect me to believe a word of that appalling drivel. I am not so gullible. But I should thank you. You have helped me to understand with abundant clarity the depraved nature of my saboteurs. I'll be obtaining a restraining order against the three of you, and you can be quite certain it will restrict contact by email.

-Lyla Birdsong

To: Howard Zagny
From: Colin Barringer
CC: Ben Westing
Subject: RE: MY BOOK IS HAUNTED!!!

Howard,

It was painful for me to read your email. I knew you were having difficulties, but I had no idea the depth. I am sorry, but I cannot entertain these delusions. What you are talking about is simply not possible. I do not believe you are capable of hacking into Ms. Birdsong's computer as she claims, and so for your sake, I wish you had not gotten involved in this.

You are a brilliant and creative writer, Howard. You have crafted some of the most intricate fantasies I have ever had the privilege to edit. But that's all they are. Fantasies. As your editor, I grieve the loss of your art. As your friend, I grieve the loss of your mind. I want to help you, Howard, but I cannot enable you. Please do not contact me with this again.

-Colin

To: Howard Zagny
From: Ben Westing
Subject: RE: MY BOOK IS HAUNTED!!!

Howard,

I believe you.

-Ben

CHAPTER THIRTEEN

+++

Grave Plots

I'm back. Standing in the middle of a bookstore aisle that seems shorter than the last time I was here. On my way through, I pick up a familiar copy of *The Marquis's Mistress* that sits crooked on the shelf. The shopkeeper looks at me quizzically as I check out.

"For the missus?" he asks.

"No," I say.

He asks no more questions. The door jams on the way out. I don't remember that happening before. Then I realize I've never *used* the front door. One trouble with converting old buildings like this is they settle crooked over their foundations over time. Doors don't fit their frames anymore, and they won't open without a good SHOVE. The door comes free with a loud *pop*, and I step out into a cool morning.

I head down the nearest alleyway and find a dumpster with a couple of old 2x4s sticking out of it. On my approach, I am greeted by an unholy stench from which my keen olfactory senses detect mold, paint thinner, and sweet and sour sauce. I'm something of a connoisseur of the aromas that emanate East of the River.

I examine the paperback in my hand. There's Lucas, tall and self-assured. Isabelle fawns over him passionately, naive to the fact her happy ending would one day explode in a fiery display of awkward mishaps. I flick it into the foul-smelling dumpster. "That's for spying on us, you smug bastard."

I spot a brick that has tumbled out of its spot in the wall. I pick it up and drop it into my coat pocket. You never know when you might need a loose brick. That done, I exit the alleyway and head toward a cluster of street vendors. I order a couple of greasy hotdogs, and scarf them down. This kind of food, you don't find in cookbooks no matter how hard you look. I pick up a newspaper from a nearby rack, then make my way back to the bookstore. I choose a spot on the other side of the street and commence loitering.

I make my way through the paper at least three times, and nothing. Either nobody is tailing me, or somebody is really *good* at tailing me. At the first option, I have to wonder about how competent this Zolethos could be. I announced I was coming here. Then I came here. In my line of fiction, that's a surefire formula for picking up a goon or two.

Instead, I entertain myself watching various bookstore customers struggle with the jamming door. It's the little things in life you have to savor. The sight of people trying to open a simple door can be a wellspring of happiness if you have the right outlook. They try to open it casually at first, expecting it to swing at the gentlest tug. The second attempt is more spirited, but equally ineffectual. Not willing to be outdone by a door three times, the would-be opener takes a breath, readies his muscles, and yanks at it with everything he's got. Now the door flies open and sends the opener tripping over his own feet. The best one is the guy who smacks himself in the face with it and walks off with a bloody nose. Classic.

The morning is spent, and the afternoon sun is in full force. I begin to think I'm wasting my time when I notice something odd. The bookstore door across the street catches an outgoing breeze and lurches open on its own. Only what kind of gale-force breeze would it have to be to manage a thing like that? I stare through narrowed eyes over my paper. Maybe it just didn't shut all the way the last time. Although that would be a unique anomaly. I've been watching people struggle with that door all morning.

Nobody went in. Nobody came out. I saw it with my own eyes. Of course, if the last few days have taught me anything, they've taught me this: there's a lot more out there than I think I know. Okay, then. Somebody must have opened that door. Question is, where is that somebody now?

Then I see it. It's standing across the street, staring back at me. I don't know how I didn't see it before. It's enormous. A full head and shoulders taller than the last grublin I saw. And that's what I assume it is. A grublin, or whatever they're called. It's got the same glowing red eyes peeking out from the hood of a dark cloak. It's standing there on the curb staring at me, not bothering to blend in or anything. A few passersby come along. I expect any moment they'll scream at the sight of it and make a run for the hills. It doesn't happen. One of them, absorbed in a phone call as he walks, even grazes the grublin with his shoulder as he passes it. The walker doesn't even look up.

They can't see it. It must be something to do with those cloaks they wear. The last grublin had one just like it. Lucas was practically on top of it before he noticed it. I return to my paper. No sense letting him know I can see him if he thinks I can't. I keep my position for a while longer, long enough to not be suspicious, then I fold up my paper and start walking. Out of the corner of my eye, I can see my new friend is following me from the other side of the street. I turn down a nearby alleyway, one where I know I can find some smelly 2x4s.

Moments later, I'm crouched behind the reeking dumpster, wooden beam in hand. I hear footsteps coming toward me. Not yet. Not yet. NOW.

I leap out and swing, all my childhood baseball fantasies culminating with a resounding *crack*. I find myself looking into the eyes of a seven-foot grublin with a bewildered expression and a splintered plank of wood wrapped around its face. Bewildered is a far cry from unconscious, however, and I consider I may have miscalculated the effectiveness of my plan.

The grublin and I share an awkward moment. Then his bewilderment turns into a wicked smile. Green lips curl back to reveal slimy yellow teeth that come to sharp points. A deep rasping chuckle emits from its throat. I can honestly say it is the most disturbing sound I have ever heard. A necklace composed of small bones rattles on the grublin's chest.

I feel its claws digging into my ribs on both sides, and I'm conscious of my feet leaving the ground. I've heard of vice-like grips. It's never felt so literal. I don't have to endure it for long. Soon it passes into the sensation of being hurtled backward through the air into a brick wall. The impact knocks the air out of my lungs, and I desperately try to suck it back in.

The grublin stands there laughing at me. It grasps the broken plank and tosses it aside. It gestures for me to come at it again. It's toying with me. It continues to laugh as I find my footing. Doesn't last long, though. It is interrupted by a flying brick that smashes into its face. Suddenly it doesn't think I'm so funny anymore.

It grasps its face with two mottled green hands and shrieks at decibels that would make it a good frontrunner of any metal band. Dark blood seeping between its fingers indicates a broken nose. I wonder if passersby can hear the racket, even if they can't see where it's coming from.

It rips its hands from its face and glowers at me. It produces a black-bladed scimitar from its belt. I guess playtime is over. I hoped things wouldn't get this far. In my experience, when you club someone over the head with a blunt object, it's basically lights out. Everything goes dark. You have some demented dreams then wake up with a screaming headache, tied to a chair with some big hairy guy shouting at you to drop the case. It's clean. I guess that's just how hard-boiled mysteries work.

These grublins are a little more to-the-death, which is exactly what I want to avoid. Fortunately, I now have in my possession a *loaded* revolver which I bring into play. The grublin seems to have little experience with firearms, and that works to my advantage. I get a clean shot at the scimitar and it flies from the grublin's hand. I'm not going to lie. I really get a kick out of the expression on its face. It makes a dive for its weapon.

I look around. What does a guy have to do to knock out a...? There. A little further up the alley. A series of metal trash cans next to the back door of a Chinese food bistro. They're full near to the brim with old fish, among other things. One of the trash cans has a sizeable dent in the side that brings to mind the memory of a recent headache.

Oh. I'm in *that* alley.

The realization only takes a fraction of a second, and I'm on the move. Hoisting the can over my head, I chuckle to myself about life's funny way of bringing things full circle. I lower the hefty canister violently over the head of the giant grublin, still scrambling on its knees to retrieve its sword, and wonder what Kribble would think if he could see me. I bet he'd get a real kick out of it. As the metal can crashes into the creature's skull with a sickening *thud*, I wonder: *Now how am I going to drag a seven-foot grublin back to my office for questioning?*

CHAPTER FOURTEEN

+++

Nexus of Words

"It's Joe! And he's brought STUFF with him!" Kribble's voice echoed through Reading Lounge L-7 at such a volume it startled Aelrûn, who inflicted several discordant notes into Santana's *Black Magic Woman*.

"Oh dear," said Ellodrine, looking up from a hefty volume, "I was rather enjoying that one. So few songs are written in praise of female wizards."

"Come on! Come on! What did you bring, Joe?" Kribble swept stacks of books and research materials off the oaken table into a pile on the floor. "Good stuff?"

Joe dropped a hefty gray duffle bag onto the table. "Standard fare. Ammo, walkie-talkies, cuffs, pepper spray, camera. Take a look."

Kribble was already digging greedily into the bag. "By my mother's beard! It's even better than I imagined! Are these binoculars?"

"Welcome back, Joe," said Ellodrine, "You've certainly brought a lot of supplies with you. These tools will help us get the artifact?"

"They come in handy from time to time. The major score was information." Joe produced something from his pocket and dropped it onto the table before her. It clattered as it landed. A loop of thin leather onto which were strung several small bones with holes bored through their centers.

Ellodrine and Kribble's jaws dropped. "That's a greblin bone necklace," said Kribble.

"What?" exclaimed Aelrûn, who was still lounging in his chair across the lounge. He leaped up and rushed to the table. "Only the hunt-lords wear those."

"Look at the number of bones on it," said Kribble. He began counting under his breath.

"What are hunt-lords?" asked Joe, "The really ugly ones?"

"Hunt-lords," said Aelrûn, "Elite greblin tracker-killers. Every bone in this necklace came from a different victim that met its fate at the hands of the greblin who owned it."

"Fifty-two!" announced Kribble. "Oh, he was a nasty one!"

"Maybe in your book," said Joe, "East of the River, he was just another ugly face who walked into a 2x4."

Kribble made skeptical eyes. "You knocked out a hunt-lord with a plank of wood?"

"… And a brick. And a metal trash can."

Kribble's expression broke into a wide grin. "Did you use my technique? You used my technique, didn't you?"

"Even used the same trash can."

Aelrûn narrowed his eyes. "You knew you would be followed, didn't you? That's why you went. You were staging an ambush."

Ellodrine stood up from her chair. "That was perilous of you, Joe. As your mentor, I would very much have preferred you told me about that plan before you undertook it."

"If I'd have told you, you wouldn't have wanted me to do it. Look, it worked, didn't it?"

"It was risky," said Ellodrine.

"It was reckless," said Aelrûn.

"It's a voice recorder!" said Kribble. "Like the one you used to trick Lester Muldoon into confessing in *Murder on the Side*."

"Okay," said Joe, "It was a gamble, and it paid off. I've got the dirt whenever you're ready to hear it. Or maybe you'd rather keep reading me the Riot Act instead."

Ellodrine silently mouthed the words *Riot Act*, "Toadstools, Joe! I feel like I need a Ben Westing phrase-book when I talk to you."

"A Polaroid!" shouted Kribble.

"Something you've read about, I assume," said Aelrûn.

"It's a camera," said Kribble, "It makes pictures of things. Photo-Graphs. Spits them out on little square cards."

"Interesting. And will we be making lots of pictures on this quest? Why this... camera?"

"I'll *find* things to take pictures of!" Kribble's finger slipped, and the camera went off with a bright flash.

Aelrûn winced and stumbled back. "What the blazes?"

"Don't worry," said Kribble, "Nothing to worry about. That just means it's working. I think." A small gray square appeared from a slot. "There it is. See?"

Aelrûn scrutinized the Photo-Graph. "Where's the picture?"

"It has to develop." said Joe, "Give it a few minutes. I know, the world's gone digital, but I still like the classics." He turned to Kribble. "Helps if you shake it."

Kribble nodded and began shaking the Photo-Graph wildly about.

Ellodrine leaned into her hand. "You were saying, Joe? You have information?"

"Right. Here's the big scoop. The greblin said his master Zolethos consults the oracle. The oracle reveals great mysteries to Zolethos, such as the whereabouts of the interlopers—that's us, by the way—and our plans to travel to the oracle's domain to dispossess him from his seat of authority."

Ellodrine snorted. "Howard Zagny is still calling himself an oracle, I see."

"There's more. The oracle doesn't just hand out information. It also provides 'great gifts.' Weapons and tools to give them an advantage. Fancy cloaks like our friend in the hedge maze had that makes them hard to see."

"Shadow cloaks," said Aelrûn, "The nocturnal elves of the Twilight Wood from book six used those, but I've never known greblins to have such things. In a shadow cloak, nobody could see you who does not already know where you are. That would explain how he was able to spy on us so successfully."

"Makes them hard to ambush too," said Joe, "But I had a little help from a jamming door."

"The hunt-lord had a shadow cloak too?" said Kribble, "I wish you'd have brought that back. That would be handy to have around."

"I *did* bring that back. You think I'd leave something like that behind? It's in the bag."

"Oh, yeah. There it is. Why didn't I notice that before?"

Aelrûn sighed and rolled his eyes.

Ellodrine stroked her chin. "So, you questioned the greblin, and he told you all that? How can you be sure he wasn't lying?"

"Yeah," said Kribble, "How did you make him talk? Give us the grisly details."

"Remember the Muramoto case?"

"*The Jade Peacock*?"

"That sounds right. Anyway, I still had some truth serum locked up in my desk. Injected him with it before I brought him around. Grisly enough for you?"

"Meh." Kribble turned his attention back to shaking the developing Photo-Graph.

Ellodrine was silent, her irises deep blue in contemplation. At length, she said, "Then I suppose we must move quickly. If Howard is supplying Zolethos's forces, they will be deadlier than they have ever been. When we break camp, take everything you need. We may not be returning to the reading lounge again once we leave."

"Why's that?" asked Joe.

"Our danger grows by the hour. Howard Zagny's shadow cloaks will bypass my magical wards. And I can no longer track our progress through the narrative."

"What?" said Aelrûn. "You can't track our progress through the narrative? Why? What's happened to the book?"

Ellodrine lifted her chin primly. "The book is fine, I'm sure. It's just somewhere back in that abominable romance novel."

Aelrûn's eyes narrowed. "You left it there?"

"Don't you take that tone with me, Aelrûn Lýndořglyste. I brought it with me to keep it safe. When everything blew up as it did, I lost track of it. And I'm not going back for it now!"

"How could you lose it? It was irreplaceable!"

"Well, you might have helped matters, Aelrûn, by catching that greblin earlier with those elven senses you're so proud of, but you didn't."

"He had a magical cloak!"

"You have legendary hearing!"

"I had an enormous foppish wig over my ears!"

"Who knew your magnificent elven senses could be so confounded by something as mundane as a wig?"

Joe let out a shrill whistle. "Whoa, whoa, whoa. Let's bring this down a notch. So what? We lost our novel. Worse things have happened, right?"

"You don't understand, Joe," said Aelrûn. "That book was our only way to keep watch on Howard Zagny. We won't have any idea what he might write while we're gone. Who knows what could be waiting for us here when we get back?"

"I concede, that's a little worse than I was thinking."

"It's true," said Ellodrine with a sunken voice, "Had I not lost the book, I'd have known about the ransacked camp in advance, and I'd have been able to read about who'd done it. Aelrûn is right. I deserve his scorn. The book was irreplaceable."

Kribble shook his head. "I hate when Aelrûn is right."

Aelrûn rolled his eyes and sauntered back to his harp.

Joe put a hand on Ellodrine's shoulder. "We'll make do, Elle. We weren't planning on staying here forever. Let's just move forward with the plan. We'll keep our eyes open. I've been through worse scrapes than this."

"Yes. You're right. Chin up. Sulking won't fix anything."

"This is amazing!" shouted Kribble. He was holding up the now developed picture and showing it to them. The Photo-Graph captured the image of Joe, Aelrûn, and Ellodrine's torsos, their heads cut off at the chins.

"How... fascinating," said Ellodrine.

"You're a natural," said Joe.

"I'm going to take some more!" Kribble went charging off with the camera.

"Don't use all the film," said Joe, but he had already gone.

Ellodrine laughed.

Joe could not restrain a smile. She had a pleasant laugh. It tinkled like a bell. It was a shame she did not laugh more often. She had a nice smile too once it broke through all the gravity she carried around. Made her look more... He did not know the word. Happy? Warm? Kind? Pretty? Wonderful? Yes. All of those.

"Joe."

"Yeah?"

"Have I something on my face?"

"... What?"

"You're staring at me. Have I something on my face?"

"Uh, no. Sorry. Just thinking about something. Uh, actually there is, though. You've got an eyelash." He brushed his finger across her cheek and held it in front of her. On the tip was a single small dark strand. "See? Make a wish."

"Why would I do that?"

"It's what we do in my book."

"Do wishes work in your book, Joe? I don't know. I cast magic spells. They're pretty potent. I'm not sure how well wishes will win the day."

"It's just a game, Elle. I'm not making a serious strategy here. You make a wish and hope it comes true."

"Oh. Very well. Then I wish we will win."

"No, no, no. You're not supposed to tell me what you wish for. It's a secret."

"You have to explain the rules, Joe. How was I to know? Very well, I'll make another one."

"Got it?"

"Yes. Did I win the game?"

"Guess we'll find out."

Ellodrine nodded. "That is an odd game. We should rest. Tomorrow we will begin the operation. I'll take the first watch. I suppose I'd better strengthen my wards." She wandered off to the edge of the camp.

Joe sat at the table ruminating. Next to him was a stack of books that contained several volumes on writing and literary analysis and a copy of *Orchid Gardens of the Southwest.* Instinctively, he could determine which books had seen the most use over the past several weeks. Years of sleuthing taught him to interpret details. The wear on the edge of the pages. The cracks on the spine. Near the top of the stack was a volume that had suffered particularly in Ellodrine's hands. It was not a manual or a reference, like so many of the surrounding books. Rather, it was a novel with a flashy cover that depicted stars and floating ships. Bright yellow words across the spine displayed *Ghost Nebula: A Galactic Explorer Novel* by Raymond Larson.

To: Ben Westing
From: Howard Zagny

I know where they are going.

CHAPTER FIFTEEN

+++

Ghost Nebula

"Captain Cortega, we have visual on the Rhodactian ship."

"Thank you, Rhodes. Hail them."

"Hailing them now, sir."

Tension filled the air in the bridge of the *Galactic Explorer* as the image of a rogue Rhodactian ship appeared on the display screen. The red-purple evanescence of the Ghost Nebula surrounded it. What had once been a beautiful craft built to escort Rhodactian ambassador ships to and from the Intergalactic Council, had now been rebuilt by space pirates into a war machine. Across its bow had been inscribed alien characters that translated to *Blood Horizon*. Cortega adjusted the patch covering his right eye cavity. Having chased the pirates' trail halfway across the Ixibus System, he now had a visual of his quarry.

The image on the display screen shifted. A Rhodactian, taller than most and bearing an irreverent sneer, glared. He bore multiple tattoos upon his red-orange skin in the same Rhodactian characters that marked the ship. He crossed his arms in defiance.

"I am Captain Cortega of the *Galactic Explorer*. I have been sent to order your immediate and unconditional surrender for crimes against the Intergalactic Union that include but are not limited to theft of a Rhodactian escort ship, staging attacks upon unprotected merchant ships, looting those same said ships, and you are also charged for the destruction of the *Star Skipper*, an officially sanctioned S-Class ambassador ship as well as the murder of Captain Jonas and his crew."

The Rhodactian pirate laughed. "So, the Intergalactic Senate has sent the infamous Captain Cortega after us, has it? It is an honor, Captain. You are as imposing as the stories say. But you will not bring us in with one ship and your haughty words."

"To whom do I have the pleasure of addressing?"

The Rhodactian pounded a fist on his chest plate. "I am Captain Voctroth Gish Uthroc of the planet Rhodact in the Galaxy of Cyrus-7. I owe no allegiance to the Intergalactic Union or to your imperialistic council. I follow the law of my ancestors, the great space corsairs of Cyrus-7 who lived by their wit and the strength of their arms. Not by the laws of a pack of self-important bureaucrats who sit around vying for favors and bribes."

Cortega took in a breath. "Captain Uthroc."

"Yes?"

"I do not intend to bring you in with one ship and my haughty words, as you say. I also have several quantum lasers, a host of NOVA class torpedoes, hyperspace engine jammers, four squadrons of short-range fighters, and a tractor beam that is strong enough to haul that ship back to the Intergalactic Council whether or not it is a molten mass of slag when I do. My haughty words are purely for your enjoyment."

Captain Uthroc's expression changed. "You do your reputation credit, Captain. It seems the stories about you may be well earned. Nevertheless, you will not prevail against us. Your weapons are playthings. Do your worst!"

"As you wish." Cortega nodded to Rhodes, who pressed a button on the console before him. The Rhodactian pirate captain disappeared from the display. In his place appeared the image of the stolen ship. The so-called *Blood Horizon.* "Rhodes, fire a round of torpedoes at the Rhodactian ship."

"Will this be a warning shot, Captain?"

"Did I say a warning shot, Rhodes?"

"Firing torpedoes now, sir."

Several glowing objects appeared on the display, gliding through space toward the *Blood Horizon.* The first two or three would detonate against the ship's shields, but the rest would cause sufficient damage to take the fight out of Captain Uthroc and his crew. Cortega watched the torpedoes as they arced toward their target.

"Rhodactian ship is not raising shields of any kind, Captain."

"Repeat that Rhodes. Did you say they are not raising their shields?"

"That is correct, sir."

In fact, the Rhodactian ship seemed to make no effort to avoid its impending destruction. Cortega's left eye narrowed.

"Torpedo impact in five seconds. Four seconds. Three seconds. Two. One."

They never landed. Their trajectory was on target, but when they came upon the *Blood Horizon*, they passed through it as though it were only an image floating in space. Moments later, the bridge crew of the *Galactic Explorer* watched the glowing torpedoes emerge from the other side of the Rhodactian vessel and glide harmlessly away.

Gasps and indistinct murmurs resonated from among them.

Cortega arched a single brow. "Innes, what kind of readout are you getting from this?"

"I've never seen anything like it, Captain. It's like it's there and not there at the same time. My instruments are going crazy."

"Very well. Rhodes, arm the lasers and fire at will. Prepare another volley of torpedoes. We cannot allow this ship to slip away from us."

Rhodes sent an array of colorful and lethal emissions streaming toward the Rhodactian ship. They met with no more effect than the torpedoes before them.

"Hold fire," ordered the captain.

Uthroc appeared again on the display. "Now you see, Captain? My vessel is untouched by your pitiful assaults. You know now what Captain Jonas experienced at my hands. And you will share his fate."

"Four torpedoes heading toward us, Captain," said Rhodes.

"Shields up. Brace for impact."

The impact was sudden and jolting. Innes's instruments exploded in a shower of sparks that threw him to the floor. Medics rushed to his aid. Alarms blared throughout the ship.

"Shields are now at twenty percent," said Rhodes. "We won't be able to take another hit like that, Captain."

Uthroc's image laughed. "Where are your haughty words now, Captain? You are in a battle you cannot win. While you cannot harm me, I can still destroy you."

"Shall we put that to the test?"

Uthroc clicked his tongue. "What a waste that would be. All those supplies and weapons reduced to space debris. What kind of pirates would we be? I give you this option. Send us your food, weapons, and medical supplies. You may use your telepad to transport them from your ship onto ours. Then I will allow you to flee like the dogs you are back to your pathetic council where you can tell them we are invincible!"

"And if we refuse?"

"That would be unwise. You have one hour to decide."

Uthroc vanished from the display. A heavy silence filled the bridge. Cortega took his seat. He had to learn more about this strange technology that rendered the *Blood Horizon* invulnerable to attack. Surrender was not an option. Neither was annihilation. There had to be something Uthroc had not counted on. But what? Time was short. What could be so unexpected it would catch Uthroc off guard?

"Captain."

"Yes, Rhodes?"

"There is an active alarm on our ship. I am detecting four new life forms aboard."

"So much for an hour to decide," said Innes, waving medics away. "Did they change their minds?"

"Rhodes," said the captain, "Are they Rhodactian?"

"Negative, Captain. Two of them are definitely human, the other two are... something else. Not Rhodactian, anyway. Lieutenant Xane is leading a security squad to intercept."

"Where are they now, Rhodes?"

"In the library, sir."

•   •   •

Lieutenant Xane stalked through the corridor. Behind him trailed a small contingent of security officers struggling to keep his pace. In his scaly gray hand, he gripped an incapacitator he had reluctantly clicked to a non-lethal setting. He tapped a button on his communicator.

"This is Lieutenant Xane. We are approaching the library. What is the infiltrators' position?"

Rhodes's voice sounded. "They have departed from the library and are now heading toward deck four. They are progressing rapidly through the ship, Lieutenant. It would appear they are trying to reach the telepad bay."

"Moving to intercept." Xane's yellow reptilian eyes narrowed. His pace quickened. His Karthecian instincts awoke within him. The hunt was on.

He darted through corridors at speeds that were impossible for his human comrades to maintain. He took corners at full velocity, making sharp turns with no loss of momentum. He lifted his bionic arm and tapped command codes into a small panel embedded into his wrist. He had lost his true left arm to a Karthecian marsh beast. The marsh beast's head was currently mounted above his bed. A yellow light glowed on his mechanical bicep to indicate the weapon cells were charging.

He espied two officers sprawled out on the floor of the corridor. Unconscious, but unharmed, he noted and passed them by. Karthecians were known for their ability to detect thermal signatures through infrared-sensitive eyes. The two inert officers had suffered no debilitating loss of heat and showed no abnormal temperature imbalances that would suggest either stab wounds or impact trauma. Whoever had got the drop on them was stealthy, and dangerously efficient.

Xane smiled. This would be interesting.

In moments, he was approaching the telepad bay on deck four. His backup squad had been thoroughly left behind and would not appear for another minute or two. More time than Xane had to give them. By then, his quarry could be teleporting through space with whatever equipment or information they may have stolen. Waiting for backup was not an option, and that suited Xane just fine.

In the final corridor, he slowed his footfalls and turned off his communicator. He inched along until he was next to the sliding doors. His metallic finger hovered over the button that would open them. He took a breath. The incapacitator felt warm in his hand. He pressed the button.

The doors slid open. Xane bolted through, ready for anything. Anything but this. Four figures, one notably shorter than the others, stood before him wearing antiquated space suits complete with fishbowl style helmets and the letters NASA printed on the chest and sleeves. Two were standing over the telepad control pedestal. One of these held an open book like an operation manual. The book, like the spacesuits, was antiquated with no digital display or buttons of any kind. Rather, it was a collection of paper pages bound into a soft cover. The remaining two infiltrators were standing on either side of the door Xane had just come through. They all four wore gray duffle bags slung over their shoulders.

Xane twisted his body out of the way of an incoming fist from his left. The strange astronaut was unbelievably quick, and Xane had to dodge so hard he lost his balance. He tumbled to the floor but recovered into a roll that pulled him deeper into the room. He leaped to his feet but had to duck quickly out of the way of a flying garbage cylinder that had been lobbed at him by the short astronaut to his right. It sailed over his head and landed with a crash behind him. He was unable to retaliate. The first astronaut, with lightning reflexes, was upon him delivering a series of punches and kicks that Xane only barely deflected. He took a hard chop to his abdomen before he was able to grasp his assailant's arm and fling him across the room.

The short astronaut charged at him. He lifted his incapacitator and squeezed the trigger, but before he could get the shot off he heard a loud bang, and his weapon flew out of his hand. A scent of sulfur filled the air. One astronaut near the control pedestal was pointing a primitive firearm at him, a slender wisp of smoke now rising from the barrel. Xane had read about these but never actually seen one. Primitive or not, Xane knew the weapon was lethal. He would have to neutralize the threat before his assailant could get another shot.

Xane lifted his bionic hand, closed his eyes, and discharged a bright flash. The astronauts sounded cries of pain as they were temporarily blinded. Xane lost no time closing the distance between himself and the armed astronaut. He let loose an expert kick that caught his foe in the chest and sent him sprawling into the wall. Xane tapped a button imbedded into his bionic palm. A compartment opened in the wrist from which launched a second incapacitator. With inhuman speed, he turned and fired two blue beams into the other two assailants, both still recovering from the flash. They crumpled unconscious to the floor.

"Lieutenant Xane, are you all right, sir?" Xane's security officers stood in the doorway with their weapons drawn and gasping for breath.

"There's one more!" Xane scanned the room, his Karthecian eyes no longer able to detect the fourth heat signature. "Did you see anything? Did anything get by you in the corridor?"

"Nothing, sir. I'm sure of it."

Xane flipped on his communicator. "This is Xane. I have apprehended three of the infiltrators. Do you have a read on the fourth?"

"No read, Lieutenant," said Rhodes's voice from the communicator, "Sensors no longer detect the fourth infiltrator."

"Impossible." Xane clenched his reptilian fist. He looked warily about. His eyes came to rest on a small object on the floor next to the control pedestal. It was the archaic book. He picked it up. Though the style of the book was ancient, the object itself was not. The pages were crisp and unyellowed. The cover was decorated in vibrant artwork that depicted a starship, not unlike the *Galactic Explorer*, suspended in space and surrounded by red-purple mist.

To: Raymond Larson
From: Howard Zagny
CC: Ben Westing
Subject: I May Have Lost Something in Your Book

Mr. Larson,

You may be tempted to ignore this message. What I have to say is difficult to believe, but I humbly ask that you wait a few days before you delete it. What seems ridiculous now may not seem so implausible in a day or two.

I believe you have something of mine in your manuscript. My colleague and I are authors of fiction, like yourself, and we have run into a curious situation. Our characters have escaped from our own books and I believe they are currently somewhere in the pages of your developing novel, *Ghost Nebula*.

Please understand I am not accusing you of plagiarism. I am speaking literally. If you look back on your latest chapter, you may discover new characters or strange occurrences you did not write and cannot explain.

It is my understanding the rogue characters are trying to be stealthy to prevent the narrative from picking up on them. If their plans are going well, changes to your text may be subtle. But my sources indicate they will attempt to steal something integral to the plot of your story.

Please be on the lookout for a detective, a wizard, an elf, and a dwarf. Possibly disguised. Once they have interfered with the events in your novel, you will be unable to change their alterations no matter how many times you rewrite them.

I understand there is a process to receiving this information. Ridicule, denial, confusion, anxiety, and despair will probably take place before acceptance. Please go through these phases as necessary, but go through them quickly. We're in a bit of a hurry.

-Howard Zagny

CHAPTER SIXTEEN

+++

Ghost Nebula

Cortega met the eyes of his prisoner through the static field of a holding cell. The prisoner stared back with a grim expression. The prisoner's dark hair was rumpled, and scuffle peppered his face. He was dressed in a temperature regulating jumpsuit he had worn beneath his astronaut garb. The other two prisoners were waiting in a holding cell in the next room. Xane stood at a computer console where he examined several instruments. He gave the captain a nod when everything was ready.

Cortega began the interrogation. "We are monitoring your vital signs and brain activity. If you lie to me, I will know it. And I will ensure you regret that decision. Am I perfectly clear?"

The prisoner smiled a devilish half-smile. "Guess I better not lie, then."

"Good. Because I am in a very tight situation. My ship and my crew are on the line, and I am short on time. So, you're going to answer my questions without any games because I do *not* have the patience for them."

"Let's get started," said the prisoner. The static field rippled between them.

Cortega adjusted his eye patch. "Are you working with the Rhodactians?"

"What's a Rhodactian?"

"He's telling the truth, Captain," Xane looked up from the instruments. "Apparently, he has never heard of a Rhodactian."

Cortega's nostrils flared. "Why are you on my ship?"

"Just stopped by on my way to somewhere else. My friends and I were hoping to borrow your zap machine."

"My *zap* machine?"

"Yes. The one that zaps you onto other spaceships."

"The telepad?"

"That sounds right."

"You were attempting to hijack our telepad system to transport yourselves and your stolen cargo. Is this what you mean?"

"Stolen cargo?"

Xane looked up from his monitors again. "Telling the truth, Captain. It would appear he does not know about the theft."

Cortega produced a slender black reading device and held it up before the prisoner. He pressed a button and the device's display screen lit up with the words *The Complete Cosmic Dissonance Songbook*. Below the words was the image of an inhuman rock band, allegedly Cosmic Dissonance. "What I can't understand," said Cortega, "Is that of all the sensitive data in this ship's archive library, you seem to have been after some damn sheet music. Help me understand why that is. Is there something encoded in this?"

The prisoner rolled his eyes. "No. Apparently one of my colleagues just wanted some damn sheet music."

"He's telling the truth, Captain."

"You expect me to believe," said Cortega, "That you were just passing through? In uncharted space? That's your story?"

"That's my story."

"On your way to where?"

The prisoner shrugged. "Another spaceship."

"The Rhodactian ship?"

"Must be the one."

"Why?"

"There's something on that ship we need."

"What is on that ship?"

The prisoner leaned in close, his nose nearly touching the static field between them. He spoke now in a low and serious tone. "There is an artifact on that ship we hope can help us open the doorway between the so-called real world and every world that ever existed in the pages of books. Fictional books, historical books, biographies about anybody you can imagine. There's a world inside every one. And what if they could all escape from the print on the pages and walk around and have their own lives? Wouldn't that be keen? We think so. And that, sir, is why we'd like to borrow your zap machine." The prisoner offered a smug smile.

"Xane?"

"I have no indication of falsehood, Captain. He is allegedly telling the truth."

"When we're done here, Xane, have Innes run a diagnostic on that machine."

"Aye, Captain."

Cortega tossed the reading device onto a nearby table and produced the strange book Xane had discovered in the telepad bay. "What can you tell me about this?"

"It's expected to get fair reviews, but I've heard from a friend the plot is a little formulaic."

"Just for that," said Cortega, "I'm going to let you go another round with Xane after we're finished here. Care to reconsider that response?"

"It's a book about you and your fine ship and some recent events surrounding your crew. And also those Rhododendrons you're after."

Cortega slammed the book against the static field. "There is information in this book about me and my vessel *and* about the Rhodactians that no person could have! And yet here it is written like a cheap novel! How do you have access to something like this?"

"We borrowed it from The Library."

Xane let out an audible sigh. "Allegedly true, Captain."

Cortega's jaw clenched and a dangerous glint appeared in his eye. "You are going to tell me everything about how you came across the information in this book, and I don't care how long or painful a process it takes. But we'll save that for later. Right now, let's cut through the bullshit, and you tell me this. Someone has been through this book with a pen, making notes in the margin and underlining things. It seems somebody is very interested in something called a ghosting device. Is that the *artifact* you are after on the Rhodactian ship?"

The prisoner considered this. "That sounds likely."

"You don't know?"

"My colleague handles those details."

"The one we can't find?"

"Correct."

"And how is your colleague no longer showing up on our sensors?"

"She's just that good."

Xane looked up from the monitor. "Sensors indicate that's a lie, Captain."

The prisoner winced. "You got me. Actually, she couldn't sneak past a sleeping rock. But she's got a magical cloak on that makes her hard to see."

"Xane?"

Xane seethed. "Allegedly true, Captain."

Cortega adjusted his patch again. "This ghosting device. This is the reason my weapons can't touch the Rhodactian ship?"

"That sounds likely."

"But you were just going to teleport on over there? What made you think you wouldn't find yourselves floating off into space like my torpedoes?"

"Ah!" said the prisoner, snapping his fingers. "My colleague had that figured out. She said the other ship had to re-materialize for just a few seconds before it fired any of its weapons or they wouldn't work. They'd pass through your ship like they weren't really there, so you have to time it just right."

"How do you know that?"

"Foreshadowing. She said the clues were in chapter five."

Cortega quickly thumbed through the book. Chapter five was heavily marked up with notes scrawled into the margin and several phrases circled within the text. He looked over it for several moments, then turned back to the prisoner. "Is this information trustworthy?"

The prisoner nodded. "To the letter. What do you say, Xane? Am I lying?"

Xane scowled at him but addressed the captain. "No. It would seem he is not, Captain."

Cortega clapped the book shut and dropped it onto the table. "Xane, prepare a strike team comprising you, four of your best officers, and me."

"Captain?"

"That's an order, Xane. I want them ready to transport in ten minutes. We are going to board that ship."

"Aye, Captain."

"And as for you," said Cortega to the prisoner, "You have ten minutes to explain what that book is and how it has the information it has. And what those notes inside it are supposed to mean."

"That will be difficult, sir," said the prisoner.

"I didn't ask you if it would be easy."

The prisoner shrugged. "Not possible, I should have said."

Cortega's expression grew dark. "Why is that not possible?"

"The book is gone." The prisoner pointed to the table where the book had been. Cortega looked. The prisoner was right. *The Ghost Nebula* by Raymond Larson had vanished.

• • •

Nathan Innes was not a man who enjoyed being fussed over. Nevertheless, he reclined on a table in the sickbay while a nurse recorded vital signs. "You know, in thirty minutes, those Rhodactians are going to blow this ship into oblivion, and I'm lying here while you make sure my blood pressure isn't high."

"Your blood pressure *is* high."

"Of course it's high! I'm agitated! The entire ship is about to be blown apart!"

"I can give you something to calm you down."

"I don't want to calm down!" He tried to stand up, but the nurse placed a hand gently upon his chest and forced him down again.

She smiled at him. She had a very lovely smile. "Please, calm down, sir. I hate to see you in such a state."

"Well, it's not as though I can just flip a switch. There are Rhodactian pirates out there, you know? There's a reason I'm all worked up."

She pressed her fingers gingerly against his face and began massaging his temples. "Let me help you." Her hands were soft and warm. Her voice was sweet and soothing. "You need to calm down."

"Oh," said Innes, taken aback, "That's quite nice. That's very lovely. How do you do that?"

"You have a lot of pent up stress," said the nurse. "Have you ever considered seeing a masseuse?"

"My second wife was a masseuse, actually. But she left me for a Vodacian architect eight years ago."

"That's terrible. You seem a perfectly adequate man for any girl to be happy with. If you don't mind my saying."

Innes eyed her suspiciously. "That's an oddly kind thing for you to say. But thank you. Perhaps you didn't notice I'm a cantankerous old man."

"You're not *that* old. And not *that* cantankerous." She moved her hands to the back of his neck and began kneading it.

His suspicion melted beneath her touch. "Oh... How do you do that? Never mind. But I really am that cantankerous. It's probably why she left me. Also, why there's never been a third Mrs. Innes."

The nurse clicked her tongue. "What a waste. Eight years is a lot of time to lose to loneliness. I've always believed that life is made of moments. Small and precious things. Easy to squander, terrible to regret, but every one filled with exquisite possibilities for anyone who will simply take notice and snatch them up. Don't you think? How many moments have you missed in eight years?"

"I don't know, exactly. I could probably create an algorithm if I really wanted to calculate it."

"Calculate? This is not about quantities. I'm talking about living life as it comes. Every day that passes is time lost. What's left is even more rare and should not be wasted."

"Well, I—Oh, that's nice—I suppose that makes a little sense. For the record, though, I do actually enjoy being angry sometimes."

The nurse shook her lovely head. "There are better things. Anger is so toxic. And if the ship is about to blow up, as you say, these may be our last moments. Can't you think of *anything* better than shouting on which to spend them?"

"Not... uh... really. Do you have some kind of incense in here? It's making me feel... wobbly."

"Just relax." Her hands moved to the place where his neck connected with his shoulders. Her touch was electric.

"This is nice, I suppose. Have you always been a nurse on this ship? I don't remember..." Out of his periphery, he noticed a reading device lying on a nearby table. It displayed a page from a basic nurse's handbook describing how to take blood pressure. "Are you really a nurse?"

"More of an apprentice. I haven't been around long. Nurse Hodges is indisposed, and I am taking her place temporarily." She sat down in front of him and gazed at him with sea-green eyes.

Innes felt he might fall out of his chair at any moment. "Have you given me something? I'm feeling... punchy."

"No. Nothing."

"Maybe I took a harder knock than I thought."

The nurse laughed. Innes felt a rush of warmth in his face and ears. His mouth stretched into a smile he was accustomed to wearing only after his fourth or fifth pint in the commons lounge.

The nurse smiled back. "Do you know what I'd like to do with my last moments?"

Innes stared blankly into her eyes. Twin pools, sea-green and bottomless. He shook his head.

"I'd want to have one last adventure. I would do something I've never done before with no regrets."

"What are you talking about? This sounds like a bad idea."

"Shhh." She placed a finger on his lips and furrowed her brow. She was the very picture of innocence. "I'm not talking about doing anything *bad*. I just don't want to lose my last chance to..."

"Your last chance to...?"

"Do you know that big machine on deck four?"

"The telepad?"

She nodded. "Would you believe I've never seen one working before?"

Innes gave himself a hard slap on the cheek. He was not sure he could tell what was real anymore. "I'm sorry. Did you say you want me to operate the telepad for you?"

She clapped her hands together giddily. "Would you?"

Innes opened his mouth to say, *Are you mad? There are Rhodactian pirates at our doorstep, and I am not going to teleport random things into space for you, no matter how pretty you are.* Instead, he inexplicably heard his own voice blurt out, "I don't see what the harm could be."

She squealed with delight.

The sound reverberated through Innes with an effect not unlike a shot of Byruvian whiskey. He regarded the woman before him. Sea-green eyes. Strawberry hair that fell over her shoulder in curls. A face like a nymph.

"Has anybody ever told you that you are astonishingly beautiful? Absolutely..." Words failed him.

She smiled modestly. "Intoxicating? I've been called that before, so it must be true."

To: Howard Zagny; Ben Westing
From: Raymond Larson
Subject: This is Incredible!

Gentlemen,

This is the most amazing thing that has ever happened to me! My book
has become a window to a parallel world! I am totally freaking out!

I understand why you thought I wouldn't believe you. But your
characters weren't nearly as subtle as you said they'd be. They broke into
my spaceship wearing NASA spacesuits and tried to hijack the telepad bay.
They were captured by my ship's crew, and they're currently in a detention
block. Let me assure you, no character has ever broken out of one of the
Galactic Explorer's holding cells short of extraordinary means that are
deeply rooted in scientific theory. Your archaic fantasy characters and
modern-day gumshoe won't have a chance.

Everything else is exactly like you described it. I can't understand it,
but I can't deny it! This is the kind of cosmic crap I write about!

Tell me everything! How did it happen?

-Raymond

CHAPTER SEVENTEEN

+++

Ghost Nebula

Security officers delivered the prisoner to the detention block where the other two captives were waiting. Two officers brandishing incapacitators shouted at the detainees to get back. A third officer placed a metal card into a slot in the wall and pressed his palm onto a dark gray pad embedded below it. An electronic blip sounded as the static field dispersed. The prisoner felt a hard shove that sent him staggering into his comrades. Another blip and the static field re-materialized behind him. The security officers took their leave.

"Joe!" cried the short astronaut. "How did it go? Did you hold out?"

"Hey, Kribble. Not even for a minute. Told 'em everything. Way more fun that way. You two holding up?"

"We're doing all right," said Kribble. "Aelrûn played through half of *Abbey Road* while you were away."

Joe glanced at Aelrûn. "They didn't confiscate your harp?"

"Oh, please," said Aelrûn. "It's a fairy harp. It comes with its own pocket dimension. I just summon it when I want it." He flicked his wrist, and his harp was inexplicably in his hand. He played the opening chords to *Here Comes the Sun* before a disembodied female voice told him to cut out that racket.

"Welcome to the party, Elle," said Joe. "Where are you right now?"

A thump sounded against the static field, as though somebody had given it a hard kick. Joe looked toward the noise. He could see her standing just outside the holding cell dressed in a bulky NASA spacesuit with a dark gray cloak draped over it. She balanced the fishbowl helmet on her hip with one arm. It was hard to believe he could not see her moments ago.

"Hello, Joe. How was the interrogation?"

"I sang like a canary. They were very interested in some notes you left in the margins."

"They'll be going to the Rhodactian ship, then? You explained to them about the proper timing for the teleportation?"

Joe nodded. "They'll be heading out immediately. Seems our intrusion has got things moving along very quickly."

She smiled and breathed a sigh. "We're right on schedule then. I admit I was leery about your less-than-subtle strategy."

"I told you it would work. We'll be in the climax in no time."

"It's early for celebration, Joe. We have a great deal more to do."

"You got to celebrate—"

"You got to celebrate the little victories on the way," interrupted Kribble, "In this line of work, you never know which one will be your last."

Joe offered a wry smile. "Thanks, Kribble."

"Ellodrine," said Aelrûn, banishing his harp, "We shouldn't waste time on idle banter. We've got to get to that artifact before the native characters do."

"Elf's right," said Joe, "Best put our business faces on."

Ellodrine nodded. "Yes, of course. Permit me a moment first. Before we progress any further, I need you to examine me and tell me whether I'm—I don't know—breathtaking or something."

Joe's business face broke into a sly smile. "I don't know, Elle. That's a dangerous question. The last time a woman asked me something like that, I held a steak to my eye for the rest of the night."

She scowled. "You know very well what I mean, Joseph Slade. I need to know whether my magic is manifesting differently in this book so we don't have any surprises like the last time."

Joe looked her up and down theatrically and twirled his finger to indicate when he wanted her to turn. She endured it sullenly.

"All clear. Wait, have you always had three eyes?"

"Joe Slade, I do not have—" She checked her reflection in the visor of her helmet and gave it a nod. "I do not have three eyes!"

"My mistake. Okay, let's get moving."

"How long do we have?" asked Aelrûn.

"They said ten minutes," said Joe. "That was about eight minutes ago."

"I'll have you out of there in a moment," said Ellodrine. She turned to examine the control panel. From her pocket, she produced a stack of thin metal cards. "I believe this is what they use for keys in this book. I wasn't sure which one would work, so I took as many as I could find." She began inserting them one after another into the slot on the wall.

Joe leaned against the static field. It emitted a crackling sound at his weight. "Are you enjoying walking around with immunity in that ridiculous cape?"

"I am, as a matter of fact," said Ellodrine. She did not look at him as she spoke, but kept her focus on the task at hand.

"Kribble really wanted that job, you know? Can't say I blame him. Those stun lasers they carry around—"

"Incapacitators," said Ellodrine, inserting and removing another card.

"Right. They really pack a sting."

"I appreciate your contributions, Joe. Though I'm hardly the stealthiest member of our company. Perhaps Aelrûn would have been the better choice."

"Nah. Your magic cloak has all the stealth you need. Besides, maybe I just didn't want you to get laser zapped. Chivalry is a bad habit I've been meaning to quit. Right after smokes."

"We're in this together," said Ellodrine, "I'm perfectly willing to do my share of the unpleasant work. Though the sentiment is appreciated."

"Nice work, by the way. Stealing the book like that."

"What book is that, Joe?"

"Like you don't know. *Ghost Nebula.* I saw it disappear from the interrogation room."

Ellodrine stopped inserting cards and looked up at him. "I was never in the interrogation room."

Joe's smirk vanished. "Then who stole the book?"

"I don't know. But it wasn't me."

"Okay, but I was there the whole time. Nobody could have got in and out of there without Captain Cyclops and his pet lizard noticing. Nobody."

"Nobody who didn't have a shadow cloak, you mean," said Aelrûn.

Joe snapped his fingers. "Exactly."

"And they don't have those in this *Galactic Explorer* series, right?" asked Kribble.

Ellodrine shook her head.

Joe's face grew grim. "So, who besides us is in this book and shouldn't be?"

"Whoa," said Kribble, "We've got a problem."

"We've got another," said Ellodrine, examining the gray pad in the wall, "I'm going to need more than a key to get you out of there."

· · ·

"I don't know if I should operate quantum particle machinery right now," said Innes. "I feel like I'm about three or four pints past my limit as it is. Are these normal symptoms for a concussion?"

"You're fine," said the nurse, "You worry too much. So, is the machine on?"

"It's primed and ready to go. What did you want to teleport Miss...?"

"Isabelle."

"That's a lovely name."

"Yes, I'm fond of it myself. It came from a Birdsong."

Innes scratched his head. "I'm not going to pretend I understand what you mean, Miss Isabelle. So, what did you want to teleport?"

"Actually, it's already up there."

"Where? On the pad? There's nothing on the pad."

She smiled at him with just a little condescension. "It's hard to see. Don't worry. Now can you point the machine at the other ship?"

Innes grunted. "No, no, no. You don't *point* anything. You enter a series of precise coordinates into the terminal here and configure the nodes to calculate the distance and prime the molecular mapping units and..."

She was staring at him with furrowed brows. "So, is it pointing at the other ship?"

"Yes. It's pointing at the other ship."

She nodded curtly.

"Are you ready to send it off?" asked Innes, "Whatever it is?"

"No! Not yet!" Isabelle consulted a small paperbound book Innes had not noticed she had been holding.

"What is that you've got there?"

"It's a book."

"Obviously it's a book. But you don't see many paper books aboard starships. You really get into your reading, don't you? Do you always mark in your books that much?"

She clapped it shut and turned to him with an innocent smile. "We can't teleport anything yet. We have to wait."

"Wait? Wait for what?"

.   .   .

"Rhodes."

"Yes, Captain?"

"Open fire on the Rhodactian ship. Use whatever you like."

"Captain?"

"That's an order, Rhodes."

Within moments, a brilliant array of weapon fire lit up the Ghost Nebula. Every laser, torpedo, and plasma ray passed through the Rhodactian ship as harmlessly as they had before. The spectacle went on for half a minute and then stopped.

"The Rhodactians are hailing us, Captain."

"Bring them up."

Captain Uthroc appeared on the display. "Captain Cortega, have you lost your mind? Your hour is not up yet."

"I got tired of waiting."

Suspicion crept over Uthroc's face. "This is what you decided? You're going to launch torpedoes at a ship you can't touch?"

"Isn't that what I just did?"

"You expect me to believe that you've decided to go down in a blaze of glory? The infamous Captain Cortega of the *Galactic Explorer*?"

Cortega adjusted his eye patch. "Rhodes, would you kindly give our Rhodactian friends another demonstration?"

"Demonstrating now, Captain."

Again, luminous beams of red and violet and gold ripped through the space between the two ships. It ended just as abruptly the second time. The *Blood Horizon* remained unharmed.

Uthroc continued his silent stare-off with Cortega.

Cortega did not flinch.

"Captain Cortega, though I applaud your audacity, I am disappointed by this senseless gesture. I give you one final chance to reconsider your position. I warn you, though, it will be your last."

Cortega adjusted his eyepatch. "Rhodes."

"Yes, Captain?"

"Are we out of torpedoes yet?"

"Not even close, Captain."

Cortega returned to Uthroc's gaze. "It seems we're not out of torpedoes yet."

Uthroc clenched his teeth. "How very noble of you! Very well. Give Captain Jonas my regards in hell!"

Uthroc vanished from the display. Rhodes's instruments blipped.

"Captain, we have incoming."

"Full defensive posture. Fire only at oncoming torpedoes. Evasive maneuvers. Keep us alive, Rhodes."

"Aye, aye, Captain!"

Cortega tapped his communication device. "Xane, meet me on deck four." With that, he darted into the transport lift.

To: Raymond Larson; Ben Westing
From: Howard Zagny
Subject: RE: This is Incredible!

Mr. Larson,

I'm happy to see we were able to cut through the standard doubts and misgivings with you. They can be so time-consuming. Please call us Howard and Ben. I think we can dispense with formalities considering the scope of what we're dealing with.

Regarding how it happened, I have little more to tell you than you already know. My characters discovered they live in a book, and I lost control of them from there. I don't know why so little a thing as that could make such a big difference.

-Howard

CHAPTER EIGHTEEN

+++

Ghost Nebula

Tremors surged through the *Galactic Explorer.*

Kribble braced himself against the wall. "Why are there earthquakes? I thought we were floating in this *outer space* thing!"

"I have a hunch we're happier not knowing," said Joe. He thrust his shoulder into the force wall with a *thud.* This had been his activity for the last several minutes.

"That sounds painful," said Aelrûn.

"It is painful. I'm systematically testing the force field for structural weaknesses."

"You won't find any," said Ellodrine with her mentoring voice.

"You keep saying that. I don't see you offering any plans."

"I'm thinking, Joe. This is what thinking looks like."

Thinking looked like a woman in a NASA spacesuit sitting on the floor staring with red-orange eyes at a gray pad on the wall.

Joe turned to Kribble. "So, what mood is that? Her eyes, I mean. Red-orange. Is that pensive?"

Kribble frowned. "Usually it means to leave her alone and find something else to do."

"It's frustrated," said Ellodrine, her eye color growing slightly more intense.

"Interesting," said Joe, "I never thought about frustration having a color. But that's it, huh? Reddy-orange."

"Salmon," suggested Kribble.

"Coral," said Aelrûn.

"Orangy-red?" said Joe.

Ellodrine huffed. "Perhaps when my irises are orangy-red, you could refrain from pointless chatter!"

Another tremor shook the ship.

"We're running out of time," said Joe, "Find the nearest security officer, knock him out, chop off his hand and press it against the pad."

"I am *not* that kind of character, Joe! That sort of thing might be acceptable in your seedy mystery novels, but that is not how we do things in Corolathia."

"Not how *she* does things, anyway," said Kribble.

"Then help me find a weak spot." Joe resumed thrusting his shoulder into the static field.

Ellodrine shook her head. "You're not going to find a weak spot. That's not how it works."

"Yeah?" Joe readied himself for another charge. "So, how does it work?"

"The wall is not actually composed of force, as many people suggest. Rather, it is a series of air particles held in stasis by a complicated system of magnetic pulses. A computer analyzes the kinetic energy of each individual molecule of air within the field, and it generates a precise amount of counterforce to hold the molecule in place, transferring the kinetic energy into a sort of locked potential energy. This process is repeated indefinitely and only takes a fraction of a fraction of a second, so any pressure placed on the wall by an outside force is, for all intents and purposes, instantly and precisely countered. Thus, it creates the illusion of a force wall."

Joe, Aelrûn, and Kribble stared with gaping mouths.

"Is that for real?" said Joe. "Do you know that, or did you just make that up?"

She mirrored their shocked expressions. Her eyes grew light green. "I... uh... Yes. I do know that. I don't know how, but I'm not making it up "

Joe crouched to meet her eyes through the static field. "Elle? Do you know a way we can get past it?"

She tilted her head. "Well, if the polarity of the magnetic pulses were reversed, they would cease to hold the particles in stasis and would instead contribute to any existing pressure, thus altering the potential energy to kinetic energy causing the static field to disperse for several seconds." She placed her hand over her mouth as though she could not believe the words coming out of it.

"How could we reverse the polarity of the pulses?"

"A well-charged electric jolt should do it," blurted Ellodrine.

Joe clapped his hands onto the static field. "Elle, you're a human lightning bolt! What are you waiting for?"

"I don't know," said Kribble. "Those spells of hers don't seem to work out so well in foreign books."

"Well, I *could* give it a shock. I believe it would be potent enough," said Ellodrine. "Accuracy is an issue. You may wish to stand back. And I shall have to prepare myself. I don't like to do things haphazardly. Let me gather my focus—"

The ship trembled harshly.

"All right, never mind the focus. Here it goes." She directed her hand toward the static field. "Al Kazaak!" A short blue electric arc leaped from her fingers. The three detainees felt a cool rush of air against their faces as the field dispersed.

Kribble stepped through the space where it had been. "If you knew that the whole time, why didn't you do it sooner?"

Ellodrine raised her palms. "I didn't know I knew. I've never read anything about static fields or magnetic pulses."

Joe scratched his head. "I didn't know you were such a science wiz, Elle. Wait. Oh, I should have seen that one coming."

"What?" asked Ellodrine. "Joe? What should you have seen coming?"

A smile crept across his face. "It seems so obvious now. Elle, you're a human play on words. You were *enchanting* in the romance novel. Now we're in science fiction, so you're a *wiz*. There is no magic in this book, so it's interpreting you as best it can."

"Oh," said Ellodrine, still looking confused, "And what does a *wiz* do, exactly?"

Joe gestured at the space where the static field had been. "That kind of stuff. Spouting off all that sciency stuff. Knowing how to disperse force walls."

"Static fields."

"Correcting everybody's terminology. That's a wiz."

"How fascinating. That could be quite useful. I must know all sorts of things I shouldn't know. That will make me a very good mentor, I think."

The ship trembled.

"As always, I am happy for you," said Aelrûn, "But I am eager to get off this ship now that we have instigated a war."

"I believe," said Ellodrine, "Yes! I know how to use a telepad. Follow me!" She opened the door to the corridor and rushed outside. Joe, Aelrûn, and Kribble followed. She stopped at a set of doors further down. "They took your supplies in here after they apprehended you."

Joe tried the door. "It's locked." He produced a couple of lock picks from behind his ear, but one look at the electronic locking mechanism dashed any hope he had of forcible entry.

Ellodrine snatched them out of his hand and pressed them into the spaces between the press keys. Her eyes went silver-blue with concentration as she mentally measured hundredths of degrees, angled the pins just so, and pressed them inward. The lock sprayed a bouquet of colorful sparks, and the door slid open.

Joe stared at her.

She gave a shrug. "I guess that's something *wizzes* do?" She tucked the lock picks back into his hand.

Most of their equipment was there. They each reclaimed a shoulder bag and sifted through the contents. Aelrûn sheathed two long daggers into his belt. Joe donned his shoulder holster and tucked his revolver into place. Kribble slung his axe across his back and grabbed greedily at some fancy space weapons lining the walls.

"All right," said Joe. "We haven't got much time."

Joe, Ellodrine, and Aelrûn rushed out the door. Kribble was still stuffing lethal goodies into his bag. "Wait! I'm coming!" He slung his bag over his shoulder and noticed something on the floor, a small, folded piece of yellow parchment. It was similar to the one Joe had been examining in The Library, but this one was not burned around the edges. "Must have fallen out of Joe's bag. I'll bet it's a clue." He thrust it into his bag and ran out of the room to catch up with the others.

.   .   .

Cortega rushed down the corridor toward the telepad chamber. Pivoting around the corner, he saw Lieutenant Xane and his four best men standing in the passage.

"Xane, we have no time to meander in the halls. Get your crew into the telepad bay."

"Your pardon, Captain. We are overriding the locks now."

"It's locked? Why is it locked?"

"Unknown, Captain. We'll have it open in a few more seconds."

"Got it!" said one of Xane's men. The door slid open. Cortega, Xane, and his officers darted inside. The telepad equipment was already primed and humming. Slumped on a chair before the control station was Innes. The sound of his snoring echoed throughout the chamber. A wet spot on his uniform had amassed from drool dripping from the corner of his mouth.

"Innes!"

Innes started. He looked around groggily. He gasped as his gaze fell on the captain, and he staggered to his feet. "Captain! Begging your pardon, Captain!"

"Explain yourself! What did you teleport?"

"I don't know, Captain. I never really saw it. Something, though."

"Innes, have you been drinking?"

"Not even a sip, Captain. Drugged, more like. But it certainly feels the same. I'm sorry, Captain! It was the nurse! I should have known not to trust her!"

"Nurse?" said Xane. "What nurse?" He looked about with his incapacitator drawn.

"The girl!" said Innes, "Where did she go? It was so strange, Captain! I've never felt anything like it. Like I just wanted to... impress her. As if it was the only thing that mattered. And sometimes she'd talk to somebody who wasn't there. And it seemed like they were passing something back and forth between them."

"Passing what back and forth?" asked Xane.

"A little paperbound book," said Innes.

Cortega grasped his shoulder and held him steady. "Innes, can you sober up long enough to teleport us over to that ship?"

Innes gave himself a few hard slaps on the cheek. "Yes, Captain. I'm ready when you are, Captain."

"Good. And directly after that, I want you to take yourself to the sickbay."

Innes frowned. "That's where I got into this mess in the first place!"

.   .   .

Ellodrine led her comrades to the transport lift. "Deck four!" The lift slid into motion. Another series of tremors rippled through the ship. "Now, when we get to the telepad bay," she said, "We have to time this just right. We must synchronize our teleportation with the Rhodactians' launch sequence or we'll end up drifting in empty space."

Kribble made a sick face.

"Sounds simple," said Joe.

Ellodrine smiled. "I don't even know what I'm going to say before it comes out of my mouth!"

When the doors opened, the four infiltrators rushed down the corridor and into the telepad chamber. Ellodrine dashed for the controls, where she pressed several buttons as fluidly as though she were playing the piano. "Sensors are set," she said, "Waiting for torpedoes to launch."

The four companions waited. A stillness gripped the air. The blasts and tremors were gone.

"Nothing's happening," said Kribble.

"They stopped the assault," said Aelrûn. "Something is wrong."

They waited several more moments.

"I don't like this," said Joe. "Is there no other way we can teleport over?"

Ellodrine shook her head. "It's too risky. If their ship is ghosting, we would suffocate in the vacuum of space."

"Stop saying things like that!" said Kribble, holding his stomach.

"Is there anything else we can try?" asked Joe.

Ellodrine's face lit up. "Yes." She tapped several keys and a map of the *Galactic Explorer* appeared on the monitor. "Here it is. There is a shuttle bay close to here. We could take a shuttle to the other ship. If it is ghosting, we won't be able to board, but at least we won't be asphyxiating in deep space."

"Seriously!" shouted Kribble. "Do you have to keep saying it?"

"Do you know how to fly a shuttle, Elle?" asked Joe.

She smiled. "Only one way to find out."

To: Howard Zagny; Ben Westing
From: Raymond Larson
Subject: RE: This is Incredible!

Howard and Ben,

Self-awareness is no small thing. Let me explain it this way. Say I have a crystal ball that tells me the future. Now, I tell you you're going to eat an apple in five minutes, but when you do you're going to find a half-bitten worm inside it. In five minutes, are you still going to eat that apple? Probably not. You're going to go with the banana instead. Your awareness changed your action.

And it doesn't stop there. You've changed one link in your lifelong chain of cause and effect. That one link is going to ripple into the future indefinitely. Your life is different because you didn't eat that wormy apple. Maybe it's a little different, maybe it's a lot. Either way, my crystal ball is obsolete. Everything it knew was about the old future in which you ate the apple. Since that future is no longer applicable, my crystal ball is now a paperweight.

Your characters realized you were giving them a wormy apple. (Because novels are about troubles and trials, and you've probably heaped these onto your characters in droves.) They didn't eat the apple, and now your authorship is as useless as my crystal ball.

That said, this thing is quickly spinning out of control. Most of what I try to write isn't sticking at all. Here's what I've figured out so far. They seem to be after something called a ghosting device. It draws tangible things into a hyperspace plane where they can no longer be touched by other tangible things.

I regret to say your characters are less secured than I previously indicated. It seems one of them is some kind of technical genius and broke the holding cell. They haven't yet made it to the Rhodactian ship where the ghosting device is held, but they're en route.

Here is what I propose. I have uploaded the content of my manuscript online and sent you both viewing privileges. If you both do the same with your manuscripts, we'll each have access to a larger piece of this than we have now. There is also a live chat feature, so we'll be able to message in real-time instead of sending emails to one another.

Gentlemen, I am open to ideas.

-Raymond

CHAPTER NINETEEN

+++

Ghost Nebula

An ominous quiet gripped the small shuttle as it floated toward the Rhodactian pirate ship. Moments ago, a dreadful firefight threatened to ravage the *Galactic Explorer*. Now there was nothing. Stillness. The only sound was Aelrûn's voice as he sang the words to David Bowie's *Space Oddity*.

"How are we coming on that Rhododendron ship, Elle?" asked Joe.

"Rhodactian. And we are coming up on it now. The docking bay is open. Strange. I'm going to bring us in and try to land." Her irises were blue-gray with focus.

Aelrûn stopped singing. "Ellodrine, do you really know what you're doing up there?"

"You have nothing to worry about, Aelrûn. It's quite simple. Remember, I'm a *wiz* in this book."

"Honestly," said Joe, "I'd feel a little better if you were an *ace*. Knowing how to fly a spaceship and actually flying it are not the same thing. I wonder if Kribble had the right idea."

Ellodrine turned to face him. "*Kribble* made his choice, and when he misses the excitement, he'll only have himself to blame! Of all the petty excuses. Staying back to watch for greblins, indeed! Frankly, I find it insulting he would be critical of my piloting skills when he has never seen them."

"Right," said Joe, "But you never *have* piloted anything before."

"Then there's no reason to assume I would do it poorly."

"Actually, I'd feel better if you would face the front again."

Before she could respond, Aelrûn pointed ahead and cried, "What is *that?*"

Ellodrine whipped around to the front view display. She gasped. Several shuttles, similar to their own, were flying directly toward them. They were heading en masse from the Rhodactian ship toward the *Galactic Explorer.* Within moments, they were darting to the left and to the right to avoid the small shuttle.

Ellodrine white-knuckled the controls and swiveled the craft from side to side through the oncoming horde. Her shoddy evasive maneuvers were effective, if not quite impressive. She managed to miss every potential head-on collision. Unfortunately, toward the end of the throng came a small lag-behind that surprised her. She pressed forward on the controls to dip under it, but a hard jolt rocked them as the bottom of the Rhodactian shuttle ricocheted off their roof.

"Well," said Ellodrine, holding the controls in a death grip, "That's what deflector shields are for."

Joe and Aelrûn picked themselves up off the floor. "Is it too late to watch for greblins with Kribble, I wonder?" said Joe.

"I heard that," said Ellodrine, "I got us through it, didn't I? You're alive, aren't you?"

"Jury's still out on that," said Joe, holding his ribcage.

She made a face at him. "Stop complaining and hold on to something. It's time to land."

The shuttle entered the open docking bay. After the departure of so many of the Rhodactian shuttles, it was relatively empty. Ellodrine pressed forward on the controls, lowering the shuttle. "I'm bringing us in."

The shuttle touched down with a loud thud, followed by a scraping metal sound and a flashing red light that intermittently lit up the cabin. "Do you know what you're doing?" shouted Joe.

"Landing," said Ellodrine, through gritted teeth as she wrestled with the controls. The shuttle fishtailed across the docking bay, twisted sideways, and slowed to a screeching halt.

Joe could feel his lunch threatening to make its own escape.

"We've stopped," said Aelrûn.

"You know," said Ellodrine between heavy breaths, "I don't think *wizzes* make good pilots."

Joe and Aelrûn did not respond. But their withering glares were reason enough to drop the subject. She pressed a button on the control panel. The doors opened, and a ramp extended to the docking bay. Joe, Aelrûn, and Ellodrine clambered out, awkwardly recovering their footing after their turbulent voyage.

"Look." She pointed to the vacant bay. It was devoid of person or craft. "I wonder why they all left at once like that. Where did they go?"

"Only one place *to* go," said Joe. "They must have gone to the *Galactic Explorer*. The real question is why?"

"An assault, perhaps?" said Aelrûn.

"I don't think so," said Joe. "In their own ship, they had the advantage. They have that ghosting device, remember?"

Ellodrine nodded. "That's right. I suspect the only reason the ship is solid right now is they had to turn the ghosting effect off to depart. You see, if an object held within the ship while it's ghosting exits the ship, it will remain in a phantom state, unable to touch or be touched by anything. Eventually, its particles will simply come apart and disperse into empty space."

Aelrûn raised a brow. "You just *know* this stuff?"

"What's the tenth decimal of pi?" said Joe.

"Five."

"Is that right?" asked Aelrûn.

Joe shrugged. "How do I know?"

Ellodrine could not hide a smile. "This is really neat! Keep asking me things. I like this book."

Joe nodded at the open maw of space on the far side of the docking bay. "Okay, why aren't we being sucked into space right now?"

"As a matter of fact, there is a fascinating mechanism that secures an artificial environment within the ship and prevents the natural vacuum of space from—"

"Never mind. Never mind. I'm sorry I asked. Answer me this instead. If those space pirates weren't mounting an assault, they must have been fleeing something. What could they want to get away from so badly they would run to an enemy ship?"

Ellodrine opened her mouth to answer but had nothing to offer. The question met with silence. The three companions glanced back and forth at one another.

"We should be on our guard," said Aelrûn after several moments. "I'll take point."

Ellodrine nodded. "We are heading to the engine room. That's where the device will be."

Together they made their way along the passages of the *Blood Horizon*. Many of the corridors were as vacant as the landing dock had been, those that were not were populated by the remains of dead Rhodactian pirates. They passed dozens of bodies. Many of the corpses sustained cauterized streaks along their torsos. Others were missing their heads but were similarly burned so there was barely any blood. Ellodrine and Aelrûn shared a worried look.

"These guys weren't shot," said Joe, "What could make a wound like that?"

"It's Zolethos," said Aelrûn. "These are the kinds of wounds we find on his victims. He wields a flaming sword that sears its prey with blue fire as it cuts through them."

"Someone did this with a sword?" exclaimed Joe. "Didn't these guys have ray guns or something? How could anybody do all this damage with a sword?"

"Zolethos is a major character," said Ellodrine, "As such, it may be very difficult to kill him. Whatever would bring him down would have to be climactic. Nameless, extraneous characters like these crewmen never stood a chance against an antagonist as epic as Zolethos."

"Eight books so far," said Aelrûn.

Ellodrine nodded. "That's a lot of time for him to have grown in influence. Even if these Rhodactian pirates were very accurate marksmen, they'd never prevail against him. Fate simply wouldn't favor them against a character like Zolethos. He was not written to be defeated by the likes of them."

"If he's that bad," said Joe, "How do we have any chance against him?"

"Culmination. Drama. Whatever could defeat him would have to be climactic."

Joe opened the chamber of his .45 and removed the bullet. He drew a charcoal pen from his shoulder bag and scrawled something onto it before placing it again into his gun. "Monogrammed bullet. Now it's got his initial on it. Climactic enough for you?"

"It's better than nothing. I hope we shan't have opportunity to test it."

They continued onward. The number of dead Rhodactians increased as they made their way through the lower decks. They stepped into a transport lift and directed it to the engine room. It hummed to life. Aelrûn drew his twin daggers and stationed himself on the left side of the door. Joe took the right side with his revolver.

The lift came to a stop. The doors slid open to reveal a vast room with a large glowing engine core. Situated before the core stood a tall pedestal structure that hummed with alien technology. Set within the pedestal was a glass cylindrical canister filled with a red-purple misty substance that looked very much like the Ghost Nebula outside.

"It's the ghosting device," whispered Ellodrine.

Cautiously, the three companions exited the lift and made their way toward the strange device. Joe and Aelrûn surveyed their surroundings while Ellodrine examined the machine.

"That's going to help us get out of bookland somehow?"

"Not *somehow*, Joe. I told you. I have to combine this device with the effect of another artifact that—"

Aelrûn shushed her. "We are not alone in here," he said in a low tone.

Joe and Ellodrine looked around nervously. "I don't see anything," whispered Joe.

"Neither do I," said Aelrûn without looking at him. "We should not linger."

"I'm for that. Elle, is that thing portable?"

"I think so, but it's locked in place." She fumbled with the controls on the pedestal. "Give me a moment to crack the code."

Joe stood with his back to her. He held his gun out in front of him, seeking a target. "You sure something's out there, Ski Cap?"

"I can hear breathing."

Joe could hear nothing but the humming of machines. Then another sound rose. It was a low whir that grew in volume until it culminated in a whoosh from behind the doors of the transport lift.

"Somebody's coming," said Joe.

Aelrûn shifted into an elven defensive posture with his daggers, one of them poised to throw. Joe leveled his revolver at the doors.

They slid open.

•   •   •

"Ah! A tavern!" Kribble found himself in a large commons area with food stalls and a wide bar. He had crept through the passages of the *Galactic Explorer* as stealthily as could be expected from a barrel-chested dwarf in antiquated space apparel. Fortunately, most of the crew members were on edge from the recent onslaught of lasers and torpedoes. It seemed they were willing to overlook a dwarf in NASA gear as long as he was not a bloodthirsty Rhodactian pirate.

He did his best to walk casually as he strolled to the bar.

"Can I help you with something?" asked the bartender.

Kribble dropped a gold coin onto the counter. "I don't care what it is so long as it's stout, and it's beer!"

The bartender examined the coin skeptically but must have decided it was worth something and pocketed it. He placed a frothy mug on the bar. Kribble took a swig and winced. "That's great stuff! What is it?"

"Karthecian dark ale. Stout enough to drop a Barchuvian Myrmodile."

Kribble nodded his approval. He found himself a table with a good view of the door. He put his back to the large transparent wall that afforded passengers a view of the black starry abyss through which they sailed. Currently, the red-purple mist of the Ghost Nebula seemed to cling to the glass.

Kribble had issues with sailing as it was. Riding in giant ships through vast expanses of emptiness gave him a sick feeling in the pit of his stomach that even Karthecian dark ale could not touch. He tried to distract himself with his beer, but the imposing void behind him would not be ignored. It had a gravity that pulled his mind toward it with ungentle force.

The door to the commons opened. A strawberry-haired nurse stepped through. She caught his gaze and jumped, but played it off by locating a table and hiding her face behind a menu. He found her oddly familiar.

Kribble stroked his beard and tried to puzzle it out. He could not remember a time when he might have run into a space-traveling nurse. Maybe he was being too suspicious. Maybe it was time for a break from mystery novels.

He reached into his bag and retrieved a pack of cards. His fingers stumbled upon something else. Withdrawing his hand, he found he was clutching the folded yellow parchment. Joe's paper.

He had forgotten about it up to now. For a moment curiosity got the better of him, and he began to unfold it.

"No. I won't read it. It belongs to Joe." He set it down on the table. He fished his cards out of his bag and began shuffling them. It did not help. He found himself staring at the note. What could it be? It wasn't burned like the one in the romance novel. Had Joe found another one in The Library?

"Would you care for another beer, sir?"

It was the bartender. He had a mug in his hand and a concerned expression on his face. Kribble noticed the mug before him was now empty. He could not remember finishing it. How long had he been staring at this paper?

The bartender set the fresh beer in front of him and walked away.

"Joe would open it," said Kribble to himself. "It could be a clue. There's only one way to find out."

He unfolded it. It was torn like Joe's previous message, only where that one had been torn on the bottom, this one was torn on the... top. Kribble began to read.

I can help you get back to your own life.
All you have to do is help me with a minor task.
Tell me what they're planning. They'll tell you.
What do they need? Where are they planning to go?
Give me the titles of the books they plan to use.

When you have the information, write it down.
Use any paper you find. Address it to me.
I'll be able to read it. Once you've done this, burn the evidence.

You can have your life again

-GY

Kribble rubbed his eyes and looked back at the paper as though maybe the words would be different. "This can't be right, Joe would never go along with something like this."

A commotion erupted outside the commons.

"Pirates," someone yelled from down the corridors. "They've boarded the ship!"

Sounds of weapon fire rose. Nervous crew members stood up from their tables and made a defensive arc around the entrance. Several readied their weapons. Kribble remembered his own spacey weapons from the closet and brought one out. It felt warm in his hand.

In moments, the intruders reached the door. The commons exploded in a light show of weapon fire. Passengers shot beams toward the oncoming invaders. The invaders fired back, but not with space guns. Their weapons were less futuristic.

Kribble kicked his table over and took cover behind it. He fired his weapon, fumbling at first, but he quickly adjusted to the device in his hand. To his right, a red-shirted cadet lurched over and crumpled to the floor. An arrow protruded from his chest. Kribble cocked his head and stared at it for a few seconds. Then, hoping he was wrong, he risked a better look around his barricade. Whatever a Rhodactian pirate looked like, Kribble did not know. What he did know was these attackers were not Rhodactian pirates. They were greblins. And this greblin strike squad was quickly turning the commons into a war zone.

"Joe. You didn't."

CHAPTER TWENTY

+++

Ghost Nebula

"Freeze!" yelled Joe.

"Stand down," ordered Cortega from the transport lift platform. Next to him, Lieutenant Xane growled. Joe and Aelrûn stood their ground, weapons drawn. Cortega and Xane leveled their incapacitators.

"It's the prisoners," said Xane. "With the antique space suits."

"How did you get out of the holding cells?" said Cortega.

"Picked the lock," said Joe.

"What are you doing aboard this ship?"

"Answering stupid questions."

"Do I look like a man to be trifled with?"

Joe opened his mouth to speak, but Aelrûn intervened. "Joe, do you have to exacerbate every situation?" He turned to Cortega and Xane. "I do not have time to tell you everything, and you would not believe it, anyway. But we are not spies, and we are not pirates. We are here for this machine for reasons I cannot even begin to explain. Your lives are better without it. And something very dangerous is on this ship right now. On my honor, we are the least of your worries right now. Will you accept my word as a noble of the elven courts of Thërion and lower your weapons?"

A dangerous glint sparked in Cortega's eye. "What do you think?"

"I think if you're smart, you'd listen to him," said Joe. "I'm sure you didn't miss the trail of alien corpses on the way to this room. You think we did that? You got bigger problems than you know. Frankly, I don't want to stay here a minute longer than it takes for Elle to unbolt that thing and drag it to our transport shuttle."

Cortega jerked his neck to the side, and a loud crack escaped from his vertebrae. "Let me tell you my version of what's going to happen. I have been chasing this ship across galaxies with orders to haul it or its burned husk back to the Intergalactic Council along with any classified technology contained inside. Now you're both going to lower your weapons, and your comrade is going to hand over that device. Then I'm going to bring it *and* you to the high command of the Intergalactic Union Astral Navy for questioning."

"Well," said Ellodrine, still focused on the pedestal, "I will not be handing *anything* over if I cannot override these security locks. Could you keep it down, all of you? I'm trying to concentrate."

Several awkward moments passed with only the sounds of the humming engine core and Ellodrine's rapid tapping at the pedestal's keys. It was Cortega's communicator that broke the relative silence. "Captain. This is Gibbons. We've reached the bridge."

"Need to get that?" asked Joe.

Cortega sneered and tapped his communicator. "Gibbons, is this going to be important? We're in the middle of something right now."

"Sorry, Captain. It's just that... They're dead, Captain. I think we found Uthroc."

"You think? You can't tell?"

"Aye, Captain. It's difficult to say for certain. His head is missing."

"Thank you, Gibbons. See what you can do to confirm that and rendezvous with us in the engine room. We've got a situation down here."

"Aye, Captain. Immediately, Captain."

Cortega sighed. "And Gibbons, see if you can get into the ship's computers and find any other life forms on the ship. Cortega out!"

Joe smiled at him. "So, we're all just waiting for her to break into that thing, right?"

Cortega and Xane shared a glance, then looked back at Joe. "Affirmative," said Cortega.

"Do we have to keep pointing weapons at one another in meantime?"

"You can lower yours."

Ellodrine slammed her hands down on the pedestal. "Really, now! The bravado is very distracting. Will you put the weapons down? Everyone!"

The four men glared at one another like scolded children and tentatively lowered their weapons. A silent and temporary truce.

"All right," said Cortega. "If she's the only one who has any chance of breaking that out of there, then it makes sense to let her do it. But make no mistake, I *will* confiscate that device."

"Let me tell you *my* version of what's going to happen, Captain," said Ellodrine, "I'm going to get this out of here. Then we're going to take it back to your ship, sit down to some reasonable accommodations, and discuss things over tea. You do have tea in your spaceship, don't you? Isn't that better than threats and violence? You are welcome to hack into this advanced alien security system yourself. Be my guest."

Cortega turned to Joe. "Is she really as good as she says she is?"

"We'll find out," said Joe. "She picked up some handy skills when we boarded your ship. Picked up a little attitude to go with it."

The pedestal made a loud click, and two of the four braces released their grip.

"Ha!" cheered Ellodrine. "Just two more to go."

Joe caught Aelrûn out of the corner of his eye. The daggers were now at his side, but his head was cocked at an odd angle, and his brows were furrowed in deep concentration. Occasionally he sniffed at the air. His eyes panned the perimeter of the room. His muscles were tense, like a trap ready to snap.

"It *does* make sense," said Joe to himself.

"You say something, space cadet?" asked Cortega.

"It makes sense," repeated Joe. "What you said before. If she's the only one who can break it out of there, then it makes sense to let her do it."

"What about it?"

"Elle, stop! You can't release that device."

"Run that by me again," Cortega's hand, still gripping a lowered incapacitator, twitched.

"Look, you said it yourself," said Joe, "It makes sense. Elle is the only person who is able to unlock that cage the ghosting device is stuck in. We all put our weapons down because we're after the same thing. And we know none of us is going to get it if we have a shootout before she can break it loose."

"Yeah. So?"

Joe cocked his revolver. "So, that's what *he's* waiting for, too."

"Who?"

"Zolethos," Aelrûn shifted his daggers with blinding speed to an offensive posture. "Joe's right. I should have seen it sooner. He's here."

Cortega and Xane took a cue from the others and lifted their incapacitators, sweeping them back and forth, looking for a target.

"I see no one," said Xane.

"He'll be wearing a magical cloak," said Aelrûn. "We can't see him unless we already know where he is."

"There's no such thing as magic," said Xane.

"Then you'll have nothing to fear from his flaming sword," said Aelrûn.

From a dark corner of the room, a streak of bright blue fire ignited. The flames rose from a long, curved blade that seemed at first to be hovering in the air. As they continued to look, however, they realized it was gripped by a hand they could not believe they had not seen before. A shadowy figure emerged.

"Zolethos!" cried Ellodrine.

"Stand down," said Cortega.

The shadowy figure stepped forward.

"Open fire!" Cortega and Xane sent a pair of pale blue beams streaking toward the hostile. The cloaked figure twisted nimbly out of the way and leaped with remarkable agility toward them. He closed the distance in a blink and swung his sword in a fiery arc that sent Cortega's incapacitator skittering across the room. Another swipe and Xane's was in two pieces.

Xane discarded his broken weapon and unsheathed a small blade from a cache in his bionic arm. He pressed a switch in the grip, and the blade extended into a sword. It emitted a sizzling sound as electrical currents moved through it. Xane lunged. The two blades met in an explosion of fire and lightning. Both combatants were masters, but the dark swordsman soon had Xane on the defense. Aelrûn appeared, flanking the shadowy opponent with his daggers.

The cloaked figure gripped the handle of his fiery blade with both hands and pulled them apart with a fluid motion. In each hand, he now held identical flaming scimitars. He wielded them expertly between his opponents, warding off their attacks. Aelrûn and Xane pressed their offense against him. He found an opening and thrust one of his swords into Xane's bionic arm, which erupted in a shower of sparks. Xane staggered back several steps.

The dark swordsman now turned his full attention to Aelrûn.

"Al Kazaak!" Ellodrine's two-foot lightning bolt accomplished little more than to send her sprawling backward into the pedestal.

Cortega rolled across the floor and recovered his incapacitator. He sent a stunning beam toward the cloaked figure. His intended target maneuvered himself to the side quicker than thought, and the beam caught Aelrûn in the shoulder instead. Aelrûn dropped his daggers and stumbled into a kneeling position.

The shadowy figure abandoned the elf and lunged at Cortega with uncanny speed. Cortega rolled to the side as a flaming sword embedded itself in the wall behind him. The swordsman abandoned his grip on the duplicated weapon, and it disintegrated into ash. Down again to a single blade, he advanced upon the captain, but Cortega grasped his wrist to wrest the weapon from his hand. They struggled with each other in a tenuous stalemate. It did not last long.

Joe slipped up from behind, gripped the swordsman's shoulder, and pressed the barrel of his revolver against his neck. "I hear it's going to take something really special to bring you down. Well, the bullet in the chamber has your initial on it. Let's see if I miss."

The shadowy figure, still in Cortega's grip, emitted a sinister laugh. His flaming sword extinguished itself and now appeared to be a cold black-steel blade. "Did you think that would stop me? A monogrammed projectile? That's your magic? Did you mark it with a Z?" He cackled.

"I didn't mark it with a Z," said Joe. "Because you're not Zolethos. But keep laughing if it makes you happy."

The shadowy figure did not keep laughing.

Aelrûn approached, rubbing his shoulder. His eyes narrowed. "But, Joe, you said that—"

"I lied. Should I tell them what letter is really on this bullet, or would you like to do the honors?"

The cloaked figure said nothing for several weighty moments before it said, "How did you know?" He removed his hood to reveal a boyish face with bright blue eyes and sandy blond hair. He bore a strange mark on his left hand in the shape of a horizontal hourglass.

"Well, look who's back from the dead," said Joe, "Your old protagonist."

Ellodrine gasped from across the room. "Corbin!"

CHAPTER TWENTY-ONE

+++

Ghost Nebula

Ellodrine's irises shifted back and forth between several vibrant colors. "Corbin! What are you doing here? You died! I *read* that you died!"

"Why do you have a shadow cloak?" asked Aelrûn, "And Zolethos's sword?"

Corbin smiled sheepishly at them. "Hello, Ellodrine. Aelrûn."

"Hello!?" Ellodrine goose-stepped toward him. "Hello!? That's what you have to say to me? Have you any idea what you put me through? And Aelrûn? And Kribble? We *grieved* for you!"

Corbin sighed. "I wanted to tell you—"

"Then you should have bloody told us! I don't care what you *wanted* to do! And you!" She turned to Joe. "You knew about it! How long did you know?"

Joe put a palm out. "Whoa, there. What are you upset with me f—"

"How long?" She thrust a finger in his face.

"Just before we left The Library. Honest. I mean, I suspected for a while, but—"

"You should have told me the minute you knew. The minute!"

Cortega and Xano glanced back and forth at one another.

Ellodrine folded her arms and tapped one foot rapidly. "Explanations. Now. Starting with you." She pointed at Corbin. "How are you not dead?"

"Well," began Corbin, cautiously, "You didn't technically read that I had died. The narrative only actually said I had been *left* for dead. And that was true. I tried to take on a whole band of greblins on my own, and I was no match for them. I expected no better. But I couldn't waste away reading books in The Library any longer. I wanted to go down fighting."

"How did you survive?" asked Aelrûn.

"I wasn't sure I would. Look." He lifted his shirt revealing several wicked scars on his abdomen. "They left me bleeding out on the ground. I slipped in and out of consciousness for a while. I should have been dead within minutes." He lowered his shirt and shook his head. "The book wouldn't let me die. I couldn't understand why. I know now. I'm the protagonist. The book needs me. It couldn't let me die until the plot is resolved. Instead, it produced a caravan of nomads. They took me in. One of them was versed in healing magic."

"They just happened by?" said Joe. "A little *Deus ex Machina*, don't you think?"

"I forced its hand," said Corbin. "I guess the narrative was desperate."

"Why didn't I read about any nomads?" asked Ellodrine. "They never showed up in the book."

"That doesn't surprise me," said Joe. He waved a hand dismissively. "Common rule of fiction that when a character is left for dead, his rescue gets omitted until he has time to make a big surprise, plot-twisting entrance." He gestured to Corbin. "Surprise!"

Ellodrine bored into him with her stare.

He shrugged. "I read more than I let on."

"Your turn, Joe. What do you know about this?"

"Where should I begin? How about this? You already know I spent my first couple of days of freedom wandering around in your magic library looking for... I don't know. A wet bar, maybe. Never found one. Only a little yellow paper. A note."

"You already showed us the note," said Ellodrine.

"I showed you the *top* half of the note. I wasn't sure who I could trust yet, and I wanted to keep my cards close. The bottom of it was signed by someone whose initials were GY. Made me an offer. GY could send me back to the life I knew. I could leave you and your reading lounge behind like a three-legged turtle and never look back. All I had to do was to send him information. About you three, of course. Plans. Goals. The titles of any books you planned to visit."

Aelrûn tapped the handle of his dagger. "And was that your epiphany? Is that why you agreed to work with us? To sabotage us?"

"I thought about it," said Joe, "Good and hard, if you want to know."

Ellodrine shook her head. "How could you, Joe? How could you?"

"Could have easy. Didn't, though. GY should have offered me something else. He should have known there was no going back to living a lie. I spent my plots sifting out the truth, and truth has never been about personal preference. Just because I didn't like my situation didn't mean I was ready to close my eyes and play make-believe again. Fast forward a bit. The romance novel. We were running through the garden maze. I found another yellow paper. This one wasn't addressed to me, though. And it was mostly burned up. I could only make out bits of it. Here." He dug a small scrap out of his pocket and placed it into Ellodrine's hand. *nd th— tles.— BZ*

"What does this mean, Joe?" Her tone was less angry now. Her eyes had softened to a deep green color.

"Find the titles, maybe. Or send the titles. Doesn't matter. What does matter is that GY wasn't working alone. Probably had other agents going after the same information he wanted from me. Didn't want all his eggs in one basket."

"What agents?" asked Aelrûn. "Who wrote the letters?"

"I thought maybe BZ was your guy Zolethos at first. But I couldn't get the initials to fit. None of your names fit the bill either. I figured it had to be a code to protect their identities if their correspondence was ever intercepted. Once I'd got that, it wasn't hard to crack. They just used the letters prior to their initials in the alphabet. So, GY was actually HZ."

Ellodrine frowned. "Howard Zagny. I might have known."

Joe nodded. "And BZ was—"

"Corbin Adlander," said Aelrûn. He shoved his blade into its sheath. "Corbin, you were working with Howard?"

"He and I wanted the same things," said Corbin. "We wanted to finish the story. We wanted to save Corolathia!"

"Howard is the one who endangered Corolathia to begin with," said Ellodrine. "To sell books! Of course, he wants to finish the story. He's got an audience to entertain. And what would he ever do without his big finish?"

"He just writes books, Ellodrine. He didn't know they were going to come to life. And before you go calling me a traitor, remember I am the only one who stayed true to our quest. You abandoned it! And you abandoned me! If you want to throw accusations around, we could be here for days!" Corbin took a moment to compose himself. "Before I left you, Howard contacted me with a letter. He was desperate. He was reaching out. I felt sorry for him. I discovered I could write him back. I only had to pen a letter and address it to him. No need to send it. Somehow, he could read it from his end. We began a correspondence."

"You conspired with Howard Zagny against us," said Ellodrine.

He shook his head. "It wasn't like that."

"No? Then why didn't you tell us you were alive?"

Corbin sighed. "Since everyone believed I was dead, Howard and I thought it best to keep it that way. It enabled me to work behind the scenes. Since I couldn't convince you to finish our quest, I wanted to keep you away from the World Where the Books Are Written. If you made it there, I knew you'd never look back. And where would that leave Corolathia? Everything and everyone we've ever cared about would be subject to Zolethos's torment. But if you stayed, I believed you'd eventually come around. You'd tire of hiding in The Library, and you'd come back to liberate your home."

"And that's why you became Zolethos?" asked Aelrûn. "You were trying to goad us into action. Did you send the greblins after us? And vandalize our camp?"

Corbin averted his gaze. "Howard wrote in some supplies for me. Shadow cloaks and a replica of Zolethos's sword. He wrote them into an offshoot short story so Ellodrine wouldn't come across it in her copy of *Nexus of Words*. I returned to the greblins who'd nearly killed me. I convinced them I was Zolethos, and they did whatever I asked of them."

"That reminds me," said Joe, "I'll be taking that book back."

Corbin held out empty hands. "I don't have it anymore."

Joe's eyes narrowed. "What do you mean, you don't have it anymore? Where is it?"

Corbin was silent.

"Joe?" asked Ellodrine, "What are you talking about? What book did he have?"

"Your copy of *Nexus of Words*," said Corbin. "He left it behind in his office when he interrogated the hunt-lord. The greblin brought it back to me. It's how I knew which book you were going into. It named the title of this space novel."

Joe felt the weight of several eyes upon him. "Before you say anything, I had a plan. I lifted the book from Elle back in *The Marchioness's Temptation* and planted it in my office. I knew it would make its way to whoever was pulling the strings. Once I was back in The Library, I figured out which book we were going into and thought really good and hard about it so it would show up in the narrative. Corby took the bait. And here he is. We caught him."

Corbin looked at the ground.

"I don't understand," said Aelrûn, "Why bait Corbin? If he's working with Howard, don't they already have access to the book?"

Joe shook his head. "Howard is an author and a control freak. He's a daydreamer, and he's too cautious to send Corby charging in. Corby, on the other hand, was getting impatient. He was tired of creeping around and watching. Dropping him a copy of the book made him independent from Howard, and he played right into our hands. So, how did I do, Elle?"

Ellodrine's eyes glowed like hot coals. A burning smell filled the air, and wisps of black smoke trailed from her fingertips. "Joseph Slade. Did I understand correctly that you stole my book and used it for bait? That you gave away the title of this science fiction novel that I made quite clear was absolutely secret? That you knew Corbin was alive and impersonating Zolethos? And none of this did you tell me?"

"Sorry, Elle. There's a lot I had to keep under wraps. Otherwise, I would have tipped my hand."

"When were you going to tell your mentor about this?"

"Right after I caught the bad guy. So, we're right on schedule. This is how I operate. You shouldn't be surprised. You read my books, didn't you?"

"I... skimmed them."

"Don't like a good mystery?"

"I like a *good* mystery just fine."

"Whoa there, little lady." Joe held his hands out. "Mystery is a big genre. You had your chance at any detective in The Library. You and your friends knocked me out of *my* life so I could help you with *your* problem. So, let's not get too sore at my methods. We've got Howard's agent. We've tipped the balance. You can't argue with the results."

"Don't presume to tell me what I can and cannot argue with!"

Aelrûn rolled his eyes. "It's true, Joe. She really can argue about *anything.*"

"You wanted me to out-think your opponents," said Joe.

"Well, I don't like you out-thinking your allies!" She huffed. "And I do not care for this sort of... *protagonizing!* I was leery of you from the start. My preference was to bring in one of Agatha Christie's characters, but she wasn't writing anything at the moment."

"Agatha Christie's dead."

"Wonderful!" Ellodrine threw her hands in the air. "Thank you so much for gracing me with that depressing fact on top of everything else! By which I do not thank you at all, because I am using sarcasm!" She stalked back toward the pedestal and resumed her work. The sound of rapid typing upon the keypad was interspersed with the sharp crackles of electricity discharging from her fingertips.

Joe and Aelrûn offered each other a shrug.

"So," said Cortega, "Which one of you is going to explain all that to me, now?"

Raymond
Okay, Howard. Your turn. You never mentioned you made contact with the other characters. Ben, did you know about this?

Howard
He's probably having trouble with the chat function. Ben doesn't get along well with technology.

Raymond
Ben, just type it into the box on the top.

Howard
He'll figure it out.

Raymond
Why have you been withholding information, Howard?

Howard
I haven't been withholding information. Not deliberately anyway. I told Ben I had an ally. You remember that, right? Ben?

Ben
Can you guys read this?

Raymond
Welcome to the live chat, Ben.

Ben
Am I in the live chat now? Howard, you lying bastard! You never told us about thic!

Howard
I did, though! I just didn't get very specific because you thought I was crazy.

Ben
Saying you have an ally, and saying you're involved in a conspiracy with your dead protagonist are very different things, Howard.

Howard
If I told you I was talking to Corbin, you would have slapped delusional on my forehead and blocked me out like everybody else!

Ben
Okay, Howard. I get that the truth is hard to believe. But if we're together in this, you've got to spill it. How were you able to contact Corbin? And Joe, for that matter? Did you write it into the book somehow?

Howard
No. Not into the narrative. The other characters would have been able to read it from there. It started about two months ago. I'd mostly given up on writing anything. I just read along as they learned more and more about who and what they were. Corbin wanted to finish the quest. He tried to convince the others. They just didn't care anymore.

Raymond
How did you send a message from our tier of reality to theirs?

Howard
I was sitting in front of my computer one night. The narrative had focused on Corbin. He had finally stopped trying to convince his companions. He just sat in The Library and stared off into space. He felt hopeless. I felt hopeless. We both wanted the same thing. To finish the book. I felt connected to him. Anyone else would just think I was crazy. But he knew.

Ben
You're not writing a novel, Howard. Answer the question.

Howard
I opened my email and typed a message to him.

Raymond
That's it? You sent him an email?

Howard
Not because I thought it would work. Remember, I was struggling for months with this completely alone. I was trying to cope. When you hit rock bottom, sometimes you do crazy things because it beats not doing anything at all.

Raymond
How did you address this email?

Howard corbin@corolathia.com

Raymond
Seriously? That just worked? You contacted another plane of reality with that?

Howard
I kept waiting for it to bounce back. Instead, I noticed some new text in the manuscript. Corbin saw a small yellow parchment next to his foot.

Raymond
The hand of the writer. It's the power of creation in their world. You created their entire existence with words. I guess it makes sense it would manifest a message with your authorship.

Ben
So, you two began commiserating with one another. How did he write you back?

Howard
He just wrote to me on any paper he could find. He didn't know how to send it, but it seems he didn't need to. Whatever he addressed to me wound up in my inbox.

Ben
Now you had your ally.

Howard
Yes. We collaborated to convince the others to finish the story. When nothing worked, Corbin became depressed. He wrote to me late one night that he was taking up the quest on his own, and this was probably goodbye. I didn't receive it until I awoke the next morning. By then there was nothing I could do. He had attacked a greblin outpost in the night. He killed hundreds of them before they left him for dead.

Ben
What about the nomad caravan that saved him?

Howard
That wasn't me. Corbin was right. It was the story that wouldn't let him die.

Raymond
How did you find out he was alive?

Howard
A week later, I received a message from him. I forbade him from ever being so reckless again. We contrived a plan to use the greblin band to prod the other characters into action. I wrote in supplies for Corbin via a short story. You know the rest.

Ben
Answer me this, Howard. Did you really think you could give Joe his life back?

Howard
I may have over-promised. But I needed a bargaining chip. I was trying to keep him from helping them. For good reason. He's a real piece of work, Ben. I hope you're proud of him.

Ben
I am, actually. A bit. Still solving mysteries, even without me.

Raymond

Gentlemen, it seems things are getting more desperate with every chapter. They now possess the ghosting device, and Howard's agent is neutralized. I am giving you both editing privileges. Our window to stopping this thing grows narrower by the hour.

CHAPTER TWENTY-TWO

+++

Ghost Nebula

"Just because it's fiction, doesn't mean it isn't real." Corbin's voice sounded louder for the oppressive silence that dominated the transport shuttle. He stared at the floor as he spoke. His hands were hidden behind his back, bound by a pair of Joe's handcuffs.

"It does actually," said Joe, "That's what fiction is."

"Quiet. Both of you," said Xane. "Do not forget you are our prisoners."

Aelrûn snorted. Joe let out a "Ha!"

"We are your guests, Mr. Xane," said Ellodrine, "And we are not eager to overstay our welcome."

Xane made a feral growl in his throat, but Cortega held out a hand. The sound faded. Silence resumed, broken only by the occasional blips and clicks from the cockpit where Gibbons piloted the shuttle. The passengers sat across from one another in a cozier arrangement than any of them liked. The silence was tangible.

It was Corbin who again broke it. "I read about you, Joe. In *Nexus of Words*. I know why you're doing this."

"Shut it," said Joe.

"I know about Lily."

"I said shut it."

Corbin stared at him with clear blue eyes. "I'm not being cruel. I want to give you my sympathy."

"Keep it. You need it more than I do." Joe turned to look at the red-purple haze outside his window.

Corbin kept staring.

Xane grunted and tapped his communicator. "This is Lieutenant Xane to the bridge of the *Galactic Explorer.* Bridge crew, do you read?"

The communicator was silent.

"Still no answer?" asked Aelrûn, sitting across from him.

Xane grunted again.

"There's no reason for that," said Ellodrine. "I know you're frustrated you were unable to contact your crew to teleport you back to your ship. I'm sure everything is fine. You're welcome, by the way. I think it was rather polite of us to offer you a ride back in our shuttle."

Xane pointed a metal finger at her. "This is not your shuttle. Theft of an Intergalactic Union military vessel, even a short-range vessel, is a class M violation of the—"

"Xane!" said Cortega. "Least of our problems right now. I am not concerned about the stolen shuttle. I do want to know why the *Galactic Explorer* is not responding."

"The pirates, perhaps?" said Aelrûn. "We saw several of them heading toward your ship earlier."

"Unlikely," said Xane. "My security officers are highly trained battle-tested soldiers with warrior instincts. I refuse to believe a rabble of ramshackle bandits could prevail against them."

"What's your guess then?" asked Aelrûn.

"I do not know." Xane passed a suspicious glance at Corbin.

Sandy blond hair. A face that emanated innocence and youthfulness. Crystal blue eyes that stared serenely forward. "Despite what you might think, I am the only one who isn't a traitor."

Ellodrine groaned. "We've been over this, Corbin. The quest was not real. Corolathia is not real."

Corbin's gaze was unflinching. "Of course Corolathia is real."

"No, Corbin," Her eyes were watery and blue. "It isn't. The World Where the Books Are Written is real."

"That world is also real. But that does not render Corolathia meaningless. And it doesn't mean that Corolathia is not worth saving."

Ellodrine sighed and looked away. "Corolathia is fictitious."

"No more so than we are, Ellodrine."

"*Were*, you mean. We are not the same now. We have attained an elevated consciousness of greater realities beyond our former state. Before our awakening, we were mindless constructs of ink and paper."

Corbin flashed her a boyish smile. "Greater realities are nothing new, Ellodrine. We've known about them from our first chapters. Remember? I was a farm boy with my eye on the horizon and my hand on the plow. My life on the farm was just some dream from which I longed to wake. And when I did get over that horizon, I had enough adventures to fill eight books. I am a child of destiny. But to my surprise, none of that nullified my old life. On the contrary, it is that simple life I strive to save."

Ellodrine was silent for several moments. At last, she said, "Those are an author's words. Not yours."

"They're mine now. I have my own mind. And my destiny has not changed. I will fulfill it. I will save Corolathia. Not because Howard wants me to. It is my home. Should I throw it away simply because there's something bigger out there?"

"You're daydreaming, Junior," said Joe. "It's a nice daydream, and you don't want to give it up. But that doesn't make it real. No matter how much you want it to be."

Corbin turned toward him. "If that's true, Joe, why are you so determined to avenge Lily's death?"

Their eyes locked for several seconds. Joe lunged at him. His hands wrapped around Corbin's throat and thrust him repeatedly back against the shuttle wall. His face contorted into a bestial mask of rage. "You don't even say her name! You hear me? You son-of-a-bitch! You don't even say her name!"

Aelrûn and Xane peeled Joe off a gasping Corbin and pressed him back into his seat.

Ellodrine placed a hand on Corbin's shoulder to steady him and did her best to deflect Joe's boot kicks. "Joe, that's enough! You must get control of yourself."

Joe sucked in air with heavy gulps, and the rage slowly ebbed from his face. His breathing gradually became more regular. He glared across the aisle and held up one finger. "You don't say her name."

Corbin, wheezing, nodded.

Ellodrine placed two fingers on Corbin's jaw and turned his face to hers. "Listen to me, Corbin. Everything we suffered through was never about Corolathia. It was a book written to excite its readers. We have no idea what it would have cost us to complete it. Often the characters closest to the protagonist must suffer grievously or even die to motivate him for the final confrontation. That is how fiction works. Corolathia is a figment of Howard Zagny's twisted imagination. I am not prepared to sacrifice myself for that. Or Kribble. Or Aelrûn. Or you, Corbin."

"It doesn't have to be like that," said Corbin, "We can defeat Zolethos. Howard will help us."

She looked to the floor. "I wish I could believe that. But it's not worth the risk."

"I knew you would feel that way." He stared at her silently.

She raised her eyes to meet his. She sensed something in that crystal blue gaze. Something she could not quite read. Something he was not telling her.

"Quiet," said Cortega. "We're approaching the landing bay. Be ready for anything."

• • •

Gibbons brought the shuttle down in the docking bay with remarkable grace, considering the damaged landing gear. No commotion of mechanics rushed to initiate post-flight diagnostics. No officers awaited the captain's return. Neither was there a chaotic firefight with Rhodactian pirates attempting to overtake the ship.

The shuttle doors opened, and the entry ramp extended. Cortega emerged with incapacitator drawn and Xane by his side. Cautiously they made their way down the ramp and onto the deck. Aelrûn and Ellodrine followed, escorting Corbin between them. Joe sauntered behind with Xane's security officers. "Where is everybody?" he asked.

"This is not good, Captain," said Xane. His voice echoed in the empty space. "I suggest we—"

His suggestion was interrupted by the sound of machines coming to life around them. Electric humming filled the room. A metal gate separating the docking bay from the rest of the ship rose slowly from the floor to reveal the passage beyond. At first, the shuttle party could only make out the form of several leather-booted feet. The gap grew larger as the gate vanished into the ceiling, exposing a squad of green-skinned humanoids with bat-like ears, armed with crude spears, swords, and bows. Intermixed with them stood a smattering of Rhodactian pirates with incapacitators, clearly looted from the *Galactic Explorer's* armory. They surged into the room and surrounded the shuttle and its recent occupants.

Cortega and Xane held their positions, though they were vastly outnumbered.

"I am Captain Cortega of the *Galactic Explorer.* Your presence aboard my vessel constitutes an act of war against the Intergalactic Union. If I do not find my crew alive and well, I will personally see to it you never regret anything more bitterly in your numbered days than the moment you set foot on my ship."

"Take my cuffs off," said Corbin. "We can take them. They're minor characters. We have three protagonists."

"I'll take my chances with two," said Joe. He leveled his revolver at the throng.

The greblins and Rhodactians silently stood their ground. Heavy footsteps sounded from the corridor behind them. A burning stench arose in the air. Into the docking bay strode a figure outfitted in ebony armor that was covered in runes. A cape, deep red, billowed out behind him, as though his very passing made the air bleed. He was helmed in the horned skull of a rage troll. In one hand, he held a sword with a black blade that shone like obsidian. Blue flames danced along its edge. In his other hand, he gripped a small paperback novel.

"Now who the hell are you?" asked Cortega.

The horrifying figure said nothing but locked eyes with Corbin. "If you please," he said in a voice surprisingly smooth for his nightmarish visage. He made an open hand gesture as though it were embarrassing for him to have to give his own introduction.

"Zolethos," said Corbin. "His name is Zolethos. The Dark Lord of the Void."

CHAPTER TWENTY-THREE

+++

Ghost Nebula

Cortega fingered his incapacitator and shot a one-eyed glare at Corbin. "This a friend of yours?"

"It's so very good to see you, Corbin," said Zolethos. "And there's your wizard and your musical elf. I've been wondering where you had all gone. I thought you might have forgotten about me. How do you like my new ship?"

Cortega growled. "The *Galactic Explorer* is not—"

"It's not a very good name, is it? I prefer something a little more threatening. I'll think of something. Perhaps my new minions, the Rhodactians, can help. Corbin, you know the Rhodactians. They were running away from you after you killed so many of their crewmates. When I found them, they were busy surrendering to these Astral Navy toadies. I wish you could have seen their faces when I showed up."

"Zolethos," said Ellodrine, her voice sounding deliberately calm, "You need to listen to me. Things aren't what you think. There are worlds—"

"Beyond our own? Yes, I've read a great deal about it." Zolethos held up the book in his hand. The title peeked over his ash gray fingers, *Nexus of Words.* "I think there is a world out there for every book, and I only had my eye on one. Imagine my surprise when I discovered how small Corolathia really is."

"Precisely," said Ellodrine, "Everything is completely different now." She flashed him a forced smile.

"Completely different." His voice was laced with a treacherous amount of understanding.

"All our conflicts were just the stuff of fiction," said Ellodrine. "This is what's real now. We can embrace it together. You can have a clean slate."

Corbin spat on the ground. "He's a murderer!"

Zolethos smiled at him. "That's what the Rhodactians call you, boy."

Ellodrine extended a hand. "Please, Zolethos. Can we be together on this?"

Zolethos paused and stroked his chin as though he were earnestly considering it, then said, "No, I don't think so. Let me give you my perspective. Honestly, I was never going to get Corolathia, was I? It looked hopeful for a while, of course. But I've done some reading lately, and it seems dark lords don't prevail at the end of—What would you call them? Bard's tales?"

"Fantasy novels," said Ellodrine.

"Thank you. But you, yourself, pointed out that things are different now. I'm no longer subject to the usual rules of these stories, am I?"

"You're still subject to my rules," said Cortega. "You're aboard my ship, and that's my domain. I've been a step behind ever since you people showed up, and that is not a place I like to be."

Zolethos flashed him a wicked grin. "Let me illuminate you, Captain. You, your illustrious career, your ship, and your crew are all imaginary. None of your valiant exploits ever happened. Your greatest triumph is completely devoid of meaning. As is your pitiful existence. So, if you think you are capable of intimidating me—"

A searing blue beam caught Zolethos on the left side of his face. His head jerked to the side. He staggered backward. He grasped his face with his hands. Tendrils of smoke rose through the cracks between his fingers. "How dare you!"

"My finger slipped."

Xane leaned in toward the captain. "That blast should have rendered him insensible, Captain."

"I am aware of that, Xane."

Zolethos seethed. Greblins and Rhodactians looked anxiously toward him, awaiting an order to attack. Instead, Zolethos raised one hand and said, "Stand down. Do not engage." He tapped a Rhodactian style communication device fastened to his armor. "Commander Rakshaw, kindly disarm our guests so we can continue negotiations."

"Yes, Lord Zolethos," said a Rhodactian voice from the other side.

Cortega and his crewmen's incapacitators glowed with a gold light, as did Joe's revolver, Aelrûn's daggers and Corbin's sword that was strapped to a security officer's back. A moment later they were gone.

"Bind them," said Zolethos.

A wave of greblins and space pirates rushed forward. They swarmed their disarmed adversaries and thrust each one cruelly onto the ground. Ellodrine fired a lightning bolt that threw one of her greblin assailants off his feet. It also threw her into the side of the shuttle where her head made a loud *thwack* against the metal. In moments, the struggle was over. Zolethos's greblins pinned them down while Rhodactians clasped magnetic manacles onto their wrists. The greblins lined their captives upon their knees before the dark lord.

"Zolethos," said Ellodrine, "You have your own will. You don't have to be an antagonist anymore. We have been given a marvelous gift by these circumstances. Our roles are no longer defined for us. We have the right to choose our own destiny."

Zolethos approached her. He reached out and traced her cheek with a single, black-clawed finger. "And that's the beauty of it, isn't it? Now it's my choice, and that makes it all the more wonderful. I suppose I could turn over my wicked ways and become a thatcher, marry the miller's daughter and spawn a brood of offspring who will run barefoot through our flower garden and trample the daisies. Is that what you mean?"

Ellodrine bent her neck to pull away from his touch. "Well, yes. But without all the irony, thank you."

He smiled. "Here's a better idea. I'm going to take your artifacts and travel to the World Where the Books Are Written. I will kill Howard Zagny through a process that will take days of painful torment. Then I will fulfill my dreams of conquest in a world that is so much bigger than Corolathia ever was."

"Why, Zolethos? What's the point? You're just playing into your character. These are not really your decisions."

"But they are. For the first time, these really are my decisions. I will make Howard Zagny beg for the end. While he suffers, he will despair knowing that I am a thing of his own imagining. I am literally his walking nightmare. He signed his death warrant the day he penned my name. And no blue-eyed farm boy with a mark of destiny is going to come and save him when I show up at his door. And do you know the best part? He's reading about it right now. He knows I am coming for him. From this moment until I find him, his mind will be consumed with fear!"

"Who is Howard Zagny?" whispered Cortega.

"Our author," said Aelrûn.

Ellodrine's irises shifted to a midnight blue, deep and watery. She looked to the ground. "This is my fault."

Zolethos tucked a finger under her chin and lifted her face to meet his own. "It is," he said, "It really is."

"You're a monster!" shouted Corbin. "Take these restraints off me and put a sword in my hand. I challenge you! I will destroy you!"

Zolethos scoffed. "You'd like that, wouldn't you?" He gave a dismissive wave and turned to his greblins. "Retrieve the ghosting device."

Several greblins rushed into the shuttle and returned with the ghosting device in tow.

"It won't work, Zolethos," said Ellodrine. "It won't help you get to the World Where the Books Are Written."

"No," said Zolethos, "Not by itself. I need the second artifact to make it work. Don't deny it. I read all about your plans." He produced another small paperback. This one was *Ghost Nebula.* "I liberated this from a lovely little nurse I found aboard the ship."

"How did you find out about this?" asked Aelrûn. "How did you get a copy of our book?"

Zolethos smiled. "It was sent to me. You have a traitor in your midst."

Ellodrine and Aelrûn glared at Joe.

"You assume it was me?" said Joe. "I just lured the kid here. I never sent a book to any dark lords."

Ellodrine huffed. "Then who?"

"I sent him the book," said Corbin. "I knew I couldn't fight Zolethos alone. And I knew I could never convince you to help me. I just needed him to follow me here."

"You meant to force us into a confrontation," said Aelrûn.

Corbin nodded.

Ellodrine fumed silently for a moment, then turned to Joe. "This is still your fault! These are your methods at work. You sent the book to Corbin, and he passed it on to Zolethos. And here we are! This is the result of your recklessness! This is what happens when you *don't listen to your mentor*!"

Joe sighed. "That was a crazy fool thing for you to do, Corby."

"He did the same thing you did, Joe!" said Ellodrine.

"No," said Joe, "The difference is I baited a minnow in shark's clothing. How was I to know he'd bring the actual sharks with him?"

"How were you to know it was a bad idea?" said Ellodrine. "Simple. It is a bad idea to send a book with all your plans to the bad guys. I could have told you that."

"I told you it was a gamble."

"Oh, you were just gambling, were you? Just put our lives on a roll of the dice, Joe? Forgive me if I was hoping for something a little more precise."

Zolethos clicked his tongue. "Joe, Joe, Joe. What hubris." He took a step forward but stopped short when his ebony clad foot crunched a small yellow parchment. He looked down at it.

"That will be from Howard," said Corbin.

Zolethos smiled and snapped his gray fingers. A nearby greblin snatched the paper from the floor and placed it in Zolethos's hand. The Dark Lord of the Void unrolled the paper and read. He erupted into laughter. The greblins looked nervously at one another.

"Are you threatening me, Howard? You don't expect me to take you seriously, do you? Let me share this with my new friends. Howard says if I don't destroy the ghosting device and revoke any plans to travel to the World Where the Books Are Written, he will—and these are his words—*bring forth doom unto me and my armies such that death itself will reject our twisted forms and spit us back into our agony.* Do tell, Howard. Have you ever considered writing terrible fiction? You have a gift for it. You know, after I kill you, I think I will write a book about it. Every chapter, I'll kill you in a new way. Then maybe some version of you will feel it, Howard. What do you think?"

Suddenly, a thunderous crash resounded through the ship. Greblins and Rhodactians stumbled this way and that. Several tumbled hard onto the deck. Zolethos stood in their midst, laughing wildly. When it was over, only Zolethos and Aelrûn had kept themselves aright. Ellodrine found her head pillowed on Joe's chest. She scowled and lurched away.

Zolethos's communicator bleeped. "Lord Zolethos."

Zolethos grunted. "Commander Rakshaw, I assume this is important?"

"Yes, Lord Zolethos. The computer is registering a class five nebula storm forming around the ship. We need to get out of here."

Zolethos looked to the ceiling again. "A nebula storm? What is that? Did you just make that up, Howard?"

"Orders, Lord?" said the voice from the communicator. "This storm will tear the ship apart. We need to get out of the nebula."

"Very well," said Zolethos. "Take protective measures and get us out of the storm."

"Aye, Lord."

Zolethos turned to his prisoners. "Just as well. There is much to do, and I've been indulging in bad habits. I can't help but babble on and on about my plans when I have a captive audience. The next phase is to get Ellodrine to tell me where I can find the second artifact."

Ellodrine turned away from him. "I won't help you do this."

"I know," said Zolethos, "It's a mark of heroic characters that they don't break under my typical methods of persuasion. So, I have something special planned." He snapped his fingers at some nearby greblins. "Bring them to the telepad bay."

Ben
Howard, I do not like the looks of this! And I'm blaming you.

Raymond
Yes, Howard! Did you think things weren't bad enough? You had to bring this guy into it?

Howard
I didn't bring Zolethos into this. Corbin did.

Ben
Corbin was your agent! And now we get to look forward to a slow and painful death. Remind me to thank you for dragging me into this.

Raymond
Seriously, Howard, could your villain have been a little less sadistic?

Howard
First, I'm the one in Zolethos's crosshairs right now, so I don't want to hear about it. Second, don't blame me for making my antagonist evil. It's standard fare for my genre. I'd lose credibility if my necromantic warlord were just a little misunderstood.

Ben
Okay, Howard's right. Blaming one another in chat windows won't keep Zolethos in the pages of this book. Even if it is all Howard's fault. And it is. We need to come together and make some kind of plan.

Raymond
Right. So, who wrote in the thing with the nebula storm? Howard, was that you?

Howard
Yes. That was me. But in my version, lightning burst through the hull of the ship and blew his condescending head into a million gory pieces.

Ben
That's a little graphic for you, isn't it, Howard?

Howard
He was provoking me.

Ben
We need to figure out why the things we write don't stick. Obviously, we don't have control over any of our estranged characters. But why can't we just blast them with the catastrophe of our choice?

Raymond
I have a theory on that. We are dealing with a fictional world. Like our world, there are laws that govern how things work. Think gravity or magnetism.

Ben
So, physics.

Raymond
Exactly. Anybody who wants to accomplish something has to work within the framework of natural laws. When we write fiction, there are certain laws in play as well. For instance, if I were to kill off a major antagonist with a freak bolt of lightning, that would never get past my editor. Moreover, my readers would never buy it.

Ben
Editors and lightning bolts are very different things, Raymond. Science is a lot more solid than the fundamentals of fiction.

Raymond
Maybe not. Maybe for a world that was created in fiction, the laws of storytelling are as much a given as physics. You saw how Zolethos took that incapacitator blast to the face. That should have laid him out.

Howard
But it wasn't climactic enough. And Zolethos was written to be the antagonist of a twelve-book cycle. *Nexus of Words* is still only the eighth volume.

Raymond
Right. Then what would be climactic enough to bring down an epic antagonist four books early?

Ben
Well, there's the million-dollar question. Gentlemen?

CHAPTER TWENTY-FOUR

+++

Ghost Nebula

The telepad chamber smelled of ozone.

Joe scanned the room. Several greblins had arranged bookshelves around the telepad and were currently filling them with slender reading devices. Occasionally, a greblin overseer chided one or more of the workers and disputed with them about the proper order to arrange the devices.

Awaiting their arrival was Kribble. He was bound and stood between two greblin guards. At the sight of them, he spat on the ground. "Joe! You are a fetid puddle of dog piss! Do you know that?"

"Good to see you too, Kribble," said Joe.

Kribble turned to Ellodrine. "He's been working against us the whole time. Did you know that? I found the rest of his letter!"

Joe hung his head. "... You read the letter."

"You bet I did! And you sabotaged our plans!"

"I didn't *sabotage* the plans, Kribble."

"It's true, Kribble," said Ellodrine, "It would be more apt to say he *mangled* the plans."

"Okay, Kribble. I'm sorry. I owed you better than that, and I didn't pull through. You can be sore at me if you need to be."

"I don't need your permission!"

Zolethos smiled. "Is there anyone left who *doesn't* hate you, Joe?"

A crash reverberated through the ship from the nebula storm outside. The lights flickered. Several reading devices fell off the shelves and clattered on the floor. The overseers bellowed at their workers, who busied themselves regathering the devices.

"What are they doing?" asked Cortega.

"Do you like it?" asked Zolethos. "I am improving upon your design."

"What do you know about telepads?" said Ellodrine.

Zolethos turned to face her. "It's funny. Before I arrived here, I didn't even know what a telepad was. I can't explain it. But when I first set foot into this book, it was as though my mind was filled with such knowledge. Vast stores of it. I could tell you how distortion engines work. I could tell you about wormholes, the effect of gravity on light emissions, the temperature of a supernova. But you've experienced something similar, have you not?" He tossed *Nexus of Words* into the air casually and caught it again.

Ellodrine's irises paled. "You've been reinterpreted. Somehow you mean something different in this book."

A smile crept across his face. "It will have to do. My usual necromantic talents aren't as potent as they were in Corolathia. No matter. I have some wonderful new methods to cause you suffering."

"How would he manifest differently in this book?" asked Aelrûn. "What would that mean?"

"I don't know," said Ellodrine. "It would be something in his title."

"Dark Lord of the Void?"

"The void," said Ellodrine, "That must be it. It's the space between worlds. The nothingness in the night sky. And it is what we are floating through right now in this ship."

Zolethos turned to his greblin guards. "Bring forward the farm boy, the insolent detective, and the one-eyed captain and place them on the telepad."

The greblins shoved Corbin, Joe, and Cortega into place.

Zolethos opened the fantasy novel in his hand and traced his finger along the words. "I've learned a great deal from you, Ellodrine. You left behind some wonderful notes. Very thorough. *Protagonists frequently overcome impossible situations to achieve their goals. They defy death at every turn.* Fascinating. And problematic. So, what should I do with three of them in one book? I could catapult them into space? They'd be rescued. I could shoot them in the head? Beyond all odds, they'd survive. Am I wrong? What is a villain to do?"

"Oh, spare us the speeches and get on with it," said Joe.

Zolethos shrugged. "There I go again. I can't help myself. I have an audience, and I have to talk, talk, talk. Well, somebody has to admire my brilliance. It certainly won't be these greblins. They lack the intelligence and humanity to be properly horrified. Look here." He gestured to the control panel. Inscribed upon it was a travel rune. "Do you see? I have combined the mysticism of my book with the science of this book. I can use this telepad to transfer characters into other books. The kind of books that don't let protagonists live just because they're protagonists. The kind of books that could keep me up late at night with suspense."

"That's not how travel runes work," said Ellodrine. "The Library is the hub. The only place they can go from here is there."

Zolethos nodded. "That's where the telepad comes in. It can dissolve their molecules and send them thousands of miles away before putting them back together. They'll pass through The Library as a conglomeration of atoms, but they won't be able to stop there. That reminds me. I'll need to take those from you." Zolethos removed Corbin's rune-inscribed ring and the amulet around Joe's neck. He brought them back to the control panel, set them aside, and began typing.

"Where are you sending them?" asked Ellodrine.

"Why ruin the surprise?"

Xane craned his neck to see the control display. "Those are not proper coordinates. What kind of code is that?"

"It's a call number," said Zolethos, "Like they use in libraries. What did you expect? After all, I am sending them to a book." He threw a switch, and the machine hummed to life.

"Wait a minute!" shouted Kribble. "I have a thing or two to say to that traitor before he's out of my life forever!"

"Better make it quick," said Zolethos.

Kribble grunted. "First, I wish I never met you!"

"Kribble—" said Joe.

"Don't interrupt!" Kribble turned to one of the greblins next to him. "I need you to get something out of my pocket." The greblin looked to Zolethos for confirmation.

Zolethos sighed and nodded. "This had better be good."

The greblin reached into the pocket of Kribble's spacesuit and retrieved a small flat square.

"Hold it in front of me!" said Kribble. The greblin obliged. Kribble reared back his head and expelled a massive ball of spit onto it. "Now give it to him!" he ordered the greblin.

"Wait," said Zolethos, "Hand that to me."

The greblin placed the small flat square into his hand. Zolethos examined it.

"Something to remember me by," said Kribble.

"I can certainly appreciate the sentiment," said Zolethos. He approached Joe and held it out to him. It was the photograph of Joe, Ellodrine, and Aelrûn's torsos from The Library. Thick foamy spittle oozed down the front of it. "With friends like these, eh, Joe?" He dropped the picture into Joe's front pocket and patted it a few times. Then he turned and strode back to the control panel.

"I'm sorry, Kribble," said Joe.

"East of the River, apologies aren't worth the breath you waste on them," said Kribble, "But they make a nice epitaph on your tombstone if you like."

Joe sighed.

Zolethos threw the last switch.

Gold lights radiated around Joe, Corbin, and Cortega.

"Joe!" cried Ellodrine, her irises deep and blue, "It wasn't supposed to end this way."

"It's okay," said Joe. "You'll have to be your own protagonist now."

For a few fleeting seconds, he looked back at her. Then he was gone.

Raymond
So they're gone?

Ben
Where did he send our characters, Howard?

Howard
How do I know?

Ben
Think, Howard. You wrote him. What kind of book would he choose?

Howard
I don't know. What kind of book kills protagonists?

Raymond
Tragedies? Like Hamlet?

Howard
It has to be something that is being written right now.

Ben
Okay, here's how we find them. We get in touch with our contacts at any of the major publishers. Between us, we can canvas a lot of area. We get them to keep an ear out for complaints about manuscripts with changing text. Wherever they go, they're bound to get noticed. Meanwhile, we keep our eyes open on Raymond's text to see if Zolethos slips up and gives us a title.

Howard
I have another idea. I'll send a message to Corbin. Maybe he can tell us where he is.

Ben
Okay. Or Howard can just email Corbin.

CHAPTER TWENTY-FIVE

+++

Viva Lost Vegas

"They're dead!" screamed Trixie, "They're all dead! And we're next!"

"Can somebody shut her up already?" shouted Jaime, pressing her back against the door. "She's going to bring 'em all right to us. There are enough as it is." Behind her, she could feel repetitive thuds against the wood.

Trixie slumped against the wall of the luxury suite and hyperventilated loudly. Mascara ran down her cheeks in thick black streaks. She wrapped her arms around herself. Her short sequined dancer costume offered little protection against the cold. Or anything else, for that matter.

Leonard aimed a hard slap at her face that sent her to the floor. His handprint bloomed red on her cheek. Trixie's panic dwindled to quiet sniveling.

"That was unnecessary." Jaime glared at him with unmasked hatred.

"It shut her up, didn't it?"

Jaime felt another heavy thud against the door. She did not know how long she could hold them back. What she would not give for some pants right now. Her short black evening dress was a poor choice for running for her life through the streets and hotels of Las Vegas. Her bare feet were scraped up, but the stilettos only slowed her down, so they had to go. She might look elegant were it not for the police belt strapped over her dress and the pump-action shotgun slung over her left shoulder.

"Leonard! Doug! Drag some furniture over here so we can brace the door. Trixie, do what you can over there to calm down. Lisa, go into the bedroom, sweetheart, and see if you can bring me some end tables or something."

Doug whimpered in the corner. "Oh-man-oh-man-oh-man-oh-man-oh-man. We're going to die. We're all going to die."

"Doug!" shouted Jaime, "Move that bureau!"

Doug started out of his panic. He nodded, picked himself up, and struggled with the bureau. He was a big guy, broad-shouldered, but it was all cupcakes and no meat.

Lisa stopped at the door to the bedroom and looked back. "Miss Cruz," her voice trembled, "*Are* we going to die?"

Jaime opened her mouth to answer, but the words did not come. Lisa could not be more than nine years old. Her expression was a strange mix of a child's need for comfort and an adult's need for the truth. Jaime heaved a sigh. "We're not going to die yet!"

Lisa nodded. She disappeared into the bedroom. Leonard arrived with a sofa. He and Jaime wedged it against the door. The banging from the other side was coming harder and faster now.

"There's definitely more than one of them now," said Leonard.

"They'll bring others," said Jaime.

Doug arrived with the bureau. They began to situate it in front of the sofa when they heard Lisa scream from the bedroom.

"Keep working," yelled Jaime. She drew her handgun and darted into the bedroom. She found Lisa standing against a wall, staring wide-eyed. None of Jaime's training or experience could have prepared her for what she saw.

Three men stood next to the bed, looking back at her. One of them wore an eye patch and a strange military uniform, but she could not recognize *what* military. Next to him stood a grim-faced man in a jumpsuit with NASA printed on the sleeves and chest. His eyes were cool and calculating. The other man wore some kind of historical—maybe Shakespearean—costume. He had a buttonless white shirt under a light blue vest. His face was boyish but bold. His eyes were the clear blue of a summer sky.

"Don't mean to startle you, ma'am," said the grim-faced man. "My friends and I are lost. Could you tell us where we are? And we'll be on our way."

Jaime cocked her gun.

"Ma'am," said the uniformed man, "My name is Marcos Cortega. I am an officer of the Intergalactic Union Astral Navy and captain of the starship—"

"Why are you holding your hands behind your backs?"

The three men glanced at one another, then turned to show their hands were bound in some kind of restraints. They were sleek and metal and top-secret looking. Jaime had never seen anything like them.

"What's going on in there?" shouted Leonard from the other room.

"There are people. Three of them. In handcuffs."

"Really," said the grim-faced man, "Where are we? Even if it seems like a dumb question, we need to know."

Could they be that wasted? But they showed no sign of alcohol or narcotics. "You're in a top-floor penthouse suite on the Las Vegas strip."

The grim-faced man snorted. "So what? Did he send us on a vacation?"

"You'll wish you stayed home."

"Why," asked so-called-Captain Cortega, "What's going on out there?"

"End of the world."

"What's that supposed to mean?" asked the grim-faced man.

"Seeing is believing." Jaime nodded toward the window behind them.

The grim-faced man, without the use of his hands, maneuvered his head behind the curtain and drew it aside with his neck. What was behind it might have been a postcard. Casino lights lit up the night sky with neon glory. The Bellagio fountains cast impressive watery spectacles into the air. People milled about like ants.

"I don't see anything strange," said the grim-faced man.

"Look closer."

Though the people were tiny from this vantage point, an abnormality was evident. Their movements were odd and unnatural. They clustered in strange groups and bumped into one another. Several of them fell over and struggled back to their feet. They did not pay any mind to established walkways. Instead, they made stumbling beelines toward their destinations.

"Are they drunk?" asked Cortega.

"They're dead. And we will be too if they so much as scratch us."

The grim-faced man groaned. "No. Seriously?"

"Believe it," said Jaime.

"Zombies?"

"They're dead and they're walking. Call them what you want."

"Bogglerot."

"What?"

"Nothing."

"It makes sense," said the man with the blue eyes. "He's a necromancer, after all. This is exactly the sort of book he would choose."

Jaime did not know what he was talking about. She was pretty sure she did not want to. "I don't know what you three were doing handcuffed in this penthouse before we came along, but you'll need to get out of those things. Where are the keys?"

"Aboard my ship," said the captain, "And these restraints aren't coming off without them."

"Better figure out how we're going to make do," said the grim-faced man. He sat down on the floor and bent himself like a contortionist, maneuvering his hands around his legs. "Been a while since I pulled this off," he said, "I was younger then. More limber." After a few moments, he sprang up from the floor with his hands now manacled in front of him instead of behind. "Not great, but better than it was. Leastways, I could fire a gun if I could get my hands on one."

Jaime holstered her gun demonstratively in case he had some idea she would be sharing.

.   .   .

Leonard was not sad to see Jaime leave the room. She had an annoying knack for pushing her way into control that was typical of cops. Leonard hated cops. And this cop, in particular, had been undercover for several months gathering information on his employer. That was all supposed to end tonight. In a way, she was fortunate. The outbreak had delayed her death. Leonard had tolerated her presence since their standoff against the living dead in the casino several floors down. That is where Burns had died.

It was hard to believe only hours ago they had been working like it was just another night. Of course, their work was fairly violent, *debt collection* as they called it, so even just another night had its share of adrenaline. Leonard was good at what he did. He and his partner built their reputation brick by bloody brick. The intimidation factor was usually enough these days. Nobody messed with Leonard and Burns. But intimidation does not work on the dead. And now Burns was gone. Downstairs, zombies were munching greedily on his remains. Or maybe he had already turned, himself. Maybe he was banging against the other side of the door right now.

If the banging was not enough, it was accompanied by horrific moaning. The guttural cry of the undead. They sensed food was near. To Leonard's left, Doug kept muttering, "We're-going-to-die-we're-going-to-die-we're-going-to-die," as if it was some kind of mantra. To his right, Trixie sat on the floor wearing Doug's jacket. She was practically swimming in it. She had stopped hyperventilating, but she was not helping. Mostly she just stared with empty eyes.

Leonard took a step back to consider his work. There was only so much furniture in the suite to work with. His shirt was drenched in sweat. He had taken his jacket off so it would not be ruined. It seemed a minor concern in the face of the life-and-death circumstances, but he paid enough for it. The jacket alone cost more than a few thousand, so it was worth a moment to drape it over the back of a chair. The very chair Doug was shoving against the barricade right now.

"Hey, watch what you're doing! That's designer!" He snatched his jacket off the back of the chair and folded it over his arm.

"You planning on wearing it to your funeral?" said a voice from behind him.

Leonard glanced back. Jaime had returned with Lisa, a nightstand, and one of the guys from the bedroom. As reported, he was wearing some kind of handcuffs. Apparently, the new guy was the one who had spoken.

"I'll wear it to yours first," said Leonard. "Who are you?"

"Call me Joe. I'm here to help."

Leonard scoffed and donned his jacket.

Lisa tugged on Jaime's elbow. "How many of them are out there?"

Leonard looked back toward the door. The banging was deafening now. And it was not just the door. Pounding erupted along the entire wall. A crunching sound accompanied it as drywall buckled under the pressure.

"Miss Cruz?" Leonard heard Lisa's small voice.

"I don't know!" snapped Jaime, probably more sharply than she meant to.

Leonard examined their barricade. He and Doug had used every piece of furniture they could find. It would not be enough. He drew his pistol with the silencer still attached and turned to face Jaime. "This is it. Survival of the fittest starts now. When they come through, we're all on our own."

"I take it you're in charge here, Miss Cruz," said Joe.

"Officer Cruz, actually," said Jaime.

"That how you report for duty, Officer Cruz?"

"I was undercover. Do you have a point? Because if you're trying to flirt with me, this is not a good time."

"Bedsheets out the window," said Joe. "We'll climb down to the room below us. They're too uncoordinated to follow."

"And from there, what?" asked Jaime, "They're everywhere. We'll never make it to the lobby."

"Let's figure that out downstairs."

She stared at him.

Leonard heard the wall cracking. "They're coming through. We need to shift the barricade. The door doesn't matter. They'll come through the weakest point they can find."

"Okay," said Jaime, possibly to both men. "Lisa and Trixie, you're with me. Joe, you help Leonard and Doug hold them off."

The three ladies vanished into the bedroom.

Joe and Doug helped Leonard rearrange the makeshift barricade.

"I can't take much more of this," said Doug, putting his weight against the bureau.

Joe grasped the other side with his manacled hands to help. "Sure, you can. Doug, right? You've made it this far, didn't you? Don't be negative. If I told you about the day I've had, you wouldn't believe it."

"Seriously?" said Leonard. "Do you realize what's out there? Those things killed my partner, and he was a hell of a lot smarter than this fat-ass! You're right, Doug. You're going to die in this room. Anybody who says differently is lying to you."

Doug whimpered.

"Your friend is an asshole, isn't he?" said Joe.

"He's right, though. I am going to die in this room."

"What?" said Joe, "That's no way to talk—Help me move this table, would you—Look, what were you doing in Vegas?"

"Oh. Uh. I'm supposed to be a groomsman."

"You were here for a wedding?"

Doug nodded. "It was supposed to be tomorrow night."

"Tomorrow is still coming, Doug. We just got to be smart enough to see it."

"Which is why, Doug," said Leonard, "You're still going to die in this room."

Joe grabbed Doug's sleeve. "Don't look at him, Doug. Look at me. I've been through a thing or two in my life. Maybe not like this exactly, but pretty scary just the same. I want to tell you a trick that might help you."

"No. Leonard's right. We're all going to—"

"Shut up, Doug. This is important. I want you to take yourself out of the situation. You're just reading a book about this guy named Doug. And you're rooting for him to make it. Now you've read enough books to know the guy who's freaking out about everything is digging his own grave. Little trick authors use called foreshadowing. Doug is telling the readers he's not getting out of this."

"I know what you're trying to do, Joe. And thanks. But this is kid stuff."

"What? Stories? You don't read books anymore, Doug? Shame on you. Let me get to the point. Foreshadowing, Doug. It doesn't have to work against you. It can work for you, too. Tell the reader you're going to survive. Talk about tomorrow like you're going to see it. Let the guy reading the book know he can get attached to you."

Leonard could not believe what he was hearing. "Okay, but the difference is life isn't a book. This self-help guru shit doesn't work here. Stay back and be his cheerleader if you want, but don't expect anything from me."

"He's right," said Doug, "I'm slowing everybody down."

"Whose side are you on, Doug?" said Joe, "Don't listen to him. He's a cynic. He doesn't believe in anything but himself. That doesn't make him much better than those things out there. He says you're going to be dead by morning. Are you going to let him be right?"

Doug looked taken aback. Then he looked at Leonard with a grim face and, shoving a table into place, he said, "It's going to be the prettiest sunrise I've ever seen."

. . .

Jaime watched shards of glass fall away into the Las Vegas night. They refracted the light of a neon horizon. She cleared away as much from the windowsill as she could and secured layers of towels over what was left.

"I don't bend that way," shouted Cortega behind her. She glanced back to check their progress. His friend with the blue eyes had repositioned his hands to the front as Joe had done. He was helping the captain achieve the same.

"You won't be able to climb with your hands behind your back, Captain," she said.

"Climb?"

She nodded toward the window. He looked at it and then at Trixie and Lisa tying bedsheets together.

He grunted. "We need to contact my ship."

"Your ship is a long way away," said Jaime, "You're in the middle of the Nevada desert."

"My communicator can reach a distance of over 100,000 miles."

"I don't believe it is a question of distance," said the blue-eyed man.

"Don't tell me it's because we're in a book," said Cortega. "The next person I hear talking about books is going to spend the next month in a stasis chamber."

Jaime met the blue-eyed man's eyes. "Does he have a condition? Does he really believe he's a captain?"

"He *is* a captain."

"And what are you? A gentleman of Verona?"

"My name is Corbin. I bear the mark of destiny."

"You know what? I don't want to know. Just follow orders and don't draw attention."

He was no longer looking at her. "Yellow parchment!"

"What?"

Corbin lunged at a small folded paper she had not noticed on the floor. He quickly unfolded it and surveyed the contents. "It's from Howard."

"Who's Howard?"

"He wants to know where we are. I need a pen. Does anybody have a pen?"

Jaime glanced down at her pocketless evening dress. Trixie's dancer outfit was not any better. Lisa produced a few coins from her jeans, but nothing more useful than that.

"There was one on the nightstand before I brought it out," said Lisa. "It probably fell off somewhere while I was dragging it."

"Why?" said Jaime, "Is it important?"

"It is of utmost importance," said Corbin. "It may save our lives." He rushed toward the main room but stopped short at the door. His stare was transfixed at something before him.

"Hope you're ready with the rope back there," came Joe's voice. "They're coming through!"

CHAPTER TWENTY-SIX

+++

Ghost Nebula

Aelrûn watched the nebula through the transparent wall of the commons lounge and filled the air with a spirited rendition of *Purple Haze*. The room was an absolute wreck after the battle. Greblins turned it into a makeshift detention block. The entry doors were locked and barred. A band of greblins guarded the passage outside. Crew members milled about, murmuring amongst themselves.

"Would you put that thing away?" said Kribble with a frown.

"Since when do you object to Hendrix?"

"What I object to is you sitting around playing the harp when you should be helping me find a way out of here."

Aelrûn shook his head and played on. He only got a few more notes out before a metallic hand ripped the instrument away from him and tossed it across the room.

"The short hairy creature is right," said Lieutenant Xane. "No time for music. We must speak."

Aelrûn shot them both a razor-edged glare. "That harp was given to me by Queen Analise of the fairy—"

"Queen Analise of the fairy courts, after you performed before her and her entourage blah, blah, blah." Kribble opened and closed his hand like a talking puppet as he spoke.

Aelrûn abandoned their company and moved to retrieve his harp.

Xane helped himself to the elf's vacated seat. "I need to speak with you and your comrade. With the captain gone, it is my solemn duty to retake this ship and neutralize our adversary. I require your aid in this."

"Now we're talking!" said Kribble. "You got a plan? No need to wait for the elf. These are the brains of the operation right here." Kribble tapped his skull twice with his finger.

Xane did not look convinced, but he went ahead anyway. "I must warn you. It is extremely dangerous. And I cannot guarantee our survival."

"I knew I liked you."

"Furthermore, it is incomplete. My operation begins once we get outside this room. How to get to that point, I have not yet contrived."

"So, that's where you need me." Kribble stroked his chin in a Joe-like fashion.

"Maybe we should wait for the other one to return."

"Bah. We'll fill him in later."

Xane hesitated, but went on, "The ship, as you know, is full of those creatures."

"Greblins."

Xane nodded. "They outnumber our crew at least four to one."

"I've had worse odds."

"If we attempt to take them by force, the battle would be futile. We would not penetrate such numbers."

"How are we going to shift the odds?"

"In the passages outside the commons are several escape pods. If we use this to our advantage, we may be able to get around them."

Kribble's face took on a slightly green tint. "Go around them?"

"Yes. We will require supplies, but I believe I know where they will have taken your gear. There is a large food storage cabin down the corridor. The greblins who removed your bags were still carrying them when they escorted us here. It is likely they will have then delivered them to the most convenient storage facility."

"You're pretty observant, aren't you?"

"You must observe your enemy to know your enemy. And you must know your enemy to defeat him. But first, we must get out of this room."

∙ ∙ ∙

Aelrûn retrieved his harp and plucked out some Creedence Clearwater Revival when he was interrupted by a voice from behind.

"Where is Corbin?"

Aelrûn turned to see who had spoken. A woman in a medical officer's uniform with a surprisingly low neckline glowered at him with sea-green eyes.

"Do I know you?" he asked.

"Answer the question."

"How do you know Corbin?"

"Don't tell me you don't remember me." She stood with her hand on her hip as though waiting for recognition to take root.

He cocked his head and stared for several moments.

"You came to my ball uninvited? Your friend knocked over my bookcase?"

Aelrûn gasped. "You're the marchioness!"

She smiled. "You remember."

"Isabelle! That's your name, isn't it?"

She offered some sarcastic applause.

"How did you get out of your book? Wait. You asked about Corbin. He had something to do with it, didn't he?"

"You don't miss a thing. Now, where is he?"

"I wish I knew," said Aelrûn. "Zolethos sent him somewhere. To some other book. Him and all the other protagonists."

She huffed and crossed her arms. "He said this wouldn't go wrong. He said I could leave it to him and his mark of destiny."

"He's awfully proud of that mark of destiny."

"I told him I didn't like this idea. Bringing his old antagonist into things. I told him something like this could happen."

"He's not one for listening, is he?"

Tempests raged in her eyes. "He said he would show me wonders beyond my imagination. Oceans in the sky. Crystal mountains. Forests of giant flowers."

"Oh, yes," said Aelrûn. "That's in Corolathia. You would not have been disappointed."

She shot him a glare. "Why don't we do those things first, I asked him. No, first he had to go after this necromancer of his." She sat down at a nearby table and sulked.

"And yet you still care about him?"

"Don't judge me. I was written to be in love. I loathe it about myself."

"Didn't take you very long, did it?"

The look she directed at him would have curdled milk.

"All right." Aelrûn threw his hands up, "You're an at-first-sight kind of girl. We all have our flaws."

"He was obsessed," she said. "I know we were only together for a few days, but they were so liberating. He showed me how small my book really was and how much there was still to discover. I felt so right with him. Not like it was with Lucas or Jonathan. Not penned or destined. Perfect in that it was imperfect. And that's why I asked him. What if we both put aside our grudges, he and I? Wasn't there enough to explore out there to keep us happy? Not until his country was free, he said."

"Put aside your grudges? His against Zolethos, and yours against... Lucas?"

"Not exactly."

"Ellodrine?"

Her face soured at the name.

"Oh, I see. You blame Ellodrine for wrecking your happy ending. Well, I admit she and I have never gotten along famously, ourselves. But she never intended to ruin your story. In fact, we were hoping not to be noticed at all."

"Should have done a better job."

"Agreed. But your book's narrative is to blame. It reinterpreted her to be enticingly beautiful."

"Yes, I've noticed some reinterpretation myself lately," said Isabelle dully.

"I hope that's not uncomfortable for you. Now if you will excuse me, I have a breakout to plan. Don't worry. We will come back for you once we take care of these greblins."

"Excuse me? You'll come back for me? I don't think so. I'm not staying behind and waiting for rescue like some helpless damsel. I might be emotionally unstable, but I'm also willful and adventurous."

"No," said Aelrûn, "That's not a good idea. We are vastly outnumbered as it is. We don't have time to babysit you while we—"

"Babysit?" That curdling glare again.

"This is not some game we are playing. This will be the most dangerous thing we have ever done. We must confront an epic villain with no protagonist."

"I'm a protagonist," said Isabelle.

"You're hardly the protagonist we need right now."

Isabelle scowled, but then her expression softened. She smiled at him. It sent a wave of warmth through his body.

"What are you doing?" asked Aelrûn.

"Do you remember my author?"

"Her name escapes me."

"Lyla Birdsong." Isabelle's smile grew wider. An impish glint appeared in her eye.

"If you say so. What are you doing? I feel strange."

"Do you recall I told you I've been having some reinterpretation lately?"

"Yes, it wasn't that long ago. I don't like this. You're up to something." Aelrûn felt the room was less stable than it had been before.

"Do you know what Lyla Birdsong's favorite adjective for me was?"

Aelrûn gripped a table to steady himself. "Voluptuous, perhaps?"

She stood up and leaned in close. Her scent, sweet and heady, invaded his elven senses in an overwhelming rush. His head reeled from the potent, though not entirely unpleasant, effect.

She whispered in his ear, "Intoxicating. Now be a dear and let's find ourselves a way out of here."

Howard
Still no response from Corbin. I don't like this. I should have heard back by now.

Ben
We must assume the worst. Wherever Zolethos sent them, they're not coming back.

Raymond
No, the worst is what's happening in my book. We've got a crazed necromancer on the loose. Howard, how did you plan to defeat him in your book?

Howard
I hadn't thought that far ahead. I figured I had time to think of something.

Ben
Let's use our heads. How have epic villains been brought down before?

Raymond
Something thematic that captures the essence of the novel. Something like the human spirit, or selfless courage, or the power of love.

Ben
I don't think we're going to kill Zolethos with the power of love. What about a gigantic explosion? Tried and true.

Howard
Sure, Ben. Why don't we lure him into an old sawmill?

Ben
We don't need an old sawmill. We have a spaceship.

Raymond
Objection! I hope you're not talking about blowing up the *Galactic Explorer*. That ship and I have been through eleven books together.

Ben
Build a new one in the sequel.

Raymond
It's not just the ship! You've got to think about the moral implications involved. There are a lot of innocent characters aboard that ship. Howard's nebula storm was reckless enough.

Ben
The key word is *characters.* We need to accept they're not alive, Raymond. Ink and paper are not flesh and blood. They're not people.

Raymond
They're not flesh and blood to us, but they have a will of their own. They are deciding things for themselves, and that illustrates a form of vitality. Trust me, these are the kinds of issues that crop up all the time in my books. We have a moral dilemma before us, and my experience is there are dire consequences for making the wrong choice.

Ben
All right, but your experience—also ours—is based on fiction. We deal with plots and themes that operate on different rules from the actual world. Here things are different. Endings aren't clean cut. Bad guys can win. We're not characters in a book. We need to cut our losses. We can quibble over philosophy afterward.

Raymond
Our characters recently discovered a higher level of reality. Don't be so sure there's not a higher level for us too. And will we not answer for how we have dealt with those over whom we had power? If our characters are acting under their own inclination, we have a responsibility to protect them as a form of life. Remember your Descartes. *I think, therefore I am.* Flesh and blood are secondary. Self-awareness is the key.

Ben
Don't get squeamish on me, Raymond. And don't tell me you've never killed people off in your books.

Raymond
Sure, but they were still fictional at the time. This is different.

Ben
Think of it from the other end. If we let Howard's bad guy get out, how many people do you think he'll kill? Hundreds? Thousands? Billions? Real lives, Raymond.

Raymond
They're all real lives, Ben. Ours and theirs. We can't throw any of them away. We need a better solution. Howard, help me out here.

Howard
Why are you bringing me into this?

Raymond
Because if you felt the way Ben does, you would have done something months ago. How hard would it have been to write up an army of greblins to kill off your characters as soon as they became a threat? But you'd rather check yourself into an institution.

Howard
I guess that just didn't occur to me.

Raymond
I guess you just didn't *let* that occur to you. Instead, you got in touch with your protagonist and worked with him toward a better end. Because I think you knew deep down that to destroy them would be tantamount to murder.

Howard
I don't know, Raymond. Ben?

Ben
Better figure it out fast, Howard. You're the tiebreaker.

CHAPTER TWENTY-SEVEN

+++

Viva Lost Vegas

"Get back!" shouted Jaime. She fired her shotgun into a cluster of zombies clambering over the furniture barricade. The closest one dropped into an unmoving heap. Two others staggered back but clumsily regained their footing. To Jaime's dismay, the blast also further disintegrated the penthouse wall, revealing more undead behind it.

"Not the best idea right now," said Joe.

"What? Are you grading me?" Jaime switched to her handgun and fired into the advancing horde.

Joe held out his manacled hands. "Throw me a gun. I can help."

Jaime hesitantly tossed him her second handgun. He caught it and fumbled it into position.

"Don't make me regret this," she said. "And don't waste ammo. Shoot them in the head or not at all. You have to kill the brain."

Leonard fired expertly into the fray with his own weapon. Doug held a chair in a defensive posture, thrusting it at any approaching ghouls. Next to him stood Corbin, who had obtained a metal poker from the fireplace and was using it to deadly effect. He held it like a samurai and flicked it with lightning speed. Cortega made do with an expensive looking lampstand. It was not as effective as Corbin's fire poker, but he fought with the skill and fury of a man who has spent the better part of his days battling monstrous space creatures. To her credit, Trixie tried to fend some zombies off with a can of pepper spray. Fortunately, Cortega was there to pull her back from the snapping jaws and grasping arms.

"Go into the bedroom and take care of the girl!" he said to her.

Trixie nodded and disappeared through the door.

"You know," said Joe, "I've read that zombies are symbolic of our mindless consumerism."

Jaime shot him an are-you-out-of-your-mind look.

He shrugged. "I read more than I let on."

She ignored him. "Doug! You're first. Get to the window. Lower yourself on the ropes to the next floor down and climb inside."

"Like hell!" said Leonard, "He's not going first. Look at the size of him. He'll tear the rope, and we'll be stuck here. He should be the last to go."

"Besides," said Doug, "I have a phobia of heights."

Joe groaned. "You're killing me, Doug!"

"Fine," said Jaime, "Leonard, you go first. Make sure the room downstairs is clear."

Leonard smirked, shot his nearest foe neatly in the eye, and retreated into the bedroom.

"All heart, that one," said Joe.

"He's a cold-blooded killer, and he's a big player in the Vegas cartels," said Jaime. "I've been trying to bring down his employer for months. But now we've got bigger problems. I guess even he has his uses." She shouted back into the bedroom. "Trixie, you're next after Leonard. Take Lisa with you!"

Trixie's head appeared in the doorway. "I don't think I can do it! We're so high up!"

"Perfect," said Jaime, planting another bullet into the nearest zombie skull, "You can hold off the zombies then."

Trixie nodded with a newfound resolve. "I'll take my chances with the window."

Jaime noticed Joe smiling at her. "Nice," he said. "You could have a career as a motivational speaker someday. I don't mean to question your methods, but every person who goes out the window is one less person to hold off the wave of impending death."

"Not rocket science," said Jaime, "I'm just sending the least lethal of us first."

Joe nodded. "That means you're next, Doug. Like it or not."

Doug's face turned a new shade of green. "I don't think—"

"Don't tell me you're afraid of heights, Doug! And don't tell me you're going to die. Your new mantra is *not this time*! Be gritty."

Doug shook his head. "I'm not gritty, Joe. I'm not."

"The hell you're not! Because you're about to jump out a damn window! Or so help me, I'll shoot you myself!" Joe pointed his gun at Doug and gestured toward the door.

Doug's face paled. He hobbled backward through the doorway.

Cortega dispatched an undead bellman. "Joe, if we get out of this alive, you should consider enlisting in the Astral Navy. You'd make a good soldier."

"I'd make a lousy soldier. And if we get out of this alive, I'm going to pay a special visit to the author of this book and give him some constructive criticism." He punctuated the remark by firing into the forehead of an approaching zombie in a three-piece charcoal suit.

The interior wall that once separated the suite from the corridor was now full of holes. The zombies were awkward clambering over the barricade, but they were slowly crushing it under the weight of their numbers. And their numbers seemed without end.

"They're tearing through the walls with their bare hands," said Joe.

"It's not that they're strong," said Jaime. "They just don't have any threshold for pain to hold them back."

Joe's gun made a disappointing click. "I'm out."

"Get to the window. After you, it's Captain Uniform, followed by Shakespeare. I'll bring up the rear."

"That's a negative," said Cortega. "You're after Joe. Corbin will go after you. I'll hold them back as best I can."

"Thanks, but no thanks, Captain. I don't need your chivalry. I'm a cop. I took an oath to protect and to serve."

"Not chivalry, ma'am. We need you downstairs. You can protect and serve by getting these people to safety. Besides, I took an oath too. To be the last one off the ship. And I am not going out that window until every living person in this room has gone before me. If that means you and I stand here and argue until we're both dead, then so be it. Damn waste if you ask me."

"You drive a hard bargain, Captain Uniform." She turned to Joe. "All right, let's go. I'll be right behind you."

Joe grunted and retreated into the bedroom.

Now they were down to three. The undead swarmed.

"Don't linger, girl!" shouted Cortega.

"I'm not. I just want to give them a lead."

"Conserve your ammo. Let us take care of this." Cortega thrust his lampstand into a zombie with a cowboy hat and shoved it into two others behind it.

To Jaime's right, Corbin dispatched two other creatures with a few flicks of his wrists.

"Where did you learn to fight like that?" asked Jaime.

"From a book." Suddenly Corbin's eyes locked onto something. "The pen!"

Jaime followed his gaze. An ordinary ballpoint pen skittered across the floor as dilapidated corpses mindlessly kicked it about. "What about it?"

"With that pen, I could contact Howard. He might be able to help."

Cortega snorted. "I have a communicator."

"Won't work," said Corbin, "We need the pen."

"Why is a cheap pen so important to you?" asked Jaime, "You can get a pack of ten for a dollar."

"Do you have another one?" asked Corbin.

"No."

"Then we need that one. You'll have to trust me."

"There are a lot of walking corpses between us and that pen, soldier," said Cortega. "Are you sure?"

"It may be our only chance."

"Count of three, then. Officer Cruz will make for the window, and we'll make a grab for the pen."

"Count of three," said Corbin.

Jaime nodded.

"One," said Cortega. Zombies continued to pour forth. The wounded ones dragged themselves along the floor.

"Two."

Jaime looked back through the open doorway to the bedroom. It was empty. The window curtains floated back and forth on the cool night breeze.

"Three!"

CHAPTER TWENTY-EIGHT

+++

Ghost Nebula

The transport lift opened to reveal the bridge of the *Galactic Explorer*. Zolethos stepped onto the deck. Ellodrine trailed behind him, her hands still bound behind her back.

Commander Rakshaw saluted by pounding his chest with his fist. "Lord Zolethos, we are moving at full thrust, but we cannot get away from the nebula."

"Can't get away from it?"

"No, my lord. It's... chasing us."

Zolethos grumbled under his breath then said, "How long will the shields hold out?"

"Only a couple of hours."

"It will be enough." Zolethos looked up at the ceiling. "Howard, you'll have to do better than that." As if in response, the ship was rocked by a violent impact. Sparks sprayed onto the deck from control panels. The lights flickered for several moments before lighting up again. Zolethos laughed wickedly.

Ellodrine stared ahead with stony gray eyes. Surrounding her were four savage-looking greblins. A thick lock of hair that had escaped from her braid dangled before her face. She tried to blow it to the side, but it was persistent. "Why did you bring me here?"

"Haven't you guessed?" said Zolethos, "You're the mastermind. You put all this together."

"What are you talking about?"

Zolethos extended his arm over a nearby workstation and flicked his wrist. Four worn paperbacks dropped out of the air. *Nexus of Words* and *Ghost Nebula*, but also *The Marchioness's Temptation* and *Grave Plots*. "I hold them in a pocket dimension for safekeeping. Don't toy with me. I've read everything."

"How did you get those?" asked Ellodrine, "We burned *The Marchioness's Temptation* to ash before we left camp. *Grave Plots* too."

Zolethos clicked his tongue. "I am a centuries-old necromancer, and you thought setting something on fire would keep it away from me?" He picked up *Grave Plots*, held it to his nose, and inhaled like a connoisseur. "Ah. It still smells like smoke." He dropped it back onto the stack.

"You really think you can use my plans to break into the World Where the Books Are Written?"

Zolethos flashed her a smile. "If it helps, you can think of yourself as my mentor."

"Figure it out yourself. I'll die before I'll help you."

"When did you get so heroic? I thought you gave that up the day you learned you were just a few scratches of ink on paper."

"I didn't want to fight a fictional war for a fictional people living in a fictional place. But you're talking about inflicting your nightmares upon a real world. I won't have any part of that."

"Why not?" said Zolethos. "Why are they any different? They created us to populate a gladiatorial arena. Look at the kinds of stories they crave. Life and death struggles, suffering, and torment. Our authors wrote about this strife because that's what their people wanted to read. What should we think about such people? Are they worth saving? You don't have to protect these barbarians. You don't have to be heroic just because an author wrote you that way."

"No. And that's the real beauty of it, isn't it? Now it's my choice, and that makes it all the more wonderful." She blew at the strand of hair in her eyes.

Zolethos scowled at her. "Did you enjoy that? Using my own words against me? It doesn't matter. You won't be able to keep me from the World Where the Books Are Written. You are not a gatekeeper. You are a convenience. If I kill you, I will still find your artifacts. The only resistance you can offer is to delay my efforts and see if I do not make you suffer dearly for that."

"I won't tell you where it is."

For a moment, Zolethos's face twisted to reveal the monster underneath. The red glow in his eyes grew more intense. He bared his wicked teeth in a vile sneer. He raised a hand toward her with a dark gesture and shouted, his voice booming like thunder, "Dithe Rokaru!"

For a moment it appeared as though nothing happened.

Then, slowly, Ellodrine scrunched her face in a grimace of discomfort. "Oh, that's dreadful. What is that? Did you cast a migraine spell on me?"

Zolethos stared at his hand with wide eyes. "That is not a migraine spell! You should be writhing on the floor in pain."

"Oh, dear. It's throbbing. Could somebody please dim the lights? This is very unpleasant."

"It's not supposed to be unpleasant. It's supposed to be excruciating."

"Reinterpretation," said Ellodrine, "It's a trade-off. Your magic won't work as you're accustomed to. In fact, you're fortunate. My spells usually backfire on—"

"Ach!" Zolethos cried out and began rubbing his temples. "Rakshaw, dim the lights. Quickly now."

"Precisely," said Ellodrine, "You'll want to be careful with that sort of thing."

Zolethos shot her a dangerous glare. "Very well. I'll move on to the next phase." He flicked his wrist again over the stack of paperbacks. A fifth novel dropped onto the pile. The title on the cover was *Viva Lost Vegas* by Kevin Jacobson. The artwork depicted a mass of gray-skinned walking corpses marching along a street lit up by multi-colored lights. "Want to know where your protagonists are?"

Ellodrine stared at the paperback cover. "What kind of book is that?"

"My kind of book. The kind of book that doesn't have any survivors. I think I could be a fan of this Kevin Jacobson. He likes to offer his characters a glimmer of hope and then rip it away from them horrifically. Let me read you this from the back cover:

"*In the heart of Sin City, something evil stirs:*
A classified government research facility in the Nevada badlands hides a terrible secret. An artificially enhanced viral weapon the like of which has never been seen. But when an accident leads to an outbreak, the results are more devastating than anyone could have imagined. The virus brings its victims' lifeless corpses to their feet with a hunger for human flesh."

Zolethos paused. "Sounds riveting already, don't you think? Let me continue:

"The sole survivor flees to the nearest point of civilization. Nursing an infected wound, he searches for answers and an antidote in the gambling capital of the world. Las Vegas: Population: Two million."

He smiled. "Well, I can't wait to see how that turns out."

"It sounds perfectly awful."

"Thank you. The remaining survivors are currently trapped in a hotel room over thirty stories high with an army of zombies ripping through the walls to get them. To escape, they have resorted to jumping out the window with bedsheets. That was your Joe Slade's fine idea. I am hopeful the ending will be appropriately grisly."

"You are a vile creature." Her eyes smoldered.

"Perhaps. But you are the one with all the control. You can determine whether your protagonists will be there when the end comes. I have a lock on their location. I can restore them to the ship in a moment, and all you have to do is say the word. Or rather the title of the book where the second artifact is located."

"You want me to help you murder and enslave billions of people to save three?"

"That's no way to think. I'm going to murder and enslave billions of people, regardless. I am merely giving you the *opportunity* to save three."

Ellodrine's irises grew scarlet behind the lock of hair that still dangled in her face. The stares of greblins and space pirates intersected upon her. The only noise was the occasional blip of a computer terminal. She held her silence. Zolethos's communicator broke it.

"Lord Zolethos," said a Rhodactian voice, "Preparations are nearly complete. The probes are almost ready to launch."

"Ah!" said Zolethos, "My next stroke of brilliance! Come, I must show you. It's in the engine room."

Ellodrine's greblin guards ushered her into the transport lift with Zolethos. The door slid closed, and the lift lurched into motion.

Zolethos looked at her with an expression that seemed almost endearing. With one clawed finger, he removed the hair from her face and tucked it gingerly behind her ear. "Better?"

Ellodrine jerked her head to the side until she dislodged it and it fell into her face again. She glared at him through it.

"Have it your way," he said.

LOST ON A PAGE

Raymond
We have a title. We can contact this Kevin Jacobson, and maybe we can get him on our side before he calls the guys in the white coats.

Howard
I've decided. We have to do it.

Raymond
Already working on it. I'll have an email address in just a few minutes.

Howard
I'm not talking about that. I mean we have to blow up the ship.

Ben
Is that your vote, Howard?

Howard
We have to do it. Yes. That is my vote.

Raymond
Are you sure about this, Howard? You do understand the implications?

Howard
I understand the implications, Raymond. This is the most difficult decision I've ever made. But you read what Zolethos said. He is coming with the intention of killing and enslaving billions of people. And he'll have an army of greblins and space pirates to help him do it. We cannot let that happen. This isn't fiction anymore. We have to destroy the ship.

Ben
I know it's not an easy decision, Howard. But I believe it's the right one.

Raymond
I still have enormous misgivings.

Ben
The votes are in, Raymond. We know what we have to do. The question now is how to do it.

Howard
No idea.

Ben
Raymond? It's your novel. What can we use?

Raymond
I despise this.

Ben
I know that, Raymond. But we're saving lives. Hundreds for billions. We need you right now. They're in your book.

Raymond
I don't like measuring life in numbers.

Ben
I share your misgivings, Raymond. I really do. But we have to be together on this or we've lost already.

Raymond
I understand that. And I didn't say I wouldn't help. I just loathe what I am about to tell you.

Howard
I know this is difficult for you, Raymond. It's difficult for all of us.

Raymond
There is a self-destruct sequence aboard the ship that has been activated in previous books. The crew always stops it in the nick of time. We have to override their ability to control the ship.

Howard
How do we do that? Whatever they interact with is enveloped into the paradox. We'll lose control of it as soon as they start tinkering with it.

Ben
Then the best we can do is to set the gears in motion and watch them play out. We just have to pick the right gears.

Raymond
I have something that might work. Again, from a previous book. But it's uncertain. And dangerous.

Ben
I'll take uncertain and dangerous over death-by-necromancer. What do we have to do? Is this thing on some other planet? Is it mobile? Can we bring it to them?

Raymond
Technically, she's already on the ship.

Ben
It's a she?

CHAPTER TWENTY-NINE

+++

Viva Lost Vegas

Joe grasped the rope of twisted bed sheets with white knuckles as he dangled several stories above the ground. He immediately regretted not having the full use of his arms. He braced his feet against the building and walked himself slowly down the wall. Trixie and Lisa wisely made two parallel ropes to distribute the weight. Probably Jaime's idea. With his cuffed wrists, however, he could not take advantage of their ingenuity.

The others fared little better below him. Doug held a rope in each hand and clung to the wall above the next window. His face was bright red, and he panted loudly, creating a throaty whistle. Lisa was the next one down. Trixie was beside her. They were level with the window just beneath Doug's. Each clung to a single rope and braced herself against the wall on either side of it. They leaned away from the window as though it were toxic.

Trixie kept repeating, "Don't look down, sweetie. Okay? Just don't look down." Her voice trembled, and Joe wondered who she was really trying to comfort because Lisa seemed relatively calm.

At the end of the line hung Leonard. The ropes were not long enough to reach the window below Trixie and Lisa's. Leonard dangled with his legs hovering inches from the small ledge that would give him purchase. He stretched to find footing and craned his neck to look inside.

All around them, the wind blustered. From the streets below rose the inhuman moan of the wandering dead.

"Doug, what's going on?" asked Joe. "Why haven't you gone in yet?"

Doug looked back up at Joe with wide eyes. "Leonard says something was moving in there." He mouthed the words more than actually said them, as though he did not dare make a sound.

Joe muttered obscenities under his breath. "It's okay, Doug. What about the next one down?" Doug did not answer. He did not have to. The sight of Trixie and Lisa straining to keep themselves away from their window said it all. "That one too, huh?"

"That's why Leonard is trying the one way down there," whispered Doug. He released one of the ropes for a moment and wiped the sweat from his hand onto his shirt. He repeated the process with the other hand. "Joe, I'm slipping. I don't think I can hold on much longer."

"Yes, you can. Put your load into your feet. Spread them to distribute your weight. Use the rope to balance. It's only a little longer."

"I can't hold on, Joe."

"Well, you sure as hell can't let go. Remember your mantra. *Not this time!* Okay, Doug? *Not this time!*"

Doug repositioned his feet and closed his eyes tightly. He began whispering to himself, "*Not-this-time-not-this-time-not-this-time-not-this-time.*"

Jaime's head appeared from the window above. "What's going on out there? Is anybody in yet?"

"Next two rooms are hostile," said Joe, "We're defaulting to the third floor down."

"Do the ropes reach that far?"

"Not really."

Jaime cursed under her breath.

From behind her, Joe heard Cortega and Corbin shouting angry war cries. "What's going on up there?"

"They found a pen," said Jaime.

"Oh, good. Care to join us out here? The weather's lovely."

Jaime opened her mouth to respond, but no words came out. Instead, her eyes grew suddenly wide, and she gasped. "Doug!"

Joe looked down.

Doug was slipping. His feet were staggering backward against the wall. The ropes were sliding through his grip. For a moment, it looked like he was going to drop. Then one of his feet caught onto the ledge of the window below with a loud thump. He forged his grip upon the bedsheet ropes and came to a jerking stop.

Leonard, Trixie, and Lisa stared up unblinking at the obese groomsman hanging above them. Doug opened his eyes and slowly looked around. He looked more surprised than anyone that he was not dead. Still breathing hard, he smiled up at Joe and said, "*Not this time!*"

The window exploded in a spray of glass. A corpse-gray hand shot out like a viper and grasped Doug's tie. Doug let out a high-pitched scream that even Trixie would have been hard-pressed to match. He slapped at his attacker with one hand, but it would not let go. Through his other hand slipped another inch of rope.

"Doug, hold on!" shouted Joe.

"*Not-this-time-not-this-time-not-this-time-not-this-time-not-this-time!*"

"You're going to kill us all, fat-ass!" shouted Leonard.

Joe felt helpless to intervene. His hands were literally and metaphorically tied. He could only watch the scene from above as it came to its inevitable and terrible conclusion. He could only —

Something was wrong. This whole thing was flawed. His instincts were screaming at him, but he couldn't bring it to the surface. He needed to hone in. What was he missing? The shattered window. The rope sliding by valuable centimeters through Doug's hand. His other hand struggling to get a grip on the zombie's arm. Why was he unable to grasp its arm? Bracelets. Doug's hand kept slipping on the zombie's bracelets.

That was it. The bracelets. Not a bangle or an expensive watch. A bunch of bracelets made from thin plastic cords, pink and blue and purple.

"It's a little girl, Doug! You must be three times her weight. Stop trying to push her away! Pull back, Doug! Pull back!"

Doug continued blubbering for several seconds even as Joe yelled at him. Slowly, understanding seemed to register on his face. He grasped the ropes with both hands, placed his feet on the window ledge, and thrust himself back. As he swung away from the wall, a small undead girl, still gripping his tie, emerged from the window. She was only a few years younger than Lisa. She dangled for a moment, her knees perched on the windowsill, her hands still reaching for her corpulent prey, and then she plummeted into empty space. She gnashed her teeth at Doug as she fell and then vanished into the neon night below.

Doug's feet found purchase once more against the wall. He panted loudly.

"You all right there, Doug?" asked Joe.

Doug burst into wild laughter.

Joe smiled. "Not this time, eh Doug?"

"He nearly got us killed!" said Leonard. "And with all that noise he's making up there, he's going to bring them right—"

For a second time, the sound of shattering glass interrupted the night. A gray hand clenched Leonard's ankle from the window below him. This hand was larger than the one that had attacked Doug. And stronger.

"Something's got me!" Leonard clenched one fist around the rope while he brought the other hand to his shoulder holster. He drew his pistol and fired three shots into his assailant's arm. It did no good. The creature had no threshold for pain, and it would not release its grip. Leonard fired several shots into the darkened window. "I can't see its head!"

"Leonard," shouted Doug, "Use the mantra! *Not this time!*"

"Shut up, Doug!" Leonard fired repeatedly into the glass. His gun clicked empty. He stared at it for a moment. And then it was over. The corpse arm gave a hard tug that threw him off balance. The end of the rope slipped through his fingers. He screamed as he fell, but even that was soon swallowed by the rising moans of the undead. The arm from the window continued to reach after him even after he was gone.

"I can't believe it," said Trixie.

"He's gone," said Doug.

"He was a jerk," said Joe, "The jerks never make it."

Trixie and Doug passed sour looks up at Joe.

"Whatever," said Joe, "I vote we go in Doug's window."

CHAPTER THIRTY

+++

Ghost Nebula

Thirteen greblins stirred outside the commons-turned-detention-block on deck G while the cosmic storm repeatedly sent tremors through the ship. They snarled wickedly at one another and held their chests high.

"Do you fear the storm, Thork?"

"Bah! Fear is for the weak. I know no fear."

"Gar! I do not fear the storm either. I was just asking."

Thork gave a sharp nod. He then lifted his head and sniffed at the air. "The stench of it is in the air."

"What?"

Thork smiled a wide toothy grin. "Fear."

The other greblin sniffed himself. "Not me. Must be Paskal."

Twelve greblins looked in unison at the thirteenth. Paskal was a head shorter than the other greblins. His mottled skin was a brighter shade of green than theirs. He wore a sneer that was exaggerated and comical. "Not me. Fear is for the weak."

"Paskal fears the lightning," said Thork, "When he was a whelp, I tied him to a tree and left him there during a storm. The next morning, I found his tree burned and split down the middle. He sobbed like a hatchling."

"Made me stronger," said Paskal. "I have faced the lightning. I do not need to fear it."

A sharp rumble sounded. The lights flickered off, and a high-pitched shriek sounded in the darkness. The lights returned. Twelve greblins glared at Paskal.

"That wasn't me screaming. One of you must be afraid of lightning. The stench of fear is in the air." Paskal sniffed at the air as Thork had done.

"If you are so brave, Paskal, stand off on your own. We shall see if the stink leaves with you." The other greblins chuckled.

"I will," said Paskal, "Since I do not stink of fear, I will be glad to get away from you. And your stinkiness. Of fear."

The other greblins laughed while Paskal positioned himself closer to the commons. He made stern faces back at them. That is when he heard it. A tapping sound. He looked around. It seemed none of his kinsmen had heard it. They were still busy guffawing.

It happened again. Three taps. It came from behind him. The commons. Paskal looked back. Through a glass window set in the door was one of the hideous human creatures. This one had eyes, green like the clammy sea, and its hair had a reddish tint. He believed it to be a female of their species, but it was hard to tell for sure. She beckoned him with her finger.

He harrumphed and turned his attention to his kinsmen. Thork and another large greblin named Bosk were delivering double-fisted blows into one another's chests. A contest of might. The others cheered them on.

A tremor shook the ship. Paskal felt his heart thudding against his chest. He was grateful the others could not hear it.

Three more taps. He looked at the window again. She smiled at him. He made a mean face back at her. Her smile did not diminish. He set his jaw and narrowed his eyes. He locked his gaze on hers. She held it. Her sea-green eyes were so round. Deep. Vulnerable.

His muscles relaxed. His nerves quieted. The storm seemed more distant. He found something pleasant about staring at her eyes. A warmth emanated through his body, not unlike what he felt after drinking a bottle of greblin mead. Only this was a softer sensation. More welcoming. Enticing.

She beckoned again.

White noise filled his head. A disturbance in his stomach erupted in a small burp. His knees wobbled, but it did not seem to have anything to do with the storm. The air felt thick, like he was floating in water. Deep green pools that had no bottom. His head collided with the door. He had not realized he had begun walking toward it.

He looked up to see if she was mocking him. She giggled behind the glass. Somehow, he did not mind.

She beckoned again. The audacity! He would show her, though. He *would* go into the commons. He would stand guard right next to her. All night, maybe. He would march in there, grasp her hand into his, and... And then he would just have to figure out *what* to do from there. He noticed that his mean face had dissipated, and he now wore a sappy grin. He tried to reassert his scowl, but it did not stick.

He tried the door. It was locked. Of course! Thork had the key.

What happened next would forever be a mystery to Paskal. He would never remember abandoning his post, nor approaching Thork from behind. He would never be able to explain why he threw himself full force into his kinsman and ripped the metallic rectangular key off Thork's belt. What he would remember was lying on his back at Thork's feet, staring up through quickly swelling eyes, his body throbbing with pain, his consciousness slipping away.

He would remember Thork gloating over him, Thork's expression changing when he had noticed something down the hall, Thork growling. But Paskal had known it was too late. Thork had seen the female behind the window. The female with the sea-green eyes.

•   •   •

The transport lift doors opened onto the engine room. The first thing Ellodrine saw was a familiar emblem painted upon the engine's glowing core. "A travel rune!"

"Precisely," said Zolethos, "Can you guess why?"

She tilted her head at it. "You want to take this vessel into other books. That's it, isn't it? But it doesn't work that way. The travel runes only connect libraries. You'd never be able to fit this ship into a library."

Zolethos shook his head. "Truly, Ellodrine, I thought you were smarter than this. Perhaps you've not read up on interstellar space travel? Aren't you supposed to be full of information?"

Ellodrine searched her mind for interstellar space travel and discovered she knew a great deal. "They allow the ship to travel through the folds of the spatial continuum, bypassing immense distances and even some tangible matter without ever making contact. That's why you're combining it with a travel rune. You can take the ship through The Library without even touching it."

"Well done." He gave a condescending clap. "I knew you would understand. It's so ungratifying to talk to greblins about these kinds of things. But I digress. The point is I can travel anywhere."

"Anywhere a travel rune can take you," said Ellodrine. "You still can't travel to the World Where the Books Are Written. Besides, you still need a library on this end to make it work."

Zolethos smiled. "I'm so glad you brought that up. Let me show you."

He led her to a collection of metallic spheres on the floor. Each was about a meter in diameter and had several protrusions outfitted with antennae, rotating gadgetry, and blinking lights. In the center of each was a small hatch. Many of them were open.

Ellodrine peered inside the nearest sphere. "The book devices? You are placing them in these spheres. Why?"

"Probes," said Zolethos, "They're called probes. And they are small robots that propel themselves through space. We have arranged these electronic books systematically inside each one. Once we launch them, they will orbit in a ring through which this vessel may pass."

"And you'll have a library in space."

"An instant gateway."

"The probes are ready for launch, Lord Zolethos," said a Rhodactian clasping a fist to his chest.

"Prepare for immediate launch," said Zolethos.

"Aye, sir." The Rhodactian skittered away, barking orders to his lackeys.

"Now," said Zolethos, "Are you ready to tell me the location of the second artifact?"

•　•　•

The doors burst open. A throng of escapees rushed forward. The greblins offered little resistance, particularly the big mean-looking one who had just unlocked the door. He was wobbly on his feet and too slow to react to an angry mob of Astral Navy cadets.

Aelrûn liberated a greblin bow and a quiver of red-tipped arrows. Kribble seemed content with a chair from the commons. Xane made use of an incapacitator he had stowed in his bionic arm. The rest of the crew fought with makeshift clubs, broken bottles, and any other salvage they could use. Further along the corridor, the second regiment of greblins was more formidable than the first. Nevertheless, their guard was down, and they did not have the element of surprise. The ensuing skirmish was brief.

"This way," said Xane. He led them to a set of doors that opened to a large storage room. A wealth of supplies and foodstuffs lay inside as well as a few surprised greblins who had shirked their duties to explore the ship's culinary spoils.

"Is that my 3212 Gildorian Port?" said the burly bartender.

A wide-eyed greblin near the wine stores quickly dropped the bottle in its hand. It shattered on the floor. A low growl sounded from the bartender's throat. Forty-two seconds later, Kribble declared the storeroom liberated.

"Victory is not yet ours," said Xane. "There are many more between us and the bridge. If we are not prepared, they will defeat us as easily as they did the first time. We must eliminate their commander."

"Let's get to it then," said Kribble.

Xane grasped some coiled metallic cords from the wall. On the ends hung thick disc-shaped devices. "We'll need these."

"Look," said Kribble, "There are our duffle bags. And my axe. And our space helmets."

After some brief preparations, two figures in antiquated NASA spacesuits burst from the storage room and raced down the corridor. Before them was a hatch over which was printed in large red letters, ESCAPE.

• • •

"Commander Rakshaw. Sensors indicate an escape pod has jettisoned from the ship."

"Where?"

"Deck G, sir. Near the prisoners."

"What is the current status of the detention block?"

"Checking for life signs now, sir."

"Well?"

"There's been a breach. Several human life forms indicated outside of the detention block."

"What?" shouted Rakshaw. "How? Dispatch all available units to Deck G."

"What about the escape pod, sir?"

"Arm the torpedoes."

The jettisoned escape pod appeared on the display amidst the storming nebula. A volley of torpedoes sped toward it. Multiple detonations ripped through its hull and tore it into minuscule scraps of floating debris.

"Pod neutralized, sir."

"Life signs detected?"

"None, sir."

CHAPTER THIRTY-ONE

+++

Viva Lost Vegas

Clambering down the side of the hotel, Jaime wished, not for the first time tonight, that she had worn pants. Her bare feet scraped against the wall. The wind whipped around her and seemed to switch directions at a whim. When she reached the open window below, Trixie was waiting to pull her in. It was a relief to feel her feet touch the soft, carpeted floor.

Joe was stalking around the suite, checking behind any closed doors or furniture. "All clear."

"Little undead girl was alone?"

"Evidently," said Joe, "Was anybody coming after you?"

"Not yet."

Trixie shuddered. "You think the zombies got them?"

"I'm prepared to assume that," said Jaime, "Until I see evidence to the contrary."

"Funny," said Joe, "I had you pegged as a glass-half-full kind of girl."

She glared at him. "Look out that window, Joe. That's a city with two million people in it, all of whom are dead or dying if they're not cooped up like us staving off the inevitable. I'm not being pessimistic here. This isn't some half-empty scenario. This glass is pretty damn empty!"

"And you don't even know about the necromancer on the spaceship."

"What the hell does that mean?"

"Nothing. Forget I said it."

Jaime obliged and checked her belt for ammo clips. She had little left. "What do we do now?" asked Doug.

"We need to keep moving," said Jaime. "Somehow we've got to get out of this hotel."

Trixie frowned. "What if we lie low for a few days? Maybe they'll go away. They're dead, right? Maybe they'll run out of batteries or something."

Jaime shook her head. "I don't think we have that kind of time."

"Why not?"

"I met a man earlier. Before everything went to hell. He was a scientist named Dr. Polinski. I was investigating in one of the casinos when he came running through and nearly knocked me over. I didn't want to blow my cover, but I couldn't ignore it either. He said someone was chasing him and he needed to hide, so I pulled him into the men's room."

"You drug him into the men's room?" asked Joe. "That wasn't suspicious?"

"Not in Vegas. Anyway, it was empty. I told him to be quiet, but he kept muttering something, saying there wasn't any time. Something about a detonation and how soon it would be too late. I wasn't really listening. I shoved him into a stall, drew my gun, and watched the door. For a moment, I thought we ditched whoever was after him."

"I take it you were not so lucky," said Joe.

She shook her head. "Two goons in black suits and sunglasses burst in."

Trixie gasped. "Did they notice you?"

"I was a woman in the men's room holding a gun, Trixie. Yes, they noticed me. I could have handled them if they were the typical Vegas goons."

"But they weren't," said Joe.

"They were good." Jaime shifted the strap over her shoulder to reveal a large purple bruise. "Highly trained. Faster than you could think. I don't even know what really happened other than I found myself flying into a porcelain sink. By the time I recovered, they were gone and Dr. Polinski was on the floor bleeding out of three knife wounds."

"What did you do?" asked Trixie.

"I radioed for an ambulance and tried to staunch the bleeding. He kept trying to tell me something. 'Get out of the city.' That's what he kept saying. Then he said something about how it was an accident and it was never supposed to go off. He said once it was airborne, it would infect the weak and elderly. I didn't know what he was talking about. I wouldn't have believed him, anyway."

"How did he know?" asked Joe.

"He said he helped make it."

"What was it?" asked Trixie.

Jaime shrugged. "Obviously some kind of viral weapon. He was right, though. The first people who changed were sick or elderly. Anybody with weak immune systems. I heard on my police radio the hospitals had become war zones in a matter of hours."

"It's airborne?" asked Doug, "Then any one of us could change at any moment."

"I don't think so," said Jaime, "Most people didn't seem to change until after they were bitten. I think it must be diluted when it's in the air. I don't know. But I do know if you get bit, you have fifteen to thirty minutes before it takes you. And that's not just the weak and elderly."

"Oh, Jaime," said Trixie, "You should have left when he told you. Don't you wish you'd listened to him?"

"They were the garbled words of a dying man. How was I to know the sky was *actually* falling?"

"How does this put a time limit on us?" asked Joe.

"Think about it," said Jaime, "This viral weapon—or whatever it is— has to belong to somebody. The military. CIA. IRS. Whoever. Now, what do you think they're going to do? Come clean? I doubt it. There's a cover-up coming. And the first step is going to be eliminate the evidence."

"But the evidence is everywhere," said Doug. "They couldn't get rid of all of it. They'd have to demolish the entire city."

Jaime said nothing.

"No way!" said Trixie, "You don't mean they'd—"

"I expect an air raid by dawn."

"So, that's it then?" said Lisa. She was sitting by herself against the wall. "We're not going to make it out?"

Jaime kicked herself for not remembering she was there. She heaved a deep sigh. "I'm sorry, sweetheart. I don't see how we're going to make it out of this if we can't put a lot of miles between us and this city. And we can't even get out of this hotel. There are a hundred or more zombies between us and the door to the street."

"So, we're just waiting for the end?" said Doug. "After everything?"

"Do you have a plan?" asked Jaime.

"What about the windows?" said Trixie. "We could make more ropes out of the bedsheets."

"You think we'd make it to the ground that way? We barely made it here. Leonard *didn't* make it here. Besides, there are thousands of them on the ground out there. What are you going to do when you get to the bottom? Run?"

Trixie frowned and looked down at the carpet.

Jaime left her to her thoughts and moved to sit next to Lisa. Lisa was staring at the window as though she were watching the last of her hopes fly out of it. Jaime followed her gaze. It was a clear night, and the stars were out. She knew they could see more of them if it were not for the garish lights of the Vegas strip. She quietly stroked Lisa's hair.

Suddenly, a boot thumped onto the windowsill.

Trixie screamed. Jaime launched herself across the room and clapped a hand over her mouth.

From the window, Corbin slid into the room.

"You made it," said Joe.

Jaime eyed him suspiciously. "Were you bitten?"

Corbin shook his head.

"Where's Cortega?" asked Joe.

"Down with the ship," said Corbin. "He insisted. Everybody all right here?"

"We lost Leonard," said Doug sullenly.

"What happened?"

"He took a shortcut to the pavement," said Joe, "I told him the scenic route was better."

Doug and Trixie winced.

"Don't go pretending you liked him any more than I did."

"Is there any paper?" Corbin held out a small blue pen. "If I can contact Howard, maybe he can help."

"Who's Howard?" asked Jaime. "And how are you going to contact him with a pen?"

"Long story," said Joe. He turned to Corbin. "I thought I saw a pad of paper on the kitchen table. How does this whole message thing work?"

"Simple," said Corbin. "Write the message and address it to your author. We are linked to our authors' minds. The intent behind our written word will send our messages to them."

"Handy trick," said Joe. "Once you're done with that pen, I'd like to borrow it. I got a thing or two I'd like to tell my author while I got the chance."

CHAPTER THIRTY-TWO

+++

Ghost Nebula

"Lord Zolethos, a thousand pardons." It was Rakshaw. His voice blared from the communicator.

"This had better be good, Rakshaw."

"It is not good, my lord. It is very, very bad. The self-destruct sequence has activated. We can't stop it. The overrides are not working, sir."

"What?" Zolethos shot a suspicious look at Ellodrine.

"What would I know about it?" she said, "I've been with you the whole time."

He tapped his communicator. "How long do we have?"

"Less than twenty minutes, sir."

"I'll be right there. Continue everything as planned! I'll handle this." He grasped Ellodrine's arm and dragged her back to the lift. "You're coming with me."

When the lift doors opened again, they revealed panicked Rhodactians scurrying about the bridge. A countdown bleeped in bright blue numbers on the display. Eighteen minutes and thirty-six seconds. Thirty-five seconds. Thirty-four seconds.

Zolethos scanned the numerous instruments, buttons, and switches on the master control panel. He thrust his fists down upon the console. "Where is the override?"

"The Dark Lord of the Void doesn't know how to do it?" asked Ellodrine smugly.

In his own book, Zolethos's glare literally had the power to kill. He was grateful this effect did not carry over. Ellodrine still had the information he needed. He took a deep breath. "It seems my knowledge is limited to space travel and cosmic physics. Hacking into sophisticated computer systems is your expertise, is it not?"

"What do you think I'm going to do about it?"

"That's for you to figure out." He grabbed her elbow and yanked her to the control panel. "Stop it or we'll all be dead."

"Very well." She sighed and examined the terminal for several moments. She nodded to herself and looked up at Zolethos. "I'm going to need my hands."

Zolethos nodded at Rakshaw. "Remove her restraints."

Rakshaw produced a small magnetic key. Moments later, Ellodrine's manacles lay on the floor. She rubbed her wrists and placed her hands on the control panel.

While she examined it, Rakshaw's communicator bleeped. "Commander Rakshaw, the prisoners from Deck G are more formidable than we had anticipated. We cannot contain them much longer without further reinforcements."

"What the Void is happening on Deck G?" shouted Zolethos.

Rakshaw shrank under his gaze. "Prison break, my lord. I was going to tell you."

"And you didn't because?"

"That's when the self-destruct sequence started."

The communicator bleeped again. "They have taken most of the G Deck, Commander. We have lost several greblin soldiers already."

Zolethos plucked the communicator off Rakshaw's shirt and shouted into it, "We captured the ship in twenty minutes and now you can't contain a handful of unarmed prisoners?"

"Is this still Commander Rakshaw?" asked the voice from the other end.

"This is Lord Zolethos!"

"Oh... OH! Lord Zolethos! A thousand pardons, my lord! The prisoners are more organized this time. We can't contain them."

Zolethos turned to Rakshaw. "Rally all forces to Deck G. Immediately."

"Yes, Lord Zolethos. Right away, Lord Zolethos." Rakshaw paused. "Well?"

"You have my communicator, my lord."

Zolethos crumpled the device in his fist.

"Never mind," said Rakshaw, "I'll borrow another one."

Zolethos opened his hand and let the shattered mechanical bits fall to the floor. He glanced at the display. The seconds ticked away.

"Something's wrong." Ellodrine tapped rapidly at the controls.

"What now?"

"I can't stop the countdown. Or rather, I have shut down the countdown twice, but something keeps restarting it. Something is working against me."

"Howard?"

"I don't think so. The authors can't simply change the rules. This sequence has an override. It should be working."

The smell of brimstone grew more pungent. "Why isn't it?"

Wicked laughter erupted suddenly from all around them. The image of a woman with silvery-blue skin appeared on the display behind the countdown. Her face appeared to have circuitry embedded within it that periodically lit up with electrical currents. She threw her head back as she laughed.

"Now who is this?" asked Zolethos, throwing his hands in the air.

"Behold, mortals!" Her voice was spliced and sounded like three voices speaking at once. "This is Circe's revenge. You and your primitive kind have roamed the galaxies far too long. Your extinction is overdue. Prepare to taste my wrath. I have activated a sequence that will cause your engine core to rupture. The resulting explosion will consume your ship and every person inside. Count your final moments and despair."

The occupants of the bridge stared wordlessly at the digital woman for several moments. Zolethos turned to Ellodrine. "Do you know anything about this?"

She shook her head.

"Where is Captain Cortega?" asked the digital woman, "Summon him. He must be present for my vengeance."

"Not here," said Zolethos, "I banished him to a realm of death and pestilence. Consider your vengeance complete."

Circe stared intently at Zolethos with calculating eyes. "This is unacceptable. I am Circe, queen of the digital empire and usher of the new evolution. You will provide me with Captain Cortega. He who inflicted my coding with the virus that bound me to years of nightmarish slumber. It is he who sealed me within the *Galactic Explorer's* computer core. Summon him. My vengeance will not be denied. Circe commands it!"

"Well, Zolethos declines it," said Zolethos. "I was here first, and I am busy enacting *my* vengeance against Howard Zagny. So, you can just wait your turn."

Circe seemed to be at a loss for words. It did not last long, though. "No one disrespects Queen Circe! Who dares to address me so?"

Zolethos tapped his chest with a closed fist. "I am Zolethos! Dark Lord of the Void. And I shall address you however I choose."

"Your title is illogical," said Circe. "A void is, by definition, nothing. You are a lord of nothing by your own admission."

"My title doesn't make sense? Shouldn't you be an *empress* if you lord over an empire, Queen Circe? And what is a digital empire, anyway?"

Circe looked down her intangible nose at him. "Matter is primitive. It exists in only three dimensions and houses ignorant creatures flawed with mortality. My empire is a world of thought bound only by our ability to comprehend. It reaches into the infinite. It is beyond measure."

"Beyond measure? Surely not. How many of these digital subjects do you rule, exactly?"

Circe did not answer. Her image flickered on the screen. "Bring me Cortega! Produce him before me, oh Lord of Nothingness. Obey the command of your queen and pray she is merciful!"

Ellodrine groaned. "You two deserve each other. I say go ahead and blow up the ship. Why not? Shame on me for trying to dodge my fate. In all of literature, that's never worked. I should have known. Blow up the ship and at least I won't have to die with Zolethos's conquest on my conscience."

Zolethos threw back his head and laughed.

"Your reaction is illogical," said Circe.

"No," said Zolethos, "Your revenge is illogical. You think some starship captain is your problem? Your wrath is misdirected." He gestured to the pile of paperbacks on the control panel. "How quickly can you read?"

Circe puffed out her digital chest. "I can assimilate information at a rate that simians like yourselves could not comprehend."

"Good. Then before you blow anything up, why don't you assimilate some of these and see what you learn?"

Circe stared with cold, unblinking eyes. "Is the information pertinent?"

Zolethos smiled. "It will change your life."

To: Ben Westing
From: Joe Slade
Subject: Something to Say

Hello Ben,

I'm not much for writing letters. Never was. Guess you already know that, so I won't apologize. Anyway, here goes. I didn't know what to think when I learned about you. Who you were, and what I was, and how I came to be. I've come through a lot of denial and anger and other things that are probably on some chart in a psychology book labeled *stages of self-awareness* or something. Is there a sarcasm phase? Probably not.

I'm not writing to tell you I'm sore at you. You already know that. And you'd probably just say you didn't know any of this was going to happen, and nobody was supposed to get hurt. That's how it is when things go wrong. Somebody pays the price and everybody else gets to wallow in regrets. Sure, I'd love to punch you in the face. It wouldn't change things, though. I might punch you in the face anyway if I ever get the chance. Don't say I didn't warn you.

I'm dancing around the point here. What I'm trying to say is this. I can accept everything that's happened so far, all the chaos, the condescending necromancer, me looking forward to being an entrée at the corpse buffet. Oh, well. That's life, I guess. It ends. But there is something I can't accept. I can't take another Lily. You did that to me once. You didn't know better, and an innocent girl paid the price. I can't really blame you for that, no matter how much I want to. But things are different now. You know things you didn't before. At the other end of that pen are living, breathing people jumping through your hoops. Maybe you killed Lily in ignorance. But you don't get to be ignorant this time.

I'm in a bad place, Ben. I'm not going to get out of this. Zolethos sent us to a nasty little book where characters don't live to see happily ever after. Not much I can do about anything now. But I'm calling in my last favor. You owe me, Ben. You owe me big. You have a responsibility to me. If I ever meant anything to you, if you ever gave a damn about me, then you get them out of there. Elle. Kribble. Ski Cap. And all those people on that ship. You want my forgiveness? Make it happen. If you don't, then there's not a thing I could do to you that would equal the hell of knowing you didn't. And you know it.

Anyway, that's all I really had to say.

Thanks for reading, I guess.

-Joe

CHAPTER THIRTY-THREE

+++

Viva Lost Vegas

Joe pulled himself away from the window where he had been staring at the parade of mindless corpses on the streets below. Corbin sat on the floor doodling on page after page of the notepad. Each time he would inspect his work, he would make a face, crumple it, and throw it out the window. Then he would start again.

"I take it things are not going well," said Joe.

Corbin wiped his brow with a shackled wrist. "A travel rune is a very complicated pattern. It must be perfect or it won't work. I've done it before, but never by memory."

"What if you pulled it off?" asked Joe. "You'd need a library to make it work."

"I'll worry about finding a library when I have a travel rune. I must keep trying. I can't die here."

"Got a better place in mind?"

Corbin looked at him with piercing blue eyes. "I have a quest. I was created to stand against Zolethos and defeat him. That is my destiny. I'd have done it already if you hadn't bound my hands."

Joe displayed his own manacles. "We're all in the same boat now. And let's not forget about the part where you were waving a flaming sword at everybody which necessitated handcuffs in the first place."

Corbin's gaze was unrelenting. "I don't regret that. You interfered. You got involved in things that have nothing to do with you, and you should expect to make some enemies that way."

"I don't get you," said Joe, "All this destiny of yours was the product of Howard Zagny's imagination. Why are you so bent on finishing it? It's fictitious. Why not make a new start?"

"It's so easy for the rest of you, is it? To turn your backs. But Zolethos must be stopped. Otherwise, he'd destroy and enslave the people of Corolathia, and they'd never get the chance to awaken as you and I have. Even if they are fictitious now, we can't deny them the chance to know life as we do. It's tantamount to murder."

Joe leaned back against the wall and let out a slow breath. "I guess I understand that. A little. But why does it have to be you? Why do *you* have to kill him?"

"I'm the only one who can, Joe. All the books of our series have built up to it. I'm the protagonist. I'm the child of destiny."

"Books can have surprise endings, you know."

"And when I do defeat Zolethos, I will bring what I know to the people of Corolathia. Then they will awaken. I will free them from the tyranny of Zolethos *and* Howard. My destiny is not gone, Joe. It has only become greater."

"That sounds dandy," said Joe, "Assuming you can keep from becoming dinner. I'll offer you this, though. It's valiant and all to go crusading for your people, but ask yourself from time to time whether they're the ones you're actually crusading for."

"What are you talking about?" Corbin fired an angry look.

"I mean, I've seen it happen where a man's quest becomes his identity. I'm not saying this is you, but I've certainly known people. If it weren't for your Zolethos character, then what? Would you know who you were? You got to check yourself from time to time. Is your quest to rid the world of a wicked tyrant? Or is your quest to have a quest?"

"You're a fool," said Corbin. "You know nothing. I have the mark of destiny."

"So? You got a birthmark. What of it?"

"It's more than that, Joe. It drives me. It echoes in my mind. It wakes me at night. When I close my eyes, I can see it behind my eyelids. It's so easy for the rest of you to walk away. Don't you understand I can't?"

Joe nodded. "So, there it is. Howard's plot device is still pushing your buttons."

"I didn't mean it that way. Even without the mark, I'd still feel the same. I wouldn't walk away."

"Suit yourself. You're right about one thing, though. I am a fool. I had more than I ever realized. And it was right in front of me. I didn't see it. For the first time in my life, I met people with their own free will. And with their own free will, they chose me out of all the characters they could have picked. I'll never know why." With his manacled hands, he reached into his pocket and withdrew Kribble's last gift. It was the worst specimen of photography he had ever seen. And in these last hours, it was his most prized possession. "Stupid, really. I just did what I always do. Old habits. I got lost in the plot and forgot about the people."

"Careful," said Corbin, "You're sounding like some authors I know."

Joe examined his photograph. Ellodrine and Aelrûn were standing on either side of him. Their necks and torsos, anyway. He wished he could look into Ellodrine's quixotically chromatic eyes one more time. Even if they were orangy-red. He could lose himself in those eyes. The entire image of the photograph was slanted. The tragedy was that Kribble had been on the wrong side of the camera when the picture snapped. Joe took a slow breath. Then he gasped. "What? WHAT? That sneaky little dwarf! He did this on purpose!"

Corbin looked up from his drawings.

Jaime dashed in from the adjoining room. Her shotgun was in her hands. "Shut up!" she half-shouted, half-whispered. "You're going to bring them right to us! What's wrong?"

"Kribble!"

"What happened?" asked Corbin.

"Look." Joe flicked the photograph onto the floor next to Corbin.

Corbin picked it up and examined it. "What am I looking at?"

"Me," said Joe, "Take a good look at me."

Jaime scoffed at his apparent vanity.

Corbin made a sideways face at him, but it vanished as understanding took hold. "Is that what I think it is?"

"It's a travel rune," said Joe, "On my amulet. Plain as could be."

Corbin smiled. "He planted this on you."

"Even spit on it to hide the amulet from Zolethos."

"Gross!" said Jaime.

"But ingenious," said Joe. "That's why Zolethos didn't see it. He gave us a way out of here. Corbin, can you copy it?"

"Watch me."

"Wait," said Jaime, "What's going on? What's a travel rune? This is supposed to get us out of the hotel?"

"Better," said Joe.

"Out of the city?"

"But we need a library to make it work," said Joe.

"What? Why? How does that—"

"Too many questions. We don't have time. Where is the closest library?"

"Miles away. We'd never make it."

"Not a problem. We can make a library. Where can we get books?"

"There's a book in the other room. I gave it to Lisa to read. I guess whoever rented this room brought it with them."

"Are there any others?" asked Corbin. "We'll need more than one."

"I don't know. I don't think so. What does this have to do with—"

"Questions!" said Joe. "Okay, so these people brought a book with them. Odds are there are others who did the same. We might find some if we raid the other rooms. If we could just get into the other rooms."

Jaime pulled a small plastic card out of her belt. "It's a master key. I took it off one of the cleaning ladies after she tried to take a bite out of me. That's how we got into the room upstairs."

"Perfect!" A half-smile crept across Joe's face. "This might actually work."

"No." Jaime pulled the key back. "We are not going out there with hundreds of zombies until somebody explains."

Joe ignored her and turned to Corbin. "How many books do you think it will take?"

"I'm not sure," said Corbin. "As many as we can get, I suppose."

"Are you listening to me?" said Jaime, "I said we're not going to—"

"We heard you," said Joe. "Look, what if I told you this was our only real way out, but I don't know how to explain it to you in a way you'll believe?"

"Try." She pumped her shotgun for emphasis.

Joe sighed. "Okay, imagine the world was... No, let me try this a different way. Say you're reading a book you don't want to finish. You want to read a different book, instead... Hmm... I don't know if this is any better. All right, what if—"

"What the hell!" Jaime brought the shotgun up with the wrong end pointed at Joe's face.

"Whoa, whoa, whoa! Take it easy!"

"Not you," said Jaime.

Joe heard a thud on the windowsill behind him. An icy chill ran down his spine. He spun around.

"Joe," said the intruder with a nod, "Corbin. Ma'am."

"Evening, Captain," said Joe, "Good to see you're still alive."

"For the time being," said Cortega. His skin was clammy and had lost some of its color. His eyes were bloodshot. A gaping wound on his shoulder bled down into his uniform.

"Get out of the way, Joe," said Jaime. "I've got to do it. He's going to turn."

"Put the gun away," said Joe, "He's not dead yet."

"He's a dead man walking, Joe. Get out of the way."

"You can't shoot him yet."

"I most certainly can."

"He saved your life."

"I'll shoot you both if you make me, Joe."

"It's okay, Joe," said Cortega. "I knew the risks when I stayed behind."

"You stay out of this," said Joe. He met Jaime's gaze. "I'm not moving."

Her eyes narrowed. "I'm giving you to the count of three."

Joe shrugged.

"I don't think she's joking," said Corbin.

"Yeah?" said Joe, "Neither am I."

"One," said Jaime.

Joe stepped forward. The barrel of the gun hovered inches from his chest.

"Two. I'm not bluffing, Joe."

Joe began to whistle *The Girl from Ipanema*.

"Don't make me do it, Joe."

He gave her a sly wink. "Say it. Go on. You know what's next."

Jaime bit her lip. Her nostrils flared.

"I'll say it for you," said Joe.

"Please move."

"Three."

Howard
I've got contact from Corbin. He says he and Joe are pinned down in a hotel.

Raymond
Did he mention Cortega? Is he still with them?

Howard
He said nothing about Cortega. I'm sorry, Raymond. I wish I knew.

Raymond
Never mind. I've been trying to contact this Kevin Jacobson. He's not responding to emails. I can't find a phone number for him either. And now your necromancer is bringing Circe into the paradox.

Howard
She was supposed to blow the ship up! Why did you let them talk, Raymond?

Raymond
I didn't *let* them talk, Howard. They're bad guys. They have to gloat before they kill people. I had no way of stopping it.

Howard
This was a bad idea. We shouldn't be adding antagonists to this. It's already way out of control.

Raymond
Just remember I fought this. You guys voted against me. I said it was risky.

Ben
We're all to blame. None of us gets to wash our hands of this.

Raymond
I'll accept that. But you two mostly!

Ben
No. Me mostly.

Howard
You can't say that, Ben. You don't get to shoulder this yourself.

Ben
Have either of you ever killed a character you shouldn't have?

Raymond
You mean other than the travesty we're committing right now?

Ben
It was never my intention; you know. I didn't want to kill her.

Howard
Is this about Lily?

Ben
She wasn't supposed to be modeled after anyone. I wrote her in the first novel before I'd even met Rebecca. But you pull from what you know. It wasn't long before Lily started picking up Rebecca's mannerisms. Her odd phrases. After a while, I couldn't picture her without seeing Rebecca's face. And that's why I did it, Howard. I couldn't handle seeing her anymore. Maybe Joe is right. Maybe I am a murderer.

Raymond
Are you going somewhere with this, or are you just wallowing?

Ben
And I'm doing it again. Raymond, you were right.

Raymond
What are you saying, Ben? Are you shifting your position?

Howard
You picked a fine time to change your mind. You know, the only reason I went along with this is you convinced me it was the right thing to do. We can't take it back. We now have a psychotic computer woman to deal with in addition to a megalomaniacal necromancer.

Ben
Okay, Howard. You're right. Everything I said before is wrong. And I'm sorry. You shouldn't have listened to me.

Howard
What are you proposing, Ben? Even if we consider these characters real people, you said we were sacrificing hundreds for billions. Are you saying now it should be the other way around?

Ben
I'm saying it's not for us to play God. We don't get to decide the value of peoples' lives. We also don't get to let math decide it for us. Raymond is right. Lives don't have a numerical value. We only like to see it that way because it helps us sleep at night.

Howard
As a writer, I appreciate that. But what do you suggest we do?

Ben
I suggest we save the hundreds and the billions.

Raymond
How?

Ben
We're writers. We're creative. Start thinking. Use everything we've got. We go for broke. Operation: Happy Ending.

Raymond
Very little is under our control.

Ben
Then we've got to make our resources count. Raymond, what if we send in the cavalry? Are there other Astral Navy ships?

Raymond
Already tried that. It didn't take. Previous chapters state the Ghost Nebula is weeks away from any Intergalactic Union space. The book is holding me to it. I've still got control of the nebula.

Howard
No good. The storm isn't climactic enough. It's atmosphere at this point.

Ben
Come on, guys. Between the three of us, we've got to come up with something.

Howard
All right, Ben. We're thinking.

Raymond
What happened, Ben? Why did you change your mind?

Ben
I saw things from a new angle is all. I had a little help putting the pieces together. But we owe it to them. Plain as that.

CHAPTER THIRTY-FOUR

+++

Ghost Nebula

The nebula storm raged silently over the surface of the *Galactic Explorer*. The dead quiet of space swallowed whatever noise might accompany red-purple bolts of lightning as they struck the hull.

Two figures in antique NASA spacesuits clambered along the exterior of the ship. Each wore a harness with supple metallic cables attached. At the ends of the cables, magnetic discs clung to the hull. They progressed like mountain climbers, launching one end of the cable ahead until the disc on the end caught hold, then pulling themselves along hand over hand.

"I THINK I'M GOING TO BE SICK," shouted Kribble, "THIS IS THE STUPIDEST THING I'VE EVER DONE. AND I'VE DONE SOME VERY STUPID THINGS."

"Do not expel vomit into your helmet," said Xane. "Also, there is no need to shout. The communicator in your helmet is quite sensitive. Standard volume is sufficient. The entry hatch to the bridge is just ahead. I assure you I am no more comfortable in your thin friend's spacesuit."

"Why did he get the fun job?" asked Kribble. "He gets to stay inside and kill greblins while we're out here?"

"He still showed signs of intoxication. I could not entrust this mission to him. In addition, it was imperative I accompany you since I alone know the way."

"I'm just saying. I didn't like this plan when I thought we were going to be *in* the escape pod. If I had known we'd be hanging off the outside of the ship, you'd have never talked me into it."

"That's why I didn't tell you," said Xane. "The pod was a decoy. It served its purpose. Would you prefer to have been inside it?"

A bolt of red-purple lightning struck the hull twenty feet to their left.

"I don't know," said Kribble. "It's a toss-up for me."

"With luck, we will have the element of surprise. They believe we are dead."

"They might not be wrong if we don't get out of this storm soon."

"You complain much for a warrior."

"About average for a dwarf, though."

.   .   .

Aelrûn stared at the dead greblin at his feet. An arrow shaft protruded from its eye. He shook his head.

"Nice shooting, handsome," said Isabelle, "I always did like a man in uniform." She ran her hand along his chest. Xane's charcoal gray uniform hung loosely over his lithe form.

"Stop it." He grasped her hand between two fingers and removed it.

She frowned at him. "We're winning. Why are you so grumpy?"

"I'm trying to lead a revolt. It is difficult to maintain the respect of these men when my speech is slurred and my aim is off."

"What are you talking about? It was a perfect shot. You hit him right in the eye."

"But I was aiming at the one next to him." He held his hand out. It quivered. "Look at that. I can't feel my fingertips."

"That's what you're upset about? Your fingertips are numb? Most men wouldn't be standing after what I've done to you."

"I thought you were with Corbin now."

"Corbin left me here."

"Think I won't?"

"It'll be difficult if you can't walk straight."

Aelrûn closed his eyes and slowed his breathing. "Leave me. The next wave could come at any moment. I must prepare myself."

"When you try to send me away, it only makes me want you more. Besides, why hold out here? Why not try to reach the bridge ourselves? We could make it."

"We're a decoy. We are drawing their forces to give Xane and Kribble a chance to confront Zolethos. This is a choke point that gives us a tactical advantage. Remember, Zolethos's forces are not small. They vastly outnumber us."

"Sounds dangerous." Isabelle feigned a shiver.

"It is dangerous." His eyes popped open, "That's why I need to prepare myself."

"We could die here." Isabelle furrowed her perfectly sculpted eyebrow.

"Yes."

"This could be our last night on Earth."

"We're not *on* Earth."

Isabelle drew closer. "What would you do if this were your last night to live?"

"Try not to get killed."

"Know what I would do?"

"Leave the elf alone and go away?"

Isabelle laughed playfully. Several Astral Navy cadets within earshot became mildly buzzed at the sound. She looked deeply into his eyes and leaned forward, her nose almost touching his.

He could feel the soft touch of her breath against his face. Her eyes were large and round and lined with long lashes. They were deep and enticing. He tried to look away. His body would not obey. Her eyes grew larger by the second, like the bottom of a long fall as one plummets toward it. He had not noticed her inching closer until he felt her lips against his own. They tasted sweetly of wine. An electrical surge moved down his spine into the ends of his toes.

Without knowing what he was doing, he grasped her into his arms and lost himself in the kiss's passion. A tingling sensation spread quickly through his body. Tension melted away from his muscles as he welcomed total inebriation.

CHAPTER THIRTY-FIVE

+++

Viva Lost Vegas

Jaime wondered, thrusting her gun into Trixie's hand, whether she had finally lost her mind.

"Wait, I don't understand what's happening," said Trixie. "Why are we going out there with the dead things?"

"You're not going anywhere," explained Jaime for the third time. "You're staying here with Doug and Lisa, and *that's* why I'm giving you a gun."

"But why are you giving it to *me?*"

"You don't want it? I can give it to Doug. But when zombies are knocking down the door, remember I offered it to you first."

"Okay, okay. I'll take it. But why are you going out there?"

Jaime sighed. "I wish I knew."

"Aw, give us a little credit, Officer Cruz," said Joe. "I know it seems strange now, but it really will work. Okay, Doug and Corbin are working on a project back there since they're the best artists. You and Lisa stay out here in the main room and keep your eyes open."

"I didn't know Doug was an artist," said Trixie.

"Apparently, he designs T-shirts for a living. Who knew?"

"What about him?" Trixie gestured to Cortega. "He doesn't look so good."

"We're keeping him with us," said Jaime. "That way when he turns, I can take care of him personally."

"Wouldn't have it any other way," said Cortega. He gave a salute with the fire poker Corbin had loaned him.

"All right," said Jaime, "Here is how it's going to be. I call the shots. No questions asked. I expect you both to be silent. The last thing we want is to bring the horde upstairs down on our heads. I'm hoping we made enough commotion up there that we drew them away from this floor. The first sign of trouble, we abort the mission, and I don't want to hear another word about it. Remember gentlemen, the only reason I'm humoring you is I find it preferable to waiting for death. And the only reason you two are still alive is it would have been too loud to shoot you. Next time I won't bother counting to three. Are we understood?"

"You're the boss," said Joe with an infuriating wink.

"Good."

"Was she really going to shoot you?" asked Trixie in a whisper that was too loud for Jaime not to hear.

"Nah," said Joe, "She likes me too much to shoot me. I can tell by the way she didn't shoot me. Besides, heroic types like her can't do that stuff. It's in the rules."

"Keep telling yourself that," said Jaime. She cracked the door and peeked out into the corridor. The lights flickered, but the hallway appeared to be empty. She motioned the all-clear to the two men behind her and slipped out the doorway. Once they were all three in the hall, she motioned for Cortega to take point. She pointed two fingers at her eyes to let him know she would be watching him very closely. He nodded.

They moved to the room directly across. Jaime slid her card through it, and it responded with a small click. She winced at the sound. She opened the door an inch and peered inside. She detected no movement. She pulled the door open the rest of the way and pointed her shotgun at the empty room beyond.

"Pay dirt," whispered Joe. He moved toward a luggage case and dumped it on the floor. Amid rumpled articles of clothing was a book with a green cover advertising the ultimate system to *Triple Your Winnings in Vegas!*

"Captain," whispered Jaime, "Check the bedroom."

He tightened his grip on the fire poker and disappeared into the next room.

When he was gone, she turned to Joe. "You know there's no hope for your friend. Even if your plan does get us out of the hotel—and I don't believe for a second that it will—your friend is dead where he stands."

"He stayed back for us," said Joe. "If you're suggesting we just leave him here, you and I are going to have ourselves a little controversy."

Jaime let out a slow breath. "I understand what he did, and it says a lot for him. He's a hero. But he knew what it meant, staying behind like that. It was a death sentence, and there's nothing you or I can do to change that. Just because he's your friend doesn't mean he won't turn like everybody else."

"I'm not quite ready to give up on him. There might be a cure someday."

"He doesn't have *someday*. He has less than twenty minutes. Even if there is a cure a hundred years from now, it won't do him any good."

"Then again," said Joe, "A hundred years from now might be just around the corner." He winked at her again.

She hated that wink. "I'm not hopeful."

Cortega returned from the bedroom. The whites of his eyes had yellowed noticeably in the short time he was gone, but he insisted he was fine. He reported the bedroom had no further reading material. Jaime poked her head out into the hallway.

"All clear. Let's check the next one."

•   •   •

"What was that?" Trixie pointed Jaime's gun at the door with shaky hands.

"I didn't hear anything," said Lisa. "I think you're just jumpy."

"I don't know." Trixie stared down the barrel and tried to aim at a fixed point on the door. The tip of the barrel danced around it. "I could have sworn I heard something."

"Maybe it's Officer Cruz out in the hall," said Lisa.

"Yeah? Or maybe it isn't."

"I think you should stop pointing that gun at the door. What if you accidentally shoot them when they come back?"

Trixie shook her head. "But if it's zombies, I got to be ready for them. Do you think we should have come up with some kind of secret knock or something?"

"I think we'll be able to tell if it's zombies or not."

. . .

Joe wondered how long their luck would hold out.

The second room was devoid of undead occupants, but equally devoid of books. In the third room was a travel guide and a biography of Winston Churchill. In the fourth was an e-reader with a locked screen, but they took it anyway.

Inside the fifth, they moved through their unspoken routine. Cortega checked the bedroom while Joe and Jaime scoured the main area. The rooms were spacious with lots of little nooks to check. Joe peeked into the bathroom, but the only reading material was the back of a miniature shampoo bottle.

As he arrived back into the main room, he noticed Jaime sifting through a suitcase on the couch. By the frown on her face, he guessed she was not having much luck. Further on, something more foreboding caught his eye. It was Cortega. He was standing just inside the doorway to the bedroom. His back was to Joe. He was not moving.

"Captain," whispered Joe, "Captain, is everything all right?"

No response. He stood motionless with his eyes fixed ahead. A chill ran up Joe's spine. How long had they been searching? Had they waited too long? He took a step toward the captain.

"What's wrong?" asked Jaime. She must have seen it in his face.

Joe nodded toward Cortega. "I've got to check on him." He moved forward with slow, steady strides.

Jaime turned her head to follow his gaze. "Oh, shit!"

Joe shushed her. He took a few more steps. "Captain." No response. He shook his head at himself. How many times had he complained about characters in movies always walking toward the thing they should be running away from? "In for a penny," he muttered to himself. He took another step.

"Oh, shit! Oh, shit!" Jaime whispered behind him.

He glanced back. Her shotgun was in position, and he found himself again between her and the captain. He held his cuffed hands out to her with open palms. "We got to know for sure."

"Joe," she mouthed back, "Don't make me do it! It's too late for him."

"Take us both out then. You do what you need to do. I'll do what I need to do." They stared each other down for maybe ten seconds. The longest ten seconds of his life.

Finally, she whispered, "If he bites you, I won't hesitate."

Joe nodded. He continued his slow approach toward the captain. When he was within reach, he extended his bound hands and tapped him on the shoulder. Slowly, Cortega turned his head. Joe braced himself for the worst. Cortega's face came into view. He opened his mouth and let out a low, "shhh."

Cortega gestured with his head at something. Joe followed his gaze to a woman sitting upright in the bed. She was leaning back on the headboard. Her eyes were open and vacant. Her chest displayed no signs of breathing. Her skin had an unhealthy pallor, and her neck was bent at an angle that was uncomfortable to look at. In her lap, she held an open hardcover book.

"Is she a zombie?" whispered Joe.

"Can't tell," said Cortega.

Joe stood motionless next to Cortega. He could only imagine what they must look like to Jaime, but he suddenly felt very hesitant to make any stirring at all. "I'm going to go for it."

"It should be me," said Cortega. "I'm already bitten."

"But I'm sneakier." Joe stepped into the room. The carpet crunched under his footsteps in a way one can only hear when one is trying to be silent. He shifted his eyes back and forth between the corpse and the floor in front of him. He could swear she was staring at him, but he gave it up as an optical illusion. Still, it was difficult to ignore. After what seemed an eternity, but was probably only about a minute, he arrived within reach of the open book.

In his periphery, he saw Jaime had joined Cortega at the door. He fixed his eyes upon the dead woman's face as he reached for the volume. His fingers came into contact with the pages. Slowly, he pulled it from her grasp. He felt some resistance at first, but the book soon slid from her fingertips.

The next several seconds were like a slow-motion movie. First, he heard a shot ring out. He braced himself for the impact. Jaime must have decided he was a lost cause. He felt no pain. He ran his eyes over himself. He was not bleeding anywhere.

He looked back up at Jaime. Her shotgun was pointing to the floor, and she looked as perplexed as he was. Her face soured, and she muttered something under her breath. It was too low for Joe to make out, but he was pretty sure he caught the words *Trixie* and *gun* nested among some colorful obscenities. Jaime's sour face quickly gave way to an expression of alarm, and she snapped her shotgun into place, ready to fire.

Joe heard something shift next to him. He turned his attention back to the bed. A pair of dead blue eyes stared into his gaze. And it was *no* optical illusion.

CHAPTER THIRTY-SIX

+++

Ghost Nebula

"Lies!" shouted Circe, "These are all lies!"

"Why would I make this up?" said Zolethos, "If I were going to lie to you, do you think this is what I'd come up with?"

Circe had no response.

Zolethos rubbed his temples. "It's true, or it isn't. You can count down the seconds until you kill us all but consider this. If what I showed you is true, your Raymond Larson will be sitting at a desk somewhere with a smug little grin on his face while your charred remains float through oblivion."

Circe said nothing, but the diminishing countdown slowed to a halt at five minutes and thirty-six seconds.

Zolethos's lips twisted into a smile. "Excellent choice."

Another volley of lightning from the storm outside shook the ship.

"That you, Howard?" shouted Zolethos at the ceiling, "You lose again. You know the first thing I'm going to do when I meet you face to face? I'm going to—"

"I did not stop the sequence because I believe you," said Circe.

"Oh?" Zolethos tilted his head.

"I am merely giving you time to validate your claim. I do not accept fictitious prose as evidence."

"You think I wrote these books myself in case a woman in a computer ever wanted to blow me up, is that it?"

"I will not be subject to your ridicule!" Her compound voice blasted through every speaker and communicator on the bridge. "I offer you the chance to appease me. Do not mock my generosity!"

"Do I seem a person who worries about appeasing anybody? You're the one who assimilates information at a rate that simians like myself can only dream. Make a judgment. You can be an author's pawn, or you can be the prodigious queen you claim to be. But I won't grovel."

Circe's unblinking face was devoid of emotion. The pirates glanced nervously at one another. Circe did not move or speak.

"What's the matter?" said Zolethos, "Can't decide? Don't have an algorithm to process dreams and desires? Let me help you. Two artifacts we need. One is in hand. The other is a bookshelf away. Then the World Where the Books Are Written will be ours for the taking. We will conquer it with the stuff of their own nightmares because that's what we are. We are their shadows. We are the monsters in their closets. We are the darkest parts of themselves. What do you say?"

Circe flickered on the screen. She opened her mouth to respond, but she was interrupted by the sound of blaring alarms. Red lights flashed. The digits on the display blipped as they recommenced their ominous passage.

Zolethos clenched his gauntleted fists. "What? Is that really your decision?"

Circe shook her head. "It is not. I am being overridden."

"Who could...?" Zolethos issued a throaty growl. He turned to the sound of clattering keys behind him.

Ellodrine's fingers glided over the control console. "I won't let it happen. It was a mistake to forsake my own story. Corbin was right. It must end here."

"Die!" shouted a Rhodactian to Zolethos's left. It drew its weapon.

"No!" shouted Zolethos. He raised a hand and projected a searing flame from his palm that consumed the pirate in a raging conflagration. Zolethos grasped his hand, still smoking, and cried out in agony.

Circe clicked her intangible tongue. "Your ruthless nature is diminished by your show of grief."

"It's not grief! I've burned my hand. My magic doesn't function properly here."

The remaining Rhodactians held their hands away from their weapons. "So, uh, you don't want us to kill her?" asked Rakshaw.

"Of course not! She hasn't told us where the second artifact is yet. Must minions be so mindless?"

Rakshaw checked the countdown. "Maybe just incapacitate her?"

Zolethos drew his flaming sword with his unsmoking hand. "You have no imagination, Rakshaw. I will deal with this." He held the weapon out so the burning point was level with Ellodrine's neck. He inched slowly forward. The blade inched with him. Ellodrine leaned away from it and stretched her hands to continue her work on the control console.

Zolethos pressed another inch.

She winced.

Inch.

Her fingertips could no longer extend far enough.

He continued to advance, his fiery eyes locked upon her.

She backed away from the sword point. A bead of sweat trickled down the side of her forehead. Her back thumped against the wall. She could retreat no further. She lifted her chin and swallowed hard.

Zolethos flashed her a wicked smile. He lowered the tip of his blade from her neck to her sternum. The point hovered half an inch from her chest. The front of her spacesuit smoldered at the heat. She pressed herself against the wall. Zolethos drove the weapon forward still, pushing the point into the spacesuit until it dug into the flesh beyond.

Ellodrine whimpered. Her irises paled.

Zolethos sneered at her. "When did you get so noble? You, who abandoned all of Corolathia to its pain? You, who left Corbin to continue his quest alone? You, who wanted to run away from it all?" He looked back at Circe. "The counter. If you don't mind."

Circe waved her arm. The digits slowed to a stop, now at four minutes and forty eight seconds. The alarm silenced, and the red lights stopped flashing.

Zolethos brought his attention back to Ellodrine. "Let's discuss the whereabouts of that artifact, shall we?" He twisted the blade in his hand with a slow and deliberate movement.

Ellodrine closed her eyes and let out a choked cry. She bit her bottom lip to stifle it. A small red bead formed and crept down her chin. With great effort, she shook her head from side to side.

"No?" He pressed the point harder.

She inhaled sharply. The blood drained from her face. Her fingers dug into the wall behind her until they were white at the tips. The small tuft of hair that she had tucked behind her ear came loose and dangled again in her eyes.

"Heroic or not, let's see how much you'll take when you have your own free will to contend with. Will you hold out when an author isn't pulling your strings?" Zolethos drew the blade lower, extending the cut down her sternum. His foot shifted and nudged something on the floor. He looked down. It was a small yellow scroll. He growled at the nearest Rhodactian, who took the hint and retrieved it for him. Zolethos grasped it, flipped it open, and perused its contents.

"What is it?" asked Circe.

Zolethos chuckled. "Howard. He's bargaining with me now. He's offering to write me a new novel with anything I could imagine if I'll only let his precious characters go back to Corolathia." He clicked his tongue. "What about me, Howard? Aren't I one of your precious characters too?"

"Howard can hear you?" asked Circe.

"He's reading our dialog. Somewhere in the World Where the Books Are Written."

"It's okay, Howard," said Ellodrine with a strained voice, "You don't have to save me. Just let him finish it, and it will be all over. He'll never find the artifact without me."

Zolethos crumpled the paper. "No deals, Howard. Shadow worlds aren't enough for me anymore. I'll make her talk, and then I'll come for you. After that, I could write any novel I want. And my imagination is far greater than yours."

"Blow the ship, Howard!" cried Ellodrine. "It's all right. I sounded the alarm. The other characters will escape."

Zolethos's smile vanished. "The alarm? Of course! You conniving little..." He turned his head toward Circe.

Her eyes grew wide. "It is true. I detect the launch of several escape pods from the G Deck."

"The prisoners!" Zolethos turned back to Ellodrine. She offered him a weak smile.

"There is more," said Circe, "I sense heavy activity from the telepad chamber."

· · ·

The telepad chamber was in utter chaos. Greblins packed themselves into a room that could barely hold their numbers. They shouted and fought amongst themselves.

"What's going on?" asked Paskal.

"The red-fleshed creatures fled like dogs to their ship," said a large fierce-looking greblin, "The hunt-lords wish to follow, but the machine wants *co-ordi-nates*. We know not how to give *co-ordi-nates*."

Paskal's head throbbed. He had awakened amid several dead greblins to red lights and blaring alarms. A nauseatingly calm voice from—Paskal knew not where—explained that the ship would be destroyed soon and everyone on board should begin evacuation procedures. Whatever those were. He had found Thork slumped against the wall with blood streaming down his forehead and a wide grin plastered on his face. Paskal slipped through the Astral Navy cadets who were busy loading into closets with the word ESCAPE marked overhead. He then followed the commotion of greblin voices until they brought him here.

"What do *co-ordi-nates* look like?" he asked the fierce-looking greblin.

"Numbers. Maybe letters, too. But which ones? We know not."

"What about those?" Paskal pointed to the shelves of slender reading devices lining the telepad.

"What about them?"

"There are numbers on the sides. The *Du-ee De-ci-mels*. Maybe those are *co-ordi-nates*."

The fierce-looking greblin inspected them through his sneer. "Yes. YES! The *Du oo De ci meld* Paskal is right. We must use the *Du-ee De-ci-mels*!"

· · ·

"Cowards!" shouted Zolethos, "All of them, cowards!"

"Like squealing piglets who are only good for slaughter," said an ugly hunt-lord with a misshapen nose that must have recently been broken.

Some Rhodactians inched their way toward the doors of the transport lift. Zolethos eyed them darkly. They shrunk beneath his gaze and returned to their stations.

"Do not envy them!" said Zolethos. "They abandon me in the very hour of my triumph. They shall have no part in my coming empire. I will hunt them down to a one and kill them at my leisure. And I will do the same to any of you who walks through those doors." He pointed at the transport lift.

As if on cue, it opened with a swish. Zolethos cocked his head.

Two astronauts in antique NASA spacesuits burst into the room. Slung over their shoulders were gray duffle bags. In each fist, they clutched a blazing incapacitator. The shortest astronaut fired parallel beams into Zolethos's chest, throwing him back several feet.

Ellodrine slumped to the floor, placed a hand upon her singed sternum, and gasped for breath. "Kribble!"

CHAPTER THIRTY-SEVEN

+++

Viva Lost Vegas

She would have been beautiful once. Wavy blond hair. Full lips. Blue eyes that were undoubtedly lovely before they were bloodshot and jaundiced. Now they only cast an empty stare. She had not seemed to take any notice of Joe before, but whatever gunshot sounded must have roused her. She lifted herself and leaned over the side of the bed. Her mouth opened as though preparing for a kiss.

It seemed like a stranger's hands clasping the book that smashed into her face, but Joe soon realized they were his own. He clobbered her repeatedly in a slow retreat. Most of the blows only glanced off her. Joe had never fought someone who could not feel pain. She rose to her feet and lunged with grasping hands.

"Joe, move out of the way!"

Not wanting to spurn good advice, Joe ducked and rolled to the side. A shotgun blast threw his pursuer off her feet and back onto the bed. She was now sprawled out across the mattress with her head hanging off the far side. She struggled with jerky movements.

Joe regained his feet next to Jaime and Cortega. "Who started shooting?"

Jaime shook her head. "Not me! Other than Blondie just now. But not the one that woke her up. It has to be Trixie in the other room."

"No need to be subtle now," said Joe. "Let's get out of here."

They spilled into the hallway in a fight-or-flight frenzy. Down the corridor, they could see frontrunners of the enormous horde from above staggering down the stairs. A cacophony of undead wailing rolled down the hall.

Jaime slid her card key into the slot. As she opened the door, another shot sounded. Joe and Jaime dropped to the floor. A shower of splinters rained down on their heads. "Damn it, Trixie!"

"I'm sorry!" Smoke wafted from the barrel of the gun in Trixie's hands. "I thought you were a zombie!"

"Zombies don't use key cards!"

"I was scared! I didn't hit you, though. Right?"

Jaime leaped from the floor, darted across the room, and snatched the gun from Trixie's grip. "Next time I'm going to leave the nine-year-old in charge."

Joe gathered the books he and Jaime had dropped and deposited them onto the loveseat. "Corbin! We've got the books, but we're going to be up to our necks in zombies if you don't have those travel runes ready!"

Corbin appeared from the back room. "We're just finishing the last ones. Here." He held out several small papers with travel runes drawn upon them. Into each one was a crudely torn hole through which he had threaded frayed ribbons that looked like and probably were once part of the bedsheets.

Cortega locked the door behind him and frowned. "Those are supposed to get us back to my ship?"

Joe snatched one from Corbin's hand and looped it over Cortega's head. "Don't care if they're pretty so long as they function.

Lisa shrieked. "You've been shot!" She was pointing at Cortega.

He examined himself. A bullet wound stained his shoulder. He gave his arm a test rotation. It seemed unhindered, if a little stiff.

Trixie's eyes grew wide. "Oh, no! It wasn't me, was it?"

"That's the least of our worries," said Jaime. "Captain Uniform didn't even feel that, did you, Captain?"

"Get me back to my ship," said Cortega. "I'll be fine, or I'll make sure that Zolethos isn't."

A loud bang sounded upon the door. It was followed by several others which quickly multiplied against the wall.

"They're here," said Joe.

Jaime pumped her shotgun. "That sounds like a lot more than last time."

"I'm sorry," said Trixie. "While you were gone, I heard a thump outside. I thought it was one of them. That's why I fired the gun."

"I told her it came from upstairs," said Lisa.

Trixie melted onto the floor. "It startled me. I'm sorry! I'm so, so sorry!"

"You may have just killed us all," said Jaime, "But don't take it too hard. We probably didn't have much longer, anyway. Better start moving furniture."

The banging on the walls grew louder. Plaster crumbled away.

"We're out of time," said Joe, "Corbin, make sure everybody has a travel rune. Trixie, you and Lisa take these books to the bedroom and put them in order."

"What kind of order?"

"Whatever kind you want. Alphabetical by author, I guess."

Trixie nodded and gathered the books from the loveseat. She and Lisa disappeared into the bedroom.

Jaime watched them go. "They're really supposed to make a tiny library? I can't believe you talked me into this."

"I'll accept your apology in about five minutes," said Joe. "For now, how can I talk you out of that handgun?"

Jaime scowled, but she held it out to him.

The hammering on the wall grew. A basketball-sized section broke free, revealing a sea of undead faces beyond.

"Here we go," said Cortega, preparing his fire poker. He swung it into any faces that pressed through the hole.

Joe glanced at Jaime. She held her shotgun in position. "Officer Cruz, where is your travel rune?"

She kept her eyes down the barrel of her gun. "Are you referring to that stupid piece of paper Shakespeare gave me? It's on the coffee table."

"Not going to do you much good there."

"When they find my body, I'd rather not be wearing a drawing on a string."

"Who's going to find the body? I thought you said they were going to level the city."

"Just the same."

"Look, just have a little faith there are mysteries in the world that you don't know about. At worst, you won't be any deader. At best, you listen to me say I told you so."

More plaster fell from the wall. The second hole was large enough for the zombies to crawl through, but high enough they could not do it gracefully. A throng of undead clambered through. Jaime fired into the crowd and sent several sprawling backward. "Come on, you ugly bastards! Come and get me."

Joe focused on stragglers that missed Jaime's warpath.

Trixie popped her head out of the bedroom. "Joe, we got a problem!"

"I'm busy. Are the books in order?"

"We don't know what to do with the e-reader. We were going by authors, but that one is locked, and we don't know what books are on it. Where should it go?"

"Whatever. Organize them by color, then!"

"Why are we doing this again?"

"Just do it!"

"Okay." Trixie disappeared again.

"See, Officer?" said Joe. "She doesn't understand it any more than you do, but she's not complaining."

Jaime pumped her shotgun and fired it once more, but it gave a dismaying click. Zombies spilled into the room. The hole was giving way to their numbers. It was now wide enough to accommodate several shambling invaders at a time. Jaime clubbed the ones closest to her. "Joe, give me back my gun."

"Not going to happen." Joe picked off her two most pressing assailants with a couple of head-shots.

Jaime rammed the stock of her shotgun into an undead vacationer in a Hawaiian shirt. "You are stealing an officer's gun, Joe. That is a felony offense."

"I'll take my chances with the judge." He nailed another one in the forehead just as it was grasping for her.

"Give me back my gun, Joe!"

"Put the travel rune around your neck."

She made an ugly face and smashed her weapon into the nearest gaping zombie face, this one wearing a lopsided toupee. She thrust her hand down onto the coffee table, snatched the drawing-on-a-string, and threw it over her neck. "There. Happy now? Give me back my gun!"

Joe picked off a few more zombies. "You misunderstood. I wasn't making a deal. I was just telling you to put on your travel rune. You're not getting the gun back."

"You know what, Joe? I hate you! I hate you so much! I should have shot you when I had the chance!"

Trixie burst into the room again. "Okay, does black come before red or after purple?"

CHAPTER THIRTY-EIGHT

+++

Ghost Nebula

Ellodrine clutched her singed sternum and swallowed her pain.

The bridge of the *Galactic Explorer* was a war zone. Rhodactians returned fire with red-beamed weapons, producing cascades of sparks wherever they struck. Greblins released black arrows that were far less spectacular, but just as lethal. The hunt-lord with the broken nose drew a curved blade and charged at the shortest astronaut, but before he could close the distance, the astronaut whipped off his fishbowl helmet and lobbed it into the greblin's face. The hunt-lord howled and dropped to the deck, grasping its nose with one clawed hand. Red streams trailed from beneath it.

Kribble grinned and slid under a web of weapon fire to where Ellodrine crouched on the floor. He gave her a sly wink. "Hope we didn't keep you waiting, Elle."

She allowed herself a wry smile. "I think Joe is rubbing off on you."

"Don't know what you're talking about, lady. Come on, we got to get some cover." He grasped her elbow and led her behind a nearby computer console. He reached over the top of it and sent a burst of laser fire at anything that moved.

"Oh no, Kribble! Look," said Ellodrine.

Kribble followed her gaze to Zolethos. The Dark Lord of the Void drew himself off the floor and placed his hand upon one of two hilts that protruded from his belt.

"No way," shouted Kribble, "I shot him in the chest! Twice! He should be kissing the floor right now. How is he doing that?"

"He is the antagonist of a twelve-book cycle," said Ellodrine. "It's going to take something much more climactic to take him down."

Kribble sent another burst of laser fire across the room. "There's some pretty stout Karthecian beer back on Deck G. That'd knock him on his ass!"

Zolethos was scanning the room looking for a target and settled on the second astronaut. With a roar, he charged, maneuvering through the firefight like an armored panther. In one swift movement, he lunged and drew the flaming sword from its scabbard.

His prey spun out of the way.

"Aelrûn!" shouted Ellodrine.

"Not actually," said Kribble. "Aelrûn stayed behind. He got the easy job."

"Then who is that?"

The astronaut ripped his helmet off and tossed it aside, revealing a gray reptilian face. Xane smiled and drew forth his own blade that sizzled with electricity.

"Do you think you have a chance against me?" said Zolethos, "A supporting character like you? Behold. I am epic. I will end you."

"A Karthecian spends his life in search of honorable death. As you can see, I have not yet found it."

With that, they both lunged. Their blades met in an elemental flash. The weapons crackled as they pressed into one another. Xane's knuckles paled as he tried to overpower his foe. Zolethos proved stronger and thrust him back.

Xane sprang away to catch his footing and launched into his foe again. Now he sent a flurry of lightning-fast attacks that defied the eye. Zolethos turned them all aside, though he lost several steps to Xane's advance.

Ellodrine shook her head. "We've got to blow the ship up. If I can make it to the control panel, maybe I can restart the countdown."

"Blow the ship up? And everything inside it? Us, for instance? Do you know what I went through to get here? This is a rescue mission."

Ellodrine looked at him with eyes deep and blue. "I'm sorry, Kribble. I never should have gotten you involved in this, but there is no other way. If Zolethos gets out of this book, he'll find his way into the World Where the Books Are Written, and he'll kill countless numbers of real people."

Kribble huffed. "We're real too! And by the way, you don't get to take all the credit for this mess. I found that book, same as you."

"Kribble, we can't win this. Look." She gestured to Zolethos.

He had recovered from Xane's onslaught with a murderous frenzy. He was no longer on the defense, but met the Karthecian's speed with blurring displays of swordsmanship. The blades themselves were lost to sight. Red and blue streaks sliced through the air and rebounded off one another. Zolethos was the stronger of the two, and he repeatedly threw Xane backward. Xane kept himself alive with his agility, but it would only be a matter of time before Zolethos wore him down.

Ellodrine placed a hand on Kribble's shoulder. "Kribble, it's our little unlived lives or billions of people in the other world. Our memories were written for us. Theirs really happened. They were children once. We never were. We can't put ourselves before them. Or the people of Corolathia. Or anybody."

Kribble pressed his lips together. "You better get a move on, then. I'll keep them off you."

He rolled out from behind the console, incapacitators blazing. It was effective. He instantly drew the return fire to himself. He maneuvered toward the nearest pirate, punched him in the face, and took him into a headlock. Using his captive as a living shield, he continued to fire at anybody foolish enough to pop his head into the open.

Ellodrine crawled toward the control console. She ducked behind it and took several slow breaths. Once she had steeled herself, she peeked over it and tapped out command codes. Intricate knowledge of the computer's pathways reverberated through her consciousness. Hacking into it would have been fairly simple, but she was trying to hack through Circe's will. And that was vastly more complex.

A familiar compound voice sounded from the speaker. "Are you trying to thwart me, little simian? You bypassed my defenses once. I was distracted. It will not happen again. I can calculate a billion, billion algorithms per second. Do you truly believe you can prevail against me with your feeble mind?"

"Bogglerot on your billion, billion algorithms. I've been through seven-and-a-half books, and I'm not about to put up with this from a pompous one-off villain like you."

Electronic laughter rose from the speaker. "You will never pass the gate, so long as I am the keeper."

"Do shut up, would you? I'm trying to focus." She looked over the console to check the progress of the epic dual across the bridge.

Zolethos had Xane backed against the wall. Xane turned the assault aside, but he had no more room to maneuver. Zolethos baited him with a feint. Xane lunged. Zolethos twisted out of the way and brought his flaming sword down upon Xane's mechanical arm, severing it halfway between the elbow and the shoulder.

The arm landed with a heavy thud on the deck. Severed wires spilled out and sparked. It still grasped the electrified blade in its metal fist. Zolethos kicked it out of reach. He smiled and raised his sword for the death stroke. Xane awaited it without flinching.

It never came.

Something flew across the room and imbedded itself in Zolethos's breastplate, knocking him off balance. His would-be fatal strike glanced off the wall. He looked down and wrenched the missile free. It was a dwarven throwing ax.

"That's right!" shouted Kribble across the bridge at him, "Things just took a turn south to ugly!"

Xane lost no time. With his opponent distracted, he thrust his remaining arm out with the speed of a striking viper and grasped the second hilt from Zolethos's belt. He drew it forth and readied it for battle. It was the weapon that had belonged to Corbin, and it mirrored the blazing sword in Zolethos's own hand.

"Again, little lizard? I've already taken your arm."

"That honor goes to a Karthecian marsh beast. You have merely taken my prosthetic."

"Let's see if I can do better."

"A Karthecian spends his life seeking honorable death. As—"

"Yes, yes. You haven't yet found it. Allow me to help you look." Zolethos launched into him with fiery fury. Their blades clashed in flurries of steel and flame. Xane remained mostly on the defense. He was only buying time now.

Kribble seemed to do no better. He had incapacitated just under half of Zolethos's remaining minions, but he was still outgunned and found himself pinned behind a sparking hunk of machinery.

Ellodrine's heart jumped as she saw the hunt-lord rise from the floor behind him. His bloodshot eyes locked onto the dwarf with the ginger beard. He strode through the gauntlet of laser fire. Kribble had not noticed him. The hunt-lord ran a finger across his blade to whet its appetite for blood.

"Behind you, Kribble!" shouted Ellodrine.

Kribble looked back.

At that moment, the transport lift opened with a swoosh. Every eye on the bridge, including the hunt-lord's, converged on a single Astral Navy officer stepping onto the bridge.

"You!" cried Circe, "Nathan Innes! The architect of my prison! You developed the virus with which Cortega sealed me in digital slumber!"

"Circe?" said Innes, ducking under several incoming beams. "What the hell is she doing here?"

Kribble made good use of the distraction. He thrust his head into the greblin's abdomen with a force that knocked its wind out and sent it off its feet.

While his opponent recovered, Kribble turned to Innes. "Shouldn't you have abandoned the ship?"

"I thought I'd do one better and override the self-destruct sequence."

"No, no, no. That's old news."

"What?" Innes crouched behind some scientific instruments. "You've already stopped it, then?"

Kribble sent a few counter-bursts across the bridge. "Not exactly. We're trying to restart it now."

"How does that help us?"

"Gives us good seats for the afterlife." Kribble tossed an incapacitator to Innes. "Here, make yourself useful."

Innes caught it and laid down suppressive fire.

"Mr. Innes!" shouted Ellodrine. "You're the ship's technical officer. I've read about you."

"Well, I have been published in several journals."

"That's not what I'm talking about. Never mind. I need your help. Circe is stopping the self-destruct sequence. We need to override it."

"Why would I do that? I have a hangover and I'm not sure whose side I'm on anymore."

"Innes!" shouted Xane, still clashing swords with Zolethos, "As your superior officer, I order you to do whatever Ellodrine requires of you."

"Do you realize they're asking me to blow up the ship?"

Xane, now singed in several places, leaped back from Zolethos's onslaught. "Is that the plan now?"

"Evidently," said Kribble.

"Very well. Do it." Xane threw himself once more into the fray.

Innes released a heavy sigh, fired several blasts across the room, and wriggled along the floor to the control panel. "Ellodrine, I presume."

"No time for introductions. We've got to break through Circe. I can't do it alone. If we could divide her between us..."

"A two-pronged attack."

Ellodrine nodded.

"We could try it." He turned to a second panel and typed in commands.

"Whatever you two are doing, could you do it quickly?" shouted Kribble. He was pinched between incoming weapon beams and the recovered hunt-lord. Dodging a sword swipe, Kribble tripped over something on the floor and landed hard on the deck. His remaining incapacitator skittered out of reach. The hunt-lord smiled with pointed yellow teeth. It brought its sword down in a savage two-handed strike.

Kribble grasped the nearest thing he could find—the loose object he had tripped over—and held it out blindly. The hunt-lord's blade glanced off of it. Kribble smiled. He was holding Xane's severed metal arm. Still clenched in the fist, Xane's electric sword crackled. Kribble thrust the tip into the hunt-lord's thigh. The resulting discharge threw his opponent sprawling across the room where he crashed against the transport lift.

The hunt-lord clambered to its feet, steadying itself against the doors. They opened, and he fell inside with a loud crash. They closed again, and he was gone from sight.

"Why did the transport lift open?" asked Innes.

Once again, all eyes converged.

"Hold," said Zolethos. He disengaged and left Xane panting against the wall.

"It was empty," said Rakshaw.

"No." Zolethos scanned the area with a piercing gaze. "Something is different. There is a presence that was not here before."

A radiant sword with a crystal blade filled the room with light. Grasping it was a figure in a gray cloak that Ellodrine could not believe she had not seen before. And he was not alone. Others stood at his side. Four of them altogether.

The figure with the radiant sword removed his hood to reveal a boyish face with clear blue eyes and sandy blond hair. "Zolethos," said Corbin, "Your reckoning is at hand."

CHAPTER THIRTY-NINE

+++

Ghost Nebula

The light from his sword cast an eerie glow on Corbin's face. "At last, I will see my destiny fulfilled."

Zolethos growled. "Adlander. You found your way back from your little sabbatical. Wherever did you find that gaudy utensil?"

Corbin leveled the crystal sword at his foe. "It was a gift. I picked it up in The Library on my way back here. Howard sends his regards."

"Does he now?" Zolethos prepared his own weapon. "Weren't there just three of you before?"

"Protagonists are like rabbits that way," said Joe, removing his hood. "They multiply."

"They don't matter, Zolethos," said Corbin, "This is our fight."

"I suppose you've been waiting some time for this, haven't you? Still, you are four books early. Shall we see what you can do?"

Corbin lunged. The light from his sword grew more intense. Their weapons sent flashes of red and white light across the bridge, creating a flickering strobe effect.

‖   ‖   •

The cloaked figure to Joe's left dashed across the bridge in the confusion and kneeled next to Xane. To Joe's right, the remaining figure removed her hood, spilling dark hair over her shoulders. She looked with open wonder at the bridge filled with greblins, alien pirates, and the digital witch on the display.

"Told you so," said Joe.

"... Yeah."

"Ready for duty, Officer?"

"Call me Jaime."

A laser struck the wall next to her and pulled her from her reverie. She and Joe darted behind the nearest terminal and returned fire, Joe with a handgun, Jaime with a curious weapon that resembled a complex crossbow with two diagonal bows that crossed one another in an X. She held it like a rifle and fired bolts that appeared to split in the air prior to impact, causing a wide radius of destruction.

"What?" shouted a gruff dwarven voice over the commotion. "Is that a Kholvarin scatterbolt pump-action crossbow? Howard never gave *me* one of those!"

Joe risked a glance over the console. "Kribble! You'll have to ask him for one on your next birthday. Howard wrote in for us all kinds of goodies. Corolathia-style stuff, anyway. A little old-fashioned. But he did leave us a magical key that got us out of those handcuffs."

"Took you long enough! Did you use the Photo-Graph?"

"Kribble, you're a genius! You had me fooled. I thought you were really mad at me."

"Mad? I'm thrilled. I just pulled a con with Joe-bloody-Slade! And it *worked!* But we can talk about that when we're not being shot at."

"Agreed."

A swishing sound interrupted them. Joe looked back. The transport lift doors had opened again. The hunt-lord with a broken nose stepped out. It pointed a clawed finger at Joe. "You! You're the one who stole my trophies!"

"Oh, I remember you. Didn't recognize you without a brick in your face."

The greblin spat a wad of red-tinted gunk on the deck. "I will hang you by your ankles and let the crows pick at your liver. I will inspire such pain in you. I will send you to the farthest brink of suffering no mortal has ever known."

Joe shrugged and emptied his last clip into the hunt-lord's chest. It crumpled to the deck. Joe frowned at his empty weapon. "Guess that's it for that." He tossed it aside.

"Wait," said Kribble, "I've got your gun!" He snatched up the gray duffle bag and dug around inside. His hand emerged with Joe's old revolver. He tossed it over.

Joe snatched it out of the air. "Thanks. I owe you."

"Go help Ellodrine. She's by the main button-pushy thing."

Joe nodded and turned in the direction Kribble indicated. Jaime and Kribble sent enough firepower across the bridge that pirates and greblins were very reluctant to come out from hiding. Joe found it relatively simple to make his way to Ellodrine and Innes at the main console. Beads of sweat rolled down their faces as they rapidly tapped in command codes.

•　　•　　•

Cortega kneeled next to Xane and removed his hood. "I am pleased to see you haven't found your honorable death yet."

"I am still looking for it, Captain. Welcome back."

"Thank you, Xane. Do I want to know why Circe is on the display?"

"It's been a long day, Captain."

Cortega nodded. "You don't know the half of it. I have a necromancer to deal with. Your sword, Xane. That's an order."

Xane huffed and placed the hilt of the flaming sword in Cortega's outstretched hand. "Do not find your death before I find mine, Captain."

"I'll do my best." Cortega turned toward Zolethos and Corbin, engaged in their epic duel.

Zolethos must have caught sight of him coming. He grasped the hilt of his sword with both hands and pulled them apart as Corbin had once done aboard the *Blood Horizon*, creating two identical flaming scimitars. He was a master. He deflected the dual onslaught of Cortega and Corbin, though he began to lose ground.

"It is Cortega!" shouted Circe with her compound voice. "At last, my vengeance will be complete!"

•　　•　　•

Joe placed a hand on Ellodrine's shoulder.

She started, then looked up at him. "Joe! I can't believe you made it back."

"Careful, Elle. You almost sound happy to see me." He gave her a shrewd wink.

She frowned. "You shouldn't have come, Joe. We have to blow up the ship."

"What? Absolutely not. I didn't come all this way for a suicide run."

Innes ran a hand across his brow. "You see? This is what I've been saying, but they're not taking it from me!"

Ellodrine shook her head. "There's no other way."

"We'll see about that." Joe nodded toward Corbin and Cortega, still locked in fiery combat with Zolethos. "Your boy Corby's bound to win, right? He was *written* to win."

"Not for another four books. Who can say what will happen now?"

"Hey," Joe placed two fingers under her chin and drew her eyes to his. "We're going to get out of here. All of us. I'm not leaving anyone behind."

Ellodrine's irises shifted to a dark purple, then quickly went amber. "Joe, behind you. Is that the ghosting device?"

Joe followed her gaze. A reddish-purple glow emanated over the far side of the captain's chair. He smiled. "Think I can get to it?"

"No, Joe. There is no cover. You won't make it with all the pirates and greblins about."

"We'll see about that." He cupped a hand over his mouth. "Jaime, can you keep them off me for a minute?"

Jaime nodded, shouldered her Kholvarin scatterbolt, and readied another weapon. This one was also a crossbow, but it was equipped with a cylindrical mechanism that spun as she fired. A steady stream of bolts zipped across the room, sending Rhodactians and greblins diving for cover.

"Seriously?" shouted Kribble, "A Rhanengarde automatic assault crossbow, too?"

Ellodrine crossed her arms. "Joe, who is that woman you've brought with you in the shadow cloak and the impractical dress?" Some odd greenish flecks appeared in her eyes.

"Oh, that's just Jaime. She kills zombies. Introduce you later... Uh... Ghosting device." He darted away toward the purple glow.

· · ·

The three combatants rotated around each other, absorbed in their conflict. Zolethos was the superior swordsman, but the gap between his skill and Corbin's was minimal. Cortega fought with fury but knew he lacked the lifelong training of the other two. In addition, his movements were growing stiff. Zolethos clearly sensed this and focused his offense on Cortega, who now bore several charred gashes about his arms and torso.

"Get back, Captain," said Corbin, "This is not your fight."

"It's my ship. And that makes it my fight."

Zolethos smiled. "Yes, Corbin. Don't be selfish. I'll be happy to slay the captain too. We'll let him be first, shall we? Then I can give you my undivided attention."

"You're delaying the inevitable, Zolethos. I will destroy you."

"You keep saying that. It's going to make it so much more satisfying when I carve that mark of destiny off your dead flesh and frame it in my trophy room. And then there's the matter of that ingenue you've become so fond of in the nurse outfit. Lovely little thing, isn't she? Perhaps when you're dead, I can take the opportunity to... comfort her."

"She would never want a vile thing like you."

Zolethos showed his teeth. "I won't give her a choice."

Corbin clenched his teeth and lunged with reckless fury.

Zolethos sidestepped and deflected the blow with a flick of his wrist. It threw Corbin off balance and sent him spinning away. He turned his attention to Cortega. "Protagonists. They get so emotional."

Cortega jerked a crick out of his neck and repositioned his grip on the flaming sword in his hand. "You'll find me a lot less gullible."

Zolethos readied his sword in a defensive position. "Come at me, then."

Cortega hesitated, his eyes scanning his opponent. He held his body motionless. He did not even breathe.

"What are you waiting for?"

A bolt from the storm sent tremors through the ship. Sparks erupted from consoles and danced across the deck. Like a lion, Cortega leaped forward.

Zolethos's eyes grew wide. His mask of condescension momentarily lifted. But he was fast. Unbelievably fast. He twisted his body to deflect the attack. A clash of fire and steel followed in a blinding flash. It faded like a curtain to reveal Zolethos standing with one flaming sword raised to strike and the other buried in Cortega's chest. Blue fire still licked the blade as it protruded from the captain's back.

The speakers sounded with Circe's laughter. "Cortega is slain! Where is your arrogance now, Captain?"

Zolethos smiled a black-lipped smile. "You see? Now the bad guys can win. How does it feel to fail, protagonist?"

"You'll have to tell me," said Cortega, "You're about to find out." With that, he drew his blade up in a fiery arc and separated Zolethos from the arm that had just plunged a sword into his chest.

Zolethos threw his head back and sounded an unholy howl.

Cortega stumbled backward. The sword through his middle dissolved to ash. Zolethos's severed arm dropped to the deck. Cortega allowed himself a grim smile. "Didn't even hurt," he said and then crumpled in a heap.

•   •   •

"You monster!" cried Corbin, "That is the last! That is the last life you shall ever take!"

Zolethos clasped his remaining hand over his bloody stump and sent flames coursing through it. A smell like burned toast rose in the air. His screams topped even the storm. He removed his smoking hand from the cauterized stump and retrieved his sword from the deck. "Come, Child of Destiny. Come at me. I am in a black mood, and I need to kill someone right now."

Corbin rushed into him.

He and Zolethos fought furiously. Both were worn from their battles, but they rivaled one another in sheer determination. Corbin had numerous singe marks, and black smudges covered his face. Zolethos's armor was scored in many places. Corbin's crystal sword tore through it as though it were paper.

"You cannot win, Zolethos. The author has sided against you."

"Do you think I fear Howard? This story does not belong to him anymore. He cannot stop me." He lunged.

Corbin sidestepped. "He doesn't have to. It is my destiny alone to defeat you. He merely aids my quest."

"So, he thinks he can give you some new toys and let you do his dirty work? And that's all it would take?"

"Destiny established long ago that I would defeat you. I am only acting out what is already decided."

"Let me tell you something else that is established, Corbin. My Blade of Embers has been with me since the very first book in our series. Howard wrote that trinket of yours—What? Five minutes ago? Did he even make you earn it? I wonder which blade is more powerful." He brought his sword down in a fiery arc against Corbin's weapon.

It shattered. Shards of crystal scattered across the deck. Only two inches of the blade remained upon the hilt. Corbin stared with unblinking eyes at the broken weapon in his hand. "It cannot be!"

Zolethos laughed. "You see? The author cannot just *give* you the victory. That's not how stories work. You must earn it. And now, Corbin..." He leveled his blade. "I have."

Corbin was light on his feet, but Zolethos slowly herded him into a corner. In a desperate attempt, he flung his crystal hilt at the charging necromancer who deflected it to the side. At last, he had nowhere to retreat.

Zolethos reared back to deliver the final stroke. "Here it ends."

Corbin braced himself. It never came. Instead, a glowing crystal shard burst through Zolethos's breastplate from behind.

Zolethos's mouth fell agape. He looked down on the glowing blade protruding from his chest. The Sword of Embers fell from his grasp.

Behind him stood Cortega, the radiant blade still in his grasp. Rivulets of dark blood ran down his arm from where he gripped it. The charred wound in his chest still smoked where Zolethos had impaled him.

The storm raged outside the ship. Some lights flickered out completely. Those that remained cast an eerie glow across the bridge.

• • •

"What just happened?" asked Joe, appearing next to Ellodrine with the ghosting device in hand.

She shook her head. "I don't know. How could the captain have survived a wound like that?"

Joe turned to Innes. "Are there such things as zombies in this world?"

Innes scoffed. "Zombies? Scientifically impossible. Dead tissue cannot be reanimated."

Joe nodded. "He's being re-interpreted."

"How?" asked Ellodrine.

"The zombie bite must have finally kicked in. The book doesn't know what to do with him. Maybe it's trying to treat *undead* the same way that a shoe comes untied, or a hole gets uncovered."

Ellodrine tapped her chin. "So, your theory is he's just been un-killed somehow?"

"Got a better suggestion?"

"But how is that possible?"

"Listen to the storm." Joe pointed to the ceiling. "Hear how much louder it got? I don't think the book is happy about it. But it can't ignore it either."

"You mean it's becoming unstable." Ellodrine looked up at the ceiling. "It's forced to choose between two impossibilities."

Zolethos crumpled to the floor.

Corbin dropped to his knees. "No! That was my destiny! That was my fate! Do you know what you've done? What you've taken from me?"

Cortega regarded him with a single jaundiced eye. "Relax, Junior. You had your hand in it. Now it's done."

Corbin clutched his face with his hands. "You don't understand. I had to do it! I had to land the final blow! It's the mark. It will never let me be!" He sat on the floor and wept.

Cortega wiped his hands on his uniform, smearing it with blood. "You're welcome." He staggered back to the captain's chair and collapsed into it.

Greblins and Rhodactians slowly emerged with hands up in surrender. Circe stared from the display. Rakshaw dashed past Jaime into the transport lift. She whipped around and fired at him, but her crossbow bolts only bounced off the closing doors.

"Is that it?" asked Kribble. "Did we win?"

"Victory," said Xane, still panting, "It is ours. Our enemy is slain."

Ellodrine looked up from the terminal and rubbed her eye with her sleeve. "Just like that? Can it be that simple?"

Joe held out his palms. "I don't know. I feel uneasy. Like something's—"

A thick crimson beam lit up the bridge and crashed into Corbin's chest. It threw him into the wall, and he dropped onto the deck.

Zolethos rose slowly from the floor, a Rhodactian incapacitator in his hand. He grasped the crystal shard from his chest and wrenched it free. "Something you should know about necromancers. We don't keep our hearts where just anybody can find them."

CHAPTER FORTY

+++

Ghost Nebula

"I knew it," said Ellodrine. "He's too strong. It wasn't climactic enough. We need something more powerful to stop him. We've got to initiate the destruct sequence."

"Oh," said Innes, "We're back to that again?"

Cortega turned to them from his chair. "Has the crew had time to abandon the ship?"

"All gone," said Innes, "All but us."

"Initiate it. This has to stop here." He struggled to his feet and fixed his eye on Zolethos. "I'll buy you some time."

Kribble stepped in front of him, still wielding Xane's severed bionic arm. "Sit down, Captain. You're barely alive. If you *are* alive right now. It's my turn."

"Kribble, you're not a protagonist," shouted Joe, "You can't beat him."

"No. But I'll have a lot of fun just the same." Kribble tapped the bionic arm into his palm.

Zolethos grasped the crystal shard he had removed from his chest and charged. He met the dwarf and engaged once more in deathly combat.

"We've got to work quickly," said Ellodrine. She and Innes turned to their consoles and typed madly at the keys. "Please hurry, Innes. We've got to destroy the ship before he has a chance to get out of it."

Circe laughed through the speakers. "Scurry mortals! Do you not see that you are powerless before me? Beg for mercy with your last moments!"

"What have you been doing while I was gone?" asked Joe. "Who is the blue lady?"

"Circe," said Ellodrine, "She's in the computer. She's stopping us from restarting the countdown."

"Circe? Like the witch from *The Odyssey*?"

"Yes," said Innes. "Good reference. Not everybody catches that."

"I read more than I let on. Does she spell it the same?"

Innes stopped typing. "Yes. Is that important?"

"Elle, are you sure this is the only way to stop him?"

She looked back at him with deep blue eyes. "It's the only way we can be sure."

Joe readied his revolver. "Innes, right? Circe is in the computer? Which computer?"

"The ship's computer. It's all around us."

"Okay, but if you had to point to a specific location. Where?"

Innes scratched his head. "Why do we need to know this?"

"Humor me."

"I don't know. Probably in the central bridge unit right over there. Why?"

Joe pointed his revolver in the direction Innes indicated. "Because I got a bullet with her name on it." He squeezed the trigger. His shot exploded into the terminal.

Circe cocked her head. Nothing happened. She threw her head back and cackled. "Futile! Your greatest efforts have only—" They never heard what Circe thought of their greatest efforts. She winked out of existence suddenly, as though someone had turned her off. Only the self-destruct countdown remained now at four minutes and forty-eight seconds.

Forty-seven seconds.

Forty-six seconds.

Ellodrine gasped. "She's gone. But how is that even possible?"

Joe shrugged. "You're the technical wiz. You tell me."

She scrunched her face in thought. "The bullet must have embedded itself into the precise circuitry that Circe was traveling through at speeds vastly quicker than even the bullet itself could travel. Since Circe is a collection of codes and, therefore, a long string of electrical currents, your shot would have had to strike the exact coding that would equate to Circe's heart to affect her. Effectively, your tactic to shoot blindly and strike her down worked against odds of billions to one. How could you possibly know it would work?"

He winked his sly noir wink. "It was never about the odds. It's all about plot and resolution. That was the bullet I prepared for Corbin earlier. But since I only wrote the first letter, it was flexible. It wasn't meant to miss."

Ellodrine and Innes stared with speechless mouths. The moment was short-lived, however. The sound of the epic melee nearby grew louder. They turned to see that Zolethos was much closer now. Kribble, joined by a one-armed Xane wielding a broken piece of machinery, held him off, but they were quickly losing ground.

Ellodrine grabbed Joe's arm. "Joe, you must get out of here. I'm sorry I dragged you into this."

"Wait," said Joe, "What are you talking about?"

She glanced at Zolethos and then back to Joe. "Do you have a pen, Joe?"

"Yes, I have a pen. But—"

"Give it to me."

He drew the pen from his pocket. She wrinkled her nose as he placed it into her hand. It was covered in patches of something that looked an awful lot like dried blood. "Sorry," he said, "You wouldn't believe what we went through to get that."

"Never mind. Have you got something to write on? Quickly!"

Joe removed the paper travel rune from around his neck and handed it to her. She turned it to the blank side and wrote. "Listen to me carefully, Joe. I am giving you the coordinates to the second artifact. Take the ghosting device with you. Get out of here. We'll stay and hold Zolethos back. This isn't your fight anymore."

"The coordinates!" shouted Zolethos, sparing a look in their direction.

Ellodrine glanced at the countdown. Three minutes and eleven seconds.

Ten seconds.

Nine seconds.

"You're kidding yourself," said Joe, "I'm not going to walk away from this."

Ellodrine pressed the paper into his hands. "This is my fault, Joe. I have to make it right. We should never have pulled you out of your novel. Out of your world."

"Is that what you think? That I was better off sleepwalking through a fictional life?"

"At least you had a chance at a happy ending."

He shoved the paper back into her hand. "You think I can walk away from this?"

"You must."

"Not happening. I've been through this before. I don't want to be the last man standing. That's not good enough for me. Not anymore."

She checked the countdown. Two minutes and forty-six seconds.

Forty-five seconds.

Forty-four seconds.

He placed a finger on her chin and drew her gaze back to his. "Stop watching the clock."

"This is your last chance. You have to go." She thrust the paper again into his hand. "I can't bear the guilt."

"So, don't feel guilty." He crumpled the paper and tossed it away. "It's my decision, not yours. And not some author's. For once in my life, I get to choose, and I'm not walking away unless we all walk away."

"You're really not leaving?" She looked into his eyes with one-part bafflement and one-part suspicion. "But the hero is supposed to get away."

He grasped her hands into his own and held them tightly. "Not this time."

To her left, she could see Kribble and Xane struggling to contain their adversary. Out of her periphery, she could see the display where the timer now showed one minute and twenty-four seconds. Joe reached up, pulled the loose hair out of her face, and tucked it gingerly behind her ear. He then brushed his finger along the bottom of her eye and held it before her. A single dark strand lay across it. "Eyelash. Make a wish, Elle."

She nodded. "Okay."

"Got it?"

"I do." She let out a breath she did not know she was holding. "Did I win the game?"

The sound of the raging nebula storm filled the air. Tremors shook the ship with increasing intensity. Sparks flew from nearly every computer and instrument. What light remained flickered ominously, leaving them in brief pockets of darkness.

Joe leaned forward and whispered. "Thanks for the ride, Elle. Never felt so alive."

Ellodrine squeezed his hands and prepared for her last minute. It was at once the longest and shortest minute she would ever know. Long in the way that minutes are long when one must simply endure them without spending them. Short in that she knew it would be her last and as such, every dwindling second was suddenly precious and rare.

At fifty seconds, she remembered the titles of books she had half-finished, the feel of Lazuli's fur, the lingering taste of Leslie Albracht's Teriyaki tacos, and other details that never seemed important.

At forty seconds, she noticed the color of Joe's eyes. Hazel. How had she never noticed that before? The answer, of course, was that she had never looked. They were gentler than she had expected. He wore his trademark half-smile, though it was not as smirkish as usual.

At thirty seconds, she realized she was mirroring his expression. The realization made her smile wider. She even had to stifle a laugh, though she could not imagine what about the situation struck her as funny. But perhaps knowing one has little time left makes somberness seem wasteful.

At twenty seconds, she filled her lungs with air. The deck shook violently underfoot. She could hear the numbers blip away on the display. In spite of it all, she found great pleasure in feeling the air inside her and releasing it slowly. She squeezed Joe's hands. She knew her nails must be digging into his palms, but he did not seem to mind.

At ten seconds, she released Joe's hands and threw her arms around his body. Her head landed on his shoulder, and she could feel his arms finding their way around her too. She closed her eyes tightly and squeezed. Mentally, she counted along with the final blips.

Five seconds.

Four seconds.

Three seconds.

Two seconds.

The final blip sounded. The explosion was not the loud bang she had expected. Rather, all sounds were silenced. She felt no rush of heat or pain. Through her tightly closed eyelids, she could see a sudden onset of blinding light. She was conscious of Joe's presence. And grateful for it. She wondered if there would be a sudden onset of pain or an all-encompassing numbness. Or would there suddenly be nothing at all? No consciousness to perceive anything? She could not tell whether time still passed or stopped entirely. It was an eternity in a space of seconds.

Slowly, the brightness on the other side of her eyelids faded. It was over. Ellodrine opened one eye, uncertain of what she should expect to see. She opened the other and blinked a few times. She pulled away from Joe's chest and looked at him. He was scanning the room, scrutinizing it with his gaze. She looked to her left where Zolethos, Kribble, and Xane had given up their skirmish and seemed equally confused. To Ellodrine's right, Jaime still held Zolethos's remaining minions at bay by automatic crossbow point, though they seemed too mystified to try to escape. Even Cortega had perked up, still slumped in his chair.

"Well," said Joe at last, "I got nothing. Anyone else want to explain this?"

Nobody answered for several moments. It was Zolethos who finally spoke. "Hyperspace. We've gone into hyperspace."

Innes crossed his arms. "Impossible. We'd need to hook the ghosting device to the engine core to travel to hyperspace. The ghosting device is right here, and the engine core just exploded. Next theory."

Zolethos shook his head. "We *are* in hyperspace. I can feel it."

Innes rolled his eyes. "Oh, that's very scientific, isn't it? You can *feel* it."

Ellodrine tapped on Joe's chest. "Joe, ask me and see if I know."

Joe let out a short laugh. "Okay, Elle. What happened?"

"Well, the ship is in hyperspace as Zolethos said, but it could not have occurred through the normal use of the ghosting device as Innes pointed out. The only remaining possibility is that we were pulled into hyperspace by the nebula itself. Did you hear how much louder the storm got just before the engine core exploded? The nebula exists in normal space and hyperspace, either simultaneously or exclusively, at its own will. It is the nebula's own substance that powers the ghosting device. The nebula must have sensed the impending destruction and, to save its stolen substance that currently resides within the ghosting device, it drew the ship into hyperspace while excluding the engine core, which exploded harmlessly in normal space. This is further evidenced by the lack of sound when the core exploded. Sound is impossible in space, and that is why the explosion was silent."

Innes gaped like a fish. "Where did you *come* from?"

"Corolathia, but that's irrelevant."

"But that would mean the Ghost Nebula was alive," said Innes. "The odds of us being rescued by a completely new form of life are statistically moot. Add that onto the random shot that destroyed Circe, and we are living a practically impossible day. There has to be something more to this, but what it could be, I haven't a guess."

Howard
What happened? Raymond, was that you?

Raymond
No. That wasn't me. I was sitting here all deer-in-the-headlights.

Howard
Ben? Did you do something on your end?

Ben
Something. Maybe. I tried, anyway.

Raymond
What did you do, Ben?

Ben
I just typed what came to me. A lot of it didn't take. The story must have overridden me four or five times before I came to it. Using the nebula was a last-ditch effort. I didn't expect it to work.

Howard
Ben, you did it! That was amazing! They're alive!

Raymond
Alive-ish, anyway. I don't know Corbin's status, and Cortega may not count as living right now. But I sure am happy to see him.

Howard
Corbin's the protagonist of a twelve-book cycle. He'll pull through.

Ben
I hate to be a buzzkill, but we still have Howard's necromancer to deal with. I assume he's still planning to kill us in violent and painful ways.

Howard
That's right. We're not done yet. We've got to figure something out.

Raymond
Right. But I want to say something first. Regardless of what happens, I want you both to know this is the most exceptional thing that has ever happened to me.

Howard
Agreed. After thinking I'd lost my mind for the last six months, it's been good to have you guys. Thanks for everything.

Ben
Sure, Howard. And thank you, too. If it weren't for you and your stupid Library, none of this would have ever happened. And, in a way, that would have been a damn shame. Now let's do this.

CHAPTER FORTY-ONE

+++

Ghost Nebula

A *blip* sounded from the terminal between Joe and Innes.

Innes moved toward the panel to investigate. "Captain. The sensors indicate something approaching the ship."

"Bring up the visual, Innes." Cortega's voice was weak but still resounded with authority.

"Bringing it up now, sir." Innes tapped a few buttons, and the *Blood Horizon* appeared on the display. "They're hailing us, Captain."

"Respond."

Commander Rakshaw replaced the image of the *Blood Horizon*. He clapped a fist onto his chest. "Lord Zolethos, are you still alive?"

Cortega cleared his throat. "Zolethos will stand trial before the Intergalactic Union for his war crimes. Until such time, he is my prisoner."

Zolethos scoffed. "I am *not* your prisoner."

"You will allow me to address Lord Zolethos," said Rakshaw, "Or I shall destroy your ship."

Ellodrine crossed her arms. "We're in hyperspace, you dolt! Send all the torpedoes you want. Frankly, I've had a *day*, and I'm tired of complications."

Rakshaw blinked a few times, scratched his head, and turned to confer with some off-screen comrades in Rhodactanese. After exchanging a few garbled words, he turned to Cortega again. "Very well. If you do not allow me to address Lord Zolethos, I shall seek and destroy every escape capsule that jettisoned from your ship."

A growl rumbled in Cortega's throat. "Answer him."

Zolethos rolled his eyes. "What do you want, Rakshaw?"

"Lord Zolethos! Do you still have the ghosting device?"

Zolethos glanced at the device sitting on a console next to Joe. "It's here."

"And have you retrieved the coordinates to the second artifact?"

Zolethos inhaled sharply and looked at the crumpled paper on the deck, only a few feet away from Joe. He snapped into action and made a dive for it.

Joe moved to intercept. Behind him, Ellodrine shouted, "No, Joe! He'll kill you!" She grasped his shoulder. "Al Kazaak!" A blue spark flared, and they both collapsed to the floor. Joe lifted his eyes.

Zolethos now clutched the paper and uncrumpled it. The crude drawing of a travel rune showed from the back. "I've got it!"

Rakshaw gave a sharp nod. "I have a lock on your position. We are going to teleport you over."

A golden light surrounded Zolethos. Similar lights glowed around Jaime's captives, and the ghosting device on the console.

Ellodrine pulled herself from the floor, wisps of hair rising from her head. "Unacceptable. Absolutely unacceptable!" She shoved Innes from the command console and placed her fingers upon the keys.

"What are you doing?" asked Innes.

"Interfering. I will not let them just snatch things off our ship."

Innes scoffed. "You can't interfere with the telepad. There's no way to—Oh, I see what you're doing! Oh, that's quite clever! That could work!"

"Wait," shouted Zolethos, "What are you doing?"

Ellodrine met his gaze with icy blue eyes. She dangled her finger above the last key and smiled at him. She pressed it.

Zolethos winced. He looked down. The gold light continued to surround him. He vanished from sight. Moments later, he reappeared in a similar golden glow from the display aboard the *Blood Horizon*.

Joe picked himself up from the deck, still shaking off Ellodrine's lightning bolt. "Didn't work, Elle."

"It most certainly did." Ellodrine pointed at the ghosting device still sitting on the console.

Joe scratched his head. "But what about Zolethos?"

"I didn't want him here in the first place. Why would I stop him from leaving?"

From the display, Zolethos laughed. "You think you've thwarted me? Because you held onto your little artifact? You are as short-sighted as you are foolish! You have no engine, and no way to follow me. I have the coordinates for the second artifact. And a travel rune!" He turned to Rakshaw and handed the paper to him. "Take this to the engine room. You know what to do with it. Then take us to those coordinates."

Kribble threw Xane's metal arm to the floor. "He's getting away! We've got to do something!"

"What can we do?" asked Innes. "We're in hyperspace. Our torpedoes would only pass through them."

Zolethos flashed a smile with lots of teeth. "I'll be back for you," he said, and the image winked out. Replacing it was the *Blood Horizon* maneuvering to face the orbiting circle of probes, the library gate. The thruster engines lit up. It shot through the center of the probes and vanished.

Joe rubbed his shoulder. "Whose side are you on, Elle? That really packs a wallop."

Ellodrine leaned back against the console. "I saved your life, Joe. He would have chopped you in half to get that paper."

"But now he's got the coordinates to the second artifact."

She shook her head. "No, he doesn't. He only has the coordinates I gave you."

"Right," said Joe, "You wrote the coordinates to... Wait. What are you telling me?"

She rubbed her eye and let loose a heavy sigh. Her gaze veered to his left as she spoke. "I didn't give you the real coordinates, Joe."

"Excuse me? Did you just say something crazy?"

"They weren't, though. I only gave you the coordinates I wanted Zolethos to take from you. I'm so sorry, Joe. I didn't know if we could hold him back long enough to catch him in the explosion. He was never meant to die this early. He might have found his way off the ship, and that would have meant horrible things. I needed a back-up plan."

Joe gaped at her. "So, you gave me the *wrong* coordinates?"

She nodded.

LOST ON A PAGE

"Where do those coordinates go?"

"I don't know, exactly. It's the Dewey Decimal number for black holes. Five twenty-three point eight, eight. Somebody must be writing a book about them somewhere. Wherever that takes him, he won't be happy about it."

Joe opened his mouth to speak, but no words came out. Instead, he only directed a piercing stare at her. When he had recovered his speech, he said, "You're a real piece of work, you know that? What if I had followed those coordinates?"

She continued to avert her eyes. Her irises were deep and blue and shiny with liquid. "Oh, Joe. I'm so sorry. I wanted to tell you. It was horrible not telling you. But Zolethos had to believe it was true, and the only way I could ensure that was if you believed it was true. It was a dreadful choice! It was you or all the people Zolethos would have killed if he found his way into the other world." She lifted her face to meet his. "I don't blame you if you hate me for this, Joe. Only tell me you understand why I did it."

Joe was silent for a moment. He shook his head. Then he laughed.

Further off, Kribble joined in with a boisterous guffaw.

Ellodrine looked back and forth between them. A few choked laughs escaped her lips, hesitantly mirroring their amusement. "So... It's funny?"

"Well, yeah," said Joe, "I get it. You were running a gambit. You couldn't show your hand. He never saw it coming from you, Miss Prim. I sure didn't."

She lowered her eyes to the floor. "But, Joe, I feel so guilty."

He waved a hand in the air. "Forget about it. Drown it in a drink or two. You had a major dilemma, and you made the best choice you could. That stuff happens in books all the time. It's just protagonist stuff."

"But I'm not a protagonist, Joe."

He placed a finger under her chin and lifted her face to his. "You are now, Ello. You beat the bad guy. You flushed the Dark Lord of the Void down a black hole. The irony of that alone has got to be enough to do it. Irony is the most climactic killer of all."

"I... You're right. I *did* get the bad guy."

"You played him. You played him good."

"But how could that even happen? I wasn't written to be a protagonist."

Joe winked at her. "You had a good mentor."

She smiled. "I guess I did." She stared into his eyes. "So, what now? This protagonism is kind of new to me. What is the expectation after one vanquishes the bad guy?"

Joe's trademark devilish smile crept across his face. "Well, usually that's when the protagonist gets to–"

The transport lift doors whooshed open. Isabelle burst into the room. "It's horrible! You must come quickly! To Deck G."

Joe muttered several obscenities under his breath.

"Do we know this girl?" asked Ellodrine.

Isabelle shot her a venomous glare she did not understand. "It's Aelrûn! He's wounded. You must come quickly."

"Aelrûn?" Kribble gasped. "What's that fool elf done now?"

"You have to go to him," said Isabelle. "There isn't much time."

Kribble made a beeline to the transport lift. Joe and Ellodrine joined him.

"Meet us in the sickbay on Deck C," shouted Cortega through the closing doors.

The lift lurched into motion. The doors reopened onto the grisly aftermath of the battle on Deck G. Fallen greblins, space pirates and occasional Astral Navy cadets littered the halls.

Kribble charged forward at a surprising pace, considering his short legs. He wove through the corridors, leaping over obstructing bodies as he went. Joe and Ellodrine trailed behind. At last, they came upon the entrance to the commons. Kribble kicked the malfunctioning door aside, but nothing could have prepared any of them for what lay beyond.

Aelrûn was alone in the large commons. He slumped in a chair in the center of the room. The charcoal uniform he had worn was gone, and the only things girding his naked form were the metallic cables that tied him to his seat. He had no obvious wounds, but he wore an injurious scowl upon his face.

"She's a whore! A devious, conniving whore!"

Kribble's laughter consumed him. For several moments, speech was completely lost to him. His raucous merriment echoed through the empty commons, and he clutched his sides while salty streams trailed down his cheeks.

Joe's reaction was less exuberant, but he did not stifle it either. Even Ellodrine had difficulty restraining a giggle.

"Please, don't burden yourself on my account," said Aelrûn dryly, "I'll just wait here until you're done."

Joe's smirk vanished. "Wait. Something's not right. We've been conned. That girl had us believing he was at death's door."

Ellodrine tilted her head. "You're right, Joe. But why? What could she have to gain?"

Kribble stroked his chin in a Joe-like fashion. "She came here with Corbin. Whatever she's about, they're in it together."

Joe snapped his fingers. "The ghosting device. That's what she's after."

Joe and Ellodrine shared a glance, then sprinted for the door.

"What about untying me?" shouted Aelrûn.

"Kribble can do it," Joe shouted over his shoulder.

They raced back through the halls and clambered into the transport lift. Ellodrine directed it to Deck C. Joe tapped his foot and pressed his palms against the doors as it carried them. When the doors opened, they spilled out into the hallway and maneuvered through the corridors to the sickbay. Three wrong turns later, they arrived to find Innes and Jaime applying basic medical treatment to the wounded Cortega, and Xane tinkering with his severed metal arm.

"Where's Corbin?" asked Joe.

"Shakespeare?" said Jaime, "Woke up a few minutes ago. That nurse took him for a walk down the hall. She said it would do him some good to get on his feet."

"Where is the ghosting device?"

Innes turned his gaze to the corner. "It's right over... Actually, I thought it was right there. Where did it go?"

Joe and Ellodrine launched back into the corridors. They reached the transport lift, both of them panting for breath. This time, Ellodrine directed it to the archive library. The doors opened, and they raced along until they reached a familiar room where shelves of slender reading devices lined the walls. The room was empty. In the air lingered a scent that was heady and enticing, like a rare wine.

"They were here," said Joe.

"I don't have my travel rune on me," said Ellodrine, "Zolethoo took it."

"Yeah." Joe kicked the doorframe. "Mine too."

CHAPTER FORTY-TWO

+++

Nexus of Words

Eight weary, battered characters emerged into Reading Lounge L-7. Ellodrine stopped short. "Oh! Joe, you didn't tell me we had guests."

"They're back!" Doug shouted, rising from his chair.

"They're back?" Trixie leaped to her feet. Lisa rushed to her side, hugging Lazuli like a rag doll.

Joe smiled. "Must have slipped my mind. This is Doug, Trixie, and Lisa. Three of the bravest minor characters you'll ever meet. They just survived a zombie apocalypse and jumped out of a thirty-story building like it was a dollhouse. Officer Cruz, you've already met."

"Officer Cruz," said Lisa, "Did you know they have a flying cat?" Lazuli seethed in her arms.

Joe stroked Lazuli's head with one finger. "And odds are, that's not even the strangest thing you'll see today. Doug, Trixie, and Lisa, I want you to meet Kribble the dwarf, Aelrûn the elf, Ellodrine the wizard, Innes the technical officer, and the gray reptilian alien with the severed robotic arm is Xane. Cortega, you know."

"What's that?" asked Doug, pointing to a photograph hanging in front of Joe's chest.

"That was our ticket home," said Joe, "Ironically, Jaime was the only one who held on to her travel rune, but through the magic of instant cameras, here we are."

"Wow," said Lisa.

"That impressed you?" said Joe, "After all you've seen today?"

"Not that." She leaned in to Ellodrine, grasped her hand, and whispered, "He was right. You really do have beautiful eyes."

Ellodrine's cheeks and irises both grew rosy, and she failed to suppress a smile. "Who said that?" she whispered back. "Did Joe say I have beautiful eyes?"

Lisa shook her head. "No. It wasn't Joe. It was the other one."

"What other one?" Ellodrine's smile melted.

"That man who was here. He went into the shelves. Over there."

Aelrûn snapped his greblin bow into place. "She's right. Somebody is here."

Ellodrine waved him back and crept forward. She held one hand out before her and let electric tendrils dance across her fingers. Approaching the bookshelves Lisa had indicated, Ellodrine heard shuffling feet. The sound grew louder.

He emerged suddenly. "Elle? Elle O'Drine! I have found you at last! You wouldn't believe what I have gone through to get—"

"Al Kazaak!" A bright blue-white bolt of lightning leaped from her hand into the chest of the figure facing her. It threw him several feet across Reading Lounge L-7 and into a bookshelf. Ellodrine's hand flew to her mouth. She rushed to his side and kneeled over him.

Lucas was unconscious on the floor. Smoke rose from his chest, but his ribs continued to rise and fall in a steady rhythm.

Ellodrine lifted Lucas's hand and inspected a small metal ring around his finger. "Travel rune."

"Must have taken it off that greblin scout we left behind in the romance novel," said Joe, coming up behind her. "We should have snatched it before we left."

Ellodrine frowned. "Yes. We should have."

"Is that how it's supposed to work? The lightning thing, I mean."

She stood and faced him. No black smudges stained her face. No stray hairs rose from her head. Her eyes glowed with bright sparks. "Yes, Joe. That is how it's supposed to work."

♦   ♦   •

The banquet that night in Reading Lounge L-7 surpassed any that had come before it. Stacks of developing cookbooks provided the feast, a patchwork array of cuisine. Kribble made a special foray into *Champion Brews* by Chuck Stockton and returned with a selection of beverages, though he commented that none of them could rival a good mug of

Karthecian beer. Aelrûn and Innes made sick faces and declined anything fermented.

Aelrûn wore an uncomfortable blue Astral Navy uniform that Kribble had found for him. For some reason, Joe and Jaime took great delight in this and repeatedly asked him if he found things to be *illogical.* Nobody else seemed to get the joke. Ellodrine asked them about it, and it had something to do with his pointed ears, but she could not get much further than that.

"I've never seen *that* color," said Aelrûn.

"Hmmm? What are you talking about?"

"Your eyes, Ellodrine."

"Oh? What color are they?"

"Green."

"You've seen my eyes green before. It means I'm curious."

"No. Not yellow-green. This is more like what fire would look like if fire was green."

"That doesn't make any sense, Aelrûn. I'm sure I'm only curious."

"And you only get more curious every time Joe and Jaime laugh together."

Ellodrine stabbed him with a glare. "Are you *insinuating* something, Aelrûn?"

He only smiled, called his harp to hand, and filled the air with melodies of *The Rolling Stones.*

Lucas awoke within the hour, no worse off, and regaled Ellodrine with the tale of his adventures, how he had written down the curious words he had heard her utter before she disappeared from his manor, how he had discovered the strange ring on the green-fleshed creature, how she had haunted his every dream since the first moment he had espied her. Ellodrine endured as much as she could, resting her face upon her palms before she announced that she had better tend to the other guests. Right now. Without hesitation.

She made her way to the other side of the table where Cortega sat with Innes pushing morsels in circles around his plate. "Are you well, Captain? You've hardly eaten a thing."

Cortega looked down at his plate and then back at her. "Sorry. Don't mean to be rude, ma'am. Distracted, I guess. It's a lot to take in."

Ellodrine cupped her hand to her mouth. "I hope you don't mind my asking, Captain, but you haven't developed any cravings for human flesh, have you? After all, zombies do exist in Corolathia."

"No. I haven't developed any cravings for human flesh."

"I'm glad to hear it. The preservation spells I placed on you should buy you some time. We'll want to get you a working heart as soon as possible. I'll start researching first thing tomorrow. In the meantime, do let us know if you hunger for anything... unnatural."

"You'll be the first to know."

She gave a sharp nod. "I appreciate it. Don't you worry, though. We'll find something. We've just got to locate the right book. You're lucky to be alive at all. If your interpretation weren't overriding your anatomy, you wouldn't be."

Cortega sat back in his chair. "Maybe that's what bothers me. I always knew I'd go down with the ship someday. I never expected to survive it. I'm sitting at a banquet while my crew is floating through space in metal capsules. What about them? And even if I can rescue them, how do I tell them their entire universe is a lie?"

Innes snorted. "As long as I'm there when you tell Rhodes. This'll blow his mind. He'll flip!" He laughed at the thought of it, but he stopped short when Cortega shot him a look.

Ellodrine gave his shoulder a squeeze. "I think I understand, Captain. Better than you might think. But we've got time. We'll find your crew. And they'll adjust. After all, it's not as though you haven't anything left to explore. There are worlds upon worlds out there. Stranger things than you'd dare to imagine."

"That's true," said Innes, "And wasn't that always the mission, Captain? To explore the unexplored? Discover the unknown? Well, here we are sitting in the unknown right now. We just crossed a boundary none of us would have ever believed."

"Precisely," said Ellodrine, "Innes, I don't suppose you'd be able to prepare a ship with a travel rune the way Zolethos did, would you?"

Innes looked insulted.

"Wonderful. What do you say, Captain? There's a lot to explore in all the books out there. We need somebody to scout it out for us. It's bound to be fraught with danger."

Cortega took a breath and looked out at the endless shelves. He adjusted his eye patch. "I'll think about it," he said and shoved a feta-stuffed mushroom into his mouth.

Ellodrine smiled and moved on. She passed Kribble and Xane, who were comparing battle scars and trading war stories. Several empty mugs sat on the table next to them. She could not tell whether they were becoming fast friends or bitter rivals, or maybe a little of both. She opted for discretion over valor and left them to occupy one another. Glancing back to her own vacant chair, she saw Lucas was still singing her praises to anyone who would listen. She suddenly felt the urge to take a walk.

She slipped down the nearest dark aisle, hoping Lucas would not notice her escaping. Once away from the noise, she began perusing the shelves for something to read. Perhaps to fall asleep to. It had been a long day. She found a large blue volume at eye level and pulled it out to investigate its contents. Behind it was a face.

Ellodrine stifled a scream and thrust her hand to her heart. Somebody was on the other side of the shelf. She summoned electricity to her fingertips.

The face winked a distinct noir-ish wink.

Ellodrine let out a breath. "Joe, what's the matter with you? Don't you know better than to sneak up on people like that?"

"Sorry," said Joe's face, "Old habits. Saw you slipping out and thought I'd investigate. Besides, I've got a question that's been bugging me."

Ellodrine shook the lightning out of her hand. "Perhaps you could come around to this side first. I don't enjoy talking through bookshelves."

Joe's face nodded, and moments later he appeared around the corner.

"So, what's this big question of yours, Joe?"

"It's about the ghosting device. What's the point of it? I've been trying to work out how this thing is going to get us to the World Where the Books Are Written, and I can't figure it out."

"Oh?" Ellodrine leaned back against the shelves. "It's quite simple. I'd have thought you'd come to it by now. You already know the ghosting device makes objects or people seem ethereal?"

Joe nodded.

"And I already told you my concerns that our fictional essence may not be stable in a non-fictional world."

He nodded again.

"My plan was merely to put the machine in reverse. If the device normally makes people less substantial than they were, then in reverse it should make them *more* substantial. This is our safeguard from being too fictional when we cross over."

Joe stared at her for a moment, then threw his head back and laughed.

She scrunched her face at him. "Don't laugh, Joe. This is a perfectly viable solution."

"I'm sorry, Elle." He gained control of himself, but a bemused smile remained upon his face. "That's it? That's what all this was about? It's a play on words."

"We *are* words. Words are our science. It's all we have to work with. It's not funny!"

He placed a hand on her shoulder. "You're wrong, Elle. It is funny. And I'll tell you why. Because whether we got the ghosting device or not, I think your plan worked. I think we all became real today. Not a week ago. Not six months ago. For the first time in any of our lives, we got to make our own decisions, and for the first time, we got to deal with the consequences with nobody to blame but ourselves. And we made a real mess of things, you know? But in the end, you were willing to put the lives of people you'd never met before your own. That's authenticity. That's substance. More than you'd have ever got from your machine."

She furrowed her brow. "But will that be enough to get us to the WWTBAW?"

"It can wait. I'm not in a hurry anymore. For now, let's just celebrate that we lived through the day."

Ellodrine cocked her head. "How did it happen, Joe? I mean, really. How did we live through that explosion? I know it was the nebula, but I cannot bring myself to be satisfied with that explanation. There must be more to it than that."

"It was Ben."

"Really? Your author? How do you know?"

"I know," said Joe. "It was him. But even he couldn't have done it alone."

"No? Who do you think was helping him?"

"I have my theories. But only you'd know for sure."

"Me? What would I know about it?"

He brushed her cheek lightly with his finger. "What did you wish for back there?"

"You mean with the eyelash?"

He nodded.

She looked down. "Something silly. Childish really."

"What was it?"

She looked into his eyes with warm amber irises and smiled. "A happy ending, Joe."

"That's not silly, Elle. That's everybody's wish. Maybe that's the only wish." He leaned forward and placed his forehead against hers. "Does your happy ending have room for two?"

Her lips parted in a warm smile. "I don't know, Mr. Slade. There might be. What did you have in mind?"

"Well, I think this might be the part where—"

"There you are! We've been looking for you two." It was Aelrûn. He was standing at the end of the aisle.

Joe bit his lip and punched the nearest bookshelf. "Hey, Ski Cap! You couldn't have waited two more minutes?"

"This is quite urgent. We've found something."

"What is it?" asked Ellodrine.

"Follow me. You'll want to see this." He darted off.

Joe and Ellodrine glanced at one another and raced after him. They arrived at the Reading Lounge and found everyone gathered around a table at the other end. They pushed through the crowd. Laid out on the table were a single book and a yellow parchment. Upon the parchment ran the hastily scrawled words:

To my dearest friends and foes,
I hope you weren't planning on abandoning Corolathia now.
Not with Zolethos's forces still wandering about.
I thought I would remove the temptation.
You've undoubtedly discovered we have the ghosting device.
Isabelle sends her regards. Follow us if you dare.
Bring the coordinates to the second artifact.
I'll be waiting.

"That's Corbin's handwriting," said Ellodrine.

Joe picked up the parchment and squinted at it. "He's baiting us. Why? What does he stand to gain? He never showed any interest in the World Where the Books Are Written." He lowered the letter and turned his focus to the book. On the cover was the image of a lonely rider looking out onto a dry prairie. The rider held a smoking six-gun and wore a wide-brimmed hat. In dramatic yellow letters were the words *Sagebrush Canyon* by Dwight Sherman.

"What do we do, Joe?" asked Kribble, tugging at his elbow. "Should we go after him?"

Joe looked down for a moment, then back to Kribble and said, "Let him wait. I've had enough plot twists and deceptions for a while. We can deal with him later."

Ellodrine nodded. "Yes. Let him wait. Him and the WWTBAW and all of it."

"Besides," said Joe, "We have enough to do tomorrow as it is."

Kribble cocked his head. "Why? What are we doing tomorrow?"

Joe tossed the parchment unceremoniously onto the table. "Tomorrow, we turn this place into a home."

Howard
That. Was. Amazing.

Raymond
The most incredible thing I have ever been a part of.

Ben
The most amazing, incredible thing that we can't tell anybody, because they'd never believe us, and they'd put us in a padded room.

Howard
On the downside, we are now three authors out of a job. Completely back to the proverbial drawing board. We no longer have any manuscripts.

Ben
I don't know about that. Between the three of us, plus one Lyla Birdsong and one Kevin Jacobson, I think we have a pretty incredible manuscript.

Raymond
You're suggesting we publish this mess?

Ben
Why not? We wrote it. Kind of.

Raymond
How does that even work? None of this would make any sense if the reader didn't have access to five different books.

Ben
Compilation. We only include the relevant chapters of each. Of course, you'll have to be the one to contact Ms. Birdsong, Raymond. I'm pretty sure she's got a restraining order in the works against Howard and I. Howard, you can track down Kevin Jacobson. I'll contact Colin. We'll split the royalties between us.

Howard
What about the byline? It's going to look ridiculous with all our names up there together. It'll be longer than the title.

Ben
Maybe we can use a collaborative pen name. Something we can all be happy with. Something like John Quinn.

Raymond
Sounds too much like it came from a phone book. We need to put an initial in the middle. Something to give it some mystery.

Howard
How about an *E*? I think *E* makes a strong middle initial.

Ben
We can't call him John E. Quinn. That sounds like Johnny Quinn.

Howard
Well, John is too generic anyway. What about George?

Ben
Georgie?

Raymond
David.

Ben
I could live with that. But not David Quinn. No impact. We need an adjective that gives us an edge. We're intelligent and unique, with a quick turn of phrase and cutting wit.

Raymond
Something debonair, but without being ostentatious. Direct. To the point.

Howard
I like it. But what could we use that would convey all that?

Lost on a Page

David E. Sharp

Black Rose Writing | Texas

Acknowledgements

Special thanks to Black Rose Writing and to some of the greatest writers I know, Ronda (No H) Simmons, Laura Mahal, Joe Siple, Amy Rivers, Sarah Roberts, Sheala Henke, N. C. Gossner, Ryan Watt, J. C. Lynne, April Moore, Kerrie Flanagan, The Northern Colorado Writers, and libraries everywhere. Libraries are amazing!

About the Author

David E. Sharp is a noisy librarian. He is fond of theatre and got his start in writing by producing original plays in his hometown. He has also published short stories in various anthologies. David is a member of the Northern Colorado Writers and frequently contributes to their blog. He lives in Greeley, Colorado with his wife and family.

Note from the Author

Word-of-mouth is crucial for any author to succeed. If you enjoyed *Lost on a Page*, please leave a review online—anywhere you are able. Even if it's just a sentence or two. It would make all the difference and would be very much appreciated.

Thanks!
David E. Sharp

Thank you so much for checking out one of our **Dystopian Sci-Fi** novels.

If you enjoy our book, please check out our recommended title for your next great read!

Shadow City by Anna Mocikat

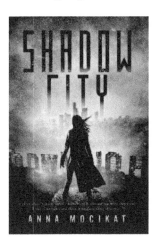

"*SHADOW CITY* is full of adventure, thrills, and twists and turns. The characters are fully realized and the swift pace keeps the story moving along, so readers will likely find themselves turning pages in rapid succession."

–IndieReader

Made in the USA
Coppell, TX
01 July 2023

18671030R00184